HOME RUN

THE HOME RUN SERIES

CHRISSY WISSLER

BLUE CEDAR PUBLISHING

Home Run
Copyright © 2018 Christen Wissler

All rights reserved.

Published 2018 by Blue Cedar Publishing
www.bluecedarpublishing.com
Cover art copyright © Yuri Arcurs/Dreamstime
Book and cover design copyright © 2018 Blue Cedar Publishing
ISBN-13: 978-1-949056-02-0
ISBN-10: 1949056023

This book was originally published under the pseudonym, Christen Anne Kelley.

This book is a work of fiction. All characters and events are fictitious and any resemblance to real persons, living or dead, is coincidental and not intended by the author.

Blue Cedar Publishing
P.O. Box 5275
Torrance, CA 90510

❀ Created with Vellum

Hidden in Time: Novel

Hidden in Lore: Collection #1

Hidden in Myth: Collection #2

Hidden in Legend: Collection #3

Little League Series

Swing Away: A Little League Novel

Prom Dates & Softball Bats

Throw Like a Girl, Catch a Date

Fly Away

No Crying in Softball

More to Life than Softball

A Pitcher's Unexpected Date

A Catcher's Christmas Wish

Stolen Bases, Stolen Kisses

Softball Baby

Off-Balance

Batter-Up Pucker-Up: Collection

Everlasting: Collection

All or Nothing: Collection

ACKNOWLEDGMENTS

Thanks, first and foremost, goes to my parents. This story wouldn't have existed without you both, for all the time, money, and love you put into me and my dreams. While my dreams may have changed, may not have involved playing in the Olympics, they still came true. Thank you. Thanks also goes to Dean Wesley Smith and Kristine Kathryn Rusch who not only showed me how to turn my writing into a business, but helped give me the courage to write this story. And finally, to Sean, my husband. You said nothing about your crazy wife when I crawled out of bed at four in the morning to write or when I asked you to read my romances and tell me what you thought. Thank you for believing in me.

To Dad—
Who taught me how not to throw like a girl.
Thank you.

CHAPTER 1

The softball cracked off the bat.

Laurie slid to the edge of her overturned bucket. Nearly tipped herself over as she leaned, closer and closer to the chain-link fence. Her metal cleats scraped on the dugout's cement floor and she pushed as if she was the one turning and running, running to catch the high, flying ball.

Just like she'd done, hundreds, no *thousands* of times before.

Laurie gripped the chain-link separating her and the field she'd practically grown up on. Gripped it hard until her own memories, of pushing off the buzzed short grass and racing to make the catch, faded. Until it was just her and her team again.

Until it was just little Suzie Turner out in right field.

Suzie, with her bouncing pigtails and smile as wide as the field, turned and ran. Her deep pink uniform, with the white lettering of her last name and the number one, reflected the heating, sweltering sun. But despite the sun and its beating-down glare, Suzie hadn't been dozing or drifting off. Not this time. This time she'd gotten a good jump. Had seen the hit. Had seen the softball flinging in her direction; the very second it'd happened.

It would be close.

Very close.

Laurie watched as Suzie glanced over her shoulder. Took in the distance. And, like Laurie had taught her, kept on running.

"Come on. Come on," Laurie chanted.

The ball arched, high, then higher. On the field, the other team's runners sprinted for the next base. Flinging dust and dry dirt into the air until it formed a cloud so thick Laurie could barely track of that white speck in the sky.

It was either the winning hit. Or the losing hit.

Meanwhile her team, her wonderful amazing team, shouted. Called out to each other. Asked for who had it.

Suzie answered.

Behind Laurie, the roar and cheer of parents froze. A collective, indrawn breath like Laurie's. Like Hugh and the handful of girls beside her in the dugout. They all waited. Watched.

Suzie, still running, still pumping as hard as she could, stretched out her arm. Opened her worn, brown leather glove—and that flying, spinning softball landed smack in the middle.

Just like they'd worked on.

Just like they'd practiced.

Laurie leapt up from her bucket. Pumped a fist into the air and let loose a walloping cheer with Hugh and her girls.

And unlike anything they could practice, it was when Suzie turned, with a face filled with so much shock Laurie could see it clear from the dugout.

Along with that big, gigantic smile.

They'd won.

Won the game, yes, but for Laurie, and what really mattered, she'd won that smile.

Except Laurie heard the unmistakable *thump, thump* behind her. So loud, so clear, it dwarfed the cheering parents.

Laurie's own smile slipped.

She glanced over her shoulder, and sure enough, there was Dan Richards, jumping down from the bleachers—yes, from the lowest step—and waddling towards the dugout. His rolling belly, and the

Slugging Angels T-shirt barely tucked into his jeans, hanging on by the slightest fold. But it was the red, scrunched face, the glinting eyes that held her.

She swallowed a curse (always mindful of her words around her girls—regardless of the currently cheering, very loud bodies).

The dust from the softball's impact hadn't yet cleared, let alone the umpire's usual shout of, "Game over!" before Richards was ready to let her have it.

Again.

Along with spewing angry spit all over her.

Just great.

She knew exactly what this was about. And how it would turn out.

Laurie fingered the sunflower seeds in her khaki shorts pocket. Just looking at Richards gave her a sour taste. And his temper. She might as well add in a mouthful of salt… except, no. She needed to deal with this. And without a mouthful of sunflower of seeds.

Yeah, she'd deal with it.

And do it the only way she knew how.

The only way she could.

She smashed her pink, *Slugging Angels* ball-cap on her head, squashing her ponytail flat, and prepared for some good ol' coach-to-parent battle.

Hugh, her co-coach and team owner, leaned against the fence. His wrinkled, leathery face was already tanned from the unrelenting southern California sun, a tan that was always better than hers.

He noticed her attention. And who it was on.

"You got this one?" Hugh asked. "He's a bit high-strung today."

"Just today? Hell, I'm surprised he hasn't blown out his knees from all the bleacher-jumping he's been doing."

Hugh lifted his eyebrows, which disappeared into his white mop of hair. "Careful there, Coach. Never know who's listening."

Referring to the five girls streaming out of the dugout, screaming and cheering at the top of their lungs. Laurie smiled and shook her head. "I think I'm safe."

Safe from being overheard (for now), but not safe from a determined and angry dad like Richards. A dad who, at times like this, hit a little too close to home.

Laurie shoved aside the memories, but they latched on. Held her. Gripped her so hard that, for a moment, it wasn't Richards stomping towards her, sneakers brushing the reddish-brown dust into the air. Wasn't Richards wearing that complete, disapproving look.

A look that said no matter how hard she worked, no matter how hard she trained, it wasn't enough.

She'd never be good enough.

Except this *was* Richards.

Not her dad.

And he was yelling at her. A coach. His daughter's coach.

Laurie dug her cleats into the cement, scraping and squashing the memory away. She wasn't a player anymore. She was a coach; a *good* coach, and she just flat out didn't have time to deal with the past—not if she expected to handle Richards.

And be nice about it, too.

Dealing with irate, know-it-all parents required a delicate touch. It was an art, one Laurie had picked up over the years. She'd seen all kinds of softball parents, from the most understanding and loving to the kind who pushed their girls until the game of softball changed from a fun sport to a job.

Those were the kinds of parents Laurie wanted to slug. And with good reason.

It didn't matter how many of these parents she'd met over the years or how many 'talks' she'd had with them. It never got easier. The memories were always there, lurking, waking up at just the right—and the wrong—moments.

"Enough, Stevens," Laurie growled to herself. "Focus."

She'd have to use her best tactic. Quick and to the point.

And it was the only way she'd get through this with her shredded self intact.

Laurie grabbed her old, reliable, 25-ounce Louisville Slugger bat and went to head Richards off.

A good bat, one she'd used in her high school days and all the way through college. Still of use to her, even now, even after that career had long ended.

Her girls ran from the field and into the dugout, all nine mingling with the other five racing out. Leaving Laurie trapped in the middle.

"We did it, Laurie!" Suzie leaped in the air, hugging Laurie around the middle. "Did you see my catch?"

"I sure did. You were great!" Laurie leaned her bat against the fence, temporarily relinquishing its comfort, and held up both hands for the team's high-five jumps.

Parents were one part of her job, this was the other. The better one.

Suzie jumped, stretching her short fingers towards Laurie's hand, and completely missed the double high-five.

Not that Suzie cared, or any of the other girls for that matter. One by one, they jumped, missed, and then tried again. Hugh gave his usual deep, barrel laugh, the one their girls loved, before shooing them into the dugout to clean and pack up.

Richards reached the field, face red, steam practically spewing from his ears. That last fold from his T-shirt finally untucked and now flapped around his middle.

Time for business.

Laurie finished the last couple of air high-fives and hefted her bat.

Lacey, the only girl who hadn't lined up for the high-fives, was standing off to the side, cleats still on, glove still clutched in her fist. Refused to enter the dugout. She towered over the other girls, both in height and size. Already pitchers on the other team were sending Lacey wary glances whenever she stepped up to the plate because any bat of Lacey's that touched the ball practically ensured it would go far.

To the *fence* far.

And she hadn't even hit her growth spurt, which meant there was a good chance she'd be a hell of a hitter once that kicked in. Not much of a runner, though, and if that attitude kept up, she'd not be much of a softball player, either.

But it was the attitude that was the problem.

A big problem.

One that, if Laurie didn't get a handle on—and on *Richards*—meant Lacey would go down a path darker than the one she'd gone down.

At least Laurie's teammates (when she'd played) had always liked her. At least they'd never been *afraid* of her.

Lacey gave Laurie a smug smile, the one kids got when they knew their parents were gonna knock some serious sense into you.

Hugh noticed Laurie's gaze and leaned closer, keeping his voice low and jolly so the girls wouldn't suspect trouble. "You sure? You know he wants Lacey to start more."

Laurie lifted her eyebrows. "You mean, this would go easier if you talked with him and not me?"

Which was true. Mostly because Hugh was male and to Richards's mindset, that meant he was much more willing to understand his position as Lacey's father.

But she understood his position just fine.

After all, she'd had a father just like him.

This was her team as much as Hugh's and whether she liked it or not, parents came with the territory. Even the ones that brought up bad memories.

"Thanks, but I'll handle this."

She needed to. Because, maybe, one day, she could move on.

Hugh glanced pointedly at the bat resting on her shoulder. "That's part of what I'm worried about, girl. You play nice, remember?"

"I always play nice." *When they do.*

Thankfully, she was saved from Hugh's response as the girls, Suzie in particular, had quite a few highlights of the game they were sure Hugh had missed seeing, and therefore had to enlighten him.

Lacey still glared at Laurie, still refusing to come into the dugout. Clearly she wanted to be near the action of her dad ripping Laurie a new one.

"Go get packed up." Laurie pointed into the dugout.

Lacey merely lifted her chin. Triumph.

Not today, kid.

With girls like Lacey, girls who thought they knew everything, there was really only one way to deal with them.

Be bigger. Stronger. Then maybe, somewhere down the line, they'd be willing to listen to something softer.

Kinder.

"Get packed or sit the next two games."

"That's not fair! I'm one of the best players. You need me out there if you want to win."

Laurie straightened. Took a deep breath to calm herself. Lacey was getting to be too much like Richards. The same arrogance. The same driving desire she'd seen countless times back on her old teams.

No matter how much she wanted to, she couldn't yell at Lacey. Couldn't even tell her how dangerous this road was and where it would lead if she wasn't careful. Because Lacey wouldn't listen.

Not yet. Maybe not ever.

For some girls, they never did.

"We're not here to win. We're here to have fun."

Lacey knew that. All her girls, and their parents, knew that. This was a team that had fun. The day it became a job for them was the day Laurie quit.

"Pack up or sit out. Your choice." Laurie spun, her cleats digging nicely into the hard-packed dirt, and headed Richards off before he reached the dugout.

This wasn't a conversation she wanted her girls to overhear.

But to appease Hugh, she gave Richards her best smile, though she did swing her bat nicely onto her shoulder. Might as well appeal to his male sensibility and appear strong. It might work in her favor.

"What can I do for you, Mr. Richards?"

"Coach," Richards growled. "This is the second game you've sat my daughter."

"Actually, I was pretty sure she was playing first base just now."

"You know what I meant." Sweat streamed from his face and his giant nostrils flared. "She should be starting. No one else on this team can pitch or hit like Lacey, and you sat her!"

Laurie's smile wobbled as her temper flared. "You know very well why I sat her."

"Do you think I'm just going to sit around and let you ruin my kid's chances? Ruin her shot at a great future?"

"Dan. Your daughter's twelve. She isn't even close to the age where—"

"Every game is important! Every game she has a chance to catch someone's eye. A coach on an 18-and-Under Team even."

"Eighteen? Christ, Richards, she's only twelve!"

But he didn't hear her. Couldn't. Already too lost in big dreams and an even bigger future.

"Maybe even scouts. High school. Hell, college. *And* if you can't teach her, if you can't be the great coach we thought you were, then you're wasting our time."

Her head swam.

Richards was honest to God thinking of Lacey for an 18-and-Under Team?

When it came to travel softball teams, age didn't exactly matter. Travel teams were the intense version of this game. More than any school or high school or league team. These were the teams that traveled to different cities, different states even, all with the end goal in mind: playing for college.

Just not Laurie's team.

Which was why she was coaching girls so young. Young enough that those big, lofty dreams didn't matter. Having fun was what mattered.

But if you were good enough to play with the big girls, and on those teams where seniors dominated, then you'd play with the big girls.

If you were good enough.

If your parents agreed it was the right move.

Laurie couldn't think of one instance where it was the right move. Not for a girl barely twelve. Not for Lacey.

It certainly hadn't been for Laurie.

The field tilted slightly. Red-brown dirt and the green, trimmed outfield temporarily trading places. How many times, for how many of her own years playing softball, had she heard Richards's exact words? Those exact same dreams?

Sometimes, they'd even come from her own, misguided lips.

Richards stepped forward, breaking the hold her past had on her. She needed to focus. Needed to be right here, right now if she was going to do Lacey any good.

She had to talk him down.

Laurie didn't back up. Not even when he pressed close enough she could practically taste his own sweat on her tongue. She squeezed the comforting rubber on the bat's handle. Dirt slid under her nails.

Focus. Stay calm.

"You still think you're some great hot shot?" Richards continued. "Well, I got news for you. You ain't in this sport anymore. You're a has-been, and the fact that anyone even remembers you playin' is a miracle."

This time, he leaned so close their noses nearly touched.

It took all of Laurie's control not to slug him. This man, no matter what she said, no matter what she did, would never understand.

Would never listen.

And *that* hit too close to home.

Enough to re-stir her anger. To push through the air that was trying to hard to catch in her throat. To clog there and keep her captive.

Not this time.

Not ever again.

"So you tell me," Richards growled, so close the sweat from his brow heated the already sun-hot air between them, "who the hell do you think you are sitting my daughter?"

"Her coach."

Laurie tapped her bat gently on her shoulder.

A reminder.

Richards's eyes zeroed in on it, but he made no move to back down or back up. Not like she'd expected him to.

"I'm the coach," she said again. "Lacey's coach, just like every other girl on this team. I'm also not going to stand here and let you yell in front of these girls. You have a problem with the way I run this team? You don't like the way I coach? That I don't measure up to your inflated expectations of me? Fine."

Another tap of the bat.

Richards's eyes jerked back to her face. They widened. Just slightly. As if *finally* realizing the danger.

That, just maybe, he'd gone too far.

"When Lacey joined this team, I made myself clear. We're not here to train your daughter for college ball. My girls are here to enjoy the game, to have fun." Laurie's breath hissed out, low and dangerous. "And if you ever yell like that in front of my girls, you and Lacey can get the hell off my team."

They glared at each other.

Richards looked away first.

Laurie risked a glance at the dugout. Hugh had done his part, keeping the young-ins away, focused on the small candy bars he was handing out on account of their second win of the season.

Even Lacey had been distracted by the promised treats. Good. Meant that they could finish this before it got any worse. Of course, quite a few of the parents had crept closer, hoping to overhear.

That was at least one thing that never changed from team to team, or parent to parent.

The gossip.

Laurie leaned back. "Do you have any problems with that?"

It was a trap question, and the way Richards's eyes narrowed, he knew it too. He and Lacey could quit the team; that was their choice.

She didn't resent them for it, but this was also her team.

She had choices too.

"Now," she gestured towards center field. "Why don't we have that talk, take a short walk, and work this out?"

She brushed past him. Her hand tightening on the bat. *Patience. Just another parent, one who if all the signs pointed correctly, wouldn't last long.*

Parents like Richards never did. They always had their own ideas, their own big dreams for their kids. The kind of dreams that usually ended up with two words: *college* and *scholarship*.

Why was she even doing this? Why was she fighting so hard when no one wanted to listen? What was the point?

They reached center field and Laurie thrust aside all her doubts. Richards would sense them, like a shark smelling blood.

Their talk went about as well as expected. Richards was furious Laurie hadn't started Lacey (again), and of course, was adamant that when Lacey had shoved their catcher Mandy, it was not in fact, a shove.

"Shove or not a shove," Laurie said. "I don't give a shit."

Richards's mouth clicked shut. He blinked. A softball coach for twelve-year-olds didn't do much swearing. It came with the job. There were times, however, when such words were needed.

Necessary, even.

Like now.

"A gentle, friendly shove is still a shove and I won't have fighting on my team. I warned Lacey and she decided to back talk to me. So, I benched her for the first half of the game. Hugh agrees with my decision."

That last comment effectively cut Richards off at the knees. He couldn't go plead his case to Hugh, not if Hugh was already on Laurie's side.

"If you want her playing," Laurie said, "then I suggest you talk to her."

Lacey's fighting habits had started almost immediately after her parents separated. That, however, wasn't Laurie's business. There were certain topics where it wasn't her place to say anything. At least not until kids like Lacey made it Laurie's business.

Richards might not be pleased, but he couldn't argue her points. He didn't say he agreed with her; no, that wouldn't be up his alley, but he nodded anyway and went to collect his daughter.

Lacey had that gleam in her eyes, the triumph for having her dad stand up for her, which immediately died when Richards shook his head.

Not this time, kid, Laurie thought to herself.

Of course, Lacey had no idea, and would never know, that the real person who'd stood up for her had been Laurie.

She watched them leave and the muscles in her right shoulder pulsed. She rubbed at the knots and hissed. A leftover reminder from her softball days, the muscles still hurt, still got tense whenever something like this happened. As if her body, along with her mind, refused to let her forget.

She lowered her arm. Right now, the last thing she needed to remember was playing softball and dealing with her dad, the coach.

"You gonna help me out here?" Hugh came up beside her and dumped a handful of softballs into the bucket.

"You bet." It was exactly the kind of distraction she needed. She and Hugh loaded up the ball buckets and equipment bags into the back of Laurie's somehow still running pick-up.

The weekend hadn't been a hard one, not for their team, anyway. Only two games on both days, though the spring season was only just getting started. They'd be soon seeing their girls once during the week for practice, then on the weekends. Switching between three and four games a day, every week until the summer season closed.

Still, the park—with its four, well-used softball fields—was already deserted. Teams, parents, and their kids seemed to vanish the second the last pitch was thrown. It made the park more relaxing, more inviting as if it needed the quiet to settle in for the night after a long day of roasting hot dogs, French fries, and mounds of ketchup.

But right now, with her shoulder pulsing and Richards's accusations rolling around her mind, not to mention her own damn memories, the last thing Laurie felt was peace.

She packed her bat and slammed the tailgate door. Her truck shook slightly.

Hugh lifted his eyebrows at her. "It went that well, huh? Got a bit of extra steam to work off?"

"Steam is too generous. Try really pissed off."

"I can see that. You want to talk about it?"

"No."

Hugh merely looked at her.

"There isn't much to say. I told him to back off. Lacey pushed Mandy, regardless of how he wants to dice it."

"I noticed he stopped yelling."

Laurie shrugged. "Not hard to do when you carry a bat."

And if you have no problem using it, if push comes to shove.

Hugh let the bat comment slide. But he looked at her, like he always did. Just like he always knew why she needed it for these talks.

The bat, as much as the softballs and the very fields her team played on, were part of her past. A direct link, and a reminder, of the kind of coach she refused to be.

"You okay?"

She knew what he was asking. And why.

"Yes. No." Laurie leaned against her truck and rubbed her shoulder, the muscles still tight, still pinching. "It'll come up again. It won't be the last talk."

"Unless he decides to take her to another team." Hugh sighed. "I'm getting too old for this. It didn't always used to be this way, you know? Parents thinkin' they know what's best, even if they don't know anything about the game."

"It's not you. And it's not me. The game's changing."

It had started to change when she was Lacey's age, when it was Laurie out there being yelled at by her father as he pushed her to do better, to excel.

She rubbed her forehead. What was wrong with her today? Why all these memories and why now? Was it just because of Richards?

Sure dealing with him usually brought on the bad times, ones that no matter how many times she buried them, just kept digging themselves free.

"I thought I could change things, make a difference in their lives."

Hugh reached over and gripped her shoulder. "You are. Why do you think parents keep lining up to join?"

They joined because regardless of what Richards thought, Laurie and Hugh were excellent coaches. They had a knack for bringing up the best talent, for nurturing girls. The problem was she and Hugh were merely the dinosaurs who refused to go extinct. That was the real problem. The one neither wanted to bring up.

Teams nowadays didn't care about having fun. They wanted results. They wanted the best chance for the kids to get that college scholarship.

It didn't matter if the kids were only twelve-freakin'-years old.

Laurie bit her tongue and kept her thoughts to herself. So did Hugh.

One day, they'd have to accept it, but until then well it didn't matter so much did it?

"Still," Hugh reached his arms up above his head, his old bones cracking and creaking as he stretched. "Sittin' all day on that damn bucket—I'm definitely too old for that."

"Whatever you say, old man."

Hugh laughed. "Old? Damn straight I'm old. Girl I remember when you were no taller than our Suzie-pie. About just as freckled too."

"I was always taller than Suzie. And I only had two freckles." She knew because she'd counted nearly every day.

Hugh scanned the empty parking lot, a lot that had been recently filled with the more expensive cars and BMW's. That was southern California living for you. Laurie's beat-up truck was the only one of its kind on game days.

"But you're right," he said. "Times are changing. It's not the same game as when you came through. A different world." He shook his head. "More kids will be like Lacey, more dads like Richards who think they know everything."

Laurie dusted off her pants a final time, not like it did much difference. She seemed to be covered in as much dirt as her girls. "It's still enough the same."

She hoped it was, that there was enough reason for her to stay, to keep playing the game she used to enjoy so much. "As long as there are kids who want to play good ball, who want to have fun, then I'll still be here."

She'd still coach. She'd make sure at least one girl had the experience she never did. As long as she never crossed that line, the line that so many coaches had no problems stepping over, she'd keep coaching.

Yes, she still spent most of her days helping out kids—or trying to. Most kids, especially the lovely high school age ones Laurie taught, didn't appreciate the help. But out here, on the field, this was still her life.

Even as hard as that life had been at times.

But she'd learned, the hard way, that she couldn't stay away.

This, *this*, was where her heart was.

On the field.

"I know you will, kid." Hugh slapped her shoulder. "I've no doubts about that."

Laurie nodded, but kept her mouth shut. She had her doubts, and Richards in all his anger, had reminded her of them.

CHAPTER 2

Jack Evans knew exactly what he was looking for. Age, attitude, and most importantly, coaching style. He leaned against the Ferrari, slipping his hands into his jean pockets and scanned the softball fields.

Throngs of people gathered, mostly around the snack stand, but quite a few hovered around field number two. A packed park. Definitely a good sign.

Somewhere, some place here, he knew was the perfect team for Elizabeth. He just had to find them.

Jack opened the Ferrari's passenger door as Elizabeth peeked her head out. "I've got a good feeling about this one. Much better than the last two."

Elizabeth worried her bottom lip, a nervous gesture she'd picked up since the divorce.

Three years. Three years and this was how far they'd gotten. But she was talking to him now, even if half the time she was asking about her mother.

The mother that had, more or less, left them both. For money. For 'greener pastures.' For players that hadn't yet realized they were living in the bowels of hell and needed to get out.

Nancy. The mother who'd left him because he'd screwed up their marriage and their daughter. The mother who'd left them because he wanted out.

Jack forced a smile. "Come on. Let's give this place a chance."

Please.

He could barely see her face over her low-pulled baseball cap, but she at least gave the fields a long look before carefully stepped out. At least this time she got out of the car.

When they'd visited Mount Crest Park, with its perfectly manicured outfields, the grass cut to a perfect, ball-bouncing height, each unused field had a shining sign warning that the field was only for authorized users.

Elizabeth had taken one look and didn't budge.

Not that he blamed her. There was something to be said for a little imperfection, to play on a field that players actually played on rather than simply admired.

"Come on, this place looks exactly like we're looking for. See," he pointed to the food stands. "Regular people are serving regular hot dogs."

And not that fancy, organic stuff the other place was selling.

Jack smiled, trying to be encouraging, but Elizabeth only ducked her head, turning her attention back to the fields.

He did his best not to notice, not to let himself feel too much. It still hurt, but he reminded himself he was doing this for Elizabeth.

He deserved to feel hurt. He didn't deserve her trust. Not yet. He had to earn it.

He'd find her the best team and then, maybe, he'd see a smile.

Or two.

Jack steered Elizabeth towards the fields and she shuffled along beside him, shoulders hunched, hands tucked in her pockets. This wouldn't work if she didn't at least try.

He studied the crowd, searching for the tell-tale signs of collared shirts and notebooks. College scouts—and not a single one in sight. Good. The last thing Elizabeth needed was a team and a place that thrilled on playing hard, on working towards college dreams.

She was too young for that. Right now, all he wanted was a damn smile.

"Are you excited?"

"No."

"That's too bad, because I am."

"Mom says softball is wasting my time."

This time, Jack bit back his anger. Nancy had no problems about wasting her own time and the money she'd gotten through the divorce.

"Your mother doesn't know the first thing about sports," Jack snapped. "Or softball."

Elizabeth flinched as his hard voice and Jack cursed himself. But he wasn't going to let her think that way; wasn't going to Nancy win over their daughter just to spite him.

"Well," he said, "I'm excited enough for the both of us."

He felt it, felt opportunity tingle in the air. It was the same thing he'd felt during those high pressure, Major League games. When each player stepped up to bat against him. The tingle had told him which pitch to throw, how to make the batter off-balance.

That's what he'd felt when baseball had been his life. That was before the drugs, before the women, before all the money had gotten to his head.

Even after all those years, he still knew the tingle.

Maybe things could work out, for both him and Elizabeth. The tingle might be a tiny, slim beacon of hope, but it was still hope.

"I don't want to be here." Elizabeth scuffed her sneakers on the cement. "Can't I just sign up for a team? Any team?"

"You know we can't do that." Jack slipped on his sunglasses. "It's got to be the right team."

And if she'd wanted any team, she would have at least gotten out of the car at Mount Crest. This was all just Nancy talking, all her poisonous words seeping into Elizabeth.

He'd stop them cold.

But he try to keep a calm, straight face while he did it. Not easy when they were talking about Nancy.

There was nothing he could do about parental visits; though, thankfully, Nancy rarely showed up, rarely cared enough to show up. But when she did...

Jack shook himself. Now wasn't the time to think about Nancy. This was about Elizabeth and finding the right team, the one that would make her smile.

Nearby, the sound of a bat cracking a ball ripped through the air. The stands cheered.

Elizabeth's head shot up, an eager light filling her eyes. "I just want to play."

"You will, sweetheart." Jack lifted back her ball-cap and kissed her forehead. This time she didn't pull away.

Jack didn't dwell on that tiny accomplishment. The day had only started. He would celebrate after he's signed her up with the best team; the right one for his daughter.

And he sure hoped he'd find it here. Sunny View Sports Park was one of the last ones before they had to look outside the area. They might even have to move if he couldn't find the right team.

And he'd move; hell, he'd do anything for Elizabeth.

Hadn't he already proven that?

"Big crowd," he murmured. Which also meant a good team.

Elizabeth merely nodded, seeming to shrink into herself. Jack pulled her closer, hoping to reassure her with his presence. He had no idea how his daughter had such a fear of crowds when for years he'd excelled on them. Thrived on them.

Of course, he knew how.

Nancy.

Jack poked at Elizabeth's small bicep muscle that her shirt didn't quite hide. A slight definition, just enough toning to stand out.

"You're growing some guns there. Do I need to take out the radar gun? See how fast you're throwing?"

"I don't have muscles."

"You could."

"I don't want big muscles. I don't want to look like a guy."

"Believe me, you'll never look like a guy." He paused. "Then again, maybe I want you to look like a guy."

She frowned, but still managed to look gorgeous. Not adult gorgeous, thank God, just the promise of beauty, the hint of it.

Elizabeth definitely had the Jack-gene. Not the Jack-guy gene, but the Jack-good-looking gene. But he truly hoped he had a few more years to worry about that particular problem.

Jack wiggled some room for them as they moved through the crowd. A gentleman was nice enough to step aside, probably when he caught sight of Elizabeth. Then he saw Jack.

"You're Jack Evans? The pitcher?"

For a second, Jack lost control of his smile. Irritation trickled in. Not now. Right now he was here with his daughter.

Still, he turned, throwing on his charming smile, barely breaking stride from Jack the Dad to Jack the ex-ballplayer. He shook the older man's hand but kept a firm grip on Elizabeth.

"Good to meet you. Jack Evans."

"Man. I saw you play back in '06 against the *Indians*. Damn good game, sir. I was real sorry to hear about your retirement. You had some great things going for you."

"Still do. Being a dad is a full-time job."

Jack kept the smile, but only from sheer and constant practice. The question came up often enough and his standard answer had been practiced just as often.

As well as making up for being a terrible one the first half of Elizabeth's life. But no one needed to hear those details. They didn't need to hear how Nancy had purposefully sent photos to the newspapers of him...cheating. With several women. At once.

A paper that eight year old Elizabeth had accidentally seen when she'd spilled her cereal on the table and used the paper to clean up the miss.

Jack gave the man's hand another good shake. This man, and all the rest like him, didn't want to hear about Jack hitting rock bottom.

All they wanted to hear about was the glitter and the shining lights. They wanted to hear about Jack the star player, the Rookie of the Year with the most promising career seen in the last decade.

"Like I said, it's not easy being a dad. I'm sure you know all about it."

"I do," the man nodded in complete understanding. "And good for you, standing up for your kid."

He leaned in though and whispered, "But I sure miss seeing you on the mound. One hell of a slider you threw."

He pumped Jack's hand another time, then passed him his buddy— also a baseball fan.

Elizabeth squeezed his hand and then slipped away before he could protest. The crowd had already swelled as his growing fans wandered over—or maybe not fans so much as curious onlookers who wanted to meet someone marginally famous.

Or once-famous for that matter.

Jack shook several hands, glossing over names as he scanned for Elizabeth. He spotted her at the top of the bleachers.

He should have known. She had either gone there so he could easily find her or because she knew how he felt about heights.

Honestly, he hoped it was the height thing because it meant they had something. At this point, even a little pre-teen vs. parent animosity would be nice.

For several minutes, that was the last time he could think about Elizabeth.

Walking the fame line was a delicate balance, and this particular gentleman had a pretty good voice. Within minutes Jack had established his own small crowd.

Which was not what he'd come to do at the ballpark.

"It was great meeting you," Jack said, smooth as ever, before Mr. Richards could introduce him to yet another friend. "I'm actually here with my daughter. We're looking for a team."

"Is that her up there?" Richards glanced up at Elizabeth. "If she's got even a smidgeon of your talent, she's a player we definitely want on our *Angels* team."

"*Angels?* Never heard of them." Other than the American League team, of course.

Richards nodded to the field in front of them, the one Elizabeth was watching.

Field Number two. The one the crowd gathered around.

The sound of metal striking bat ripped through the air again. Richards and the crowd cheered, and in that moment, they completely forgot Jack existed.

All that mattered was this team and the girl rounding the bases. She touched second, hitting the corner at a nice, lean angle. She was fast off the base, sprinting towards third. She might even make it a triple.

The coach at third base circled her arms, pushing her run to stretch the hit, to make it count.

Pushing.

Driving.

Jack leaned forward. He kept silent, but the tingle was back, swirling through him.

Just like that, he was taken back to the game. He felt wind roaring through his helmet, drowning out all noise, all the cheers. Felt his arms pumping up and down. All he could see, all he could focus on, was what in front of him.

He blinked. The memory still clung to him, as if he could feel the dirt scratching at his arms.

The third-baseman stretched her glove out, wide and waiting as the softball raced in. The runner reached with her arm as she slid and caught the corner of third base.

The third-baseman's glove crashed down, smacking into the runner's side. Hard from the sound of it.

Jack smiled. Even before the umpire made the call, he knew she was safe.

The umpire swung his arms out, a cross motion once, then a second time. Jack couldn't hear the call, not over Richards and his band of fellow parents.

Jack clapped along with them. It was a professional courtesy. That was a damn fine hit and some good base running, but if it hadn't been for the third-base coach, that runner would never have taken the chance.

He watched as the coach helped the girl up and gave her a high-five. Tall and lean, even from this distance he could see the coach's sculpted legs before they disappeared into a pair of black, comfortable-looking shorts.

He clapped again. That was some damn fine coaching. Only someone on top of their players, someone who understood their strengths, their weakness, as well as those of their opponents, could pull off a tight play like that.

And make it look like just another day. A no-big-deal kind of move.

The coach turned to the next batter, clapping and cheering her on.

Jack's eyebrows rose and he leaned forward, not because of the game or the cheering parents as (from what he could tell) their big-hitter stepped up to the plate.

It was the coach's gaze that held him. That intensity, that focus. The kind of gaze that only came from someone who knew the game, who'd lived it.

And if he were honest with himself, that intense gaze also happened to belong to a very surprising—and beautiful—woman.

'Beauty' didn't quite cover it. 'Beauty' didn't apply to the strong, female athletes he'd known throughout his career. Call it exotic if you wanted, Amazonian even, but not beauty.

Unlike the one woman he'd married (and then soon divorced)—but that had been part of Jack's problem. Nancy had beauty in spades, but that was about all.

No, this woman was definitely not Nancy.

Tall, defined, with the kind of body any sports player would recognize. More breathtaking than Nancy with her fine jewelry and fancy dolled-up hair.

Jack edged his way to Richards, who nodded at the batter. "That's my kid there. She's got talent. She's going places."

Jack smiled, hoping for a neutral response. That girl was a giant for her age. If she could actually hit the ball she would go places.

"So, who's the coach?" Jack tried for a casual nod, hoping not to appear too interested.

"Her." Richards's smile fell. "A coach who wouldn't know good if it bit her on the ass."

A woman half Richards' size of slapped his arm. "Knock it off, Dan. Just because you didn't like that she benched Lacey—for shoving my Courtney, I'll remind you—doesn't give you the right to bad-mouth her."

"You don't bench your best player," Dan growled.

"We do on this team. Especially for fighting." The woman truly only came to Richards's chest, but man, it didn't take a star pitcher to realize this was one spit-fire he wanted to give wide berth to.

Jack's eyebrows lifted. "Nice to meet you, and you are...?"

"Courtney's mother." She shook Jack's hand. "I've heard of you Mr. Evans. News already made its way down from the snack stand. Now, if you want my advice—and this is true advice—I'd suggest you sit your butt down and make your own decisions about this team."

She released Jack's hand and glared at Dan. "You never know who's got a chip on their shoulder."

Jack nodded. He would have tipped his hat to the lady if he'd had a hat, but he knew good advice when he heard it. And he also knew how to steer-clear of trouble—a talent he'd acquired thanks to Nancy.

"I think I'll do that."

Richards scowled, but he moved away from them, getting closer to the fence as he cheered his daughter on. Courtney's mother clapped, but it didn't have the same enthusiasm.

"You're not sitting." She paused mid-clap.

"I was hoping you could tell me a little about this team. And about the coach." The coach was the heart and soul of a team. You could tell a lot about the players if you understood the coach.

"Laurie Stevens. She used to play ball herself, once upon a time. Back in college."

Jack's eyes narrowed as he studied Laurie. Calm movements, sure and confident. Never showed any nerves, never showed her players any of her thoughts other than they could do their best.

Not traits he'd seen often since he and Elizabeth had started this hunt.

"I can see that."

"After staring at her for thirty seconds?" Courtney's mother asked.

Jack shrugged. "It's a gift."

"Hmph. Well, are you gonna stay?"

Jack didn't appreciate the knowing look she gave him. Of course, whether she knew he was thinking about Stevens' coaching ability or how great she looked in her snug uniform shirt was a different story.

Then again, anyone with half a brain would notice both. So, Jack merely pointed to his daughter.

"I think my daughter has a seat picked out." Nice and high, of course. "It's her decision."

"Good for you. It shouldn't be anyone else's but hers. And it looks to be a damn fine game." Then Courtney's mother smiled. "I'm Diane, by the way. If your daughter fits in, it'd be nice having another parent around."

This time she shot Richards's back another glare. "You just let me know if you have any questions. That's Courtney to the left. She's small like me, but she's about to hit her growth spurt. She'll be a great hitter, especially with Laurie working with her."

"I bet she will—and thanks." Jack shook Courtney's hand. "I think I'll see what she's made out of."

He didn't specify if he'd meant the team or Laurie. In reality, the coach was one and the same.

Jack was more than happy to join Elizabeth as he carefully made his way up the metal steps, gripping the handhold. Elizabeth shrugged, not quite apologizing for the height but at least admitting she'd chosen the spot on purpose.

As if he could blame her. He had dragged her all around these soft-ball fields for several weekends.

"Looks like these guys might be promising." Jack slid beside her, back pressed against the metal railing. At least it wasn't an open-backed bleacher. Then he'd have made her move.

"I don't want to be here."

"We've talked about this."

Elizabeth pulled her knees into her chest. Clearly going into her silent mode, a mode that didn't solve anything.

"Elizabeth. Talk to me."

Elizabeth bit her bottom lip. He waited her out, even excusing himself from an interested fan. Finally, she caved.

"You'll just pull me again. As soon as I start playing you'll decide you don't like the coach, or the girls, or a parent and you'll pull me."

Well, that was a start. And she was talking to him, which was what he wanted. Except now he needed to talk to her.

"I told you why the last team didn't work out." He hadn't, actually, but there was no way he was going to mention the way Coach Marks had looked at his daughter as if calculating just what kind of player Jack Evans's daughter would turn into.

And how it'd profit his team.

Maybe Jack was being silly, and maybe his punching Marks was a slight over reaction, but he was doing his best.

Elizabeth rested her head on her knees and glanced up at him. "So what makes this team so different?"

The coach was a very good looking female who at least knew how to direct her base runners, which was more than Marks had done.

Jack shook his head. "I don't know yet, that's why we're here. Everyone else seems to like this team."

Elizabeth said nothing as she closed up. Damn it.

"Do you want something to eat? Hot dog? Sunflower seeds?"

"No."

Jack pulled out his wallet. "We're gonna be here for a while. You might as well eat something."

"I had cereal before we left."

He pulled out a $20 bill. He hadn't noticed the breakfast. He'd been so preoccupied researching teams online and who was playing that he hadn't even noticed her eating breakfast.

What had she eaten? Cereal? A bowl of chocolate fudge ice cream? When was he going to start noticing these things?

Elizabeth shook her head at the money, tucking her hands under armpits. "I don't want it."

"Don't be difficult."

He could feel the nearest crowd goers leaning towards them. Ex-baseball player Jack Evans and his daughter having a nice public disagreement at a softball game. Not the way he wanted to introduce himself to Coach Stevens either. At least, if this was the team he wanted for Elizabeth.

Elizabeth didn't budge.

"Fine." He smashed the money back in his wallet. "What do you want? Food? A drink?"

Coward, Jack thought. What he wanted was her to smile, and if there was anything in the world that could make his little girl laugh.

"My mother."

CHAPTER 3

"**Y**our mom's busy."

Nancy was busy, always busy, but Jack wasn't. He was here and he would always be here.

Jack gazed at the field, watched as the pitcher threw another pitch, this one high and to the outside of home plate. The batter miscalculated and swung anyway.

Strike three.

This was something Nancy would never see—Elizabeth striking out, hitting her first ever home-run. Even when they'd been married, Nancy had found a way to miss every game, every practice.

Leaving Elizabeth alone.

But then, he hadn't been much better.

"She's always busy." Elizabeth wiped her eyes. "But I guess it doesn't matter. Playing softball doesn't matter."

Jack tensed. "Why do you say that? I thought you liked playing softball."

Elizabeth shrugged. "That's what mom always said: 'girls sports don't matter.'"

"They sure as hell *do* matter."

Jack took a deep breath and tugged Elizabeth closer to him. He needed her to understand, to see that what Nancy said wasn't true.

"It's true you can't make a ton of money like I did, but that doesn't mean you playing and having fun don't matter."

"Really?"

The hopeful look she gave him nearly did him in. Jack squeezed her shoulder. "Really."

The *Angels* team went to bat, their cheering and bright faces at complete odds with the wounded look on his daughter's face. A look he wanted to wipe away, taking all the pain with it.

"They look like they're having fun," Elizabeth whispered. There was no hiding the agony in her voice, or the longing.

Great. This wasn't what he wanted their Saturday outing to be like, with the ghost of Nancy leeching all his daughter's sunshine.

"They do. Do you want to sit closer? Maybe talk to one of the parents? I'll bet they'll know if their kids are having fun."

"Maybe."

But she didn't move to sit closer or to talk with Courtney's mom, Diane. Jack left her alone with her thoughts. What was he going to do? How was he going to fix this?

He'd thought it'd be easy, finding her the right team, a team she could relax and be herself on. He hadn't realized he needed to fix what Nancy had unknowingly, or, shit, maybe even knowingly, broken. Their daughter's confidence.

He wanted to help, needed to help, and there wasn't a damn thing he could do if she didn't let him.

The game moved on and Jack settled into to simply watch. No studying, no taking notes on performance or tactics. He just watched, and after another inning, was surprised to see Elizabeth was right.

The kids were having fun. So was the coach. Laurie Stevens never stopped smiling.

Jack leaned towards Elizabeth, intending to point out why the batter hit that last ball as a weak grounder to the third baseman, and froze when he saw her face.

Her ball-cap was still pulled low, but it couldn't hide the smile shining from her face. Elizabeth was smiling.

It wasn't a big smile, but by damn it was a smile.

Afraid to break the spell, afraid to call her back to herself, Jack simply watched her. He forgot about the game until she looked up.

Oh, yes. That was definitely a smile.

"Can I, Dad?" Wistful, soft voice. Afraid. "Can I play for them?"

"Is that what you want?" Jack hardly dared breath.

Elizabeth nodded.

"Then I'll talk with the coach." He stood, pulling off his sunglasses and tucking them into his pocket.

"Right now?" Elizabeth half raised out of her seat.

"Right now."

Elizabeth's face lit up and she nearly knocked him off the bleachers as she flew into his arms hugging him. In public. Hell, forget 'in public,' she was just hugging him.

He carefully wrapped his arms around her and hugged her back.

He could do this. He could do the Dad-thing. And what's more, he'd show Nancy that he was good at it.

Neither he nor Elizabeth were failures.

And if he was going to put his daughter's happiness in this team's hands, well, he'd sure see if that coach was as good as everyone thought she was.

CHAPTER 4

*L*aurie jogged into the dugout, cleats easily digging into the dirt, as her girls streamed out, taking the field. Gloves smacking into backs for comfort, luck, and more importantly, connection. Teamwork.

Dust lifted off the leather. Clung to her face, to her hands.

The dirt was a part of the game, helped make it real. But nothing felt more real, more right, then seeing the excitement.

And *damn*, for an at-bat inning, they hadn't done bad.

Scored two runs and Lacey hadn't punched the other team's second baseman when she stretched for the ball, getting Lacey out before she'd touched the base.

Progress, Laurie thought, happened one step at a time. And when it came to Lacey, Laurie knew progress would go very, *very* slow.

But it was still progress.

What mattered most, though, was that all her girls—even Lacey—were smiling. Laughing. Having fun.

The unhappiness that had dogged Laurie for the past week (making her school week—and the legion of homework a sludge to get through) had *finally* lifted. Sure Richards made a point of glaring at her when she'd arrived at the field this morning, but Lacey had offered no snide remarks, no glaring looks at Laurie or her team-mates. Instead, she'd suited up and took the field in the second inning.

She hadn't complained. And top of it, *all* her girls were having fun.

Whatever problems other teams were having as they pushed to make the game more competitive, working their girls too hard and too fast. Well, it wasn't happening here. Not on her team.

Laurie pulled her upside-down bucket closer the fence so she could give pitching signs to their tough-cookie catcher, Mandy. It scraped at the ground, catching between dirt and cement, but Laurie didn't pay much attention.

Her focus was on the field.

On her girls.

A smiled pulled at her lips. She let it.

A Saturday game day couldn't get much better than this. Mid-game, and they were already ahead. It was a good time to let loose and have some fun.

Laurie watched Heather warming up, pitching a few fastballs, then adding a change-up which lifted off too high, forcing Mandy to stand for the catch. And while Mandy shared in Lacey's overall size, they didn't match in height. She had to spring up just to catch the fly-away pitch.

Laurie frowned, making a mental note to work on that pitch at Wednesday's private pitching lesson. She definitely needed to call a few change-ups this inning. The only way to get better was practice.

"No kidding," she heard Hugh say from the other side of the dugout.

She blinked. Finally realizing that Hugh wasn't beside her like normal.

"Your girl's looking for a team?"

Laurie frowned. A parent asking about the team? And mid-game? That was more than just odd. It was flat rude.

Laurie didn't turn. Even though she was tempted, if only to glare at Hugh. Laurie had learned, quite early, that parents who wanted to chat during a game also had a habit of offering coaching advice. Offering, which soon, turned into demands.

Like Richards just last week.

However, the temptation to sneak a peak over her shoulder itched against her spine—especially when she heard the softer, but deeper, rumbling response.

A response too low for her to pick up without actually turning.

And she couldn't. Right now, Heather needed her attention.

Not to mention, turning meant an interest on her part in the conversation and she wasn't interested.

Besides, Hugh knew how she felt about meeting prospective parents—*especially* during a game.

Parents were a package deal. If she wanted kids to play on her team, then the parents came with them.

She accepted that, grudgingly.

However, she didn't need to have her game interrupted to meet them.

Besides, keeping Richards in-line was more than enough. Adding a parent who insisted on giving coaching advice—

"Come on in," Hugh was saying. "Let me introduce you to Laurie Stevens. Coach Stevens was one hell of a ball player in her days. Sorta like you."

What the hell? She was coaching!

Laurie sprang from her bucket. Mouth open, ready to snap at Hugh and this new 'parent.' She turned, got an eyeful of the parent, and her mouth clicked closed.

This wasn't just any parent.

She recognized the face, the stride, hell the perfectly muscled arms (yes, she could tell from underneath his smooth, leather jacket).

This was Jack Evans.

The Jack Evans.

Former pitcher for Major League teams, the guy who'd led the league in strike-outs as a rookie. A man who looked nothing like the poster she used to have on her wall.

Laurie was really glad she'd closed her mouth instead of standing there, mouth hanging open, unable to look away. Well, she couldn't look away, but at least she didn't look like an idiot.

She hoped.

But why did he have to look even better in person? Even the scattering of gray in his hair merely added to his features, making him look more, deeper somehow, than when he was ten years younger.

Jack followed Hugh into the dugout, nodding to each girl. They smiled at him. To them, Jack was just another parent. They had no idea who Jack was.

A few girls gave Laurie a questioning look, a 'who is this guy?' look. They knew the dugout rules—no parents allowed—and Hugh knew the rules. So whoever this guy was, Hugh was breaking those rules, and what was worse, was bringing the parent to meet Laurie.

During a game.

Lacey nudged Suzie in the stomach, practically sending the poor girl sprawling off the bench. "Watch this. It's gonna be good."

There was almost a dare in Lacey's eyes. Probably because of what had happened last week with her own dad.

Laurie clenched her jaw. Could feel the slight, tentative relationship she had with Lacey rubbing away.

All because of a famous parent walking in *her* dugout.

Jack waltzed into the dugout, smooth and confident, not a single step out of place. As if he belonged there. Didn't seem at all bothered how his fancy, and probably expensive, shiny black shoes already carried a sheen of red-brown dirt dusting along their sides. A man like Jack Evans belonged in the dugout, as if he was born with some special ability that made him 'fit.'

Which was fine.

So long as it wasn't her dugout.

Laurie spun back around and promptly planted her butt on the bucket. She didn't need a parent like Jack Evans attached to her team. One look at him was enough and she knew, simply knew he'd be trouble.

He'd want a big and flashy team. The kind of team that attracted talent and had their sights set on out-of-state tournaments and college exposure.

It was everything she stood against.

Everything she'd fought against.

The home plate umpire called for batter up, snapping Laurie from her thoughts. Time to get to business.

Laurie flashed the first sign to Mandy, who passed it along to Heather.

Fast-ball. To the low, outside corner of the plate.

Before every game they discussed what the new 'code' would be—their secret conversation between coach and pitcher. After all, can't have the other team stealing their signs. Even with kids this young, people still cheated. Human nature.

Hugh ambled up beside her.

She didn't look up.

"There's someone I'd like to introduce you to, Laurie."

"In the middle of a game?"

Hugh winced. Oh, yes, Hugh knew exactly what he was doing and knew it'd piss her off. Still, he held out his hand as Jack slid up beside him.

"He's a special guy, not the kind you meet on any old field. I'd like you to meet him."

"I see."

And yes, she did see. Fame still got you a few things in life, especially when it was a person who dazzled old men like Hugh.

She set her scowl in place, glanced up at both men, and was glad she'd prepared herself, along with taking an extra moment to catch her breath so her surprise wouldn't show.

Because she definitely, *definitely* hadn't expected her breath to be stolen.

Jack looked even better closer up. Their eyes met, held. His a deep blue, like an evening in spring. Neither moved as they stared at each other, that assessing intensity Laurie usually reserved for the game.

Hugh cleared his throat.

Laurie shook herself free and got to her feet. She held out her hand, hoping to cover up her fluster and her very obvious staring.

"Jack Evans, right?"

His eyebrows shot up, clearly surprised, but then he smiled. "I am. Good to meet you."

Yes, it was the same smile she remembered from watching him on TV and the four times she'd seen him play in person. It was the same smile. Still gorgeous, still made her heart beat a tiny bit faster.

Jack clasped her hand, a nice and firm grip. The kind of grip that said 'confidence' and 'control.' Not the kind of grip easily forgotten.

Her pulse quickened.

"I hear you're the coach to play for." Jack didn't let go of her hand.

"It depends on what kind of team you're looking for." Laurie tried to smile and absolutely failed.

Yes, he was gorgeous, but she didn't want him here.

He had a look in his eyes, that intense concentration. Jack Evans was a man who knew exactly what he wanted and how to get it. She recognized the look from her days of playing softball.

The same look she recognized in herself before she walked away from the field.

And she wanted it nowhere near her team.

"I watched you play a few times," she said. "You were quite the player."

There, wasn't that nice and professional?

Of course, he still held her hand.

Laurie's smile wobbled when she realized it. "You'll have to excuse me. We don't usually meet parents during a game."

She shot Hugh a look, who immediately backed away.

"Sorry about interrupting," Jack replied. He still hadn't let go.

"It's fine," Laurie lied.

Finally, finally Jack released her hand, a hand that now tingled, and nodded towards the catcher. "Looks like you're needed."

"Right. Thanks." She managed a nod, then knelt down and flashed Mandy the next sign. Time to get back to work.

Hugh returned to his nice, friendly conversation with Jack Evans. A conversation that continued behind her as they sat on the metal bench. Once in a while they were drowned out by the cheering girls, but Laurie still heard enough.

Jack was looking for a team for his daughter.

Laurie's breath caught. The minute the words left Jack's mouth, she knew she'd lost. Hugh would offer Jack's daughter, Elizabeth, a spot. Regardless of the girl's talent, regardless of whether she'd fit in with the other girls, Hugh would offer it to Jack.

Laurie flashed another sign.

That meant Jack wasn't going to be leaving any time soon. She thought of their handshake and the confidence practically radiating from Jack. He knew it, too. He knew Hugh wouldn't turn him down.

She glanced at her hand and it warmed, as if remembering his touch.

Laurie crossed her arms, shoving the betraying hand under her armpit.

This was fine. She could deal with Jack Evans so long as he remained a parent. An unobtrusive, quiet parent in the bleachers.

Jack knelt beside her, his leather jacket, softer than butter, brushing her arm. She hadn't even heard him approach.

Laurie refused to acknowledge him, but that didn't matter, not to someone like Jack.

"The batter's crowding the plate."

Duh, she wanted to tell him. She wasn't a first year coach.

"Why not go for a nice screwball inside, throw the batter off balance a little?"

"Because the pitcher only has two pitches," Laurie snapped. This was *exactly* what she knew would happen. "She hasn't even heard of a screwball."

Realizing she'd broken her silence, Laurie settled for glaring at Jack—who was quite close to her right now. The smell of pine and warm leather drifted to her, surrounded her; underneath it was the subtle smell of sweat. Of the field.

She managed, barely, not to reach for her trusty Louisville Slugger bat. She needed to get him away from her.

"Of course." Jack flashed a smile, the smile she had plastered on her wall for years. The famous smile.

She tightened her fists. That bat looked really, really tempting.

Jack was everything, *everything* she hated about the game. Everything her father had wanted for her, for her future.

And Jack was too damn gorgeous for an ex-ballplayer.

Jack's smile grew as if he knew what she was thinking of. The posters and her teen crush. Clearly not the bat within grabbing reach.

Hugh, however, knew what she *was* thinking and clapped Jack on the back. Either that or he just knew her really well. "Why don't we head out for a while, Jack? Let Laurie do her thing and you can tell me about Elizabeth?"

Jack's face changed. One moment he was the suave player, and the next... Laurie shook her head. She didn't know what to call it. Proud father? Jack Evans?

"Sounds great."

Hugh kept his promise and kept Jack away from her. She gave her attention to her girls and to the great game they played, even though they ended up losing.

Losing was part of life. What mattered were those smiles and that meant she'd done her job.

Even if she'd felt Jack watching her, felt his gaze on her back, studying her, weighing her. She refused to blush, even when she felt her face heat. God. She could practically see that knowing smile.

The jerk.

She'd hoped her rude attitude had scared him off, or at least made him reconsider his daughter's request. Hugh, however, had done his job well.

When Laurie picked up the last equipment bag and turned, Jack stood there. Hands in his trouser pockets, leaning against the fence, a strand of silky brown hair dangling in his face. He locked fantastic, as if he'd just stepped out of limo arriving at the stadium.

In contrast, she had dirt caked into her uniform shirt, dirt under her nails and she'd lost the battle with her ponytail some time ago. But it wasn't her looks that bothered her. Really, it wasn't. It was that she'd lost more than the game today.

"Something I can help you with?"

"Looks like you could use some help." Jack nodded to the bag.

"I got it." She hefted it further up her shoulder. "Thanks, though."

He shook his head. "My gentleman sensibilities won't allow me to stand aside and let you carry a bag half your weight."

"It's fine—"

Except her protest didn't mean a damn thing. Jack, smooth as ever, swept the bag from her. She ignored the spark when his fingers brushed her shoulder.

"I'll walk you to your car and then you can meet my daughter."

Oh, was that right? How very thoughtful of him. Considerate. A man who expected everything he wanted in life just because he was a famous player, even an old famous player.

"How do you know this team's right for your daughter?"

Jack glanced back. "I don't. Which one is your car?"

Laurie stomped to her truck, forcing him to follow. "If you don't know, then why are you here?"

"Because Elizabeth and I made a deal. She wants your team." This time, his deadly, way-too-gorgeous smile was safely tucked away.

Good. Then that meant her anger could run wild without any distractions. Any distractions with this man, like his smile or when his gaze focused on her, for some unknown reason, were actual distractions.

"Why does she want my team?" Laurie opened the tailgate.

She noticed Hugh lingering by his car, shifting from one foot to the other. He wouldn't get near her until Jack left.

Fine. If everyone insisted she have this conversation, so be it.

Jack didn't answer her question. "Great game you played today."

Except that wasn't what he was saying.

She felt it, felt it in the weight of his gaze. It had been a test. One she and her *Angels* had apparently passed.

"We lost," Laurie pointed out.

Jack shrugged. "Can't win them all. Besides, the best games are the ones when the fans are on the edge of their seats. That back there," he nodded to the field. "Was a great game."

"I thought so too." She waited as Jack lifted the bag into her truck, then slammed the back shut. "Now. Why do you want my team?"

"I don't want anything. She wants it." Jack's blue eyes, eyes his posters had done little justice to match the color, met hers. "You haven't convinced me you're right for Elizabeth, but she thinks you are."

"Yes, but why?"

This was an important question, one that told Laurie whether or not a girl would be a good fit. She refused to let even Jack Evans dodge.

Jack clearly didn't like her forthcoming attitude, or the fact she stepped up and met him head to head. At least, if the way those sparkling blue eyes narrowing was any indication.

Laurie raised her hand, stalling him. "I ask this of any parent, even the famous ones. Mr. Evans—"

"Jack."

"Jack." She did not like the way his name rolled off her tongue, or the way her stomach twisted.

Laurie squashed both the thought and the reaction. "Jack. I know what I want for my team. I've met a lot of parents and I know you all want the world for your kids. So do I. But this team isn't about their future softball career or playing in college. It's about having fun."

Jack tensed. "Fun? Is that right?"

Then, the tension seemed to drain from him. His attention turned to the sleek, black sports car—Laurie had no doubt it was his—and the girl, waiting beside it, wringing her hands.

Even from here, there was no mistaking that she was his daughter. One corner of his mouth lifted up in a smile, which brought Laurie right back to being pissed-off. Pissed that Hugh had forced her into this position, pissed that someone like Jack—who had no business wanting a boring little team like the *Angels*, was here.

"Yeah, fun," Laurie snapped. "If Elizabeth or you don't fit with this team, I'll have to ask you to leave."

"Really?" Jack leaned against her truck. That half-smile didn't go away, instead it got bigger. "You'll ask us to leave?"

Damn him and damn that smile. "Yes. My girls have fun. They're still kids and I'm not here to push them or to make them work every day, non-stop."

She couldn't help the emotion leaking through in her voice, couldn't stop it. Jack's smile slipped and she looked away before he realized that she was talking about more than being a coach, that she was talking about herself. About her dad.

About those damn memories that picked today of all days to keep haunting her.

Somehow, she knew it was Jack's fault.

The game was always meant to be fun. It wasn't a job. Later on, sure, when they had something to work towards, like college scholarships, but not now.

"Coach Stevens, I hate to say this, but it looks like you've got yourself another player."

"But I haven't—"

"You've made your point, very clear." He reached for her hand. "And I know I won't find a better team."

He was fast. Faster than she'd expected otherwise he wouldn't have gotten hold of her. Jack leaned towards her, pinning her both with his gaze and his grip.

"Is that so?" Somehow, Laurie found her voice. And the spark of anger she needed to use it. "I never said I needed another player."

"No, you didn't." Another inch closer.

Laurie wanted to pull back and grab her bat—which she'd carelessly zipped away in her bag. She needed it. Needed the lifeline. She should have known this conversation was coming.

"I don't need another player. And what makes you think I'll take Elizabeth?"

"You will."

He let her go. Suddenly it was a lot easier to breath. Until she met Jack's gaze and froze. Crap. This was no longer the famous baseball player. She knew this look, had seen it in every parent who'd introduced themselves and their daughters to her.

"You will because she needs you."

It was the look of a parent who cared about their kid, who loved them. And she knew, damn it, she knew she couldn't say no even if everything inside her was screaming for her to.

But she couldn't, because he was right.

Elizabeth, for whatever reason, needed Laurie. She needed her *Angels.*

CHAPTER 5

"Now, Laurie." Hugh raised his hands as Laurie stomped across the parking lot. "There ain't no need for this."

She'd barely waited for Jack to slide into his car, if a Ferrari could be called a 'car,' and drive off. He'd put her into a corner and there wasn't a damn thing she could do about it.

Her cleats clicked against the pavement. She hadn't had a moment to even change into her tennis shoes. "No need? What the hell do you think you were doing?"

"I was having a nice chat with a parent, one who had a particular interest in seeing his kid play on our team."

"You brought him into the dugout!"

Hugh tried to make more smoothing motions with his hands, either that or he was protecting his face. "Well, he was insistent, and he *is* Jack Evans."

"I don't care who he is. You don't bring parents into the dugout, especially during games. The next thing I know every damn one of them will want to be there."

Dan Richards would be one of those parents, and every time he had something to say, every time he disagreed with Laurie, he'd come barreling in.

Laurie groaned. She'd quit first. "How could you do this to me? You backed me into a corner, Hugh. How could I tell him no?"

"That's not true, Laurie. You have the final word. If Elizabeth doesn't measure up, then that's all there is to it. I told Jack as much."

Like that would mean a damn thing. Jack got whatever he wanted. It took only a passing glance to see that about him.

"And Elizabeth is very nice" Hugh opened his car door.

Slipping away, huh? Laurie crossed her arms.

"She's a little shy, but I'm not surprised. Jack's a bit…"

"Hard to see around?" Laurie asked.

"If you want to put it that way. Anyway, it's your call and I thought you'd need some time to think about this more. Discuss it, even."

"There's nothing to…" Wait a minute. There was something else going on here. She could smell it. "Discuss what?"

"That's right. You know, tomorrow's Sunday and we can't break with tradition."

The tradition being that every Sunday after a game weekend, she and Hugh relaxed at his place (or hers) drinking beer while he fired up the grill.

"I was planning on coming."

"Good." Hugh smiled, big and proud, and just a tiny bit wobbly.

Laurie stepped closer. "What did you do?"

"Do?"

Oh, he wasn't about to go all innocent on her. She'd known him for way too many years. "You invited him, didn't you? You invited Jack to our coaches' barbecue?"

Hugh slammed his door shut and through the closed window, gave her another shrug. "It'll be good for you. A chance to get to know your newest parent. And… a chance to let go some of that baggage you're always pulling behind you. 'Sides, he's a bit nice to look at."

He winked at her.

Winked at *her.*

"No!" Laurie smacked the window with her open palm. "Hugh you listen to me right now. There's no way I'm coming over if Jack is."

"And his daughter!" Hugh turned the engine on, drowning out her protests. "I'll see you tomorrow. Get some rest tonight. I'm sure you and Jack will have lots to talk about."

Then, Hugh was gone. Speeding out of the parking lot as fast as his rickety car would take him, which wasn't very fast.

"I'm a damn dinosaur," Laurie muttered. That was the only way to describe herself—and her situation. Now, she was about to go extinct.

"And I'm so screwed."

Even on teams with girls this young, the vultures were already sinking their claws in. Looking at the next hot girl, the competition, changing the game from being fun to work.

That was everything Jack represented. Like every parent, he wanted what was best for his daughter, and now he was here, insisting his girl play on Laurie's team.

Laurie untied her ponytail and stuffed the band in her pocket. It did nothing to relieve her creeping headache. Or her tense shoulder muscle. She rubbed at it, thinking all her luck to have it act up twice in two weeks.

Now with Jack here? She might just need a standing date with a massage therapist if she was going to survive the season.

There wasn't much she could do about it, or Hugh's decision about Elizabeth. So, she had to look at the next best thing: a long, hot soak in a bath with a terrific glass (or glasses) of Syrah.

That'd be her reward for getting up tomorrow, for dealing with another upcoming week of teenagers and pop quizzes. She may love her job, both on and off the field, but even she needed a break (and a very long, bubbling bath).

Laurie turned, tugging her keys from her pocket, cleats clicking as she headed back to her truck. And stopped when she saw Suzie slumped on the ground beside it. The truck's tire nearly dwarfed her as she pressed her knees to her chest. Her bat bag was discarded beside her.

Her wine and bath could wait.

In only two strides, Laurie reached her. "Suzie? Are you all right?"

Suzie glanced up. Her eyes filled with tears.

Silly, stupid question. Of course she wasn't all right.

"Honey, what's wrong?" She knelt in front of Suzie, but waited for permission before she came any closer.

Suzie's bottom lip trembled.

Laurie glanced at the darkening sky. It was late. The sun had sunk behind the mountains while she and Hugh had talked. Now evening stretched on. Even the park lights had turned on.

Laurie's truck was the last in the lot. That's when she understood. "Did your mom have to work late again?"

Suzie shrugged. "I don't know. She didn't tell me."

"Do you want to call her and find out? You can use my phone."

"Her cell's broken."

And probably no money for a replacement.

Okay, then. Time for Plan B. "Well, we can't leave in case she comes by and worries that you're not here. I guess that means we wait."

"I don't want to keep you." Slowly, Suzie raised her head. The hope, and that tiny smudge of fear, was enough to break Laurie's heart.

"Nonsense. This is part of my job." Laurie opened her truck and fished out her glove and a ball. Maybe it was a good thing she hadn't changed her shoes. "But there's no point in us waiting around doing nothing. Grab your mitt."

"Why?"

"I'm gonna teach you how to pitch." *The basics anyway.*

"But, I can't pay, I mean I can't…"

"I'm not charging you. We're just killing some time, okay?"

Yes, Laurie was Suzie's coach and got all kinds of help at practice and at games, but Laurie also taught private lessons. The extra income was nice, especially when it came to padding out her teacher's salary (not to mention the constant wear on team equipment and her summer, dry months when school was out).

Laurie motioned her over. "Come on. It'll be fun."

Suzie scrambled to her feet, wiping off the rest of her tears with her dirt-stained uniform. "I can't pitch."

"Why not?"

"I'm too old. Everyone's been pitching for years."

"Old?" Laurie laughed and tossed the softball, which Suzie easily caught. "You're only 12! I was much older than you when I threw my first underhand pitch. Besides, you think those other girls are born knowing how to throw a curve ball?"

"I guess not." Suzie glanced at the parking lot, searching for a pair of headlights and a car to come pulling through.

Nothing.

She had to take Suzie's mind off her mother. "I heard you tell Lacey just the other day you would love to be a pitcher. I'll show you some basic moves, something you could even practice with your mom."

"Really?"

"Only if you like." Laurie nodded to the field. "We've got the whole field to ourselves. Just the two of us."

Suzie bounced to her feet, slinging her bag over her shoulder. "How old were you? When you know, when you started?"

"Young enough to realize that's where the action is. Everyone else —other than the catcher—stands around waiting for the ball to be hit."

"Yeah, but how old were you?"

Laurie laughed. "I was just about your age, but a couple inches taller."

"Oh."

Suzie chewed on this for a while, at least until the next question came up. Laurie let her have at it, asking whatever she liked, showing her how to snap her wrist and release the ball, how to time her arm movement with her hips.

"What about the girl today? The one in the stands?" Suzie flipped the softball using her wrist and hips, just like Laurie had shown her.

"You mean, Elizabeth?" Laurie tossed the ball back.

"Is that her name? Is she going to play with us?"

"How do you hear about her?" Laurie asked, unable to hide the suspicion in her tone.

Suzie blushed. "Lacey's dad."

"Lacey's dad has a big mouth." This made Suzie laugh, which was a good start. Much better than crying.

It turned out, all the girls already knew about Jack Evans and his daughter—except for her name, apparently.

Laurie felt the ground wobble around her, just a little. Suzie's questions, though curious seemed to be a bit too probing for a 'casual' question. "I'm inviting her to try-out and see how she does with you girls."

Suzie flicked the ball back to Laurie, accidentally hitting her hip making the ball go into the dirt. "What about her dad?"

Okay. Laurie had been fine chatting about Elizabeth and assuring Suzie she'd treat both Elizabeth and the team fairly. Each side would check out the other.

Jack, however, was not a topic of conversation. Especially the way her stomach did a quick, then sideways, flip.

Definitely not up for discussion.

"Well, her dad's not trying out for the team." Laurie threw the ball back and squatted for another pitch. "He's only driving her to the games."

Suzie smirked. The little kid smirk, the one that says, 'ya, right adults. I'm not stupid.'

Laurie was definitely finished with this conversation and all this thinking about Jack. That's when she remembered Hugh and his complete betrayal. Inviting Jack to their coaches' barbecue.

What was she going to do?

Before Suzie could make another comment about Jack, her mother drove into the parking lot.

Saved by the headlights.

Suzie grinned and ran towards the car, completely forgetting about Laurie, and, thankfully, Jack Evans.

Another crisis averted and who knew, she might even get another developing pitcher out of the deal. Laurie picked up the discarded balls and gloves and made her way to Suzie's mother.

Still, she couldn't help but wonder, if Jack had been a coach, how he would have handled the situation tonight, specifically, Suzie and her tears.

Not Suzie's questions about Laurie.

CHAPTER 6

$\mathcal{A}$s usual, Jack opened the car door for Elizabeth. But this time, instead of slinking out, head bowed, ball-cap pulled down low, Elizabeth skipped out of the car.

Jack nearly fell over. He blinked, trying to make sure he wasn't seeing anything. When Elizabeth's bouncing didn't disappear, he rubbed his eyes.

No, he wasn't seeing things. This was his daughter and not some imposter.

She hadn't been happy last night when he told her in the car about his talk with Laurie and Hugh. Elizabeth had been subdued then. Maybe she'd been afraid to believe it was true, that they wanted her to play.

Elizabeth collected her glove and her softball cleats with more energy than he'd seen in months.

He rubbed at his eyes again. If this was the kind of mood swings he needed to expect as she got older...shit, he was in big trouble.

Elizabeth turned. Jack's hand slipped off the door.

She smiled at him, one of the brightest smiles he'd seen since Nancy had walked out on them. Good thing he'd left the coffee tray in the car or he'd have spilled it all over himself. Not at all a good first, or in this case, second impression for Coach Laurie.

Not that he was looking to impress her. There was no need. Even if she was stunning to watch on the field.

"Here, let me help." Elizabeth reached in and offered the very coffee he'd just been grateful for not holding.

"Thanks." He'd already finished his own coffee on the way over; these, however, weren't for him.

He balanced the two drinks, one coffee and one sugar-free vanilla late (with regular milk), a special order thanks to the hint Hugh had dropped after yesterday's game. See? Impressing Laurie was not needed, not when he had bribery on his side.

The latte also happened to be a fantastic excuse to talk with her, and if he was lucky, maybe see another blush or two. Oh, yes, Jack knew she'd been a fan. If she recognized him after all these years, with him being away from the celebrity circuit it meant she'd been a true fan.

There weren't a whole lot of those. The last place he expected to find one was on Elizabeth's (hopefully) new team.

Elizabeth gave him her second smile of the day and he nearly did spill the coffee. "You really think she'll cave for coffee?"

"Your mother always did."

"Oh." Her smiled wobbled and Jack wanted to kick himself.

Damn it. He knew better. "Looks like it's going to be a great day for ball."

In fact, it was already so damn sunny he needed his sunglasses just to see past the bright glare.

"Dad. It's southern California. It's always sunny." Elizabeth peeked in the car. "Are you sure I should leave the bag here? What if I need something else?"

What she'd meant was her bat bag, a bag she wouldn't need until she was officially on the team. Her glove, and the cleats, was a compromise.

"If you need it, you can get my keys and grab it."

Not that he expected Elizabeth to be playing today. He'd seen first-hand just how defensive Laurie was about her team. She wasn't going to let anyone play without making sure they were a good fit.

The park was just as crowded as yesterday and it took some jostling to make his way through the crowd with coffee intact and unspilled. The unmistakable smell of French fries sizzling in oil and hamburgers already on the grill filled the air.

Jack took a long deep breath, breathing in the familiar scents, the scents of home.

He hadn't been lying when he told Elizabeth it was a great day for ball. Part of him wished he could be out there right now. This time, though, he didn't want to be pitching in some giant stadium, but standing on the field, giving Elizabeth tips and helping her.

That would be a great day. Still, even he admitted his step was a lighter since he found Laurie and her *Angels*.

Both teams were already in their dugouts, bags and bats unpacked, then one trickle after another, headed to the outfield for warm-ups. Every team had a different way of doing things, a different mantra, a different set of drills. Most started with stretches and then did some running exercises to get the muscles moving.

Laurie's team, her *Angels*, tossed a few balls around and some girls stretched. His eyes scanned the field, searching for the familiar, tall, lean body. He found her in the dugout, already at work, her head bent over what looked like the batting lineup.

She hadn't tied her hair up yet, and that blonde hair practically hid her from the world. Hugh headed in, placing his bag next to her and she gave him a warm, friendly smile.

The same kind of smile Elizabeth had given him. The smile that said she didn't want to be any place in the world but here, at a ball game.

Jack looked away. He'd forgotten what it was like to feel that way. He didn't think he'd see it again, not here. But he had and twice in less than twenty minutes.

Maybe it was a good sign that this was the right team for Elizabeth, that maybe Laurie was the right coach.

He shook his head. There was no point thinking about Laurie or her team, not until it was official and Elizabeth was on the field warming up.

Jack focused on the girls. They were still moving at a nice, leisurely pace, still waking up, still chatting. Girls always seemed to be chatting about something.

Not so much Elizabeth, but he hoped that would change. He hoped she'd have a reason to have her friends come over or call them late at night. It'd mean she was getting better, that she was finding her own happiness—one that didn't include Nancy.

Jack snuck a glance at Elizabeth, who stood on her tip-toes, trying to see better. He could practically feel her need to be out there, that humming, vibrating energy.

His daughter was happy. The thought distracted him so he misjudged one of the steps leading down to the field. The coffee sloshed and he made a quick recovery to save both himself and the coffee.

Thankfully, Elizabeth didn't notice. "You think she'll come?"

"Who?" Jack balanced the coffee, especially careful not to tip the all-important latte.

"Mom."

Jack smacked into a trashcan and nearly lost both cups. A few drops of the latte spilled onto his hand, burning him. He winced, just grateful he hadn't asked for extra hot.

Elizabeth paused. "You okay?"

"Yeah. Have to pay attention where I'm going."

More like pay attention to where his daughter was going—with questions she had no business asking so early in the damn morning.

"Well?" She asked again. "Do you think she'll come?"

"Elizabeth." He attempted calm, attempted patience and utter understanding. "We've talked about this."

Their talk, apparently, hadn't been much of a talk. At least from the look she gave him now. The talk had clearly only been to appease *him* and had nothing to do with *her* agreeing, or for that matter under-standing, Nancy and her decisions. Like not wanting to spend time with her daughter.

He didn't understand it, didn't understand Elizabeth's need to be with her mother, especially when Nancy made no secret—to either him or Elizabeth—that being a mother was the last thing she wanted.

Still, Elizabeth held on, almost hoping that one day Nancy would realize she wanted Elizabeth in her life.

His shoulders fell and he knew he couldn't destroy that hopeful face. "Fine. I'll ask."

Jack, had also apparently, not thought much of this so called talk either.

"Later, though," he said. "I have some drinks to deliver and we don't want me spilling it all over myself." Again.

Elizabeth considered this and then nodded, face solemn. "I don't think Laurie would like that very much."

Forget about how daddy would feel about wearing the coffee. "Come on, let's go find us some seats."

Seats that weren't on the very top of the bleachers.

He looked up as Laurie headed onto the field, the same bounce in her step that Elizabeth had. At least, there was one until she noticed Jack. She faltered, mid-step, clearly breaking her concentration. She scowled at him, which was a damn shame since she really had a nice smile.

Deceptive, sure. It was the kind of smile that hid the unrelenting, determined woman underneath. Her scowl, however, hid none of that.

Maybe he should rethink that 'true fan' thought.

Elizabeth played with the end of her braid as she peered around Jack to see Laurie heading towards them. "I told you. You should have ordered the grande."

"You know, there was a time when women liked me."

Back then, he'd had dates—and partners—whenever he wanted one. In any city the team stayed in. Any time of the year. Hell, he had more dates than there were games in the season—and that's saying a lot.

Course, Elizabeth didn't need to know that.

"Mom said it was because of the money."

"Yeah, she would know." And then regretted his words and his stupid male pride for saying it. "Elizabeth, I didn't mean it."

"Yes, you did."

No, he thought. He couldn't lie to her. "Yeah, I did mean it. And she took off pretty quick when the money was going to dry up."

"She took off because of the pictures." Elizabeth closed off, flipping her braid over her shoulder, and floated up the bleachers. Right to the top.

"Damn it to hell." He'd talk with Elizabeth later and apologize, but that wouldn't go over too well. Not when he'd only be apologizing for the sake of apologizing.

Especially when he didn't want to tell her the truth, that Nancy had been the one responsible for those pictures. Yeah, Jack did some pretty stupid things. Fame. Money. It went to his head, just like it did a lot of other players. But he'd cared about Elizabeth. Had made sure she, at least, didn't find out. At least, until Nancy decided to change the game.

Even though she'd let his fame and money get to her head too.

More so than him.

And hadn't cared a whit about Elizabeth being in the crossfire.

But Jack kept his mouth shut on that last. He didn't want to ruin Elizabeth's hope that her mother was a good person; a mother who cared.

"You'll have to come clean at some point, Jack," he said to himself.

That conversation, he knew, wouldn't go over well at all. Especially when he knew she wouldn't believe him.

Jack headed towards the dugout. He might as well go deal with the other angry female and get this over with. He'd give her the damn espresso, and then do what he could to convince his daughter he wasn't a complete asshole.

There'd been a time when he'd had a way with women. Smooth, confident. Some even called him disarming. Even Nancy.

Then he'd become a father and he'd been screwing up ever since.

Jack walked onto the field and faced his next challenge: to somehow convince Laurie she wanted his daughter on her team.

That part, he thought as he kicked up some dirt, was easy. Convincing her he wasn't the scumbag she clearly thought he was, was another matter.

At least, he was a reformed scumbag.

Laurie waited on the field, not quite willing to step off her territory. She wore the same team uniform, the red color bringing out her hair—hair she'd unfortunately now tied back.

But a strand slipped free and she reached up, an automatic gesture, to tuck it behind her ear. A delicate, gentle movement.

Probably the only delicate thing about her.

He tried not to think about why that made him smile.

CHAPTER 7

*L*aurie had thought she'd prepared herself for the sight of Jack, thought the glass of wine—okay, two glasses of wine—she had last night would do the trick. But seeing him here, watching as he easily moved onto her field without the slightest hesitation, and she knew the whole bottle wouldn't have been enough.

There was no preparing for a guy like Jack Evans, especially when said guy knew exactly the kind of person he was. Tall, and still as beautiful and perfect as he was yesterday, leather jacket and all.

And he had the kind of walk that said he was in charge.

A ball-player, through-in-through.

She headed out of the dugout, grabbing her bat along the way. She needed it. Needed the comfort that everything would be all right. That just because Jack Evans was now a team-parent didn't mean her team would change. That just because she'd had a crush on him ten years ago didn't mean she'd go weak in the knees now.

Even though her knees felt a little on the weak side.

But there was no avoiding this meeting. She needed to get some things said and she might as well do it now.

"Morning to you, too, Coach." Jack nodded to her and was careful to keep the coffee tray upright.

She placed her hands on her hips, tried to drum up the tiniest speck of confidence (and wondered where the hell it went), and gave him her 'too early in the morning to talk to a parent smile.' Usually, parents tended to take the hint and back off.

"Can I do something for you, Mr. Evans?"

"Jack."

Now it was his turn to switch on the smile, but where hers was warning people away, his was inviting.

She forced herself to scowl, to glare right back, to not swallow at the sudden spike in temperature or how it was getting difficult to breathe. She was determined, absolutely determined, to not allow her stomach to flutter.

Which was exactly what the damn thing was doing.

"Okay, *Jack*." His name came out more like growl which was better than airhead and fluttery. Much better. "What can I do for you?"

"Smile." He held out one of the coffee cups. "I'd really like to see you smile."

This time, she had absolutely no control over her stomach butterflies or her involuntary swallow reflex.

"Excuse me?"

"You have a terrific smile. At least, until you lay eyes on me, which means I've got to help with that, so here." He held out the coffee again.

Laurie was aware that they were standing on the field, right in front of the parents who had perfect, front row seats to her and Jack's high morning duel.

She crossed her arms, mostly to look intimidating, but also to put some pressure on the damn fluttering area.

She was not attracted to this man. Couldn't be. He represented everything she absolutely hated about softball. Or baseball, or any sport really. He was the guy who pushed himself, who practiced every day, who forgot how much fun the game was until it all became about the bottom line.

The career. The success.

He reminded her too much of herself. Of who she could have become.

Laurie wanted nothing to do with him. Not on her team, not in her life, and certainly not the cause of any smile she wore.

Or the fluttering.

"Do you always start with bribes this early in the morning?"

"Only when necessary. Especially since we started off on the wrong foot."

"You're the one who set which foot we started on." She kept her voice down, her tone still pleasant, knowing the whispering had already started.

Why did he have to do this now of all places?

"You interrupted my game to pitch your daughter's qualifications for my team, and then preceded to instruct me on which pitches to throw—"

Jack held up both hands, meaning both coffees, in surrender. "Hey. That was Hugh's idea. Not mine. I thought we should wait until after the game before I introduced myself. And I always thought good coaches liked to hear different opinions. Advice. Excuse me for being out of line."

Out of line?

The muscle in Laurie's face twitched. "Out of line? Out of line? Why you arrogant, stuck up—"

Dan Richards's deep laugh boomed from the stands. Laurie snapped her mouth closed.

Jack cocked an eyebrow, causally glancing at the stands. "Are they always this bad?"

Her nostrils flared. How did he get under her nerves like this? She needed to end this, whatever this was, and get back to her team.

"Look, if I wanted advice I would ask the pros. Not some has-been baseball player who had the audacity to instruct me on how to coach my girls after watching us play less than an hour."

Jack's back tensed, but his warm smile didn't budge. "Ouch. I guess that means you noticed, huh?"

Laurie sputtered. She was going to kill him. Absolutely going to kill him.

"I came to bring you coffee."

He raised the drink and stepped towards her, closing the suddenly very short distance between them. There was hardly room for the coffee.

"I came to bring you coffee," he said. "Not to start a fight. I've had enough fights since I woke up this morning so if you don't mind."

Again, he pushed the coffee towards her, but she didn't move. "Laurie, just take the damn coffee. Pretend like you're grateful, and we can continue this conversation after the game."

This time, the smile was gone and for the first time, she felt like she saw the real Jack. The Jack who was tired, spent all night dealing with his daughter and had gotten up earlier to deal with a bitchy (rightfully bitchy) softball coach.

He paused, looking once over her shoulder. Towards the stands. "I don't think you'd appreciate the crowd watching—and listening to us."

Laurie cursed herself and her temper. And this stupid fluttering that got her into this damn mess in the first place. "Fine, but I want you off my field."

"No problem." Except he didn't move, just held up the tray.

"Thank you." She snatched one coffee, leaving the second for him, though she was careful not to spill any on her. Or him. "Now go."

No luck. Jack merely ran a free-hand through his hair, just slightly disheveled as if he really had had a few fights—and had already did the hair-run through a few times.

"I really used to be better at this," he muttered to himself. "Look. I don't want to fight. All I want is my daughter to be happy and she thinks your team is the answer."

Laurie, feeling all those eyes on her but refusing to look, sipped the offered drink. Vanilla latte. Hugh. He'd tipped Jack off, probably yesterday, on her choice of morning wake-up drink.

She sighed.

The truth was she didn't want to fight with him either except she couldn't seem to help it. Not when every time she looked at him she remembered, remembered what it was like playing for the big teams.

The pressure. The job.

Remembered her dad standing on this very field, hands on his hips, his anger radiating off him, so deep and penetrating it nearly knocked her over. All because she'd ignored his pitching signs. Again.

Laurie sucked in a breath of cool air.

"Hey. Are you okay?" he asked. "I really didn't mean to upset you."

"I know, it's just..."

It's just your very presence was a reminder of a time in her life that still hurt, even a decade later. She said none of this, though. She didn't even talk about this with Hugh, if she could help it.

Jack had lived that life, lived it and one day had walked away. It wasn't much different than her choices.

And it wasn't fair to hold who he was—who he'd been—against him.

She hoped for calm and confidence, especially when she didn't feel either at the moment. "You did your job well. Hugh already made his decision. This," she indicated the latte, "wasn't necessary."

Jack rocked back on his heels, still holding the tray and his coffee, and glanced back at the stands where his daughter sat on the highest bleacher.

This close to him she could smell the leather from his jacket, the same smell from yesterday, the same jacket. A jacket that fit him a little too well around his arms, revealing a tiny hint of a muscled chest.

She snapped her eyes back to his face.

If Jack noticed her staring at his chest, he didn't show it. But considering his attention was on his daughter, she didn't think he had.

"It's *your* decision. You're the coach." Jack's turned his bright blue gaze on her, his very startling blue eyes. "The coach always matters, especially when you make the decision whether to bench my daughter to get back at me or let her play."

"I'd never do that!"

"No?"

"Absolutely not. And if you think I would then you sure as hell don't know me or how I coach."

Jack considered her words. A softness crossed his features and then disappeared again. He shrugged. "You're right. I don't know you, but then, you don't know me either."

He leaned towards her, closing the space she'd given them when she'd accepted the latte. "Knowing me doesn't matter. Just know my daughter. Let her play."

This close, Laurie smelled a hell lot more than Jack's leather jacket. She could smell Jack.

Her head spun from the closeness of him, of his size, his strength. Of his challenge.

She forced a breath. A careful, controlled one so he wouldn't know how much his nearness affected her. *Which it didn't.*

"If your daughter plays anything like you did," Laurie whispered. "I'm gonna have to let her play."

And then, Jack did something that truly took her breath away.

He smiled. At her.

"She's even better. Better than I ever hoped to be."

He reached towards her and lifted the bat from Laurie's fingers, the bat she'd completely forgotten and now hung lifeless in her hands. She let him take it. As if she could possibly protest. Not when he was this close, this serious.

Jack set down his tray and coffee on the moist ground with the tufts of trodden grass poking through the dirt. He tested the bat's weight, though his gaze never left Laurie's. "Elizabeth's good, but she needs a good coach."

"I think..." Laurie swallowed. "I think the rest is for Elizabeth to decide."

"You'll let her play?"

Laurie nearly laughed. As if this decision was up to her anymore. "She had a place on the team the minute you introduced yourself to Hugh."

Yes, she hated that, hated the way Jack had completely gone around her and her rules. Laurie held her hand out for the bat, and after a moment, Jack gave it to her.

"This is a good bat," he said. "Has seen some hard days. Lots of hard hits."

"It won't pass regulation anymore. Too many dents." None of the girls would use it; it was too heavy for them.

"Yours?"

She nodded. "My playing days, yes."

"In college?"

She shrugged. Hardly any news, though it wasn't something she ever enjoyed talking about. "If you want to hear about my game days, I'd suggest you Google it."

"I'd prefer hearing it from you. How about tonight? At Hugh's barbecue?"

As if she could possibly forget that little dinner engagement. "I don't ruin a good beer by talking about my college days."

That, she noticed, sparked his interest. It wasn't so much a change in expression, but a change in his intensity. As if he scented something, something that drew him.

Laurie pulled herself back. Anything that drew Jack to her was bad, bad news.

"I've got to get back. To work."

"Of course, if you'd need hel—"

Jack cut off when his phone rang. He gave her a quick apology, but he'd clearly recognized the ring. The intensity he'd just directed at her disappeared.

No. Not disappeared, shifted. Turned darker. Whoever was calling him wasn't someone he wanted to talk with. But he did excuse himself, wished Laurie a great game and stalked—yes, stalked—off the field.

Laurie swallowed, unable to help herself. Rage radiated off the man, pent-up and restrained, though barely.

A powerful, intense man. A man who'd shone that same intensity on her.

How the hell was she going to survive Jack Evans being a parent on her team?

"Laurie?" Hugh asked behind her, voice tentative and unsure. "Everything all right?"

"Hell if I know," she whispered. She couldn't take her eyes off Jack or the way his shoulders tensed. "But I'm really glad I'm not the one calling him right now."

Hugh slid up beside her, both of them watching Jack. "Anything I need to know about?"

Except that he'd gone over her and signed on a girl with a parent who she probably shouldn't have any contact with?

Laurie shook her head. That wasn't fair. Jack hadn't done anything yet, regardless of the warning bells his very presence set off in her. Right now, he was a parent looking for the best team for his girl.

A girl who wanted Laurie and Laurie's team.

That wasn't Jack's fault.

"No, Hugh, everything's fine."

In truth, she was simply glad that intensity was no longer on her.

Laurie closed her eyes and breathed a long, deep sigh of relief. Get through the game, that was all she had to do.

The rest, well she could figure out what to do later. Maybe tonight, over beer and hamburgers, she and Jack could compromise. Figure out somehow to work this out between them, whatever this was.

Not the fluttering thing, hell no way was she bringing *that* up, but the team thing. They need ground rules.

Laurie, if she were honest with herself, was the one who needed the rules.

CHAPTER 8

*J*ack snatched up coffee and tray from the ground and hurried off the field, digging out his smart phone from his jacket pocket. He didn't need to see the screen to see who was calling, not when he'd attached the Imperial March ringtone from *Star Wars* to the one person it fit perfectly: his ex-wife.

Jack's good mood vanished. Not that he'd call the near argument with Laurie 'good,' but he sure as hell enjoyed bantering with her, riling her up. A complex, interesting woman, and one he was determined to charm—even if she did want to beat him with a bat.

Another two rings. Nancy still hadn't hung up.

Jack growled, pushing his way through the crowd who'd gather to eavesdrop on him and Laurie. Diane, Courtney's mother, gave him a questioning eyebrow raise, but she merely pushed Dan aside for him.

He nodded his thanks, then tossed the full cup of coffee—the one he'd picked up for Hugh—into the trash. Probably cold by now anyway.

From the stands, Elizabeth perked up even as he silenced the phone. Eyes wide and hopeful, she scrambled down from the bleachers.

Damn. He should have picked it up before Elizabeth heard, before she realized who was calling.

Jack pressed the phone to his ear, hurrying towards the food stand and as far away from Elizabeth as possible. "Nancy. Isn't it a little early for you?"

"Don't you dare start with me this early in the morning."

Up and angry. How'd he get so lucky?

"I'm not the one who called." As if that meant anything to this woman. To her, everything was his fault. Their marriage. Their divorce. Their daughter. "What do you want?"

"Elizabeth called me."

Jack veered off to some obscure bench. Not a soul in sight. Everyone was at the field. He paced around the bench, covered with white bird-droppings and speckles of moss.

"She didn't tell me."

"She called last night," Nancy snapped. "Barry heard her message this morning. Jack. He woke me up. We've talked about this. She's not supposed to call me unless there's an emergency."

Her idea of an emergency was him falling down dead and her being foisted with Elizabeth.

"For whatever reason I can't fathom," Jack said, "she wants to talk to you. Probably has to do with you being her damn mother."

"Don't you do swear at me, Jack, and don't use that mother excuse either."

Of course not. Because being a mother was, after all, an excuse. All he wanted was to chuck the phone into the field—and Nancy with it.

"Fine. Tell me what she wanted and I'll see what I can do."

"How should I know?" Nancy asked. "She only left a message. Something about a softball team and wanting me to show up. Today. *This* morning."

Jack cursed, the pieces clicking into place. Elizabeth had called to tell her mother the good news. She'd found a team. She'd wanted to share her excitement with her mother.

A mother who didn't give a damn unless it was him signing her another check.

"She's excited," Jack growled. "She wanted you here."

"Well, I'm certainly not coming."

Fine by him. "Then why did you call?"

Jack couldn't help gazing at the field, his eyes searching for Laurie before he realized he was doing it. There she was, heading out the outfield with...with Elizabeth right behind her.

Jack lowered the phone and Nancy's sharp, cutting voice drifted away. Elizabeth had her glove with her. She was smiling.

He slumped onto the bench, bird droppings and all, his legs no longer able to hold him. He could buy new pants. He couldn't buy that smile on his daughter's face.

"Are you listening to me?" Nancy's barely controlled anger lashed at him again.

"No. I'm busy enjoying our daughter's happiness. Oh, that's right. You don't give a shit."

There was a sharp intake of breath and Jack expected a shrill tirade that would scare even the crows, who hopped on the tree's branches above his head, scanning Jack for hot dog treats.

"I called because Barry insisted I come down to see this, this *game*. I don't even know which sport she's talking about. I, of course, refused to go."

Which still didn't answer his question about her calling. "Nancy."

"I'm getting to it!" Sharp, piercing.

Jack winced. He had to hand it to Barry for putting up with her for three years now, even if the guy was a womanizing jerk. Far as Jack was concerned, they were perfect for each other.

"I'm busy this morning, at which point Barry insisted I...I make it up to her. To Elizabeth. You both can come over for dinner. Tonight."

"Dinner."

"Yes. Chantal will have it ready by 6:00. Sharp. Don't be late."

"I didn't say we were coming."

"You will," Nancy purred. "Even if I have to call Elizabeth myself."

She was right. Damn it, she was right. "Should I expect company?"

Meaning Barry.

"No. Barry stepped out for the evening. Had some sort of plans with his teammates. You remember, your *former* teammates."

Jack let the dig slid past him. He was done caring about that life.

"Anyway," she continued, "I'll have your scotch waiting, no need to pick up any. I always have some for just such an occasion."

"Fine." Jack clicked the phone off.

If Nancy was sincere about a family dinner, how could he not at least try to get along?

Jack watched Elizabeth, watched as Laurie introduced her to the other girls. Tentative, shy Elizabeth, who practically hid behind Laurie. If Jack let her, Elizabeth would always hide in the background, never stepping forward, never being herself.

And somehow, Laurie seemed to know this. She smiled at Elizabeth, giving her a friendly pat on the shoulder. It was a great smile, he realized, and it did just the trick.

Elizabeth glanced up from behind her hat, still shy and tentative. Unsure if she was welcome. Laurie only encouraged her, finally tossing a ball to another girl, a girl who barely reached Elizabeth's chin. The two ran off to play catch.

Jack shook his head, breaking the spell Laurie's smile seemed to hold over him.

No matter how he looked at it, he was going to have dinner with a woman who hated him. That meant no barbecue with Laurie and Hugh.

At least Laurie should be thrilled he wasn't showing up.

A shame really, since she was the one he actually wanted to have dinner with, to find out why she'd gotten so defensive with him. And why she felt she needed to.

Jack stood, grimacing at the specks of outfield mud and dirt circling the bottom of his jeans. Nancy would expect perfection. Too bad—she was just going to get him just as he was.

Eating dinner with Nancy was nothing short of eating sharp spines and hot sauce. Dinner with Laurie, even when wielding that heavy-ass bat of hers, would have been a much more pleasant experience.

Jack tucked his hands in his pockets. He was a father. That meant his daughter's needs came before his, even if it meant a dinner with a viper.

He'd be the only one forced to suffer. Lucky him.

CHAPTER 9

$\mathcal{L}$aurie watched as Jack left the field, heart still pounding, as he pulled out his phone. Her shoulders sagged and she took a long, deep breath.

Finally, she had some space. Space to figure out what she was going to do about Jack and how she was going to survive him.

Hugh, however, was really not helping matters.

Hugh gestured to her drink with the clipboard. "Nice of him, bringing you a coffee and all."

"It's not coffee. It's a vanilla latte, and if my guess is right, it's also sugar-free. Stop lying. You knew damn well where Jack got his espresso tip from."

Hugh shrugged. "I'm just trying to help."

"Help? You're the one who wrangled me into this mess." Her temper rose, yet again. Jack seemed to have that effect on her, even when she wasn't talking to him.

Laurie took a calming sip of her latte. It was good. Probably from some specialty place and not the drive-thru she usually went to.

Nothing cheap for a man like Jack Evans. She glanced after him, not wanting to and yet unable to help herself. There was no expensive leather jacket in sight.

A smile tugged at her lips before she could force it down. Too bad for her, Hugh noticed.

"Ah-ha! You do like him."

"Don't be ridiculous. I nearly smacked him with a bat."

"You have a tendency to do that. With everyone." He pointed to her latte. "Drink. You're way too grumpy without your caffeine. I can't have you scaring the girls this early in the morning."

"I'm not scary," Laurie muttered to herself. She did, however, drink. And since it was getting cold, she finished it a little faster than she usually liked.

Already both teams were getting a move on, warming-up and casting aside the rest of their sleep. Getting ready to play. The hum of the game swirled through her. Anticipation. The *Rascals* were a good, solid team. Not push overs, for sure.

Laurie never knew what kind of game she'd expect from them, or what kind of game she'd expect her girls to play. That was one of her small, secret joys.

They headed into the dugout, putting together the final touches on the starting line-up and who would be playing where. She leaned back on the metal bench, the chill seeping through her favorite, well-used pair of shorts.

She tossed the empty cup into the trashcan, the dull *thunk* the only other noise except for the distant chatter of her team, their opponents, the parents. Hugh waved her to sit and relax while he gave the girls the pre-game pep talk.

From across the field, Kent, the *Rascals's* coach, set aside his own clipboard and waved, a wave which she returned. He wasn't bad looking, which was why quite a few of the single mothers foisted their kids onto Kent's team.

Still...Laurie rested her elbows on her knees, studying him. Compared to Jack, Kent barely hit average in the good-look factor. Not that many people could compare to Jack Evans and that body he'd somehow managed to keep in shape.

Kent's smile curled up. Laurie blushed and immediately looked away. *Great, Laurie, just great.* Now he'd definitely ask her to dinner after the game.

Not that he didn't do that after every game, but she'd just given him quite the invitation.

She shook herself. What was she thinking?

"That's the problem," she muttered. "I'm not thinking."

And I'm lonely. If she was honest with herself, maybe this whole thing with Jack was just her being lonely. What else could it be? After only one day and she was this distracted by him?

Maybe she should just say yes to Kent for dinner and get this loneliness-distraction thing over and done with.

"Time to get moving, Coach," Laurie said to herself. "No more feeling sorry. No more thinking about Mr. Jack Evans."

After all, she had a day of games ahead of her. A day filled with balancing the ever shifting moods of young, nearly teenage girls.

See? How could she possibly be lonely?

Laurie grabbed her ball-cap, adjusted her ponytail; but when she turned to find Hugh—she found Jack instead. She spotted him by the bench, not far from where her girls warmed-up. Whoever he was chatting with on the phone, the call must have been going exactly as he'd expected it. Badly.

Even at this distance—she felt his rage. His unhappiness.

Laurie shook her head. Or maybe because she saw too much of herself—her old self—in him. There was being successful, and then there was being happy.

They were not always one and the same.

Be fair, Laurie told herself as she unpacked the rest of the bats and helmets, setting them besides hers. She didn't know him, as he so eloquently put it. And did she really want too?

No. Laurie shoved another bat in place. She didn't want to know him. She didn't want him or his kind anywhere near her team.

She couldn't trust that he'd keep his word, that he'd let Elizabeth have fun instead of being sucked down that road—the one he walked as a pro baseball player. The same road she'd walked all through her softball career.

"Do you need help?"

Laurie glanced up. A tall, young girl peeked into the dugout, hands clasped behind her back. There was no mistaking that face, especially when it was a face she couldn't seem to get out of her head.

Elizabeth was a little thing—with the exception of those long legs. Good muscles there. A pitcher for sure.

"Sure," Laurie said. "Help would be great."

After all, it was this kid's dad who was distracting her; Laurie might as well get some help.

"I'm Elizabeth."

Elizabeth held out her hand, which Laurie shook. If you could call it a shake. The girl's hold was tentative at best, as if she thought Laurie was about to bite her.

"I'm Laurie. I hear you want to play for us."

"I do... if you want me, of course." Elizabeth bobbed her head. "What would you like me to do?"

Laurie knew a change of subject when she heard one. She let it drop, instead directing Elizabeth to take out the catching gear. She was pleasant and nice, though only answered Laurie's questions with one or two words.

She didn't push, though she caught Elizabeth sneaking one or two glances at her father, who was still on the phone, still silently raging.

Time for a distraction. For all of them.

"How long have you been playing?" Laurie asked.

Elizabeth shrugged. "A few years. Ever since I was little, but I wanted to be a baseball player."

Laurie raised her head from where she bent over her gear. That was definitely more than a few words.

"A baseball player, huh? Like your dad?"

Elizabeth nodded. "Just like him. And a pitcher."

"I can tell he's proud of you."

Elizabeth smiled and Laurie nearly fell back onto her butt. That was some smile. A happy one.

"He was thrilled when I told him. Mom though..." Now the smile died. Another gaze flicked back to Jack.

It didn't take a wild guess for Laurie to figure out just who Jack was talking too. Jack hadn't been kidding when he'd talked to her last night.

Elizabeth needed this team.

Laurie stood, dusting off her shorts. "From what I can see, he's still proud of you."

"Yeah. I know."

Watching this girl, so unsure, so hesitant, Laurie began to understand why Jack was so determined that Elizabeth play on this team. If he wasn't careful; hell, if Laurie wasn't careful, this little girl would have very similar scars to Laurie's, the kind that never went away even if you walked away from the field.

She didn't know how the mother fit into the equation, but Jack was right about one thing. Elizabeth needed to play—and have fun—with softball.

"I told him to get a larger latte," Elizabeth said, breaking the silence. "He was really... pushing yesterday. I know he can be pushy sometimes."

"Pushy," Laurie echoed. "I'd say that's putting it nicely."

Another smile, this time with a tad more confidence. "I wanted to ask if I could play today, but Dad told me not to. Though I did bring my stuff, just in case."

"He told you no, huh?" Interesting. She'd expected the opposite.

"Well, he did say something along the lines of maybe next week."

Was that so? Not even twenty-four hours, and already he was weaseling his way onto her team?

Elizabeth pushed on. "But I told him no. It's not fair, to the other girls I mean."

Under Hugh's direction, their team finished their running drills and were now warming up their arms, throwing the balls back and forth to a partner. One group had three players.

It was an opportunity, Laurie realized. And it was an opportunity to distract the girls who were now watching Laurie and Elizabeth. The same girls, if not the entire team, who'd probably overheard her conversation with Jack.

They were, apparently, the newest gossip.

Elizabeth swept off her hat and scrunched it in her hands, not looking at Laurie. "Anyway, I just thought I could maybe help out. I brought my mitt, so if you need me... I mean... I can if you like..."

"It just so happens I could use you."

Laurie tossed Elizabeth a ball, which Elizabeth easily caught. Elizabeth didn't grab for the ball, but gently cradled it, using the natural movement to slow it down. Soft hands.

"It'll give you a chance to get to know the girls," Laurie said.

Elizabeth brightened. "Really? You mean, I can?"

Who could ever say no to you? Laurie thought. "You bet. We'll see you at practice on Wednesday, right?"

"Really? I mean, I can?" When Laurie nodded, Elizabeth danced to her feet and nearly ran out the dugout before sliding to a stop. She waited for Laurie.

Jack might have the manners of a toad, but at least he passed on some to his daughter. Or maybe Elizabeth got those from her mother.

By the time they reached the outfield, her girls had already gathered, clearly expecting to meet the newest player. And with the exception of Lacey, which wasn't much of a surprise, everyone was welcoming.

Then again, Laurie wondered how long it would take for her girls to see Elizabeth for herself, and not the famous, and rich, ex-ballplayer dad of hers.

There was nothing she could do to help Elizabeth with that one. That part was on her and the rest of the team.

Jack had finally left his spot on the bench. She couldn't see his leather jacket in the parent crowd and he wasn't in the bleachers.

Her part, however, was much more difficult.

She had to apologize.

CHAPTER 10

*A*s much as Laurie loathed admitting it, the game went...surprisingly well. And Jack had, surprisingly, behaved himself.

Hugh clapped for Lacey, who pitched the final inning. They ended up playing the *Rascals* a second time, mostly because the *Lady Lucks* didn't have enough girls. It happened sometimes in their league, mostly because they weren't as competitive as other leagues and they didn't do any 'traveling' to distant tournaments.

Still, it was good practice and the kids were having fun. As far as Laurie was concerned, that was all that mattered.

From her spot in the dugout, she watched as Jack stretched out his legs. Maybe she'd been wrong about him. He'd simply sat there and enjoyed the games along with the rest of the parents. Sometimes he clapped, sometimes he offered encouragement.

Not that she'd noticed, of course.

In fact, he'd merely sat on the bleachers—the lowest one—and watched the games. Just like any regular parent.

"Something wrong?" Hugh leaned closer to her.

Laurie jerked her attention back to the game. "No, why?"

Hugh hummed to himself, glancing at the stands—and at Jack.

"Well, I wanted to make sure nothing was wrong. After all, we're up by three runs and our newest bat-girl seems to be having the time of her life."

Sure enough, for the second time today, Elizabeth rearranged the bats to her liking. She hadn't stopped smiling since Jack had pulled her out of the dugout, whispered something to her...and she'd been all smiles since.

Did it have to do with the phone call? Talking with his ex-wife?

"It's nothing."

She wasn't about to explain any of these strange (who knew what they were, certainly not feelings) about Jack. Certainly not to Hugh who'd merely use it as leverage.

Laurie gave Lacey the next pitching sign, and covertly snuck another glance at Jack, who was once again the center of the parents' attention. Okay, maybe not so much all the parents but the female variety.

From both teams. Kent, she'd noticed earlier, wasn't pleased about this turn of events. After all, the single moms came to his game for a reason, while the single dads, well... they came to Laurie's games.

Laurie hid her head in her hands as her stomach fluttered again. Was this what games with Jack would be like?

Hugh nudged her in the ribs. "Need another sign, Coach. You sure you're all right?"

"Yeah."

Shit. Jack was distracting her and the man wasn't doing anything but *sitting* there. She gave Lacey the sign for a change-up and this time, she made sure to pay attention.

"Seems to me like you're distracted. Not much different than those others."

"I'm not distracted. I didn't leave until late last night. I'm tired, that's all."

"Of course." Hugh flashed her his all-knowing, sweet-old-man smile and patted her shoulder. "We've got this game in the bag, Coach. Loosen up a little. I'll handle Lacey if you want to go chat with the parents."

"I don't need to chat." She purposefully gave Lacey another sign. "And I'm fine right where I am."

Hugh merely shrugged. And Laurie, with her traitorous eyes, couldn't help a second glance at Jack—who was just being introduced to Claire, Suzie's mom.

Laurie perked up, pleased to see that Claire had made it. And it meant she wouldn't have to stay late today. Of course, Jack seemed to hold Claire's a hand a bit longer than usual and there was that smile of his...

Not that Laurie cared. Why would she? If the mothers on her team wanted to swoon over Jack, that was their decision. Grown women, all of them.

How could they not flock to him? Jeez, he was every female parent's dream come true. Not hers.

Definitely not hers.

That was precisely what Laurie kept telling herself, even when it was time to shake the other team's hands. The *Angels* had won, but all the girls played great—even Kent's girls.

When Laurie shook Kent's hand, thanking him for a great game, it was his turn to hold her hand a little too long.

"Well done, Laurie. I'm not surprised in the least."

"You did good yourself." She tried to pull back, except Kent, once again, wasn't quite ready for her to go. "Kent. I've got to clean up and have a team meeting."

"Course. I just wanted to know if you were free. Tonight. A little after-game drink or two."

Laurie glanced at her girls, already putting the helmets and bats away for her. Elizabeth ran out the dugout and grabbed Jack's hand, practically pulling him to the car.

Where were they going? Weren't they coming to Hugh's?

"Laurie?" Kent pressed.

"Yes, sorry."

Kent glanced at the parking lot, at Jack and Elizabeth. "Ah. I'd heard a rumor Jack Evans had walked onto your team. I didn't believe it, even when I saw him. He looks different now."

He looks the same, Laurie thought. Better, even. "His daughter, actually. She walked onto my team. Not Jack."

"Jack." Kent still had her hand. "First name basis already? I'd spotted him looking for a team yesterday, but by the time I went to introduce myself he'd already approached you."

"He did." Laurie tried to pay attention to Kent. She really did, but she couldn't stop thinking of how she'd ended things earlier.

Was he leaving for good? Before she had a chance to tell him—and heaven help her—that he was right?

No. Elizabeth needed the *Angels.* She couldn't let Jack leave, not without hearing the truth.

"Sorry, Kent. I have plans tonight. Can you please excuse me? I have to talk to someone?"

"Sure thing." He dropped her hand. "You go do your coach thing. I'll see you next weekend? At the Artesia tournament?"

"Yeah. Of course."

Laurie ran off the field, not bothering with propriety. She was a damn softball coach and if she wanted to run off the field, well then'd she simply draw attention. The hell with it.

Even if that attention was now on her and Jack.

He couldn't leave until she apologized.

She ran into the parking lot, careful not to let her metal cleats slip on the asphalt. Plastic ones like her girls wore would be safer—except she didn't usually run after a parents.

A parent who also happened to be a very good looking, ex-ballplayer.

"Jack! Wait up."

They'd already reached his car—a freakin' Ferrari—with Elizabeth slamming her door shut. Jack, however, heard her and paused. He turned, a smile tugging at his lips.

Laurie stopped on the other side of the car. Elizabeth's side. She needed to talk, yes, but distance would also be good about now. Especially with everyone watching.

Laurie's face heated at the thought, a thought she shoved aside. She was here, running across the parking lot—running after Jack—because of Elizabeth.

"Couldn't let me leave without saying goodbye?"

"No." *Yes.* Why did he have to open with that damn arrogance of his? "I mean, yes."

Jack's smile widened. "Good to know."

"Why do you have to make this so difficult? Can I just talk with you for a moment?"

He didn't say anything at first, merely stood there half-in, half-out of his car. Finally, he leaned in and she thought she'd lost him. Maybe if she'd kept a rein on her temper, even a little, it wouldn't have come to this.

"Jack, please. About earlier. I'm sorry."

He straightened, his eyes meeting hers—holding hers—and she felt for sure like she was going to turn into a gooey puddle of nothing. Just like the Wicked Witch or something.

"Give me a minute, Elizabeth," Jack said. "Coach Laurie needs to talk with me."

Laurie didn't hear Elizabeth's answer as Jack closed his door and made his way over. To Laurie. On Laurie's side of the car.

"I must have misheard. You just said something like an apology."

Jack came closer. Too close. If she could smell him, if she could feel his heat, then that was definitely way too close.

Laurie shifted back and Jack smirked. The bastard knew what he was doing. He knew exactly what he was doing to her.

"If you weren't such an arrogant ass," Laurie snapped, "I'm sure you'd hear a lot more apologies."

"*That* was definitely *not* an apology."

She crossed her arms. "That wasn't meant to be an apology. That was telling you to stop being an ass."

Jack lifted his hands in surrender. "I see. You have an interesting way about you, Coach Stevens."

She couldn't believe it. He was toying with her. Like a cat batting with a frightened mouse.

The only difference was she wasn't afraid. Not in the least.

"This, what you're doing with this," Laurie motioned the space between the two of them. "I don't know what your life was like when you were playing ball, but don't play it with me."

"I didn't realize I was."

"That's bullshit and you know it."

Jack tucked his hands into his jean pockets. Not a touch of dirt on him. Not like Laurie. "Fair enough, but I'm betting this wasn't why you chased after me?"

Turning it back around her, was he? Except she had run after him.

"I wanted to apologize for earlier. You were right," she said quickly, already seeing his arrogance snap back into place. All he needed was her to add to his ego. "About Elizabeth. You were right."

The good-looking and confident image Jack had projected to the women of the softball fields, vanished. He was back to being Jack-the-Dad and he wasn't at all relaxed. Far from it.

"You talked with her?"

Laurie nodded. "She needs this team."

For a moment, Jack lost his focus, as if he saw something from the past or something else Laurie couldn't see. She glanced at the field. Her girls were already leaving the green, making way from the next team.

"Jack?" Laurie asked.

"I'd like her to play. For you." He blinked, as if coming back to himself. "Does this mean she's official?"

As if Laurie ever had a say. "She's official. Did Hugh tell you about the practice schedule?"

"Yesterday."

Of course.

"Thank you. It'll mean a lot to Elizabeth." He pulled out his keys and turned around. Cold, abrupt, as if talking to her meant nothing to him which was silly. Of course it meant nothing.

"You're leaving? I thought...I thought Hugh invited you to the after-game dinner?"

With that one, simple question, Jack-the-Dad disappeared and sexy, suave Jack returned. Laurie nearly tripped over her own feet. She couldn't tell which of the two was more dangerous.

One reminded her of her own childhood, reminded her of everything she'd lost. The other reminded her that she was indeed a woman, and apparently, a rather attractive woman.

No, she decided. Both versions of Jack were equally dangerous and she wanted nothing to do with either of them.

"Change of plans, though I look forward to next time."

Laurie steeled her will and resisted with everything she had. "That's *if* I invite you."

Jack shrugged. "Hugh seemed game for another go at it."

"Except next weekend it's my turn to host." Meaning she got to invite whoever the hell she wanted.

Jack flashed her his special smile, the poster smile. "Sounds like a plan. We'll see you then. Six, right?"

"What?"

He didn't wait for a confirmation on the time, or to explain. No. The damn, infuriating man slammed his door shut.

"I didn't invite you!"

And he didn't hear her. Not when he revved his engine like a teenage boy looking to impress some airhead girl. Of course, he did have the audacity to roll his window and give her one final wave before driving off.

"Why that asshole. I'm going to kill him!"

Claire, who Laurie hadn't heard sneak up on her, tugged on Laurie's uniform. "I really hope you don't kill him. He's quite the looker."

Laurie's flush deepened, but not from anger. Try mortification. "Claire, I didn't mean. I mean... I didn't invite him."

Claire, who was hardly bigger than Suzie and who only came up to Laurie's chin, gave Laurie a friendly punch in the arm. "You better have invited him! Because if you didn't, than I surely will before the next unattached mother does."

Laurie sighed. There was no way, none at all, she was going to survive Jack Evans as a parent on her team.

"Is there something you needed, Claire?"

"Actually, I wanted to talk with you about some extra lessons for Suzie and, if you wouldn't mind—I feel terrible about last night."

She didn't mention the money. Or the coast.

That was the kind of mom Claire was. She'd scrounge up the money if it made Suzie happy. Even if it meant Claire being bone-tired, week-in and week-out.

"It's no problem. Really, I was glad to help."

Claire linked her arm with Laurie, pulling her away from the parking lot, now empty of Jack's Ferrari. "And I want to help you, too, and I really don't think yelling at the man is going to win you any points."

"I don't want to win points. I don't even want him near me."

Claire gave her a long, look. "Sure you don't. That was why you ran after him, practically leaving poor Kent on the field all by his lonesome."

"That's... that's not it at all." It wasn't, but nothing Laurie said seemed to convince Claire of that.

But then, if she couldn't convince herself, how was she supposed to convince anyone else?

CHAPTER 11

$\mathcal{J}$ack pulled into Nancy's long, cobblestone driveway. An impressive, expensive-looking driveway—stones probably imported from some European castle or something. Expensive or not, the actually driving sucked as he and Elizabeth bounced up and down, jarring them both.

He also bit his tongue, too.

Lights decorated the drive, giving off an inviting atmosphere which did nothing to lessen the pain in his mouth. Of course, the lights were merely for decoration and had nothing to do with actually being inviting.

Though, for once, they had been invited.

His hands tightened on the steering wheel. He was doing this for Elizabeth. He'd canceled on dinner with an interesting woman (and Hugh) for Elizabeth.

But seeing the way Nancy spent his hard-earned money did not make him feel better. The damn woman would probably never marry again—or even live with a guy—just so she could keep sucking him dry.

The hell with that. With her.

There was no way she was getting another dime out of him. Not after the shit she just pulled.

They'd gone home after the game and freshened up. Well, he'd changed his jeans for a nice pair of slacks. Elizabeth, however, could barely sit still long enough to swap her cleats for her shoes.

Evening had come at a much slower pace than either of them wanted. Elizabeth, in eager anticipation, Jack, in eager dread.

He didn't get far up the driveway, couldn't because the way was blocked. At least two dozen cars lined up to the grand front steps.

"Son of a bitch."

"Dad?"

"Nothing." Yeah right this wasn't nothing. Just like this wasn't some damn simple family gathering.

Jack wasn't much of a car person, at least not the type who could pick out the make, model, and whatever else those car people ogled at, but he knew for a fact these were not Nancy's cars. At least not all of them.

He may not have known cars, but he knew money. Nearly every car there cost a shit ton of cash—way more than his own.

He also knew the kind of people who drove these cars. The kind of people Nancy called 'friends.' The kind of people Nancy wanted to throw in his face and to 'remind' him of his former life. Remind him of what he'd turned his back on.

Even after all these years, she still didn't get it.

One car in particular caught his eye. A Bugatti Veyron.

That was one car he knew. Knew, because he'd been with Barry when he'd bought it, both so trashed Jack had a hard time remembering what they were even doing at the dealer lot.

"Dad?" Elizabeth leaned forward in her seat. "I thought you said Mom wanted us for dinner?"

"I did."

"And… and didn't she say it was just going to be us?"

"That's what she said."

Elizabeth worried her bottom lip. "Maybe… maybe she got the time wrong or something."

Jack couldn't let go of the steering wheel. Couldn't because if he did he'd find Nancy and strangle her.

His good mood, the lingering one from a beautiful softball coach chasing after him, was a distant memory. As if it had never been. That's where they should be right now, not dealing with Nancy's shit.

"Your mother," he said—as calmly as possible, "didn't get the time wrong."

"She could have."

"No, Elizabeth. She didn't. She did this on purpose."

Somehow, Jack released his death grip on the wheel and yanked off his seat belt. "Wait here. I'll go see what this is about."

He slammed the door behind him.

The unmistakable booming of Nancy's high-definition sound system echoed in the once-quiet twilight. It grated on his nerves, setting both his teeth and temper on edge.

Too many memories. Too many decisions he'd left buried in the past.

He took two steps and realized Elizabeth hadn't listened. She followed him, softball glove clutched to her chest, eyes wide and staring at the large expanse of Nancy's house. If four stories, more bedrooms than any sane person would know what to do with, and a handful of hand-cut and trimmed gardens, could be considered a house.

"I asked you to wait in the car."

"I want to see Mom."

"No, you don't." If Elizabeth saw Nancy right now... No daughter, especially Elizabeth's age, should see what was going on in there.

Elizabeth's eyes narrowed and for a second there was steel in his usual timid daughter. "Why? Is this going to be like the newspaper? Like those photos?"

The pictures of him.

"I wouldn't be surprised."

Glass shattered, which was then followed by even louder laughter.

Elizabeth flinched, the steel in her eyes disappearing as quickly as it had appeared. This was no place for his daughter.

"In the car." Jack pointed.

"But—"

"Now."

It took more energy, more than he thought possible, to keep from lashing out. Elizabeth didn't deserve his anger, especially when he was trying to earn her trust. Trust she so easily gave to Nancy.

"Trust me. Just, get in the car. Please." Jack spun, trusting Elizabeth wouldn't follow him, and stormed towards the house. The closer he got, the more he knew he didn't want to open that door.

He knew what awaited him. The best he could hope for was finding Nancy and getting the hell out of there before their daughter saw too much.

Or he remembered too much.

Knocking was pointless, so Jack let himself in, then wished he hadn't. Smoke billowed around him, rushing towards the cool, open night air. It surrounded him in a tantalizing cloud.

He didn't want to remember, didn't want to yearn, even if briefly, for those lounging days in the open air of his yacht. The half-finished bottle of scotch, the taste of lime and tequila tingling his lips from where the newest girl had kissed him.

He and Barry celebrating another win, another out of town, three-game trip.

Jack coughed and his eyes watered. The memory dissolved with the cloud.

That had been another life. One he didn't want back. One that had no place for Elizabeth.

Unsurprisingly, the foyer was empty. After all, the action, and the booze, was further in. Coats hung sleek on the nearby rack, and even with the warming spring weather, he spotted one or two furs.

Jack squinted in the dim lighting, letting his eyes adjust. The tendrils of smoke showed him where to go, as if the music alone wasn't enough of a guide.

Jack steeled his will, forced aside every scrap of memory lurking near the surface, and plunged into the world of smoke, music, and celebrities who had way too much money and way too much time on their hands.

The way he'd once been.

Jack picked his way towards the party, stepping over discarded clothes, beer bottles, and unmentionable puddles on the marble floor. Voices echoed from the back deck and the pool.

Jack clenched his fists. He didn't want to go anywhere near the pool. Any pool for that matter. As if he needed the reminder of where he had met Nancy.

Or where their first time had been.

Two shadows lingered near the doorway, just outside the glow from the outside lights. Arms clasped in a tight—very tight embrace— to the point where they could simply be one shape.

He slowed, not wanting to interrupt anything. Or more truthfully, not wanting to see anything.

The smaller of the two paused and turned towards him, a slender, silky body Jack would recognize anywhere.

Nancy.

She detached from the shadows, the slender slip of a red dress—if Jack was gracious enough to call it a dress—hugging her thin form in all the right places. The kind of places Jack had also liked back in the day, before he gotten a heap of sense.

"Jack," Nancy purred. "I'm so glad you came."

Screw calm. "Not exactly the kind of family dinner I was expecting."

"No?" She smiled.

It wasn't a real smile. Not once had he seen this woman give him a genuine smile. A smile that was simply a smile and not something with a hidden agenda.

"That's right," he said. "This wasn't the kind of family dinner I thought we agreed on. You know, the one where I brought our twelve-year old daughter."

Nancy pretended surprise. She was always good at that. "Elizabeth? You brought *Elizabeth* here?"

Then there was that smile again and she purposefully searched over Jack's shoulder. "Well, where is she? Where is my darling daughter?"

"In the car, away from your claws. Did you actually think I'd bring her in here?"

Her smile slipped, just a tad, but enough to let Jack know he'd gotten to her.

The second shadow finally joined Nancy, and by the height, Jack should have known who was standing beside her.

Barry White. Star pitcher—and starter—for any damn team he played for. And that had been quite a few teams.

And unlike Barry, who gave Jack his lazy, I'm-the-king-of-the-world smile, Jack hadn't quite kept his pro-baseball physique. Sure he still worked out, but his guns looked nothing like that shiny mess Barry carried around.

But unlike Jack, Barry had apparently never pulled himself away from the dark side.

"You still haven't changed have you, Jack?" Barry leaned against Nancy, wrapping his possessive hand around her shoulder and pulling her close. "You're still an ass to this beautiful woman."

"Damn straight I am. As long as she's a bitch to her daughter than I get to be an ass."

Nancy pushed away from Barry. "Why you—"

"Your daughter's in the car," Jack snarled. "She's crying because she thought she'd have a nice evening with her mother and instead, you throw the whole damn thing in her face."

Barry stepped forward. "Now wait a minute here."

"Stay out of this, Barry. From what I heard, this stupid dinner was your idea."

Barry's eyes narrowed. Jack felt the tension growing between them, his challenge echoing in the small space separating them as if the stupid music and drinking in the background had simply fallen away.

The same way it was always between them. Only one could come out on top.

This, he realized, was why Nancy had invited him. For the fight.

Well, Jack wasn't going to play, not with Elizabeth waiting for him.

"Forget it. Both of you. Have your damn party. Elizabeth and I have somewhere else we can be. Some place where there happens to be another beautiful woman—one who actually wants to spend time with our daughter."

His words had their intended effect. Nancy's eyes narrowed, practically glowed a bright red.

That, of course, was when Barry threw the punch. All 200 lbs. of packed-in muscle doped up on steroids, crashing towards Jack's face.

Just like old times. And like old times, Jack was still the faster of the two.

Jack pivoted. Air rushed past his head as Barry swung. He slipped behind Barry, used Barry's momentum against him, and pushed.

Jack drew power from the ground, the same way he used to do when he pitched, and shoved Barry.

Barry went flying and smacked right into the wall.

Nancy screamed and ran to Barry's side, trying to help him stand. It was actually kinda funny and Jack smiled. She couldn't do a whole lot in in ten-inch heels or whatever-the-hell they were.

Barry clutched his head. Like usual, his thick skull saved him from any serious damage. Except maybe a concussion, but then Barry was probably drugged out on something and probably hadn't felt a thing.

Just like old times.

"Shut up, Nancy," Barry growled. "You're hurting my head."

"I will not." She spun on Jack, red, dangerous finger nail thrusting at him. "This is all your fault."

Handling Barry and his usual temper swings was one thing. Handling his ex-wife was another and required greater caution.

Nancy was not above eye-gouging.

"I'm not the one who lied about a cozy dinner gathering." Jack raised his hands, backing away, specifically to keep those claws away from his vulnerable parts.

Nancy straightened. She smoothed out her dress, never once taking her eyes off Jack.

"If you hadn't quit baseball, if you hadn't walked away from all this, forced us all to walk away with you, then I wouldn't have to shove it in your face."

"I quit baseball for Elizabeth."

"You did it for yourself. All because you couldn't hack it anymore."

Nancy leaned in. The strap of her dress slipped further down her shoulder, revealing the small curve of her breast. Jack kept his gaze locked on her face.

She smiled. "Elizabeth was only an excuse, a cover up."

She inched closer. Close enough that he could smell the booze, smell the smoke clinging to her, mixing with her lavender perfume.

His stomach churned. He tasted bile at the back of his throat.

Barry leaned against the wall, not moving from where he'd fallen, arms across his chest. Watching. Watching and enjoying the entertainment.

"I quit because someone handed a reporter a stack of photos wrapped in a pink bow which included quite a handful of lovely supporting commentary." This time, it was his turn to lean forward, his turn to tower over her.

"Photos," he growled, "that Elizabeth happened to see. Or did you conveniently forget that part? Or where you the one who left the newspaper on the table just for her to find?"

"I did no such thing," Nancy snapped. "It was meant for you. It's not my fault she saw them. I have some decency in me. Those photos were never meant for a child, especially my child. But I had to make you see, had to make you realize that you were blowing everything."

Surprisingly, he believed her, at least about Elizabeth seeing the newspaper. Elizabeth had been only a casualty in Nancy's deadly game, a game where she didn't like to lose her control, her hold over Jack.

"That's one you're right about." Jack forced a deep breath in, forced himself to take another. "I did blow it. I failed my family. I failed my daughter."

He'd still be locked in that world, the same as Barry, if it hadn't been for Elizabeth. His daughter. His shining light who'd finally grabbed him by the balls and forced him to wake up.

Or more accurately, to grow up.

"I should be thanking you. If Elizabeth hadn't seen it...I'd probably still be where I was. I left for Elizabeth and I haven't regretted it since."

"You walked away from our life," Nancy snapped. "Baseball was everything."

"*The money* was everything," Jack said. "The money was all that mattered to you.

She pursed her lips, but he recognized the glint in her eye, the same stubbornness she'd always had. "Your secret is you lost your game. You weren't good anymore and no matter what you did, no matter how hard you tried, you couldn't get it back."

"I never lost my game." He glared at Nancy. "The game lost me."

Or more truthfully, he'd gotten caught up in the other world, the darker side of the game. He hadn't been able to fight his way back, and when he finally could, he decided to walk away and be the father he should have been from the very beginning.

That was the truth. That was the reason Jack Evans, star player retired. It was a truth Nancy still refused to understand.

Not his problem.

"If you want that life," he told her, "fine." Jack waved towards Barry. "Have at it, but don't you dare try to bring Elizabeth back into this or I swear, Nancy, I will see you in court."

His anger rode him, hard. He wanted to hit something, wanted to smash Barry's face into the wall.

Jack stormed out of the house, slamming the doors behind him, causing the nearby windows to shake. The hell with Nancy, with Barry, with baseball.

He'd walked away from that life and hadn't looked back since. There was no way in hell he was going to start now. And if she thought setting up the perfect mood, the perfect party, was going to eat him alive—well she could forget it.

Elizabeth sat in the car, waiting for him like he'd asked. Her cheeks and eyes were red from crying. As soon as he sat down, her eyes teared-up again.

"She didn't get the time wrong," Elizabeth whispered.

"No."

Jack took a long, slow breath. Had a hard time breathing past his anger. That wasn't what she needed to see right now. "She's busy. With other things."

Elizabeth swallowed. "Other men?"

There was no point answering. Elizabeth didn't want to hear the truth, not with her already mentioning the newspaper photos.

"We're leaving."

Elizabeth sniffed and rubbed her eyes. "I don't want to go home."

He turned the car on and carefully backed out. Although the urge to smash into Barry's Bugatti was tempting. Very tempting. And yes, while he still had more than enough money from investing and real estate, he didn't quite have that much money laying around.

There was only one person who could help him right now, one person who Elizabeth would want to see—would smile to see. Even if that person did want to smack him with a bat.

But maybe, just maybe she could help him forget the memories the smoke had awoken.

CHAPTER 12

The last thing Laurie expected when she answered Hugh's door was the red-faced, barely held-in temper of Jack Evans. Her hand slid from the doorknob. She didn't think. She reached for him.

"Jack?"

His eyes, their blue color now darker than midnight, pierced hers. She forced herself to remain still, to not instinctively step back. This wasn't the same man who'd driven off, leaving her in the parking lot as she yelled at him.

"Jack?"

She watched as he swallowed, as he attempted to regain control. When he finally spoke there was an edge to his voice, like thunderclouds on the horizon.

"You still have room for two guests?"

She shivered. This wasn't a man you wanted to get angry. Especially this angry.

"Of course. Hugh's just putting on some hot dogs." What was going on? What happened? "Jack. I thought you were—"

"Something came up. I thought this the best place to go." He glanced back at the car. "Elizabeth didn't want to go home."

Elizabeth? Laurie peered around Jack and saw the Elizabeth hunched in the car. Arms hiding her head. Her small frame wracking with sobs.

She rushed past Jack, practically leaping for the car, except Jack caught her elbow. She froze mid-movement, which caused her to crash back into Jack. They collided and her breath whooshed out. He didn't move. A solid, rock wall.

"Don't mention her mother."

His fingers dug into Laurie's bicep. Not hurting, but firm.

Laurie nodded. "I understand."

Jack let her go and that was the last Laurie thought of Jack. Though later, when she'd gotten Elizabeth to calm down, had convinced her to come inside and have a hotdog with her and Hugh, she realized her arm hadn't forgotten Jack's touch.

His fingers still burned on her skin. Scorching.

Laurie's face flushed and she rummaged in the cooler for another beer, hoping no one saw.

They were on the deck, enjoying the warming spring night. Elizabeth had finally fallen asleep on the cushioned lawn chair propped up on Hugh's deck. She'd scarfed down her share of the hot dogs and then crashed.

That was good. It was what her body and soul needed.

Hugh lounged in his favorite deck chair, even though it was missing a leg stand, making it a tad off-balance. Jack, however, wasn't nearly as comfortable. His back was still just as straight as when he'd first stalked in the door. Not even the three beers had made a dent. Still just as rigid, just as angry.

Laurie popped open the cap and took another long swig. She'd need it for this conversation. She and Hugh hadn't said anything to each other about how they were going to deal with this. But then, they hadn't needed to either. He'd taken one look at Elizabeth, who'd had a tight grip on Laurie's middle, and nodded.

This was for her to deal with.

Why, she had no idea. Hugh was the one who'd practically signed Jack onto the team.

Probably because she'd played as close to professional ball as a woman could, that should could better relate to someone like Jack.

Ha. There was no relation between Major League baseball players and whatever-the-hell she'd been.

Hugh stood and stretched. "Well, that was one good meal. Nice to relax after a long game weekend."

Laurie rose and he waved her down.

"No, sit. I'll clean up. You be a guest for once and entertain our new team member."

"You sure?"

Jack offered to help as well, but Hugh put his foot down and got Jack another beer.

"I do have to drive you know."

"Not any time soon, you don't. You've had a rough evening and she's done for." Hugh raised his hand when Jack protested. "I'm old, but I'm not blind. Whatever your ex-wife did, it was a piss-poor thing to do to a kid."

Hugh pulled out a blanket and tucked it around Elizabeth. He kept his voice quiet so as not to wake her. "You took care of her, now let us take care of you. Meanwhile, I'll take care of the dishes."

Hugh disappeared into the house leaving Laurie alone with Jack—except for Elizabeth who was fast asleep.

She might as well get this over with. It would help if she wasn't sitting quite so close to him.

She needed space so she could think a little. It was a problem she'd been having ever since he'd walked into her life. Actually, tonight Elizabeth had distracted Laurie enough where she couldn't think about Jack.

But now?

She took another long sip. Now was definitely a different story.

"Do you want to tell me what happened?" she asked.

"No."

Just the reaction she'd been expecting. This would be easy as pie. Not.

"I think," she said, "doing the dishes was the easier of the two jobs, and I think, I got screwed on this deal."

As she'd expected, that caught Jack's attention. "What deal?"

She gestured with her bottle towards him. "Who got to be the one who got to talk with you."

"I don't need to talk."

"Look, Jack. When you come over, your daughter crying hysterically—"

"She wasn't hysterical."

Laurie merely looked at him until he finally dropped his gaze. "As I was saying, we're a family here. The team's a family. So when you show up, clearly needing our help—don't interrupt, you needed our help—we're going to get involved."

She put her beer down on the small table. "Even if you don't want us to."

"It's not necessary." Jack rose and Laurie practically felt flames crackling as his temper seemed to get its second wind. Lucky her, indeed. *Thanks, Hugh.*

"It's late. I should be getting Elizabeth to bed."

She rose as well, and when he moved towards Elizabeth, Laurie slid in front of him. She held out her palm and when he would have touched her, he flinched back.

Okay. She didn't think her presence was that terrible. No. She needed to focus on helping both Jack and Elizabeth—not focus on this attraction. A very, clearly unwanted attraction.

"Don't run. Really, don't run," Laurie said. "We want to help."

Jack stared at her hand, still raised, before finally wrenching his gaze away. "I told you. I don't need help."

Of all the arrogant...

"Fine. Then why did you come over? Why, after your ex clearly shredded both Elizabeth and you to pieces, did you come here? Why did you bring your daughter here?"

"It was a mistake. Obviously. Clearly I shouldn't have brought her here."

"Is that right?" Laurie stepped closer, fist clenching at her side. She could practically feel the solid grip of her bat—ready to pound some since into the man.

"Yes."

"I see. So that's how you align your priorities? Suddenly coming here is a mistake because I'm pushing to help you? Even though your daughter has clearly relaxed, is sleeping comfortably, even actually smiled a handful of times—you're telling me you think you made a mistake?"

Now she was closer, so close she could smell the beer on his breath, could pick out the definite outline of his chest muscles through his shirt—silk, maybe?

Jack didn't move. His body was taunt, standing straight and ready to explode. She could feel it rolling off him, deep waves, strong waves. Breathtaking.

"Yeah," he whispered, voice now hoarse. "That sounds about right."

"Okay, then." It wasn't okay. It was far from okay; not the way he was looking at her right now. "So long as that's clear, if you still want to leave..."

She stepped aside, motioning to Elizabeth. "Then you can go."

He didn't go. Far from it. Instead of collecting his daughter, carefully picking her up and taking her to the car, he collected Laurie.

Actually, his hand slipped around her wrist. A strong grip. A pitcher's grip, like hers.

He pulled her to him.

This time when her fingers touched his chest, he didn't flinch. The same scorching feeling flared up her wrist, all the way to the top of her head.

Breathing became suddenly very difficult.

"This wasn't," she swallowed. He was way too close. "This wasn't what I meant."

"I know."

He kissed her. Jack Evans, former Major League baseball player and heartthrob to many teenage girls and women of all ages—including Laurie—kissed Laurie Stevens on the mouth.

The scorching heat changed into a blinding blaze. His touch, his lips. She couldn't feel anything beyond the burn. Couldn't hear over her own heartbeat.

Her body melted. It was like every muscle in her body turned to goo and she could barely hold herself up.

Laurie sagged against his chest, leaning into the kiss. He wrapped his arms around, pulling her closer.

Hugh cleared his throat from the door.

Laurie and Jack sprang back. She knocked into the table, spilling her beer. She cursed and quickly picked it up.

"Well, glad to see that went well." Hugh rubbed his chin, glancing at one and then the other. "Much better than I could have done."

Jack ran a hand through his hair. He didn't look at Laurie. "I can pretty much guarantee that."

Hugh snorted. "Why the hell you'd think I let her do the talking? And don't think this conversation's done." He waved his sponge at Jack. "That might be a mighty fine distraction, but you've still got yerself a problem."

And just like that, Laurie saw the change. Jack went from the slightly-embarrassed man who'd just thoroughly—yes, thoroughly—kissed her, to the stranger. The dad who didn't know them, the dad who saw them only as coaches and nothing more.

Hugh's smile folded in on itself, clearly realizing he'd overstepped his bounds—and the situation.

Laurie grabbed some napkins and dumped them on the beer puddle she'd created. Well, wasn't this just great? She was good enough to kiss but obviously not good enough to trust.

"We should get going," Jack said. "It's late and tomorrow's school."

Laurie squeezed her eyes shut, thankful she was kneeling, her head at angle so Jack couldn't see. The school line. She'd been fed that one a handful of times.

Except, she couldn't remember any of them hurting quite this bad, striking her quite so deep. "Yeah, of course."

Her voice hadn't cracked. *Take that Jack Evans.* As if his rejection could possibly hurt her.

Not a chance.

Laurie tossed the soaked napkins on the floor and held out her hand. "Thanks for coming by."

Jack stared at her hand as if not quite sure what it was doing held in front of him. She refused to let her smile waver. Not even in the slightest. He hadn't upset her.

After a brief moment, Jack shook her hand.

The kiss, if he even called that a kiss, had apparently been erased from his memory. Hadn't happened.

That was exactly how he looked at her.

"Thanks again. And thanks for inviting us."

She hadn't invited him. She'd also make sure Hugh didn't extend the offer again. Unless Elizabeth needed help. That was acceptable, but spending time with Jack, was not.

Hugh gave her a look, the look that wanted to give her a good kick in the pants, but for once he kept his mouth shut. Right now, she could only deal with one male at a time.

By the time Jack and Elizabeth left, the back taillights of his car barely pulling away, Hugh threw his sponge on the ground and rounded on Laurie. "What the hell were you doing?"

"Saying goodbye." She collected the empty bottles and dumped them into the recycle bin. "And making sure he was still bringing Elizabeth to practice."

"That's not what I meant and you know it."

Laurie sighed. Hugh stood barely a foot from her, arms on his hips, looking like he was ready to tackle her. She knew from experience he wouldn't let this go. Not until he said his peace.

She tossed the last bottle in. "I know what you meant and I really don't care."

"I saw enough of that kiss to make my own toes curl. You let him walk away from you."

"Yeah. I did." She was fine with that. Totally fine. She didn't want a guy like Jack in her life anyway, right? "The kiss was unexpected, but it shouldn't have happened, and it won't happen again. That's as close as I'm ever going to get."

Hugh snorted. "You actually believe that crap?"

Now it was her turn to get mad. "You were the one who invited him in the first place. In fact, you didn't even ask how I felt about it, and now you want to lecture me about a kiss?"

A kiss she hadn't started.

Even if she enjoyed it.

"Forget it." She threw down the soaked napkins. "I'm out of here. Next time you invite a girl—and her arrogant parent—onto the team without consulting me I'm out of here for good."

Laurie snatched her purse from the chair and shoved past Hugh. She steered clear of the beer puddle and sponge, and slammed the front door behind her. This was supposed to have been a relaxing barbecue.

Maybe she should have gone out with Kent instead. And if he'd tried kissing her she could at least slug him.

She refused to think about why she hadn't slugged Jack.

CHAPTER 13

*L*aurie stared into her empty coffee cup. Why hadn't she gotten the bigger espresso?

Her girls slowly arrived at the field, parents in tow, everyone still yawning, still waking up for another Saturday of softball games. A few girls were already in right field, throwing balls back and forth to each other. The sound of balls smacking into the leather gloves swept over her.

Laurie held in her fourth yawn in at least that many minutes. This had been the worst recorded softball week on record.

Four canceled pitching lessons, one ankle sprained her at practice, and good ol' Dan Richards had started up again about Lacey not getting in enough pitching time.

Of course, none of that compared to the 1:00 a.m. wake-up call from a distressed parent who had no idea what to do with her daughter (Laurie's former player) who'd decided to toss away her college scholarship to join the Marines.

When the cup didn't magically refill itself, she gave up and tossed it into the trashcan. At least they had a break between games today. As soon as this wonderful eight o'clock game was over she was dashing to the nearest coffee stand.

If she could survive that long.

Hugh leaned against the fence, grabbing hold of the chain-link, and studied her. "You look like hell."

"It just about fits my week. How the heck do we keep ending up with all the morning games?"

Today was one of those days when she should be staying in bed, sleeping in, or even better—reading a book. Nope. Instead she was here, waiting for another weekend of games to start.

"You gonna tell me what happened?"

Laurie stifled a yawn and failed miserably. Man she was tired. "I got a call about Janice. This morning, early."

"Janice? Just got a softball scholarship to UCLA, Janice?"

"Yeah. She turned it down and signed up for the Air Force. She told her mom last night." When she'd gotten home after partying with her girlfriends—hence the freaked out mom calling Laurie at one o'clock.

Hugh winced. "And they called you, huh?"

"They sure did."

Once Janice's mother had realized the high school and travel team coaches weren't going to change Janice's mind, that's when she got desperate and called Laurie.

Not like Laurie could do anything. It was Janice's choice.

Not to mention the fact the girl had already signed up. What's done, was done.

All Laurie could hope to do was help her parents understand, which was silly since when she'd made the same decisions she hadn't been able to get *her* parents to listen to her.

Still, she'd tried with Janice's parent, even if it meant being up way, way past her bedtime.

"Then it's good I thought of you." Hugh lifted two coffees.

Laurie sighed in complete, blissful relief. "You're an angel."

Hugh held the latte away from her. "I'm actually the manager of the *Angels*, and my offer shows I've forgiven you for your stormy attitude at Sunday's barbecue. Which means no more stormy attitude right now. You're scaring the girls."

"I am not."

Laurie could practically smell the caffeine goodness. She resisted, though. He wasn't about to win her over so easily.

"And I'm not grumpy. Besides, I wasn't the one who started it."

He held the latte further from her. "Not good enough. After a kiss like that you sure as hell better not be storming around my field."

"If you recall, it wasn't the kiss I was pissed about." Laurie snatched the latte from him.

It was what came after the kiss. The part that mattered. The part where someone like Jack realized what he had impulsively done—and it was clearly an impulse—and backed away (or in his case, ran) from Laurie and the awkward situation.

"You're also still pissed about Wednesday's practice." Hugh gave her the-arms-folded-over-his-chest glare. "That he didn't show up."

"Technically, he did." He just hadn't stayed. "And I'm not mad. Why would I be mad? I'm glad he's away from my field."

It was her field. Her team. Her girls.

And she was not pissed. How could she be? It wasn't like she'd even seen Jack. He'd dropped Elizabeth off at the curb, like every other parent, and the moment practice was done, he'd swooped right in and picked her back up.

She was not mad at all.

"Just drop it about the kiss," Laurie said. "It meant nothing to him and I wish like hell it hadn't happened."

Hugh leaned across and tapped her forehead. It was their gesture, their 'talk-to-me' gesture. "You don't believe that, do you?"

As if Jack's running away Sunday night and his avoidance on Wednesday (not like she knew he was avoiding her), wasn't enough of a clue.

"Just let it go. We have games to play and..."

Laurie scanned the rows of cars and the parents slowly streaming into the park. She couldn't help but look for his Ferrari. Damn it.

"We have games to play," she said. Firmly. "And I can't be a good coach if I'm thinking about kissing a parent."

Which, of course, was the perfect timing for Lacey and her own darling dad to show up. Dan's eyes widened, clearly catching the last bit of their conversation. Someone who had absolutely no business, none whatsoever, knowing who Laurie did or did not kiss.

He just better not be thinking she was thinking of kissing him!

Definitely the softball week from hell.

She tossed the lid of her latte into the trash. "Just get them warmed up. I'm gonna go for a walk."

Hugh touched his hat and nodded. "Whatever you say, Coach."

The *Angels'* girls were starting to show up and a few stragglers were heading into the dugout. But not Elizabeth.

At least by herself, Laurie could admit the truth. She was looking for Jack and he clearly wasn't looking for her.

She picked out a spot close enough to the girls, but far enough away to give her some privacy. It also happened to be the same table Jack had sat at last Sunday. Had it seriously been only a week?

Ugh. She was so screwed.

Laurie took a long, luxurious sip of her latte. She closed her eyes and listened to the sounds of the field coming to life. Balls smacking into gloves, the snap of leather as it closed around the ball. The tiny sharp sounds of plastic whiffle balls hitting bats.

Good sounds. Even if they didn't always bring up the most pleasant memories, memories of her days on the field instead of just coaching. Days she'd long since shoved behind her.

Yet, without even trying she remembered the last day she stood on the field, on the pitcher's mound at her college's championship game. The game she hadn't finished.

Her stomach twisted. Why was she thinking of this now?

"Morning, Coach." Claire said, as she strolled up to the bench.

Laurie was more than glad to shove the memory aside and, thanks to Hugh's refreshing latte, managed a fairly nice smile and not the grimace she given to everyone else this morning.

"Hey there. How's Suzie?"

"At home, grumpy and sick in bed. Do you mind if I sit?" Claire motioned to the bench.

Laurie scooted over, but gave Claire fair warning she wasn't the best of company. Claire merely laughed. Laurie wished she could laugh like that, beautiful and carefree. At least, Claire laughed when she wasn't exhausted from working two jobs.

Working two jobs so she could pay for Suzie could play with the *Angels.* It wasn't that the team was expensive, but there were expenses and they added up—especially when they had to travel. Traveling to a handful of tournaments had been the only concession on growing and becoming more competitive, that Laurie was willing to make.

Claire tucked a strand of her short red hair behind her hair. "Believe me, I could see your mood the minute I stepped out of my car."

"That bad, huh?"

Claire shrugged. "It happens to the best of us, but I thought it looked like you could use some company."

"I'll take your word for it."

Actually, Claire's company wasn't too bad. She was a pleasant person to be around, always smiling (when she wasn't exhausted), and she gave Laurie her space. Claire even let Laurie finish her latte before she started in on the real reasons for her visit.

"You're probably wondering why I'm here."

Laurie nodded into her empty cup. Definitely empty. "I figured you'd tell me when you were ready."

Claire gave Laurie a half-smile. "So long as you tell me what's between you and Jack."

Laurie started and dropped her cup.

"When you're ready of course."

"There's nothing between me and Jack." Laurie retrieved her cup from the ground. At least it was empty. "Why does everyone keep asking about me and Jack? I've known the guy for a week."

Claire lifted an eyebrow. "None of us single women are blind. The man could barely take his eyes off you."

Laurie rubbed the back of her neck. "More like testing my coaching techniques. Trust me, I know when I'm being studied for my looks and when my coaching abilities are being studied."

"There's a difference?"

"Yes and besides, I don't like him or his type."

"Now he is a 'type'?"

"Yes. The very rich, baseball-snobbery type." Which he hadn't actually acted on since she'd met him, but Laurie knew it was in there. She'd seen that intense gaze of his as he studied her, as he studied the game.

It was in there, just waiting to come out.

Laurie waved towards the field. "Why don't we walk and you can tell me why you've come to the game, even though Suzie's in bed, sick."

Claire slipped from the bench. "Fair enough."

What was one more conversation? After all, Laurie knew when she'd agreed to coach with Hugh she'd be more than just a softball coach. She'd spent nearly as much time coaching off the field as well as on it.

Turns out, Claire needed her support as much as Suzie.

They circled the outer field so Laurie could keep an eye on the girls—and on Hugh—and did her best to ease Claire's fears. It hadn't taken much guessing to find out problem.

Lacey had taken to picking on Suzie, mostly because of her size, but also because Suzie had told some of her classmates—who also went to the same school—about Laurie showing her some pitching basics.

Laurie rubbed her forehead. She should have known Lacey would be a problem, would get defensive and, instead of talking to Laurie, would take it out on Suzie.

"I'll handle this, Claire. It's mostly my fault anyway." They had reached the parking lot, a good place to end the conversation so Claire could get back to her sick daughter.

Claire snorted. "I think the fault lies with her bossy, arrogant father."

"True." This time, benching Lacey clearly wouldn't be enough. She'd have to find some way to get to the stubborn girl. "Thanks for talking to me, and tell Suzie not to worry. As soon as she's better I'll give her another lesson."

"You don't have to. I mean, you know I can't...."

Pay.

Laurie nodded. "I know. Just that if you're ever running late again we'll have something to do to pass the time."

Claire smiled. It was more a smile of relief than a happy smile. Not like Laurie could blame her. The woman gave everything she had, and then some, to her daughter.

For some reason, that dedication reminded her of Jack.

As if on cue, a familiar rumbling engine roared around the corner before entering the parking lot. More than a handful of women jumped up from the seats and one or two even reached for their purses to powder their noses.

Claire clutched Laurie's arm, her squeak drowning as the Ferrari slide into almost two parking spots.

Well. That apparently answered the question of where Jack was.

Late.

Elizabeth sprang from her door, snatching her bat bag and raced towards the field. She glimpsed the wide eyes and absolute terror on Elizabeth's face.

The look smacked right into Laurie's stomach. She doubled over, her body freezing. She squeezed her eyes closed, unable to help the flow of memories. Her own feeling of terror, of being yet another disappointment, another failure to her father.

No, she told herself, that's not fair to Jack. Anything could have happened; it didn't necessarily mean it was his fault.

Claire dug her fingers into Laurie's arm, pulling her back. "Laurie? Are you okay?"

She managed a nod, kind of. It took a moment for her breathing to even out and by that time Elizabeth had reached the field.

"Laurie?" Claire whispered. "You're not going to say anything, are you?"

"She'll be fine." Laurie tried for her most soothing voice, even as she felt her insides turn to iron.

Jack slipped out from his car, sliding on his sunglasses. All business, ready for action. His posture said it clear enough: stay the hell away from me.

Laurie moved towards Jack, but Claire dug in again. "I wouldn't. Anything will set him off."

Laurie gave Claire a questioning look and it was enough that Claire immediately let go.

"My ex-husband."

Another place Laurie didn't go with parents. Not unless they called her asking for help.

"Just, just be careful." Claire unlocked her car door and slid inside. "I think he might like you—at least, if you don't kill each other first."

"Well, I don't like him but I promise, I won't kill him." Laurie closed the door for Claire.

Until she found out what he'd said to Elizabeth. Then, she'd kill him.

Jack, as if sensing her, tucked his sunglasses into his pocket and faced her. Dark rims circled his eyes, nearly identical to hers.

For some reason, it didn't make her feel any better.

CHAPTER 14

Jack knew he was late. In fact, as soon as he gave in to Elizabeth's pleading eyes yesterday, he'd known they'd be late.

His daughter, whose eyes were still puffy and red, his daughter who barely waited for the car to stop before she launched herself out of the car, yanked back the seat, and then yanked her bat bag out. She'd ignored him completely.

"Elizabeth, let me—"

"I got it."

That was all. No apology, no 'I'm sorry, I didn't mean what I said in the car.'

And why not?

Because she'd meant it. Just like Nancy had meant what she said about him being a terrible father and a cheat.

Jack slammed his car door shut. What was he supposed to do? If Nancy had asked him if Elizabeth could spend the night, that would have been one thing. He'd have told her no. Not with an early softball game the next day.

But she'd asked Elizabeth—not him.

Laurie's team was well into their warm-ups. Elizabeth hurled her bag into the dugout. She'd probably forget to tie her shoes. She always forgot when she was upset.

Against his better judgment he'd dropped Elizabeth off last night for a 'girls night sleepover'—after making sure it would actually be a girls-only event and that Nancy didn't have any anonymous guests over. It had been one 'request' that Nancy was smart enough not to contest.

Nancy had promised to have Elizabeth up early, dressed, and fed. She'd wanted to apologize for dinner last week, wanted to make it up to her little girl.

Jack slammed his palm onto the steering wheel and winced. His hands, still sore from pounding on the front door, trying to wake them up. It'd been Nancy's plan from the start, a way to get back at him from walking out last Sunday and making her look like a fool in front of Barry.

When he'd finally gotten inside, temper flying, he hadn't been careful with his words. He hadn't noticed that Elizabeth was smiling, as if she and her mother had a fun time together.

He hadn't noticed. And he'd said some pretty mean, but truthful, words about Nancy. Of course, Nancy gave back as good as she got. Somehow managed to tie in his dark days in baseball and making Elizabeth feel worthless at the same time. Reminded Jack what his days on the road had been like, leaving the Nancy and Elizabeth behind.

What his behavior had been like. Who he'd been with. Slept with.

They'd both gotten so caught up in the argument, they'd forgotten Elizabeth standing right there. Listening. Crying.

The knuckles on his right hand were split open in a few places. A white bubble had formed during the drive from where he'd hit the door wrong. He'd heal.

He wasn't sure Elizabeth would. And once again, it was his fault. His and Nancy's.

Jack got out of his car, slamming the door behind him. A couple walking their yellow Labrador glanced up, and then walked faster.

The dog, though, merely wagged its tail. Clearly Jack was someone who had too much energy and needed to play.

Play.

He'd forgotten that word a long time ago. Jack ran a hand through his hair.

At least Elizabeth had the game. It'd help her, guide her. The same way it had for him.

She'd be happy. That was what mattered. And he'd make damn sure she had everything—everything—she needed to succeed.

So, yes. He was late to the game.

And that was why, when he saw Laurie heading towards him, Jack's very short temper got a hell of a lot shorter.

"I know we're late."

And knowing she'd probably have her own hackles up, gearing for a fight, a fight Jack didn't want to start, he stalked towards the bleachers.

If Laurie wanted to make a scene, fine. It was her choice. But right now, he really needed to stay away from females before he wiped them off the planet.

It was a good plan. A solid plan. At least until Laurie touched his arm.

He knew it was her. Knew because of the flare of heat, burning as hot and wild as his temper, immediately drawing his thoughts back to that kiss last week.

A kiss he shouldn't have started.

A kiss he couldn't stop thinking about.

A kiss he had no business thinking about when his daughter was pissed at him and when he'd nearly killed his bitch of an ex-wife.

He had enough female problems to last him a lifetime.

Jack turned, slowly and deliberately. "Now is really not a good time."

"I can see that." She didn't let go of his arm. "And I think you should take a walk. Before you head over there."

She didn't back down from his glare, not like most women did—

the ones smart enough to figure out that only fools played with fire. Apparently, Laurie wasn't one of them. Either that, or she didn't care.

"Worried I'll upset your parents?" he asked.

"Worried you'll upset my girls."

"They're practicing in right field."

"Not for long. Jack," she paused, as if trying to phrase her words so he wouldn't snap.

He was close, though. Very close.

Her hand tightened. The heat grew. Jack ignored it.

"Jack, I can feel how pissed you are from the outfield. You need to take a break and walk it off."

Jack didn't move.

"Okay, fine." Laurie's eyes narrowed. "You want me to be mean, I'll be mean. I don't give a damn what happened this morning, why Elizabeth is practically sobbing and trying to tie her shoes, but you're not going anywhere near that field until you've calmed down."

"Anything else?"

Laurie looked away. "Yes. I'm sorry. I'm sorry that I thought...that I thought you were the one who upset her."

She would think that. Just like everyone.

"Forget it."

"I mean it. Whatever she said, I'm sorry."

Jack straightened, felt himself pull away from her. "That's none of your business."

He saw the flash in her eyes, the temper she'd kept tucked below the surface. He felt himself draw closer, felt himself pulled in by that spark—the flash of determination, of competition?

He felt his own spark answering in turn.

"You're right. It's not my business." She glanced down at her hand, as if only now realizing she still touched him.

The leather from his jacket creaked as she removed her fingers. One by one, he felt each finger pull away. The heat between them lessened. It didn't go away—no, that would be asking too much—but enough so he could concentrate.

Concentrate on his anger and not the kiss.

"Just, just take a walk," Laurie said. "You both need it."

"All right." It made him feel better knowing she was right. "I'll take a walk."

Laurie didn't smile, didn't gloat or try to wheedle out what had happened like Nancy would have.

Instead, she merely nodded. "I'll get Elizabeth warmed up and get her on the field. She's got a good arm, but I think I'll put her at first base this morning—I think that will be enough action to get her mind off things."

Now that he was this close, and now that he could see without the red haze clouding his vision, he noticed shadows darkening Laurie's eyes. They didn't detract from the beauty he'd seen last week, but it did make her seem more…human.

Normal. Someone with actual emotions who could stay up late and worry—and not just about where the PR studio executives were going to sit her in front of the cameras. Not like Nancy.

Laurie shifted back and he immediately felt the separation, the distance between them. Breathing also became a little easier.

"Thanks for showing up," she said.

And as quietly as she'd caught up with him, she left. He still felt her touch on his arm, even through the smooth leather, he felt her. Which, of course, was the last thing he wanted to be feeling right now.

Attraction and anger, Jack shook his head; not a good combination. At least not for a guy who was doing his damn best to be a good father.

Yeah. Like that was working well for him.

Jack glanced at his cut-up knuckles. Maybe she was right about that walk. He wouldn't be good company for anyone right now. He'd walk the perimeter, maybe scope out some of the other teams.

He wouldn't stray far. He wanted to see Elizabeth, see how she was holding up. After his harsh comments about Nancy this morning…

Jack pivoted. He'd just stay close. Close enough where he could see her.

By the time he made his third loop around the park, circled all four fields, and in general kept his distance from the park population, his temper had cooled. It hadn't fully burnt itself out, only another steamy kiss—which Jack was not thinking about and was not on the table as an option—or a full-on fight with Nancy, would do the trick.

He settled for tolerable. Yes, he was now tolerable and could interact with other parents, all of who were much better at parenting than he was.

Jack's shoulders tensed.

No. He wasn't going on another walk. The game was about to start, and if saw right, Laurie had started Elizabeth like she said, on first base.

It was a good coaching move. Elizabeth couldn't possibly pitch right now. She wasn't like Jack had been when he was on the mound. She couldn't block out the world or channel those emotions into every pitch.

Jack tucked his hands into his pockets as he made his way to the stands. That had been half the reason he'd been such a damn good ballplayer. Or had been until his life turned upside-down and everything he'd known or wanted was tossed out the window.

Because he'd gotten caught up in the fame.

Being a father was the best thing that had happened to him.

It just hadn't been good for his ball career or for his marriage.

Or maybe it had been just what he needed, just like Laurie seemed to be the right thing for Elizabeth. And maybe, for him too.

CHAPTER 15

$\mathcal{H}$ugh met Laurie before her feet even touched the field. If she didn't do some fast thinking, and fast talking, she'd be in for another round of interrogation about Jack and their second confrontation.

This wasn't what her tired, aching brain needed right now. Not when it was still trying to process exactly what had happened between her and Jack—and the way he'd looked at her.

She was so not ready to talk about that just yet.

"You just gonna let that go?" Hugh gave his glove a firm, fisted slap.

'That' meaning her little exchange with Jack. She easily spotted his tall shape and familiar leather jacket as he walked away from her girls, heading towards the legion of empty benches.

He'd walked away, just like she'd asked.

"He's walking it off. That's what matters."

Hugh studied her, then rubbed his chin in the way that said 'I'm thinking, and right now I'm thinking you're not being honest with me.' "You want to tell me about it?"

"There's nothing to tell." She especially didn't want to tell Hugh how her fingers still sizzled from where she'd touched Jack. That was none of his business.

Laurie shrugged, attempted to appear relaxed. She knew more people than just Hugh were watching her, waiting for her reaction. Nosy parents.

"More ex-wife problems," she said. "I didn't ask for details."

"The same ex-wife who had Elizabeth in tears last Sunday while Jack nearly blew up the world?"

"I hope to hell he only has one ex-wife," she growled. Neither she, nor the team, could survive more than one. "Jack will be fine. It's Elizabeth I'm worried about."

Elizabeth, who scrambled in the dugout, pulling on knee pads, face red and practically in tears. Laurie's chest twisted.

Laurie couldn't do much for Jack. She could, however, help Elizabeth.

"I think our newest player should start today," Laurie said. "What do you think?"

"As if I run the team or anything. But yeah, that's a good plan. It'll keep the kid's mind off things and batting's good for letting off steam. But then, you'd know that part well yourself."

Yes, she knew.

Laurie watched as Elizabeth fumbled with her shoelaces, trying to hurry and making it worse. Jack could take care of himself. She, however, had a little girl to help out.

If Elizabeth would let her.

"Grab your glove." Laurie tossed a ball to Elizabeth who'd finally gotten her shoes laces, sort of, tied. "I'll warm you up."

"But, I'm…" Elizabeth stared longingly at the girls.

"They're already warmed. You can join them when you are."

Still Elizabeth didn't move. She seemed trapped on the cusp of being an angry teenager and a frightened deer. No wonder Jack didn't know what to do with her.

"Look," Laurie said. "You're mad at your dad. That's fine. I had more days of being mad at my dad than I can remember. Grab your glove and let's go have some fun."

"But I was late."

"Was that your fault?"

Elizabeth's eyes widened and she glanced away. "No."

"Then I don't see any reason why I should take it out on you."

Elizabeth stood, clutching her worn glove to her chest. "It wasn't my dad's fault."

"It still wasn't yours, either. Now come on, or did you not want to play first base?"

"You mean, you're letting me start?"

As if Laurie could say no to that hopeful, pleading look. "Yeah, I am. If we get moving."

That was all the incentive Elizabeth needed. Before Laurie could blink, Elizabeth dashed off and was waiting on the grass. She tossed a softball up and caught it. No smiles yet, but there'd be one before long.

Smiles were Laurie's specialty. Smiles meant she'd done her job, and if she got one out of Elizabeth today, that was more than enough reason to celebrate.

Laurie shook her head. Whatever had happened this morning, she knew it wasn't Jack's fault.

Elizabeth waved for Laurie to hurry up.

The first game of the day and they were already off to one hell of a start. She might, if she were lucky, actually survive.

If she didn't get any more Jack-kisses.

Oh, wait, he didn't want to kiss her anymore. Which was perfectly fine. She wasn't supposed to go around kissing parents anyway. Or thinking about kissing them.

Still, the thought of Jack, even in his volcano of a mood, sent her stomach rolling.

"Survive?" Laurie muttered to herself. "Not a chance in hell."

To Laurie's relief, the game went without a hitch. No angry parents to calm down—even Dan and Lacey behaved themselves. Of course, it probably had something to do with Samantha getting creamed on the mound, which forced Laurie to bring in Lacey earlier than she wanted.

Oh, well. She couldn't win them all.

Elizabeth on the other hand, was a definite win.

Laurie watched as Elizabeth slipped on her flip-flops and bounded out of the dugout, only to turn right back around because she'd forgotten her bat bag.

Smiles. All smiles.

Laurie glanced at Jack, who still sat perfectly behaved in the stands. His eyes were all for Elizabeth.

It didn't take a mind reader to see how much he loved his little girl. Nor did it take a mind reader to understand why he'd walked away from baseball.

"That was a good game," Laurie said to Hugh as she untied her own cleats. Not all the coaches wore them, but for Laurie, well it made her feel closer to the game, closer to the girls.

Even if some of the memories weren't all that great—okay most memories from the time she turned fourteen and started playing on an 18-and-under team—but somehow, she still loved the game.

That was why she was here.

"Good game?" Hugh snorted. "Coach, that was a damn fine game and some mighty fine coaching there at the end."

Laurie laughed. "All I did was wave my arms. Elizabeth's the one who got the winning run in."

She nodded towards Elizabeth who practically threw her bag down to jump into Jack's arms. He held her to him, tighter than Laurie had seen before, as if he'd lose her if he let go.

Laurie's breath hitched and then she quickly looked away, hoping no one had noticed. She was paying too much attention to Jack, especially after he'd already made his intentions towards her clear.

Still, after a nice pick-me-up latte—and yes, she did drink a ton of caffeine, no point in denying it—Laurie was ready to go for the next game.

At least, she was until she turned and noticed a familiar, white-collared shirt in the stands, and the embroidered initials of 'MFU.' Mount Forest College.

Laurie's old school.

The cleats slipped free from her hand. The metal struck the concrete. Charles hadn't noticed that she'd seen him; too busy tucking his glasses into his shirt pocket.

Laurie's stomach hit about rock bottom. Her breath had disappeared somewhere and she didn't quite know where.

Hugh paused as he was putting away the catching gear. "You okay?"

Like she could answer. Or speak for that matter.

Charles. Her college scout, back from the days when she used to play. The man hadn't changed a bit. Still slightly overweight, still leaning forward with his eyes slightly pinched together as if trying to see some secret with x-ray vision.

Charles, the scout who'd found her.

Laurie squeezed her eyes shut. What was he doing here?

"Ahh," Hugh murmured. "I was wondering when you'd notice him."

"Was he...was he watching our game?"

Surely she would have noticed. At least, she would have a week ago before she'd met Elizabeth. Before she'd kissed Jack.

"Showed up about a half-hour ago. Long enough to scope out the fields. I said hello, though. Wanted to find out what he was doing here."

Hugh wouldn't meet her eyes. That meant this was bad, bad news.

She really wanted the comfort of her bat, the bat she'd slugged her way with through travel ball, through high school, and then... and then through her stint—short stint—at MFU.

At least, until she'd decided to quit and walk away from a career, from the Olympics.

"What does he want?"

"I'm sorry, Laurie. I don't know how to say this." Hugh ran a hand through his hair. "Ah, hell. You and I both know you don't want the answer to that. Why don't you just talk with him yourself? Maybe, seeing as how you played for the guys school, could get some sense into him."

So, it had happened.

It had finally happened.

College scouts had found their way to the twelve-and-under softball teams. Charles had found his way to Laurie's girls.

CHAPTER 16

The worst part, the absolute worst part, was that as soon as Charles sat down, flashing his shirt's little MFU initials, parents flocked to him. It was like a gun went off where instead of people running away, they ran towards the shooter.

It didn't matter that he'd chosen to sit and scout Laurie's team—everyone (from coaches to parents) came rushing towards him. She'd probably been the only one in the park who hadn't been aware that Charles had arrived.

If she had more strength, meaning if her legs could have held her, Laurie would have stomped over there, grabbed him by the collar and hauled him to the nearest dumpster.

Since that wasn't an option, she rested her head in her hands. What was she going to do?

Charles was actually a nice guy. She liked Charles. That wasn't the problem. The problem was what he represented and the chain-effect she knew, simply knew, would follow.

"What does he want?" Laurie asked again.

"He's a scout, Laurie." Hugh patted her back. "What do you think he wants?"

She knew. She wasn't a fool, but hearing Hugh say it, hearing the finality in his tone. She just couldn't take it.

Laurie shot to her feet. "They are twelve-years old. Why. Is. He. Here?"

Hugh dropped the bag he'd been stuffing with the catcher's gear. More than a few heads turned, including Charles.

"I imagine he's here because of you. He's a smart a guy and figured out the kind of girls you coach here, the kind of girls you taught to be amazing softball players."

"I didn't—"

Hugh stepped in. "You're the heart and soul of this team. You know how to not only coach these girls and make them into fabulous ballplayers, but you help them cope, help them prepare for what's coming. Me? I'm just the guy who brings you enough latte to wake you up."

Her throat closed.

She remembered the MFU championship game, standing there, her dad yelling from the other side of the fence, telling her everything she'd done wrong in that last inning.

She hadn't stood tall, she wasn't pushing hard enough of the mound.

Even to this day, she remembered every word.

And she remembered, as if it were yesterday, throwing down her glove and the final, soul-wrenching words. "I quit."

She remembered and she knew Charles remembered too. He'd been there.

And so had Hugh.

Tears pricked her eyes the way they always did when she allowed herself to remember, to go back to that day. "I wouldn't be here if it weren't for you. I would have walked away and never looked back."

Hugh touched the brim of his *Angels* cap. "Maybe, but regardless, I'm not the one who kept you here. You kept coming back all on your own."

He gazed at the field, his expression longing. "It's the game that kept you here. Not me. It's the game, it's the girls, and the fact that you still have something left to teach, that keeps you coming back."

It hadn't been the game for a long, long time. Back when she was Elizabeth's age. Still having fun, still enjoying life.

Before softball became a job. Something she had to work at several hours every day. Before softball had become her life: from vacation and holidays, to the choice of what she'd major in college. All that had mattered was softball.

Hugh had helped her past that; he'd been the one to convince her coaching was the way to go. That she still had a place on the field, just not on it.

"It's not the game," she whispered. "It's not the game that keeps me coming back."

It was her dad.

It was her promise that she'd have a team who remembered to smile, to have fun, to laugh. To have a team where her dad's words had no power over them.

Over her.

Hugh gave a long, tired sigh. The kind of sigh that spoke more than of just a long day, but of exhaustion. Was Hugh tired of coaching? Was that what this was about?

It wasn't a comforting thought. Not when her panic rose just thinking about it. He had to stay. She couldn't do this without him.

Hugh helped her remember, every day on the field, why she became a coach, why she agreed to deal with parents like Dan Richards, why she taught girls like Suzie how to pitch.

"All I'm saying," Hugh said, "is there's a reason why Charles parked his bottom on our bench, and there's a reason why someone like Jack Evans picked your team over some other high-and-mighty team."

Hugh nodded at Charles, who watched them both, a pencil tapping against his chin. He had to know they were discussing him. "You'll just need to come to terms with that. And with your dad. No one else can but you."

Hugh didn't give Laurie a chance to respond, didn't even let her process this very much one-sided conversation before he left. She slumped down her bench, head bent low.

"I came to terms with it. With him." She rubbed her eyes, hoping to rub away the headache she already felt coming like a herd of wild, and frightened, horses.

It may have taken nearly twelve years, but she'd come to terms. After all, she was here coaching instead of pretending like this part of her life hadn't existed, right?

Not to mention she did see her own parents for holidays like Christmas. She even got her dad his own present every year.

He never came to her games though. He knew she didn't want him here.

"Agh." She slapped her hands onto the metal bench. "I hate it when he's right."

About the only things she'd come to terms with were that she'd never throw a decent knuckle-ball (the damn thing hurt too much), she'd never convince a coach she could be both a great pitcher and short-stop (believed to be mutually exclusive), and she'd known when she was finished.

Done with the game forever.

As for the rest, yes, she still had issues.

And if she knew Hugh, he wouldn't be letting her near their games until she talked with Charles.

Like a Band-Aid, Laurie decided it was best to rip it off as fast as possible, even if it meant you had to look away. She didn't waste time as she stormed towards Charles—she tried to be nice and friendly, really, but even she wasn't convinced.

Charles, however, was a smart guy and he'd known what kind of greeting to expect. The parents and other coaches flocking around him had vanished by the time Laurie made it to him. They weren't idiots.

Jack, she noticed, remained on the stands. He leaned back, muscular arms crossed over his chest—and yes, she could see those muscles even with the jacket on.

Jack hadn't been one of the flocking parents. If anything, Charles had flocked to him.

Not a good sign.

Charles, his hands free of the notebook, stood and shook Laurie's hand. He appeared just the same as she last saw him, at this very field, when she was only a few years older than Elizabeth.

"Laurie Stevens. It's been a while."

There was also a reason for it.

His grip, firm and confident, hadn't changed either. If only she'd known what this meeting would have meant back then and wondered how differently her life would have turned out.

A crystal ball would have come in handy.

Laurie kept her mouth shut. Polite. She needed to be polite. "It's good to see you, Charles."

"We both know how you feel about seeing me." Charles grinned. "As if I could possibly forget what you said that day you quit."

He chuckled, releasing her hand so he could hold his stomach. "They still talk about it, every once in a while. The coaches, the regulars."

She never thought she was that funny.

Jack didn't laugh either, merely watched the two of them, not bothering to hide the fact that he was eavesdropping.

Laurie shifted. She could ask to speak privately with Charles, but that would only draw more attention. Any attention towards this man was the last thing she wanted.

In fact, she didn't even want her girls to know he existed.

Like that was going to happen. Not with Dan Richards toddling towards Lacey, practically overflowing with the news. A college scout from one of the big schools, here, watching them!

Pain, sharp like lightning, sizzled through her. Came right out of her long buried-past to strike her. Unable to move, unable to stop the ground falling away from her feet.

She could do nothing but fall.

Hugh had known. That was why he'd sent her to Charles. To get this out now while she could still hold onto a few anchors of safety.

Laurie knew better. She knew this world, the softball world, would never allow even the illusion of safety.

Within an hour, her entire team would know about Charles. Lacey would tell the rest. From there the competition, even the back-stabbing, would begin.

Any hope Laurie had of keeping this a secret, of holding back the inevitable for a few years of softball fun, died the moment Charles had stepped out of his car.

Charles mirth slowly faded. The pleasantries gone. He was, after all, here on business.

Time to discuss the real reason he was here and how there was nothing, absolutely nothing Laurie could do to stop it. Charles waited, giving her the first move in acknowledgment of this being her home field. Only problem was she didn't know what move to take, or which tactic to try.

Jack saved her.

Jack. Of all people. Of all the people she'd thought would swarm over Charles… he didn't.

Instead, he leaned forward, as if attempting to read the embroidered gold and blue initials on Charles's shirt. "MFU, huh? Aren't these girls a bit young? I doubt you'll find yourself a freshman starter in this group."

"No, of course not," Charles stammered. "I'm not expecting anything like that at all."

Laurie breathed a sigh of relief and gave Jack a small smile. Almost, couldn't believe what she'd heard. Was hearing.

Had she been wrong about him? About the fame? About his passion for the game? After all, he didn't have to intervene; he could have left her to deal with this.

"Oh, well that's good," Jack said. "These girls are way too young. They're barely thinking about high school let alone college."

Not to mention that she didn't want them thinking about college. Not for another two or three years at least.

Charles was slowly recovering. He'd apparently known who Jack was and must have hoped for some bigger support—support Jack had given to Laurie instead.

"Competition is fierce," Charles explained. "We've found ourselves needing to look at younger and younger girls, approach them early."

Laurie's eyes narrowed. Translation: offer promises and routinely follow up so no one poaches the talent they spotted first. When Charles had approached her all those years ago, even she'd been too young.

Her dad hadn't thought so, hadn't realized the long-term harm it would cause her. If only she'd listened to her gut.

"Why are you here?" she asked. "Why are you watching my team?"

Charles fiddled with the collar of his shirt, the same as he'd done that day he'd met Laurie. "Stacey Mills. She's a freshman starter. Bats second and plays in center field for our school. She's one of the best ball players we've seen in some time."

A chill settled over Laurie. Stacey Mills. She was one of Laurie's girls. *Was*, because it had been six years since Stacey last played for Laurie.

In general, Laurie didn't keep tabs on her girls after they left the *Angels*, not because she didn't care what happened to them, but because it hurt too much.

Hurt to see nearly half eventually break away from softball forever. Then there were those who wouldn't let Laurie go, like Janice, because they needed a friend. They needed someone on their side.

Jack lifted his gaze, taking in her hunched form, the white grip she had on her arms. He said nothing, merely waited for her response. Charles waited too.

"Stacey," she said. "She played for me nearly six years ago. Almost seven. What does she have to do with you watching my team?"

She didn't want an answer, not really, because she'd known what Charles' answer would be. It was the kind of answer Laurie couldn't walk away from. No matter how hard she wanted to.

"You coach quality girls. Stacey isn't the first we've noticed."

Laurie closed her eyes, felt the verdict slam down around her.

"They're too young, Charles. They have no business thinking about college."

They needed to have fun. They needed to be kids and enjoy the game.

Charles paused, licked his lips. "I've got myself quite a few parents who think differently."

Only because they don't know better, Laurie thought. *And by the time they realized it?*

It'd be too late for the girls. Just like it'd been too late for her.

CHAPTER 17

*J*ack knew he was stepping over the line, knew he should have just stayed in the background and let Laurie have her chat with Charles. He didn't. Couldn't.

And he wasn't the only one.

Parent after parent, from Richards to even small, mouth-pinched Diane, inched their way closer. Curious and excited, yes, but maybe… maybe even a little worried. Well, not Richards. He was practically taking notes on his used hot dog napkin, complete with ketchup stains, fawning over every word out of Charles's mouth.

Jack should walk away. Should let Laurie have her space—and considering how she felt about him butting into her game, he should have walked.

But didn't.

Couldn't.

Not when he'd heard every line, every smooth reassurance in the book coming out of this scout's mouth while Laurie stood frozen.

He didn't know what had happened to her, why she'd thrown her glove down and quit. Sure, he could have gone on the internet done a quick search but that felt like breaking her trust.

If she wanted him, or anyone else for that matter, to know she'd tell him.

"I'm sorry, Laurie," Charles said. "Like I told you, I have quite a few parents who think differently and I can't pass up this opportunity. You're producing great ballplayers out here."

Jack watched as her eyes narrowed and the Laurie he knew—the one who'd stood up to him a few short hours ago—came back. This time, he knew he didn't need to step in and defend her.

His softball goddess could take care of herself, even if she'd let behind her trusty bat.

"Are you telling me," she asked, "the only reason you're here is because of me? Because of the way I coach?"

Charles beamed. "I knew you'd see reason. We must have done something right for you to come back to softball after all these years. You're teaching the best group of girls I've seen... well, since your dad took up coaching."

When Laurie's entire posture tensed, ready to face-off against the league's biggest, meanest heavy hitters, the pieces clicked into place.

He may not have known Laurie's personal story, but he knew what had happened. He knew because he'd been there himself.

"My dad and his great coaching, huh?"

Those parents who stayed, who'd lingered to listen, ducked their heads and walked—quickly—the food stands, bathrooms, or whatever. Any place that wasn't here.

Jack stayed. He didn't know why, but he simply knew she'd need him here. That she needed support.

"Let me tell you about my dad," Laurie said. "A dad who started out just as a dad, but who stepped into the coaching role. Why? Because he's good at it. He's got some great tips and strategy to offer the team, but there's something else he's great at. Pushing his daughter. He doesn't mean to and for a while it's okay because she wants to get better."

Laurie crossed her arms and leaned over Charles. "But then it becomes too much. He pushes his daughter harder than the other girls. Nothing she does is good enough. There's always some mistake, always something she could do better. Pushing her until there was nothing fun left in the game."

Laurie took a deep breath, as if this last bit was the hardest. "He pushed her until there was nothing left but to walk away."

Jack closed his eyes. She had no idea that what she'd said had hit so close to home for him. And not just for him. He knew a few dozen guys who'd had the same experience.

Some had worked through it, like him; had found some measure of success and the will to keep going.

But not everyone did. Like Laurie, he realized. She'd walked away.

"There's a reason my father doesn't coach anymore," Laurie said. "And I'll give you a hint. It's because he screwed up with me and dealing with scouts like you."

Charles blinked. "I don't think that's—"

"Now," she cut him off. "If you're saying the only reason you're here, scouting my girls, is because I'm a coach. I guess the only thing left for me to do is quit."

Jack's head snapped up. Beside him, he heard Diane's voice catch and then whisper, "Jack! She can't do that."

No, she couldn't. Not when Elizabeth needed her so desperately.

Jack stood, but Charles beat him to it—as well as spilling his notebook and pencils onto the floor. "Laurie, now there's no need to be rash."

"I guarantee there's nothing rash about this. I swore I would never let another girl go through the experience I did, and I'm damn well not going to let it happen on my team. So if you're here because of me and me alone. Fine."

Laurie ripped her *Angels* hat off her head and threw it at Charles. "I quit. Again."

She swerved on her cleats, the metal digging into the concrete as she stomped off.

"Jack!" Diane gripped his arm. "You have to stop her."

He didn't need the prodding. Like hell he was going to let Laurie walk away from them, from him.

Charles reached for him, but Jack yanked his arm away.

"I think you've said enough for one day? Maybe you should just get the hell out of here."

"I have every right to be here." Charles tucked his glasses back into his shirt pocket.

"Not if you being here costs us our coach." Jack stepped forward, towering over the middle-aged, mousey man. "Now. Go."

He didn't wait to see if Charles listened, not when Laurie stormed towards her truck. She didn't even bother to pick up her bag.

Hugh was coming out of the dugout, but he'd never reach Laurie in time. Not when she was in a mood like this.

"Ah, hell," Jack muttered and ran after her. It looked like it was his day to deal with women. But at least this was a woman he was determined to deal with; a woman he couldn't let walk away from him.

By the time he reached her, Laurie had thrown open her truck's door. He grabbed her shoulder, preventing her from getting in.

"Damn it, Jack. Let go of me."

"Not a chance. Not until you've walked this off."

"There's nothing to walk-off. I made my decision."

His hands on her arm tightened. He felt the heat again, so hot it practically burned his fingers. He didn't need this right now, not when he needed her to understand.

"If you think me or any other parent on this team is going to let you quit, you've got another thing coming."

She stopping struggling. He leaned in, pressing her against the car door. She smelled like leather, sweat, and dirt. Like the ballgame, and it was damn distracting.

"This is my choice." She didn't look up at him, not even when he slid in closer and there were only inches separating them.

"No, it's not. It's the team's choice and I can promise you, they won't let you go."

She bit her bottom lip. Just like Elizabeth would do when she was upset. Jack nearly rocked back, taking her with him. He refused to let this strong, independent woman look like his hurting daughter, not when he needed her to get through this.

"I promised myself," she whispered. "I promised I would never let this happen."

There were tears in her eyes, and they cut through him, deep.

He wanted to pull her into a hug, wanted to sooth away those fears and tell her it wouldn't happen. Except, that would be a lie.

"You leaving isn't going to change things."

"You don't know that."

His hold on her arm loosened, not holding her quite so closely, quite so tightly. He didn't let go, though. He needed contact with her and, he hoped, she needed it with him too.

"Yeah," he said, "I do know. And so do you."

She looked away. A tear rolled down each cheek. His hand moved without thinking, collecting the first tear and then the second.

"I don't... I don't know what to do."

"I don't either."

Laurie reached up and griped his hand, pulling it away from her cheek. He thought she'd push him away, but she didn't. Instead, she closed that last tiny distance separating them, laying her head on his chest.

Jack didn't care that the whole park was probably watching this, including Elizabeth. He just didn't care.

He wrapped his arms around her waist, holding her, giving her what small amount of comfort he could.

"Nothing I do will make Charles go away will it?"

She wasn't talking just about Charles. She was talking about the competition, the team in-fighting and jealousy as each girl worked to get the scouts' attention on them and them alone.

He wished he could tell her yes, that it would go away. "No, it won't."

She nodded. "And I can't fight it either, can I?"

"Not alone, no." He lifted her chin, staring into her eyes—eyes now filled with tears. "But we can fight it, as a team. If you let us. If you let me."

He didn't know what she would say, didn't know how she'd react to his very open, very unconcealed emotions. But he had to say it, had to tell her that she wasn't alone in this fight.

Footsteps padded up behind them. Laurie turned to see around Jack's shoulder and after a slight hesitation, he released her.

The second he did he missed her in his arms, missed feeling her strength and her vulnerability.

The whole team stood behind them, Elizabeth standing up front. Her gaze flicked between Jack and Laurie, who still stood close to him, and Elizabeth gave him a small, shy smile.

Diane stepped forward for the parents, gripping Courtney's hand in her own. "Jack's right. We won't let you quit and we're not going to let you fight this alone."

No, they wouldn't. He would make sure of it, regardless of what Laurie had to say about it.

This was his team too.

CHAPTER 18

*I*f it hadn't been for Jack last week, if he hadn't gone after her—and if the team hadn't gone after her—Laurie knew she wouldn't be here right now.

Laurie snuck another glance at the stands. Even for this early in the morning (yes, yet another early morning game—who'd have thought she had such terrible luck?), all the best seats were taken. Packed.

Why?

Because of the collared shirts.

Perfectly pressed, white shirts with a crisp collar all the way around the neck and each university's initials below the pocket. The initials were always embroidered, always in some kind of flowing script you had to squint to see.

This morning, there were two more collared shirts. Both from big, fancy schools, both who had no business scouting twelve-year-old girls.

Charles sat in his usual spot, as if he didn't have any other team to be scouting, you know, like girls at an age he could actually scout. But no, he was here, watching Laurie's team—yet again.

Proving his point most likely: that Laurie couldn't run him off.

Laurie shoved her hair back into a ponytail. Well, he couldn't run her off either, even if that's what she wanted. Her team wouldn't let her.

Jack wouldn't let her.

She gazed at him, unable to help herself. Felt her heart pound the second she laid eyes on him.

He lounged on the bench, long legs spread out before him. Easy going, comfortable Jack, acted like he was holding court on her field. Always with that confidence. That surety. Which is what made her so nervous, so unsure.

The other two white shirts lingered nearby, inching closer, wanting to speak with Jack, wanting to get his attention.

They wanted to talk about Elizabeth.

Laurie could tell from the way their eyes darted back and forth between each other, hidden behind charming, friendly smiles.

She sucked in a breath. Her hands tightened on the fence-post, so hard her knuckles went white.

It didn't matter that Jack had made his point clear last week, they still circled him like vultures.

But was this all a game? An act to further draw in their interest?

She wouldn't put it past parents. She'd seen it before.

But from Jack?

She just didn't know. Couldn't trust what she hoped, that spark that simmered, *always simmered*, between them.

So, she'd avoided him all week. Even at practice when he'd purposefully stayed to talk with her. Sure, it was childish, but she couldn't do it. Couldn't. She'd opened up so much of herself... a small hole into the whole mess that was her life.

And she hadn't wanted him to see.

She'd used every excuse in the book to sneak away without speaking to him, without dealing with what had sparked between them last weekend. And what she felt right now—even though he wasn't telling the scouts to take a hike. Which is what she'd have expected after last week. A loud, very deliberate demonstration that he wasn't interested.

Except, he said nothing to them. Nothing.

So was it a game, then? A play?

And that was the problem. Laurie didn't know and she was afraid that maybe, just maybe she was wrong.

Or right.

When it came to softball, when it came to this game, she was all tied in knots. Like the past and present intertwined until she couldn't tell where one ended and the other began.

Or how to unravel them.

Jack's eyes flicked to her, a smile tugging at his lips. He continued to ignore the scouts, his attention completely on her. It didn't make her feel better, not when she didn't know the truth, didn't know whether or not he'd been... he'd been what?

Honest with her?

Charles also finished his coffee and had started on his second—a coffee which Richards had conveniently offered to him.

Laurie forced her hands to loosen. On Sunday, everything had seemed so clear. She thought she'd been wrong about Jack. That he'd taken her side against the college scouts, that he believed in the way she coached her girls and not the way someone like Richards wanted, pushing for the competition, for the glory.

Everything he'd done, defending her, then running after but now...?

She didn't know what to think.

Laurie flipped her ponytail over her shoulder and swung her attention back to her pre-game preparations. Jack laughed, deep and resonating, and her stomach curled as if his laugh wrapped around her, tantalizing and warm.

That day he'd come after her, when he held her... she'd thought he was going to kiss her again.

Him. The formerly famous baseball player, a man who Laurie barely knew. And what was worse, she'd wanted him to kiss her.

Laurie shoved the thought away. She needed to focus on the scouts and what the hell she was going to do about Charles.

She was too riled up to think about pre-game prep, so she shoved the bats against the fence. They made several loud, and rather satisfying, slamming noises. The kind of noise only aluminum striking cement could make.

Any other time, the sound would make her cringe—memories of her own father kicking bats around after she'd pitched a fat, please-hit-me fast-ball right over the middle of the plate when it should have been low and inside.

"Damn it. What am I doing?"

She was a freakin' mess. First the college scouts, then this... this *thing* with her and Jack, and now memories—those memories that wouldn't leave her alone.

Hugh entered the dugout, line-up chart tucked under his arm, and gave Laurie a long look. "You're scowling again. And you're looking at Jack."

"I am putting out the bats, which is in the complete opposite direction of Jack."

Making it therefore impossible for her to look at him.

And anger was easier. Anger she could understand. Could hold onto. At the very least it'd give her the energy until she figured out what was going on in her life.

And maybe even her heart.

Damn it.

She'd been doing just fine, *just fine*, until Jack had come along.

"You sure? Sounds like you're beating something to death in here." Hugh clipped the chart onto the fence. "Of course, it's interesting that if you weren't looking at Jack, you still knew exactly where he was sitting."

"Every woman here is aware of exactly where Jack is sitting."

It was a fact. Laurie had no problem admitting to it, so long as she made a general comment about the entire female population and not a population that only had her in it.

"Is there a reason why this particular woman," he tapped her head, "has been avoiding Jack all week?"

"Who said I'm avoiding Jack?"

"It's rather obvious."

"I'm not avoiding him."

She stayed focused on what she was doing—which was now rearranging the bats (no slamming this time) in order of weight and height.

"Jack just asked me about it."

Laurie shrugged. She didn't want to talk about the way he'd held her or that she'd cried in front of him and how even now she felt herself losing all sense.

And now watching him with the scouts? She had no idea what to think.

Hugh sighed. "Look, I know this is tough. Seeing Charles, and then with all that…" He waved his hand towards Jack. "All those big dreams that literally walk beside Jack. I get it, kiddo, but you've got to give him a chance. You've got to give yourself a chance."

Laurie gripped the worn, leather handle of the bat she was currently holding. "I don't know if I can do that."

She didn't know if she ever could.

"Yeah, I know. But trying never hurt anyone. Can you please just talk with him after the game? Some of the girls are picking up on it. Elizabeth," he said with great care, "is picking up on it."

Laurie's hand stilled and she lowered the bat. "There's nothing to talk about. Really."

Nothing she *could* talk about. "I'm fine."

Hugh merely scrunched his wrinkled brows, waited a beat, and then sighed his weary, old-man sigh. "Just to keep Elizabeth happy, okay? She's finally getting her groove, and doesn't need thoughts of her coach not liking her dad messing it up."

It wasn't that she didn't like him. It was because she liked him a little too much.

Hugh steered the conversation back to what mattered most—the game. Of course, the game was about the only topic where she wouldn't (at the moment), bite Hugh's head off. And it was nice because just for a moment, Laurie lost herself in the upcoming game, the strategy.

She forgot the scouts, the parents, and most importantly, forgot Jack.

In general, she liked to keep the strategy simple. Sure she could have made the *Angels* into a hardcore, cut-throat team, but Laurie would hang up her glove before she let that happen.

She'd played for teams like that and she wanted no part of them.

Instead, she focused on a strategy that would be fun for the girls, but still allow them to pick up on the more advanced skills and techniques. Stuff they'd need later on.

More or less, the *Angels* games were competitive practice. It was one of the reasons she had agreed to help Hugh with the team when he first started it.

Laurie glanced at the line-up and noticed Lacey had been moved to position four, the standard for a clean-up hitter. A typical team's best and hardest hitter was usually the clean-up. Not Laurie's team. She liked to sprinkle talent throughout her line-up and not just keep a top-heavy focus—all the best players batting in the first through five positions.

Laurie's way made for a well-rounded team. This line-up, however, was not well-rounded. It was a standard line-up and now that she was looking closer, noticed two other changes.

Hugh was heading out to the girls when Laurie called him over. "You moved Lacey to clean-up."

"Uh, nothing much. Just an idea I had."

"An idea?" She unclipped the chart. "This looks like a standard line-up. You even moved Samantha to ninth."

Samantha was this game's starting pitcher. Pitchers were notoriously terrible hitters, mostly because coaches only pushed them to be good pitchers and not well-rounded players. And because of bad coaching, this usually meant pitchers hit at the bottom of the line-up, which was again not the way Laurie coached.

"Samantha's one of our most consistent hitters," Laurie said. "She's great at putting a ball in play. Why'd you move her to the bottom?"

She closed in on Hugh. He wouldn't meet her eyes. Instead, he glanced at the stands where the parents sat.

Parents—and in particular, one pair of long legs and the usual leather jacket. Jack? Had Hugh been getting advice from Jack?

"Hugh? Was this your idea?"

"You know, I thought I'd give the traditional approach a try against the *Rascals* and see how we do."

He hadn't answered her question. "Was this Jack's idea?"

"What, uh, what makes you think that?"

"I thought we talked about this."

"We did talk, but then I got to talkin' with Jack and he had some pretty good points." Hugh nodded towards the chart. "Don't see the problem about giving his suggestion a try."

"No. I guess you wouldn't." But Hugh didn't see, didn't understand. First the scouts, then the competition between the girls, the jealousy.

This was how it always started out. Started, but never ended.

Jack had come to her defense against Charles. He believed in what she was doing. She'd almost trusted him. Almost, because, trust didn't come easily with her.

But still, her breathe caught in her throat and her heart hammered. *What if she was wrong?* And wasn't this, this right here, proof enough?

Fear worked its way in, rolling in her belly. It didn't go away.

Jack was, once again, working his way onto her team.

Why?

"Since when did you start listening to parents?" Laurie rubbed at her suddenly tight shoulder muscle, working out the knots from her former pitching arm. "And since when did you start taking that parent's advice before consulting with your coach?"

"I'm not listening to parents. I'm listening to suggestions from a guy who knows his way around the game."

"Baseball is not softball."

"There are more than enough similarities and you know that."

Hugh jerked his hand towards the stands. "And like it or not, he knows his game. I'm a big enough man to admit I don't know it all. So yes, I did listen to his suggestions and thought to give them a try."

A try.

Laurie's head spun. She glanced at Jack. Saw him straighten, push off the bench. The scouts immediately drew back. He stared at her, a frown darkening his face. Concerned. Was he coming towards them?

No. She didn't want him too; didn't want him near her. The pounding in her head grew but she hadn't a clue if it was because of the memories, her anger, or just because of Jack.

She pushed Hugh aside. "If you want to take advice from Jack, maybe you should just get it over with and make him a coach. Right after he signs Elizabeth up for the next college team."

"Laurie."

He grabbed for her arm, but she easily slipped past him and stormed towards the bathroom. The far bathroom, the one where she'd have some small sliver of privacy.

Not that it mattered. She probably had both teams, the stands, and every nosy parent's attention right about now.

"Damn it." She shoved a tear aside. How could this still affect her? After all these freakin' years?

She almost made it to safety. Almost. But then, she'd have stomped faster if she'd known Jack was going to run after her.

The problem was, she didn't know.

At least, not until he touched her hand. By then it was too late and she couldn't run.

CHAPTER 19

Heat flared where Jack's fingers grabbed her wrist. A tentative, light touch as if he was unsure of his welcome—which she had absolutely no problem making clear.

Laurie jerked her hand back, but his fingers merely tightened, pulling him closer to her.

There was, however, nothing tentative or light in Jack's gaze. Nothing at all. Those eyes burned through her, almost as much as his touch. Laurie stumbled back, couldn't remember the last time any man had ever looked at her like that.

Jack didn't let go. Instead, his grip tightened. "This has gone on long enough. Are you going to tell me what's bothering you?"

"I don't have any idea what you're—"

"Talking about? That's right. Talking. You haven't said a word to me that wasn't 'hello' or 'goodbye' this whole week."

He was the absolute last person she wanted or could talk to right now. Not with what she'd heard from Hugh, not after seeing him with those scouts.

"There's a lot going on right now. I'm sorry if you felt I was ignoring you." Laurie waved her other hand (the hand not being claimed by Jack) towards the stands, to the—well, that was quite a group of parents whose heads had turned their way.

"Shit," she whispered.

He glanced over his shoulder, swore, and pulled her towards the other end of the bathroom—the end facing away from the field. Even as he yanked her away from prying eyes, heat still radiated from his touch.

She couldn't face him like this, not when she was cracking at the seams, her memories spilling from more holes than she could close. She didn't have the willpower to fight all these battles, on all these fronts.

"Jack, I don't think..."

"Damn nosy parents," he growled. "How the hell do you put up with them?"

She wanted to mention it wasn't that bad, or wasn't normally. But then, normally she didn't have a famous guy running after her or pulling her behind a bathroom.

And normally she wasn't having a fight with the famous guy. No, that wasn't true—she always seemed to be fighting with Jack, even when they weren't actually fighting.

That was part of the problem. She couldn't think past him, couldn't clear her head long enough to get her sense of direction, of who she was.

She had to get out of here. She had to get away from him.

"I'd think you'd be used to the attention," Laurie said. "You've had more experience than the rest of us."

And if she recalled, there'd been several tabloid features as well—in some very unflattering circumstances.

Jack's eyes narrowed as if he knew exactly what she was thinking of. "Not at my daughter's game."

He closed the gap between them and her back pressed against the cement wall. The cold leeching through her *Angels* shirt did nothing to alleviate the full-on heat wave rolling through her body.

Rolling through parts which had no business having rolling heat.

"And, in case you forgot, I put that life behind me." His voice dropped and his gaze flicked once to her lips.

The earthy, rugged smell of leather and male surrounded her, made it harder to breathe, to think.

"Why are you pushing me away?" His fingers brushed her cheek.

This was definitely too close. She tried to use her hands to separate them, to put some distance between them—or at the very least, cool air to dampen this... this heat.

Jack wasn't having it. He pushed her suddenly weak hands aside. Then there was no escape. No place for her to run. Or dodge. She had no choice but to face him.

Which she didn't want to do, and damn it—he was making her. It was as if that sparked something in her, maybe it had to do with the memories and all those times she hadn't stood up for herself, even when pushed into a corner.

To hell with this.

"Fine. You want to know why I'm not speaking with you? It's because you're courting the god-damned scouts. After everything that happened last weekend and you're, you're courting them."

His hand stilled. "Courting the scouts?"

She took a deep breath. Her stomach knotted, hearing his lowering voice.

"You heard me," she snapped. "Elizabeth's only twelve. The last thing she needs is to be thinking about college."

The hand on her cheek fell away, taking it with it all the heat. Jack backed away. Freed, she couldn't help but realize how cold she suddenly was—and the cold way Jack stared at her.

"You don't think I know that? You don't think I'm a good father."

"I didn't say that."

But she had—it had been implied. The look he gave her said the same.

"Okay, but that wasn't what I meant." Now she reached for him, but Jack yanked his hand before she could touch him.

"I think that's what you meant. You don't think I know when it's too much? When I've put too much pressure on her? I stood up for you last weekend and you don't trust me."

Every inch of Laurie wanted to cringe, his rising temper and voice reminding her of how many times she'd stood behind the bathrooms with her father yelling at her.

God, it hurt.

"Elizabeth is my daughter and I know what's best for her. I know better than some coach we just met. And since you wouldn't talk to me, I told Hugh what I'd be doing—that I'd keep the scouts occupied so they wouldn't talk to the other parents."

She needed him to stop yelling so she could simply think and apologize for the mess she'd made of this. "Jack, can you please—"

"She's happy. And don't you dare try to take that away from her. Or from me."

He didn't give her the chance to explain; he didn't give her the chance to do much of anything, not when he grabbed her chin and practically pulled her into his arms.

Laurie stumbled. Only his chest saved her from falling over. That and the look in his eyes, intense and hurting.

Hurting because of her.

"Damn it, Laurie." He barely spoke. "I don't need this from you, too."

Then, he kissed her. Hard and hot and desperate.

She should have hit him. That's what she would have done if it had been any other person. If this was someone other than Jack, the one person she *wanted* to kiss her.

She kissed him back, matching his desperation, needing to apologize for hurting him, for doubting.

She kissed him, until her lips grew numb and her legs shook from holding her upright. Kissed him until this heat burnt the last, lingering memories of her father away; until the only thought she had was *Jack.*

Laurie arched up to meet him, as if she could pull him in closer, deeper. Never wanted him to stop.

His arms tightened around her and he answered with a groan of his own. And then, before she could sink deeper into him, Jack pulled back. Still holding her, but at arms' length now as he gasped for air. Laurie was gasping too, both from her need to breathe, but also because of what had just happened. Again.

Jack ran a hand through his hair, the exact same place her hands had just been. He stared at his hand, as if realizing it as well.

"Damn it."

That wasn't the reaction she wanted to hear, not after she'd just had a serious, toe-curling kiss.

In the distance, she heard the sounds of girls cheering, the distinct hit of softball off a bat. The game. She'd completely forgotten—and forgotten the audience who was probably getting mighty curious.

She blushed. This time, those parents had something to be curious about. She and Jack seriously needed to deal with this. Whatever this was between them, it was getting out of hand.

"Jack."

"No. Forget it." He straightened. "That was me this time. I stepped over the line."

Again, not the reaction she wanted to hear, especially with her heart pounding as if she'd just rounded third base and headed towards home.

"I think," she swallowed, finding her voice. "I'm fairly certain there was some of me in there, too. We should talk about this."

Why was this so hard?

He turned, shoving his hands in his pockets, and the smoldering look he gave practically challenged her: *do you want to talk about this?*

Hell, no, but it wasn't like she had a choice.

Laurie was a coach and he was one of her player's parents. And she'd hurt him, badly.

He was also Elizabeth's father, and they both knew Elizabeth had enough to deal with right now.

Laurie took a deep breath. She could only explain one thing at a time—hard to believe the kiss and her attraction to him was the easiest one to deal with?

"I don't normally do this, I mean, go around kissing the parents."

His eyes darkened and she could feel his lips on hers, bruising her, seeking entry into every part of her.

"Not many seem worth kissing," he said. "Is there a reason you don't kiss parents often?"

Lots of reasons, hundreds of reasons, and damn her, she could only think of one. "The others, they might see it as preferential treatment."

"Right. And how is that different if I were a coach and allowing my daughter to start all the games, even if she was one of the best players? How is that different?"

He wasn't helping.

"It is different. You're not a coach."

Jack hadn't stepped closer, but oh man, it felt like he was right there, so close she was practically against the bathroom wall again.

"And... if I was a coach?" His voice, so quiet and deep and dangerous, she barely heard him.

She had no problem getting coffee with parents. The problem was she and Jack would do more than drink coffee. "You're not a coach, and besides I don't date—"

"Any coaches either, huh?" He snorted. "How about Kent and dinner?"

Kent? How in the world did he...?

"There's nothing saying men can't ask me to dinner, but that doesn't mean I'll say yes. And why do you care about Kent?"

"I don't."

Agh! He was so frustrating. Why couldn't he at least *try* to pretend he understood her position? The last thing she needed was to compromise the team and reputation she'd worked so hard to build.

"Look, Jack, all I'm trying to say is—"

"It's fine." He held up his hand.

"Fine. *Fine?*" Laurie slapped her hands on her hips. "This coming from the guy who, after *he* kisses *me*, decides his next words would be 'Damn it.' Now you have the nerve to question my ethics?"

He didn't even bother apologizing, or even trying for an excuse. The jerk.

"It's complicated," he said.

"Why do you think I'm trying to un-complicate it by not kissing you anymore?"

Again, those eyes narrowed. "I thought I kissed you."

Oh, this was just ridiculous. Laurie stomped over to him, ready to let him have it—that slug in the gut she should have given him earlier instead of kissing him.

"Dad?" Elizabeth's voice, tentative and worried.

They both froze and Laurie immediately hid her fist behind her back, as if hiding her fist would hide what had nearly happened.

Elizabeth poked her head from around the bathroom, eyes wide.

Shit. This was exactly, *exactly* what Laurie wanted to prevent. She didn't get the chance to apologize.

Jack, smooth as ever, slid in front of Laurie. "Coach Laurie and I were having a discussion."

Elizabeth tilted her head. "That didn't sound like a discussion."

No, it sure the hell didn't.

"It was. We were only talking about some new opportunities." He glanced back at Laurie. There was no heat in his eyes, but something else. Something she thought might be much, much worse.

Stubbornness.

Elizabeth glanced at Laurie, before darting her eyes away again. "Is everything okay, now?"

Fear. She was afraid Laurie was going to bench her. Laurie hated that look more than anything; she should never have let this get so far. "Of course, it's fine. Are you all warmed-up and ready to play?"

Elizabeth nodded.

"Laurie's right," Jack said. "We've got some things to work through, like trust, but it's settled now."

Laurie's head jerked up and she glared at him. "We haven't—"

She snapped her mouth shut when she saw Elizabeth biting her lip.

Had Elizabeth seen them kissing? Laurie's face reddened. Damn Jack and his stupid, steamy kisses. They were a worse addiction than the excitement she'd felt after striking-out batters.

The problem was although she'd walked away from softball—and striking-out batters—Laurie wasn't so sure, deep down in that place she refused to believe existed, that she could walk away again.

Not from Jack. Not from that look he sent her, the one that promised more.

CHAPTER 20

Jack was positive that if he'd had one favor all day, it was the walk back from the bathroom. Slow. Deliberate. Plodding. First, he had a chance to burn of some anger. And second, it gave his pants a chance to loosen before he had to face the most inquisitive parents on the face of the planet.

Laurie stormed ahead of them, fists clenched at her side. At least she gave the impression that they'd had a fight and not that he'd nearly taken off her uniform behind the park's bathroom.

Even if she hadn't trusted him, even if she'd thought even for a second that he didn't care about Elizabeth's happiness.

His fists clenched at the thought. He had enough of women who didn't trust him, who didn't believe he could be a good father.

So why couldn't he just forget Laurie and move on? Why did he have to keep kissing her?

Elizabeth dragged her feet beside him, scuffling her cleats in the grass. Every once in a while, she glanced up at him before quickly looking away.

Not at all rushing to get back to the game because... because of what she had nearly seen, and almost as important, what she must sense between him and Laurie.

After the fourth time, he'd ran out of patience. "You can ask me, you know. What is it?"

"Oh, I was just... I was just wondering if you think Laurie will still let me play." Elizabeth grabbed a fistful of her uniform and squeezed as if she couldn't take the answer.

Jack paused, mid-step, before recovering. Did Elizabeth actually think—yes, of course she did. That's what Nancy liked to do.

"That's silly. Of course she'll still let you play." And if she didn't he and Laurie would have a serious discussion.

"Really?"

Jack sighed and half-arm hugged Elizabeth. "Yeah, really. She'll still let you play."

"It's just when you and Mom fight, Mom gets mad at me ..."

"Laurie's not like Mom." He tried to keep the low growl out of his voice, but knew he failed when Elizabeth stiffened. "Laurie cares about you and every girl on that team. She'd pin me to home-plate if I ever did anything to hurt you."

Fool woman would do it, too. He ignored how *that* image made him feel. No way; now wasn't the time for Laurie-type fantasies, not when Elizabeth needed him.

Laurie actually gave a shit about his daughter—and everyone else's girl on the team. The only thing Nancy cared about was whether or not her nails had chipped.

After a moment, Elizabeth relaxed. "I'm glad she invited us to dinner tomorrow, too."

"Me too."

Of course, he didn't mention the fact that Laurie hadn't invited them. Hugh had.

He also didn't mention that he doubted Laurie knew about it yet. If she had, she probably would have slugged him the moment they were out of sight.

At least, then she'd have had a reason to hit him, and not some misguided thought that he was seriously talking with the scouts.

Elizabeth was on a roll now, and kept talking about all the great things Laurie had done, and how Elizabeth hoped Jack would start helping out with the team.

This past week, he and Elizabeth had been practicing together. Throwing the balls, passing on some of his favorite secrets. He thought it was helping, repairing the trust between them.

He hoped Elizabeth told Nancy all about their 'quality time' together, to prove to her that she hadn't ruined things for him and Elizabeth.

"Do you think she'll listen to the suggestions you gave Hugh about the batting lineup?"

Jack chuckled. "You little eavesdropper."

She shrugged. "Well, you weren't exactly talking quietly and it wasn't my fault I overheard."

That was his daughter for you. Already he could see her nervousness dropping away, as if each step closer to the field was returning her confidence.

"We'll see, won't we?"

It was the perfect, non-committal parent response. Generally, Elizabeth would have picked up on it and narrowed her eyes at him before he squirmed and gave her a real answer.

This time, she merely hugged him, already growing distracted as the first inning wrapped up while Laurie jogged to the field.

Jack slowed as he watched Kent smile at her, the kind of smile that was way beyond friendly, but he couldn't tell if she noticed or not—or what her reaction was. Not when her back was to him.

The college scouts had already taken their places in the stands even as parents respectfully closed in on them.

Jack frowned, thinking back to what Laurie said. "I was thinking about the scouts. Are you okay with them watching you?"

She shrugged. "I haven't really thought about it."

She scrunched her face in a way that made her ten times cuter and was every bit the reminder she was still his little girl. Thank God she was only twelve or he'd have much bigger problems on his hands.

"I guess I don't mind," Elizabeth said. "I think the other girls care more, like Lacey. She's always talking about scouts watching her."

Jack nodded and told Elizabeth to let him know if she changed her mind. If the pressure got too much, they could always find another team, just in case.

Elizabeth paled. "I don't want to leave. I want to stay on this team."

"And we will, but I wanted you to know that your happiness comes first. Even above the team's. Okay?"

Of course, that also meant dealing with Laurie for another year or two until Elizabeth got too old for the division. That was an awfully long time to just be a regular parent, especially when that kiss had promised so much more.

He wasn't sure if that was good enough for him.

Elizabeth hugged him and dashed off the field, joining her teammates in the dug-out. Laurie, he noticed, never looked back at him.

That was fine. She knew he was there.

Why? Because he could still feel her lips burning against his and knew she'd felt it too.

But, it was just a kiss, right? And if being a parent was too complicated for her, well, he could always un-complicate it, along with proving to her that he could be trusted. That he was a good father.

Besides, it had been ages since he'd done some serious coaching.

THE REST of the weekend flew by and Jack found himself more involved with watching the game, studying the girls. The more he watched, the more excited he got.

This, he knew, was what he should be doing.

And Hugh was right—Jack did have something more to give. He might be done with baseball, but there was a great deal he could pass on to the girls; when he mentioned the idea to see what she'd thought... Elizabeth, she'd jumped into his arms. Had begged him to coach. As if, for her, it had already been decided.

Jack had stumbled, barely holding her up from the shock. He couldn't remember the last time he'd seen her so excited, so happy. And happy... about him?

What else could he say but yes, that he'd meant it? That he wanted to be her coach? That he would talk with Hugh, and God help him, talk with Laurie?

As Jack had expected Hugh thought the idea was marvelous, had even mentioned it was time he step down anyway. He was getting tired, having a hard time keeping up with the changing game... of course, there was still the matter of Laurie. And kind of how they hadn't told her.

Yet.

For good reason, too. Jack was fairly certain she was going to kill him—or at least try really, really hard.

At least she hadn't gone for her bat when Hugh mentioned he'd invited Jack and Elizabeth over for Sunday's after-game dinner. Her eyes had narrowed to tiny slits, and yes, her hand had clenched and unclenched a few times, before she spun on her heel and stormed off.

Elizabeth tapped her chin. "Dad. Laurie seems to do that a lot around you. Why?"

"I drive her crazy."

Hugh had only laughed. Good ol' Hugh, always staying out of the line of fire, which was also why, he was sure, when Jack and Elizabeth arrived at Laurie's, they learned Hugh had bailed.

Laurie shrugged and said he didn't feel well.

"I see." Jack did his best to contain his frown, but this only seemed to make Laurie happier.

"Of course, if you don't want to stay for dinner that's fine. I haven't even started so—"

"No. We'd love to stay."

She looked like she was about to protest; was even beginning to ease the door shut, but Elizabeth yelled in excitement and dashed inside.

"See? Looks like we're staying."

For now; until he told her about his conversation with Hugh. He doubted even Elizabeth could save him from Laurie's fury when she learned she'd not only have a new co-coach, but a new team co-owner. That her travel team, the *Slugging Angels*, would now be shared with a guy she could barely stand. Most of the time, anyway.

Yeah, he couldn't wait to break the good news.

CHAPTER 21

*L*aurie leaned back in her comfy lawn chair, finished her third beer, and did her best to ignore Jack, who stretched out beside her. Both their legs were propped up on the same lawn table and every once in a while, his shoes would brush her bare feet.

It was way too close, way to intimate. She couldn't make herself move.

She could just make out the muffled noise from the movie Elizabeth was watching. Actually, the movie she had been watching. The last time Jack stuck his head in to check on her, she'd fallen asleep.

Even the distant car horns and traffic barely dented the quiet, and slightly tense air that seemed to surround them.

That's right. *Them,* alone on her deck, with that kiss from Saturday's game lingering between them.

Laurie groaned and closed her eyes. This was one giant mess. A mess she could fix if she was brave enough to step up to the plate and tell him.

Yes or no. It was completely up to her. He'd given her space all weekend, though she'd done her best not to be alone with him—and he hadn't pursued her.

She wasn't fooling herself though. All evening, ever since she put the hot dogs on the grill, he'd given her 'that look.' The kind of look every woman wanted, especially from a man like Jack Evans.

Even now, she felt his gaze on her. Hungry, but quiet, as if lying in wait. Waiting for what, she hadn't a clue, but she'd hoped it was for her answer.

Laurie gave her beer another longing look, decided having another wasn't good if she wanted to keep her head on straight. If they were going to talk about this, now was the time.

"Jack. We need to talk about yesterday."

"I didn't think there was much to talk about."

She glanced up, surprised. She'd been expecting resistance, not this... this calm acceptance. "You mean, you're fine with it?"

Wow, wasn't that a lame way to put it? Gee, thanks for being so attractive but you're a parent, and therefore not allowed on the dating field.

"You said you couldn't date a parent. I can understand that." Jack lowered his legs from the table, putting down his half-finished beer bottle instead.

Still his first one, she noticed, and long gone warm. She sat up and her head spun slightly. Not much, but enough that she didn't trust herself so close to him.

Didn't trust herself to say no. Not when he was looking at her like that.

"Besides jealously with the parents, you'd risk everything you've built. People respect you. The other coaches, parents, heck even the umpires respect you. I get that."

She released a breath she hadn't realized she'd been holding. "Thanks."

She meant it, honest. He was giving her what she asked for; respected her enough to back off.

So then why did her stomach plummet about sixty feet?

"Thank you," she said again.

Jack ran a hand through his hair. "Damn. If I'd known Hugh was gonna bail..."

"Hugh?" What did Hugh have to do with this? "What are you talking about?"

Jack stood suddenly and paced back and forth on her short deck. "Tonight. We were supposed to talk to you about this together."

Now, it wasn't just her stomach plummeting, it was her heart too. Dread swept through. Somehow, she got to her feet, stood and faced him.

"Talk to me about what?"

"The team. The *Angels*." Jack turned, so tall and handsome, commanding the attention from every person who looked at him.

That wasn't what had her attention though, it was his nervousness. From the first minute she met him, she'd known Jack was the kind of person who'd look anyone in the eye. The kind of person who wouldn't walk away, who stand tall and face forward.

He was the kind of person who'd fight until he got what he wanted. And from the way he'd been acting, he'd shouted loud and clear that he wanted her.

Except now he wouldn't look her in the eyes and it worried her. "What about my team?"

"That's the thing. And I don't want you to think it's just because, well, that it's just because of the kiss."

"Kisses," she whispered. "There's been more than one."

What was going on? Why wouldn't he look at her? And why did her stomach clench like this?

"Yeah. There have been more than one. But I wanted you to know, it wasn't just because of that. I've been working a lot with Elizabeth, and I'm enjoying it. A lot."

Laurie stepped forward, took his chin and made him look at her. "Jack."

His eyes bore into her, so strong and forceful she nearly backed away. It was like he'd been avoiding looking at her just so she wouldn't see this look—a look that made her want to bail towards safety. Even though there was no safety, not with Jack.

"Hugh was supposed to tell you. I'm sorry, Laurie, if I'd known..."

"Tell me what?"

"The *Angels*. Hugh's retiring. He wants me to take over as coach...as the team's manager."

The stubble from his evening beard scratched her hand as she stepped back. She kept backing up until she knocked into the lawn table. Her beer tipped over.

She didn't hear if it broke or not. She shook her head and couldn't say a word. Hugh? He'd...he'd really done this? And he couldn't even tell her in person?

"Shit, Laurie. I'm sorry. I knew this was wrong, but I didn't want to lie and..." Jack moved towards her.

"Don't. Don't touch me."

He froze, inches from her. The only thing keeping him at bay was her hand and her words.

"Please don't touch me."

His hand lowered. "I should go."

Yes, yes, he should go. Already she felt the tears welling up in her eyes—traitorous female emotions. She would not cry in front of Jack. She wouldn't show him just how hurt she was—by him, by Hugh.

Hugh, who should have known better. Hugh, who should have known exactly what this betrayal would do to her.

"Please go."

For a brief moment, it looked like he might change his mind, like he might disregard her request and take her into her arms. Laurie's heart thudded.

He couldn't touch her right now and he must have seen it because he only nodded and left. She heard him waking Elizabeth, telling her it was time to go because Laurie wasn't feeling well.

Wasn't feeling well, ha! More like being ripped in half by someone she trusted more than anyone else.

The minute she heard the door close, she stopped fighting. She sank into her chair, the same one she'd bought when she and Hugh came up with this crazy, wonderful idea of starting a team together, of getting together after games to relax, chat, and sometimes celebrate.

She leaned over and let herself cry. She cried until the hurt became a dull ache, but even then the ache couldn't take away the betrayal or the sadness as Jack looked at her, knowing what he said was really, really going to hurt.

Her choice, the yes or no, just got a lot more difficult. Now it wasn't just yes or no to dating Jack. It was yes or no to her team.

Her girls.

CHAPTER 22

Hugh banged on Laurie's door four times before she finally answered it. Actually, she about yanked the door off its hinges. "Go away."

Hugh hunched over, hands on his knees, panting. His beard was more disheveled than usual, making her feel a tad bit better, but not nearly enough to even think about forgiving him.

"Laurie—"

"No. You don't get to talk to me, you don't get to apologize. Not after the shit you pulled."

Tears welled up in her eyes again. Damn it! She wiped at them even as his face fell even more. He had no right to see her upset like this.

"Just go away."

"I'd like to talk with you." Hugh slipped into her house before she could slam the door, which only made her more upset, more mad, more like needing to cry.

"Get out."

"I will, I promise, but first I have to explain."

"There's nothing to explain." She slammed the door closed. "You walked out on me. You! After all you did to get me on this damn team, and you're the one who walks away."

She'd spent the whole week bottling all this inside her, keeping her smiles as normal as possible, going about her usual teaching routine, putting up with her high school kids with as much as her wavering-smile would allow, acting like there was nothing wrong. Nothing at all.

She also hadn't returned any of Hugh's calls. Or Jack's.

And now he thought he could simply come over? No, he didn't get to do this. Not when he couldn't even tell her the truth, couldn't even break the news to her in person.

She rounded on him, finally her need to vent taking over, finally pushing away those stupid useless tears. How many times had she cried to her father, tried to get him to understand how she felt about softball and the scouts and playing year round, non-stop, without a break?

He hadn't listened, but Hugh would. She'd make sure that he listened and understood just how much he'd hurt her.

"How could you do this to me?" She poked him hard in the chest.

Hugh fumbled backwards until he ran into her kitchen wall and hit his head against the hanging copper pots. They banged and rang against each other. A sympathy that just couldn't quite quit.

"Laurie, if you'll just give me a chance."

"You had your chance to tell me, but instead of telling me yourself, you made Jack do it."

It should have been Hugh. Hadn't she earned that at least?

"And what am I supposed to tell the girls? I bet you were going to leave that one to me, too. You just disappear without a word, without an explanation and I get to pick up the pieces."

Hugh lowered his hands and sighed. "You'll tell them the truth, that's what you'll do."

"The truth?" She practically spat the word. "And what the hell is the truth?"

"It's that I'm old and tired. And you can deny it all you want, but I haven't been running this team in years. How do you think that makes a man feel?"

It was the worst excuse she'd ever heard. "You're not old. My father's older than—"

She cut herself off. Looked away.

"Yeah, he's older than me, and I know for a fact he's not as happy as me. After all, I'm the one you still let into your life. At least, I used to be."

Laurie bit her bottom lip. Hugh had been a coach when she was Elizabeth's age, just some random coach on a random team they'd played every couple of weeks.

And Hugh had been the only one to stand up to her father. The only one who stood up for Laurie's happiness. That was why this hurt so bad.

Laurie shook her head. "How could you? How could you not tell me?"

"Because it hurt. Just like now it's hurting, knowing I'd never be the coach these fancy college scouts would come to watch, never be the kind of coach someone famous like Jack Evans would want for his daughter's team."

Hugh sighed, stepping away from the copper pots, still quietly banging against each other but with less intensity, less force. It was the only sound in her kitchen, the only sound except for his feet shuffling on the tile.

"It was *you* that caught their attention. It was *you*, because you made every girl shine even if she wasn't a good enough or very talented, even if she always swung at the wrong pitches or missed the batting signs. Your patience and your hard work made them laugh, make them enjoy themselves.

"You turned each of those girls into great ballplayers."

"That's not true," Laurie's voice broke. Had he always felt this way? How long, and she'd never even noticed? "You're as much a part of this team as me."

He chuckled. He sounded old, defeated, and sad. "It's not right for me to feel this way, not when I'm the one who pulled your arm until you agreed to coach with me. And," he smiled, his wrinkled face showing the same kindness as it had all those years ago. "I knew you'd be great at it."

He stepped forward, gave her shoulder a good squeeze. He'd given her that squeeze, too, after her dad had told him to mind his own damn business.

Laurie's swallowed. "You can't walk away from me now. You can't walk away from this team."

She needed him, even if he didn't believe the team did.

"You're a great coach," Hugh said. "So great you outshone me, but I knew it'd happen. How could I not? I knew how you played, I knew how much you loved the game."

"I stopped loving the game a long time ago," she said.

"Nah, you didn't. Just thought you did for a while. I knew I couldn't let your talent die, not when there are tons of girls out there who need someone like you, someone to advocate for them."

Hugh gave her shoulder another squeeze before stepping around her and opening the front door. She didn't move. Her feet were rooted to the floor.

"I'll talk to the girls," he said. "Let them know I'll still be around, still watching, but from the sidelines. I think it's what I'm good at."

He left, closing the door behind him while Laurie still stood in her kitchen, alone.

"But you're wrong," she said. "You changed at least one girl's life."

Even though he hadn't been her coach, even though in the end, it hadn't changed her father's mind or made him listen to her. Hugh had given her the foundation, the strength to one day stand up and walk away.

"Damn you, Hugh." She wiped her eyes, and the stupid tears that just kept coming.

Even if she resigned, she knew Hugh wouldn't come back. Damn old goat was even more stubborn than her.

That meant, she had a decision to make. Stay on the team and pass on what she could to girls who still wanted her help, who still wanted to enjoy a few years of softball.

Or she could walk away, just like Hugh had just done.

Laurie clenched her fists, squeezed her eyes closed. Then she took a deep breath and walked into her living room.

On the mantle, hanging nice and neat in its frame, was her scholarship offer. Her dad had framed it, along with a picture of her pitching at one of her many games, and a picture of her signing the document. The contract.

She'd kept it as a reminder and a promise. A promise she'd break if she walked away, especially with scouts like Charles who already had their eyes on younger players, parents who didn't know any better, who didn't know when to back off and just let the girls have fun.

"Damn all you stupid men. What am I supposed to do?"

Actually, she was the stupid one. It was a stupid question to ask, especially when she already knew the answer.

Laurie reached for her cell phone and called Jack. If they were going to do this, they were going to do this right. And if he so much as tried to kiss her, she'd just have to apologize to Elizabeth for killing her father.

CHAPTER 23

The last person in the world Jack expected to hear from was Laurie, and the last thing he expected to see was her, standing on his front porch, arms crossed and glaring at him, while wearing one of the cutest skirts he'd seen in ages.

Cute mostly because it showed off a shapely waist and long legs— but in a different way than her shorts.

A sexier way.

And thoughts like that, with her eyes narrowing as if she knew exactly what he was thinking about, would not help his survivability chances.

"Is it safe if I invite you in?" he asked.

"That depends." She lifted her chin, which only made him want to swallow his impulse to kiss her.

"Depends?"

"Depends if you try and kiss me."

Right. She was still pissed—and she had every reason in the world to be pissed.

"I promise. I'll keep my hands to myself."

He would because this was more than just an attraction now. He wanted to work with Laurie; he wanted to coach the *Angels* with her. He still wanted more, wanted to her to have a place in his life. He hadn't a clue why or why he was even drawn to someone as bristly and stubborn as her.

He hoped someday she might feel the same. Or at least not want to kill him on-sight.

Jack opened the door for her. "Come on in. Elizabeth will be thrilled to see you."

Laurie gave a curt nod before brushing past him. Not actually brushing though, as she swerved to avoid touching him. That was fine; she needed her space and he'd give it to her.

For now. Until she showed the slightest interest back.

Jack closed the door. Hadn't he just offered to keep his hands to himself?

He shook his head. *What was it with this woman?*

He turned and found Laurie staring open-mouthed at his home, the marble flooring, the giant staircase, the framed artwork he'd had commissioned over the years.

He smiled. Despite his efforts to remain unattached and professional, he couldn't help it. He was damn pleased. "I'm glad you like it."

Laurie spun, clicking her mouth closed. As if she could possibly hide what he'd already seen. "It's very nice."

He lifted an eyebrow. She'd have to do a heck of a lot better than 'nice' considering he'd designed the stupid place.

"I mean, even from the outside I knew it'd look great."

Great, was better. He gestured for her to follow, reaching for the small of her back to guide her, but she sidestepped out of his way. He swallowed a sigh. *Right, no touching.*

"This way." He gestured for her to follow. If she was going to jump away every time he touched her it was going to make coaching more difficult.

"I thought there'd be more pictures of… you know, well… you."

He knew she meant when he'd played baseball and the awards he'd garnered over the years.

"There are, just not in the receiving room. If you like, I can show you."

"I'd like that."

He remembered that she'd been a fan, back in the day. That was the only reason, he told himself, why he was showing her.

It had nothing to do with wanting to impress. Or the fact that he led her through the house the long way, passing through a kitchen large enough to accommodate the whole team, the living room with its mounted, plasma TV.

Finally, they reached his study, which opened up to the backyard and pool. He opened the door, indicating she should go first, and smiled at her involuntary gasp.

He couldn't help himself, honest. She'd asked to see his 'pictures' and like a good host, he'd merely provided. Showing off had only been a side benefit.

The room itself, with its high-walled ceiling and perfectly lighted, framed pictures of him and his team. Medals and trophies, carefully arranged behind glass, from years playing in T-ball, up through Elizabeth's age, to his Major League career.

His study was his place, but not a place of regret. He may have walked away from baseball, but he refused to regret his time there. Or his decision to leave.

Above his barely-used fireplace was a portrait of Elizabeth. He'd had it commissioned the year he decided to quit baseball, the year he decided to become a full-time father and not some half-remembered shadow.

It hung across from his desk so that every time he looked up, he saw her first—first and far above his baseball career.

His study was a place of remembrance for everything he'd accomplished, and everything he still had ahead of him. And right now that included Laurie, whether she wanted it to or not.

Laurie turned in a small circle, mouth open as she took in his baseball career. He leaned against his desk, studying her the way she studied his baseball remembrances.

He may have promised to keep his hands off, but he'd said nothing about his eyes, and right now he took in every inch of her, every turn of her lips, every time her eyes slightly widened when she saw something amazing.

Nancy had never once looked at this room with the same excitement and joy Laurie now did.

"Jack," she whispered.

It was the first time she hadn't said his name in some kind of hostile or threatening way.

She paused in her spin, the largest glass case catching her eye. She headed over and her mouth hung open in wonder. She reached out, tentative and shy, as her long fingers brushed the glass.

"Is this...? Is this your Rookie of the Year award?"

The way she spoke, almost fearful and nervous, brought him back to the moment. Back to her. He came forward, unlocking the case. "It is."

"Don't. You don't need to... I mean." Laurie immediately backed away.

He smirked and took the award out anyway. The polished metal gleamed, and, like always, the baseball with its gold stitching caught his eye and held it. After all these years, it still felt heavy.

He'd had no idea, not even when he held it for the first time, what it would mean.

Jack's shoulders tightened. While he never hid his baseball legacy, he also didn't dwell on the memories. Better to look to the future.

"It's fine. Really. Please." He held it out to her.

She hesitated a moment, eyes glued to the baseball, before finally accepting it. "I never imagined it would feel like this. It's *heavy*."

Yes, it was.

"I had my guesses, but now I really need to know. You were a fan of mine, weren't you? Not many people know—or remember—about this." He nodded to the Rookie of the Year award.

To her credit, she didn't fumble or drop the irreplaceable trophy. Instead, her fingers tightened around the base and finally sighed. "I guess that was pretty obvious."

Jack smiled. "Not at all. It's nice to know people still remember me."

Laurie snorted. "Everyone still remembers you."

He didn't care about everyone. He cared about her.

She blushed, as if she knew exactly what he was thinking. "You were one of the best. I remember...," she hesitated. "I remember listening to my dad talking about you for years. The kid who came from nowhere and blew everyone's socks off."

It was a story Jack hated to remember, hated because of what the sudden, instant fame had done to him. He hadn't been ready. Yes, he'd been ready for the game, but not everything that came with it.

"One of your ex-teammates was in the paper today. Threw another no-hitter. I remember him too." She gave him a small smirk. "And I remember how angry he was that you beat him out of this."

She nodded towards the baseball in her hands.

Jack's mood darkened. "Let me guess, Barry White."

"Yeah. How did you know?" She glanced up. "Do you still follow the games?"

He tried not to, but after seeing him at Nancy's... wasn't it just Jack's luck Barry had a whole string of home games? "No, I don't keep up anymore, but I saw him recently. He's still at the top of his game."

All because of drugs and arrogance and Jack's ex-wife jacking his ego. A man living on that kind of high couldn't help but throw no-hitters. After all, that's what Jack had done.

She tilted her head, a strand of hair curling by her cheek. "Do you miss it? Do you miss playing?"

"No."

Laurie met his eyes, her lips pinched in a tight line, and then she nodded. "I don't either. I miss parts of it...I miss the game. I miss the joy of rounding third or feeling the perfect pitch."

She closed her eyes and sighed. "I knew, even before I released the ball, where the pitch would go. I could feel myself leaning forward or if my hips were closed."

She looked at him and smiled. "But I could also tell when I threw the perfect curve ball. The second it came off my fingers, I'd know."

He'd know it, too. Every time, he'd known.

"So," she asked, "do you miss any of that?"

He didn't want to miss baseball, didn't want to feel the slight coiling in his stomach. But it was there, just as those very brief yearnings when he'd walked into Nancy's home and remembered the life he'd left behind.

"All that stuff you just said? Yeah, I miss that. The rest? Never. Besides, if you were a fan then you knew about my fall from grace."

She nodded. "I remember, but don't forget I had my own fall—though not quite as flashy and as…"

"Well publicized?" Jack offered.

"Yeah, that's it. Besides, you have Elizabeth now." She handed him back the trophy, now much heavier than when he'd taken it out.

"Elizabeth is worth more than a thousand baseball games. I wouldn't change my decision and I've never regretted it."

There were smudge stains from their fingers on the trophy, but he'd clean it later. For now, he'd leave them as yet another reminder.

"You're a good father. She's lucky to have you."

Jack straightened and turned his back to Laurie as he locked up the case. He tried to ignore the way his heart quickened. Or the feeling of pleasure that someone like her thought he was a good father.

"I'm guessing you came here for a reason and not to gaze into my former, shady life."

When he turned back around, Laurie's relaxed posture had vanished and been replaced by her get-down-to-business stance. It was his fault, but right at this moment, he didn't care. She was the one who'd come into his home and brought up memories—innocently or not—he'd buried in the deepest, darkest corner of the earth.

"You're right," she said. "I came on business."

They might as well cut to the chase. Hugh had given the team to Jack, putting both him and Laurie in a tight, uncomfortable space. Right now, with this hanging between them, even his spacious study felt closed-in. Cramped.

He wouldn't sugar-coat it. He'd ask her straight out, coach-to-coach.

"Are you going to quit?"

Laurie's eyes narrowed, and Jack wondered if she had a bat in the car or if she'd grab the one from the wall. With Laurie, he didn't discount anything.

At least she didn't know it was nailed-on.

"No. I'm not quitting, and if you think I'm going to walk away from my girls—*my* girls who I've worked hard for—you've got another thing coming." Laurie stepped forward and thrust her finger into his chest.

It didn't hurt at all, but anger was much better, much easier to deal with than regret. Both for him, and for her.

"This is my team," she said. "Neither you or anybody else is going to take that away from me."

"It's my team, too, now." Jack's hand circled hers, trapping her. "And I'm not going to walk away either. I guess that means we're going to have to learn to work together."

She was so close. A spitfire of fury that he really, really wanted to kiss. No, *needed* to kiss.

His hand tightened around hers. She lifted her chin, a challenge that if he so much as thought it, she'd hurt him.

"I might have walked away from baseball, but there's no way I'm walking away from this team." It was Elizabeth's team. His team. "And I'm sure as hell not walking away from you, either."

He didn't give a shit about his earlier promise, not when he needed her, right now. Right here.

He needed Laurie and he needed this team.

Jack leaned in, even as he felt Laurie shifting her weight to hit him (or knee him, that was definitely a possibility), or, possibly, even kiss him right back.

He didn't know and didn't care.

At least, not until the sliding glass door to his study opened and Elizabeth asked, "Dad?"

CHAPTER 24

"*D*ad?"

Laurie changed the direction of her knee, which was heading straight for Jack's groin. She stumbled and nearly landed against his chest. Somehow she found enough balance to pull away.

Sort of.

He still held her wrist and he wasn't letting go, not even with Elizabeth standing there, a beach towel wrapped around her waist. Water dripped from her hair and purple floral bathing suit. A puddle formed on the wooden deck outside Jack's study.

Elizabeth gazed at Jack, then at Laurie, a small blush reddening her face. "Uhh...Laurie, what are you doing here?"

Trying not to kill your father for trying to kiss me again? Laurie thought, but wisely kept her mouth shut. Oh, dear. This was not what she wanted.

"I came here to talk to your dad." *Talk only. No kissing.* At least that had been her intent.

Laurie tried to pull free, but Jack's grip only tightened. What the hell was he playing at? His daughter was right there—his emotional, fragile daughter.

181

"Jack?" Laurie hissed. Her heart raced like she'd just hit the game-winning run.

Jack, master of calm, didn't radiate even a smidgen of the tension she'd felt from him earlier. Or the desire, as he'd looked at her, leaning in for another kiss.

"Laurie came to talk about the team," Jack said.

"Why?"

Elizabeth still hadn't taken her eyes off their interlocked hands. If he didn't let go in two seconds, Elizabeth or no Elizabeth, she would hit him.

"Well, Elizabeth, I'm going to be your new coach. That is, if you're okay with it."

The way he said it, so commanding, so permanent made it real. For the first time since he'd told her, Laurie knew it was real. Real, and wouldn't change.

Elizabeth's eyes went wide.

Jack was staying. He was staying with her team. Her girls.

"And," Jack added quickly, "if Laurie doesn't kill me first. It's your call." He said this to Elizabeth, before turning his smoldering gaze back to Laurie. "And yours as well."

Laurie's body went slack just as Elizabeth jumped forward with a squeal. The towel went flying and the wet teenage girl flew at her father. He released Laurie just in time to catch Elizabeth.

He spun her around in a circle. All smiles, all laughter.

"You mean it?" Elizabeth asked. "You're really going to be a coach?"

Jack laughed and hugged her again. He didn't seem to care about his sodden clothes, just held her closer.

Laurie backed up until she thumped into his desk. She forced her gaze away, giving them some privacy for this moment. And by the way Jack smiled, the complete and utter joy he radiated, Laurie knew this was a moment.

"Of course you're a great dad," Laurie whispered to herself. How could he possibly think otherwise?

Elizabeth jerked her attention to Laurie. "Laurie, is it true? Is my dad going to be a coach?"

"Yes, yes it is."

Jack grinned at her and suddenly it became much harder to breathe. Yes, she'd seen him sexy as all hell, and unshakably determined, but she'd never seen him like this. The happy father.

Elizabeth jumped down leaving behind an Elizabeth-shaped wet stain on Jack's shirt and pants. "I'm gonna call Mom."

Then she took off. She dashed out so fast she missed seeing the way Jack's smiled vanished. He stood there, hands still open, staring down at his white shirt—a shirt which was now a more pinkish color, showing his bare skin underneath.

Laurie blushed and looked away. She also didn't need to see that.

"Right. Your mother."

Jack ran a hand through his hair, and then stomped to his desk. He maneuvered around Laurie so skillfully he didn't even touch her.

He may not have touched her, but she felt his rage. It seared through her, so strong and fast she sank into a chair, stunned.

"Jack?"

"Her mother."

It was all he said as he grabbed a beer from a small fridge, partially hidden behind the desk. He glanced up at Laurie and grabbed another beer. "I'm sure you need one just for being here."

"Actually, I'm—"

"Here." He thrust the open bottle in her hands and ushered her to the couch. "If you don't drink with me, I'm afraid I'll reach for something stronger."

Right. The ex-wife problems. So, on top of them now being co-coaches with this annoying attraction between them, there was also recovering, still-fragile Elizabeth, and then the evil ex-wife.

Great. Laurie sank into the couch. And she hadn't even gone into her own problems yet. This was such a mess.

Jack took a long swig from his beer, then another. "She'll call and leave a message. Then, she'll try again in another hour after leaving two more on Nancy's cell phone."

Laurie's head snapped up. "You're telling me she won't even talk to her own daughter?"

"Not unless there's something in it for her. Mostly money or... favors from me."

She had a feeling he'd meant to say something else.

"I'm sure it'll be fine," Laurie said. "I've known a few parents like her. They never go to the games, pretty much leave the kids alone. It's almost easier to deal with."

Easier than the ones who didn't let go, who got too close and pushed and pushed until there was nothing left.

Laurie immediately let go of her poor, captive beer bottle and placed it on the table. "I'm sorry. It's really too early to be drinking."

"If we're having a conversation about my ex-wife, which we are, then it's never too early."

"I'd rather not have a conversation about your ex-wife." She'd said it hoping to say, *'this topic of conversation is too personal so let's not have it.'* Instead, she was pretty certain it had the opposite effect.

Like the way Jack's intense gaze turned hungry as he looked at her. "You're right, of course. Except the disappointment is almost unbearable. For Elizabeth." He took a long drink from his beer. "Not me."

Sure enough, Laurie could already hear Elizabeth's feet padding back down the stairs. She'd thrown a shirt on over the bathing suit and now it was plastered to her body.

Very much like Jack's—except for the muscular, sculpted chest his white shirt now did absolutely nothing at all to hide.

"What's wrong?" he asked.

Seconds ago, Elizabeth had been all smiles, now she hung her head and a resigned, defeated sigh escaped her. "She didn't pick up."

"It's all right. Your mother's usually busy this time of day. Why don't you go change? We'll go out to dinner to celebrate."

"Really?" Elizabeth wiggled her wet hair between her fingers. "Can Laurie come too?"

Laurie straightened up so fast she only sank further into the giant, cushioned couch. "Ah, wait. I can't... I mean..."

Jack pointed at Elizabeth. "*I* think that's a great idea, but I think you'll need to convince her to come."

"Oh, please come, Laurie! Say you'll come. It won't be a celebration without you."

"Ah, no. I don't think it's a good idea and I have..." her voice trailed off as Jack took two steps toward the couch, and then leaned over her.

She could make out the fine, softly defined chest muscles through his still-damp shirt.

"If you have plans, we understand. How about tomorrow?" he asked.

"I'm not sure."

"The day after?"

His eyes told her he'd keep going. He'd push until she said yes. They both knew she would; both knew that she had no chance, not in this conversation.

They were co-coaches now, co-coaches unless she wanted to step down.

They'd have to talk some time, and they really needed to talk. Both about the team and their plans for the *Angels* as well as this little thing called 'boundaries.'

That was definitely something Jack needed to learn.

If she wanted him to. And right now, with him so close his breath curled with hers, she didn't know if she wanted him to.

"Tonight's fine." Laurie pushed to her feet, hoping it'd make Jack back off a little. It didn't, only gave her enough room to breathe without her breasts brushing against his chest.

Oh, man, this was such a bad idea.

"Don't make me regret this," she whispered.

He smiled, a tiny pull of his lips. "I promise."

Her stomach curled and she asked herself, yet again, why she'd agreed to any of this.

No, she knew why. It was because with Jack, and being this close to him, she suddenly lost all reasoning and thinking ability. He also had one heck of an adorable daughter.

Elizabeth flung herself into Laurie's arm, pushing Jack away, now getting Laurie all nice and wet. But she only laughed, letting Elizabeth dance her around in a circle. She had more energy than even little

Suzie. Or maybe it was because she didn't have too many reasons to dance, too many reasons to smile and sing.

Seeing Elizabeth happy and smiling was worth it.

Laurie looked over Elizabeth's head and met Jack's gaze.

This was why Laurie stayed on the team. She stayed to help young girls find their way.

She stayed to help girls hold onto that happiness with everything they had, even if they didn't realize what happiness was until they touched it.

Honestly, Jack hadn't expected dinner to go so well. He leaned back on his deck, feet propped on a footstool, finishing off his portion of the pizza (he'd decided on delivery—too much could go wrong between his house and the restaurant, especially where Laurie was concerned). Still, he smiled.

Because nothing had gone wrong.

Laurie and Elizabeth swayed back and forth in the hammock. Actually, it was Elizabeth doing the swaying and while Laurie tried to squirm out and kept falling back in.

He hadn't been able to stop smiling all night, ever since Elizabeth had practically yanked her unsuspecting coach into the hammock. It was a good night, better than he could have hoped for.

Why? Other than his two favorite, beautiful women spending the evening with him, Nancy hadn't called.

Elizabeth hadn't remembered either.

Jack left the pieces of crust on his plate and put it to the side. He'd have to thank Laurie later. It wasn't anything he could make up to her for, not after the way he'd hurt her by stepping onto her team like this.

He'd do his best though.

He stood, collecting the used plates. No silverware. Not with pizza.

Not the way Nancy had always liked to eat hers with fork and knife (when she'd deemed it appropriate to settle for plain-old pizza).

The inside phone rang and Elizabeth's eyes widened. His hopes of Elizabeth forgetting about her mother were dashed when she scrambled out of the hammock, slipped passed the cracked-open glass door, and disappeared inside. Unfortunately she'd moved so fast Laurie nearly went flying.

Jack jumped forward, catching Laurie by the arm before she tumbled out, face first. "Hold on."

"Believe me, I'm trying." Laurie grabbed hold of his wrist just as her legs twisted in the netting. "Help. I'm…I'm… I think I'm trapped."

He couldn't help it. Jack laughed. His softball goddess was able to handle anything, from big shots like Jack to angry parents like Dan Richards. But it was a hammock that defeated her.

"You look stuck," Jack pointed out, even as he slowly righted her. "And if I'd known that this was all it took for you to be nice to me, I'd have gotten you in this thing sooner."

Laurie's eyes narrowed and before Jack could move, she yanked on his wrist. The hammock rocked with her movement and suddenly he landed on top of her.

"This was not what I'd had in mind," she muttered.

The blush now lighting Laurie's face was more beautiful, more arousing than just staring at her. And being this close to her was more than he could have hoped for.

"Are you sure?" His voice dropped as he lowered his head, nose brushing against hers.

She gazed at him, her chest heaving as if she'd just run a mile. "Pretty sure."

Jack breathed her in, the scent that was just Laurie. He had an incredibly hard time remembering to focus, even on simple facts like Elizabeth being just inside the house.

He even had a harder time remembering why he cared.

This time, it was him who breathed heavy, breathing in who she was—softball and hard work and something else, something that was only Laurie.

His eyes flicked to her lips, so close to hers. He should look away; in fact, he should get off of her, but his body and his brain seemed to have two very different ideas.

So did another part of his body.

Laurie's blush deepened, but if she felt his arousal, now pressing against her leg—and he was pretty certain she could at this point—she didn't say anything.

"Get off; you way a ton."

"Sorry."

He shifted, trying to get off her lap. He only sank further into the hammock's devilish netting while the contraption seemed to throw her into his lap. At least he wasn't crushing her, but he was damn sure she could feel him now—every damn inch of him.

It wasn't exactly the way he'd imagined sweeping her off her feet. He'd been hoping to go a little more slowly, start working on her not being pissed at him about the *Angels*.

"I should never have let her get you in this death-trap," Jack said. The truth was, he didn't mean it. This was the best damn idea Elizabeth had ever had. He was pretty sure she thought so, too.

"Jack." Her hand pressed against his chest, sending heat wave after wave through him. God, he just wanted to kiss her silly.

She tried shoving him, which only made her fall further into his arms—a place he didn't mind her being, even if she was pissed-off. Her fingers curled in his shirt. "Will. You. Get. Off?"

He had a hard time telling if she was mad or, or something else....

So, he went with the something else.

"Well, I certainly like this much better than the couch." He circled his arms around her waist. She wiggled away and he laughed. "Dear, that's really not helping."

Laurie froze, glanced down at their laps, and jerked her head back up. "Damn it, Jack. This is what I came over to talk about."

He leaned into her neck, taking a long, deep breath of her. God, she smelled so good. But it was more than the smell, more than the way she stirred him.

It was how relaxed he felt around her, even when they were having arguments, it never felt personal. Jack touched his lips to her neck, tasted the salt on her skin.

Laurie shivered. His hands tightened around her waist, pulling her into him. "Jack?"

If it was a protest, it wasn't the kind he listened to, not when she practically purred his name. He kissed her neck again, couldn't help but slightly move his hips against hers.

Laurie tilted her head back and groaned.

He nearly lost it. He didn't, because somehow through the haze he heard Elizabeth talking.

Yes, he wanted—no needed—to take Laurie into his arms, into his bed and probably never let her go. But not here. Not with Elizabeth just in the next room.

Elizabeth might be okay with him being a coach; he didn't know how she'd feel about him dating the other coach. He'd talk with her later. Right now, his lips had a mind of their own, trailing long, lingering kisses down Laurie's neck.

He'd talk with Elizabeth soon; damn soon.

With strength that would make Hercules and any other red-blooded male proud, Jack released Laurie's waist.

"I'm sorry. You're right we need to talk about this. I'll get off."

Except he didn't. He wanted to move, told his body to get into gear. He couldn't seem to let go of her.

"I can, uh, see that you're trying." She didn't move a muscle either, though, which he was grateful for. "This is...this is a real mess isn't it?"

He wasn't entirely sure which part she was talking about, him being a coach, him ready to pull off all her clothes and take her on the hammock, or just the whole damn thing.

"At least you're not dating a parent," he pointed out.

"I'm not dating a coach either. And definitely not *you*." She'd found her fire again, probably now that she had a chance to catch her breath. The 'something else' was, unfortunately, gone now.

"And you're getting off."

Mostly.

Jack grinned. He held up his hands. "By all means."

She punched him in the arm and he winced. She definitely hadn't lost her softball strength.

"Look," she said. "I don't want to do this... this *thing*. This awkwardness between us and this," she indicated them in the hammock, "isn't helping."

No, it wasn't. But he knew a remedy for that, and it involved her being thoroughly kissed and naked in his bed.

However, he doubted she wanted to hear that; and since Elizabeth could come back any minute, with Laurie still on his lap and his pants being as tight as they were, it was best to not bring up the 'naked' part.

For now.

"Okay. What do you want to do?"

"Other than get me out of this thing?"

"That, I can do."

He helped her out of the hammock. There was more cursing, and some minor, accidental groping, which he apologized each and every time for. It wasn't his fault the woman had no balance at all and that he needed to literally shove her out by her butt. Although, he was careful to make sure the skirt part stayed down.

He was still a gentleman, after all.

Mostly.

But even with the groping, tripping, and stumbling out of the hammock, they laughed. He couldn't help it, feeling so ridiculous that this rope netting made him look like such a fool.

And Laurie was right there with him. She grabbed onto his shirt and yanked him out between fits of giggles. Maybe it was the beer, maybe it was the way their bodies had rubbed against each other just seconds before.

He didn't give a shit. Not when her laughter faded, not when her eyes raised and met his. Not when he felt her breath on his cheek.

His hands tightened on her arms and he felt her arms tremble.

"Laurie," he whispered.

He needed her, but more than that, he needed to find some way to show her they could work together. Find some way to make her comfortable.

That she could trust him.

Of course, he needed to do the same. To trust her as well.

Jack dropped her arms and stepped back.

Laurie rubbed her bare arms. Even from here he could pick out the tiny goose bumps. "This is exactly what I'm talking about. How do you expect us to play on the same field without...without this happening every time?"

"Is that such a problem?"

Jack heard a glass door slide all the way open—all the way from that small opening his little Elizabeth had clearly left open during her dash to reach the phone. And hadn't closed behind her.

Shit.

Jack glanced over Laurie's shoulder and all feelings of calm and comfort vanished.

He'd expected Elizabeth. Expected her shock. Probably even her hurt.

He hadn't, however, expected Nancy as she slipped outside, a silky half-dress wrapped around her too-thin body, He also hadn't expected Barry White and Elizabeth, trailing after them both, phone clutched to her chest as she stared at Jack.

Nancy tucked her hot-pink cell phone into her rhinestone (or possibly diamond) coated purse.

Double shit.

Once again, Nancy had managed to ruin a perfectly great evening.

"Yes, Jack," Nancy crooned. "I'm curious to know myself. How are you going to handle this, this little situation?"

CHAPTER 26

*L*aurie spun around, hearing Nancy's voice. Jack reached out a hand to steady her, keeping her from falling back into the hammock.

The second he steadied her, he immediately let go. He didn't dare do anything more, not with Nancy there watching with her curious, predator's eyes.

"Nancy." Jack's attention flicked to Barry. "Barry. What are you doing here?"

Nancy waved her little shawl thing at him. "Jack, dear, is that any way to treat your guests?"

Beside him, Laurie tensed, the surprise at Jack's unexpected 'guests' fading as she slipped into her own mask, one he was already becoming uncomfortably familiar with: easy-going, friendly coach.

He hated that mask, hated that she hid who she was. Hated that Nancy was the reason she now wore it. Already, it felt like Laurie was an entire field away from him.

"You," he spat at Nancy, "are my *ex*-wife, not my guest, and you, Barry, will never again be a guest in this house."

Barry's eyes narrowed. Already Jack could see the slight strain in the bigger man's suit, a suit that was much too tight around the chest

—and definitely too tight for any serious arm-swinging fistfights. Which, of course, was the point.

The ladies always liked gazing at Barry's muscles.

It was the last thing he wanted, not here with Elizabeth....

"Dad! Mom's here." She pushed past the two adults and began talking so fast Jack couldn't keep up. He was sure Laurie's name was in there somewhere, because Laurie stiffened at the mention.

Or, that could be because of the narrowed look Nancy was shooting at Laurie. But Laurie, damn fine woman that she was, was giving back just as good as she got.

Jack ran a hand through his hair. This was going to get out of hand. On one side of the pool, there'd be a fistfight between him and Barry. On the other side would be the world's deadliest cat fight...hell, that would be the actual fistfight. He and Barry's match wouldn't stand a chance.

Jack had no problem betting on Laurie to beat Nancy's skinny ass.

But that left Elizabeth right in the middle.

Jack stepped between the two women. "Is there something I can help you with? As you can see, Elizabeth and I already have company over."

Wanted company, he thought. *Not scum of the earth.*

Nancy frowned, her bright red lips matching the color of a righteous fury if he didn't end this soon. "I stopped by to see my daughter."

Bullshit. "She's busy."

"Dad!" Elizabeth tugged on his arm.

"No," he said. "Just showing up is rude. Your mother can call ahead of time like everybody else."

Barry growled from the sidelines, warning Jack he'd best be careful, but it was Laurie's gentle touch on his arm that brought him back.

"It's all right, Jack. I know how much Elizabeth wants to spend time with her mother."

And before he could stop her, Laurie swept past him, hand extended and smiled at Nancy. "Laurie Stevens. I'm Elizabeth's softball coach. It's so nice to finally meet you."

Nancy tossed her curled hair over her shoulder and shook Laurie's hand without actually touching it.

"Nancy Edmonds. And I can see how nice it must be for you to meet Jack. He used to be so famous, you know. Rich, too. I'll bet Elizabeth has been a tremendous addition to your... team."

Laurie murmured something that could have been either 'thank you' or 'screw you' and withdrew her hand from Nancy's deadly embrace.

Laurie shrugged off the 'rich' comment. "I can't say he's done too badly. But then, I work on a teacher's salary and have managed to live a happy, satisfying life so far."

If there was one insult Laurie could have shot at Nancy and actually do damage, that was the one. To Nancy, money meant everything.

Jack tried to angle between the two women again, but Laurie spread her feet wide, placed her hands on her hips, and ignored him.

"The team absolutely adores Elizabeth," Laurie continued, charging on. "She's already one of my best players. You should be so proud of her."

Nancy straightened. "Of course. I'm always proud of her."

Elizabeth bit her lip, peeking around Laurie to stare up at her mother. "Really?"

The hope, the desperation in that one small plea made Jack want to grab Nancy by the hair and throw her into the deepest, darkest hole.

"Yes, Pumpkin," Nancy said. "I'm proud."

"I'll bet you are." Laurie wrapped a hand around Elizabeth's shoulders and squeezed. "So proud that we'll see you at next weekend's game, right? Saturday morning?"

"What?" Nancy's smile fell.

Jack placed a hand on Elizabeth's other shoulder, hoping to draw her away before the real claws came out. "That's a great idea, Laurie. What better way to show your daughter how proud you are, right Nancy?"

And, right on cue, Elizabeth jumped into the air, arms up high as she hugged Nancy. "Oh, mom, will you? Please?"

Backed into the corner with no way out, Nancy had no choice but to agree. Of course, agreeing and actually showing up were two different things. She glared at Jack but the deal was done.

Laurie took advantage of the break in the conversation to mention the time and that she should be off—a school day tomorrow and all; the summer hadn't started for all of them yet.

Jack stepped forward, intending to walk her to her car, both apologizing and thanking her for this. He didn't get the chance. Barry reached a hand out, stopping him.

"I'm a gentleman. I can walk the lady to her car. After all, your ex-wife came all this way to talk with you."

Jack glared at Barry. Gentleman his ass. He didn't want Barry anywhere near Laurie.

Laurie gave the tiniest shake of her head, her mouth whispering, "It's okay."

Trust. He didn't trust Barry with her, but he could trust Laurie to look after herself.

And if she didn't... no. Barry would keep his distance. But that wouldn't stop Barry from saying things, things that could damage the tenuous friendship between him and Laurie.

She lightly touched his shoulder. "We'll talk tomorrow about the girls. Maybe we can even have team party here or something."

He could tell she was trying to be both generous towards him and positive in front of Nancy. He reached for her hand, but she was already pulling away.

All he could do was nod and watch them go.

Before the door even slid closed behind them, Nancy dropped her hands on her hips. "A softball coach, huh? Don't give me that crap. Who the hell is she?"

Jack glared right back at her. "She's none of your damn business."

"Mom!" Elizabeth said. "That's Laurie. She's my softball coach, honest."

Nancy sniffed. "Well, I suppose she must be. But if I'd known you had a thing for softball coaches I wouldn't have wasted my time."

Elizabeth reddened. Already he could see her eyes water at Nancy's usual, cruel words. He kept hold of his temper. Barely.

"Elizabeth, why don't you go upstairs and pick a movie to watch."

"I don't want to watch a movie." She rubbed her eyes, but it wasn't helping. He knew her too well for her to hide her tears.

"We'll watch one together."

Elizabeth didn't even say goodnight to Nancy, just ducked her head and dashed into the house. Jack grabbed Nancy's arm and hauled her closer to the pool, the place that up until five minutes ago had been warm and comforting.

Now it felt cold and hollow, exactly how Jack felt.

"Let me go!"

"Fine." He did and she stumbled closer to the pool, but, unfortunately, managed to find her balance on those six-inch spikes she called heels.

"What is...what is your problem? I just came over to see my darling and daughter and there you are, practically naked with the softball coach!"

"Cut the act." Jack stepped closer, eyes narrowing. "You don't give a shit about your daughter. The only time she was 'darling' to you was when the new baby made you the center of attention."

"And second," he growled, "that piece of cloth you call a dress is a hell lot more naked than either Laurie or I were. You want to pass judgment? Fine. Put on some clothes and then we'll talk."

"If you think you can talk to me like this." Nancy poked him in the chest with a red, dagger-pointed nail. "I'll send you to court before you can blink. The minute any judge hears about you acting indecent in front of your daughter..."

Jack wrapped his hand around hers. His grip tightened. "Nancy. You are more than welcome to try and I'll flatten you. Threaten my daughter, threaten my family, and I'll destroy you."

For a brief moment, uncertainty crossed her face. "I used to be part of this family too."

"Not for a long time."

Not for years; not since he became famous and everything they were, everything she was, changed. He'd found his way back, but

Nancy had always preferred the glitter and the dreams. She'd stayed and he'd moved on.

Jack released her hand. "And you'll never be part of this family again. Who I date, who I'm interested in, and whoever I bring into this house, is none of your concern."

"Elizabeth is my concern."

"No," he said, "your only concern is staying in control. She's the last tie you have to me, the last little hold you have over me. Now, I suggest you and Barry both leave. You want to spend time with your daughter? Call."

And he'd have to call Laurie, too. Call and apologize. For everything.

But first, he had a daughter to cheer up, a daughter who needed her father because her mother didn't give a shit.

CHAPTER 27

Barry White stood a little too close as he opened the front door for Laurie. When he gestured her ahead, his hand purposefully brushed her arm. She ground her teeth and managed not to elbow him as she strode past.

However, if she felt so much as a feather touch on her ass, she was going to back-kick him.

A shiny black car, probably worth three times what her house cost, was parked behind Laurie's solid, reliable truck. Good. If he touched her she'd put it in reverse and smash it like an accordion.

No big-bucks fancy car could withstand solid steel.

"Thanks for walking me out." Laurie swerved to her car, hoping that'd be the end of his little escort, but then Barry was there, his hips blocking her path.

"Not a problem Ms. Stevens."

She shot him a smile. It had a good mix of 'get the hell out of my way look' and a dollop of 'touch me and I'll kill you,' but the ass didn't move out of her way.

Fine. She'd play nice; kind of. "Look. It's been a long day and I have work to do."

"I just wanted to make sure you were all right, is all."

"Trust me. I'm fine." She sidestepped around him and this time he let her.

"I just wanted to make sure you knew what you were getting into with Jack and all. We were buds back when, and he's a pretty wild guy."

"I'm pretty sure an adorable daughter has tamed him." Not to mention that she knew how wild Barry still was. Not exactly the kind of guy to pass judgment.

But Barry wouldn't leave it there. He leaned against her truck, all manly and in control, but she noticed his tense shoulder muscles and the way his smile would slip every few seconds, a struggle he eventually dropped.

"Jack isn't good with women. He doesn't treat them right."

Laurie lifted her eyebrows. This coming from the guy who was just stroking Jack's ex-wife's ass?

"Thanks again for you concern, but I'm fine."

There. She was polite to the superstar baseball player. Even her dad would have been proud. She swallowed that thought, but then jumped back when Barry slammed his fist onto her truck.

"You don't know the first thing about Jack. He'll use you, be your best friend, then chuck you the first chance he gets." He leaned closer to Laurie, using his larger frame to intimidate her.

Laurie's hands tightened around her keys. One pointed outwards. Even a big, muscular guy had weak spots.

Soft spots.

"And you know what he'll dump you for?" Barry growled. "The game. He can deny it all he wants, but he can't let it go. Even now he's swooping in and stealing your team right from under you."

Laurie straightened, felt her jaw clench. Barry was lying. There was bad blood between him and Jack and she couldn't believe anything he said.

"He's not stealing my team."

But hadn't he? Hadn't he, within a matter of weeks, taken over for Hugh?

"You sure about that?" Barry asked.

"He's doing this to be a better father." That's right, she reminded herself. He was doing this for Elizabeth.

"You think I'm saying all this because of what happened in there," Barry jerked his head towards the house. "I couldn't give a fuck who he fucks. But you seem to love your team and if you do, you'd best steer clear of Jack."

Barry stepped away from her truck. "Your call, though. If you want to keep your team that is. There's a reason he beat me out of that award, why they picked him Rookie of the Year over me."

"You're right," she said. "It's because he was the better player."

Barry's eyes darkened. "I just thought I'd warn you. I'm done here."

He left her alone outside.

She stayed where she was. Couldn't help it.

Barry hadn't said anything she hadn't already secretly feared. Jack had swooped in and within an eye-blink, was at the Sunday barbecue. He was in her stands, chatting with the scouts.

"Damn it." Laurie slapped her palm on the truck's hood. Barry might not like Jack, and that was sure as hell clear enough, but it didn't mean he was lying.

The opposite in fact. Barry had been telling the truth.

Laurie was going to lose her team.

She ran a hand through her ponytail and froze when she noticed her shaking fingers. If she wasn't careful, she was going to lose more than her team.

If she hadn't already.

LAURIE KNEW when she was beat. Any decent coach knew that. It was the good ones who managed to pick themselves up and keep playing.

After Wednesday's practice, with her butt resting on an overturned bucket, she told the girls about Hugh—who at least managed to make a farewell appearance. She also told them who his replacement would be, both as coach and as manager.

And she knew she was beaten.

The girls launched themselves into the air, screamed and giggled in a way only girls knew how, and the rest was history. Jack was here to stay. As her coach. As her manager.

Laurie nearly ran to the bathroom, her stomach churning at the thought. She couldn't get the conversation with Barry out of her head. It had haunted her the past few days, replayed every time she picked up the phone to call Jack.

And had immediately put it back down.

But Barry had only been part of the issue. The other part was her own reaction to calling Jack. The way her heart beat picked up, the way her face flushed.

She both wanted to call him and to never speak to him again. It was an unfair and completely unreasonable reaction.

So what did that leave her with? Fear. Absolute and complete fear and she had no idea what she was going to do.

She watched as Dan Richards's shook Jack's hand, a couple of giant pumps as if to show the whole world—look, we've got a new coach now. A real coach.

No one glanced at her, not even Elizabeth. Definitely not Jack.

Was that part of her problem? That here he was, the center of attention, and he didn't seem to remember her?

"You're being unfair," she whispered. This was his moment; not hers.

He stood in the spotlight, accepting congratulations and already she could hear parents offering suggestions, tactics and ideas that would best utilize their child's ability. Ideas that had gone ignored up to this point, but they were hoping Jack would listen, that he'd be open to *new* ideas.

When had this happened? She hadn't seen the change, the subtle shift in her parents. Yes, there were the college scouts and that was fairly obvious, but this?

Her hands couldn't stop shaking. She buried them in her lap.

It was just like before, when her dad was officially announced as a couch. Back then, she'd been one of those smiling, excited girls. She was the one celebrating. She was Elizabeth, thrilled that her dad was now one of the coaches.

Laurie's throat tightened. She had to get out of here.

She stood, knocking over her bucket. Barry was wrong about Jack. He wasn't here to take over her team. He was here for Elizabeth, and as soon as Elizabeth got too old for the *Angels'* division, he'd move on. Just this summer season.

Unless, of course Elizabeth made the birthday cut-off... but no, that wouldn't happen. Even if she did, Jack and Elizabeth would be moving on. Just like Lacey. Suzie. All her twelve-year-olds. And Laurie would have another slew of girls coming in.

Just like Jack would move on with this... this *thing* between them.

She tried to reassure herself, tried to ease her mind. It didn't happen.

"A lot can happen in a year," she murmured. A lot had happened in a matter of weeks.

Stop it, she chided herself. Jack hadn't done anything wrong. All she had was Barry's accusations and her fears. That wasn't fair to Jack.

Claire peeled off from the group of parents and headed towards Laurie, picking up Suzie's discarded cleats and winked. "I have to say, coach, you don't look too happy. If that was me and he was my new co-coach, I'd be having my own party."

"I'm not." The words sort of jumped out on their own. That wasn't what she'd intended to say. She'd meant to smile and talk about how happy she was.

Claire's eyebrows quirked up.

"I'm not," Laurie said again, "happy or having a party."

"That's really too bad. I think you're missing out. On both." Claire nodded towards the group. The girls had circled around Jack and he was busy giving them jumping high-fives.

Laurie's high-fives.

This was her team. She felt tears swelling in her eyes. Damn it, she hated crying. Of course, that only made it worse.

"I can't do this."

Claire gently touched Laurie's hand and her smile vanished. She stared at Laurie, concerned. "Why not? From everything I can see, Jack will make a fine coach and I'm sure Hugh wouldn't have stepped down if he didn't feel Jack was a right fit."

"It's...it's not just the team."

"Oh." Claire smirked. "Well, even Richards could see *that* between you two."

"No!" Laurie's voice rose and she immediately squished it back down. Thankfully everyone was still focused on Jack and didn't hear.

Would this be what it's like from now on? Everyone's eyes on Jack?

"Yes. No. It's everything." And she couldn't stop her stupid eyes from filling with water. She wasn't going to cry. Not here, not in front of everyone—and especially not in front of Jack. "Everything about this is a giant mess. I'm a mess."

She used to know everything, used to know how to deal with everything. Now she had no idea where to start.

Claire deposited Suzie's cleats in her bag, then snaked her hand through Laurie's and led her away from the group. "You might be my daughter's coach, but I'm also your friend. And right now, as your friend you need some one-on-one girl time."

"Girl time." Laurie couldn't remember the last time she'd done that. Was it in college? Right before she'd quit the team?

"Will a walk in the park work? Or do we need to see a fun, romantic comedy or something? I think there are one or two playing that would fit the criteria."

Romance was the last thing, the very last thing, she needed right now.

"A walk will do just fine," Laurie said.

Still, she couldn't help but glance over her shoulder. Jack and Hugh were handling both the girls and the parents. Laurie's stomach twisted and looked away.

"Stop that." Claire pinched Laurie's arm.

"Hey!"

"I mean it. You're looking down on yourself. You're acting just like me and you can't do that."

"You're right. About Jack, I mean. He'll make the team better."

"But...?"

"It's just that everything...first Jack, and then the college scouts. Now Hugh's admitted he's been walking in my shadow for years and steps down. I just don't know what to do."

After a slight hesitation, she told Claire about her meeting with Barry and her own fears about Jack changing her girls. Changing her team.

Claire pursed her lips and shook her head. "I think you're right to distrust Jack. You don't know what went on between those two, but you know, Barry's not exactly un-opinioned in this situation, dating Jack ex-wife and all."

"First there's Jack, and then, all the college scouts... it's just bringing up memories. I'm having a hard time seeing around them. I know you're right, but I'm still... still scared."

"I don't think you need to be, at least not of Jack stealing the team. Besides, you're forgetting about the steamy attraction."

Laurie snorted. "Believe me, I didn't forget. I'm trying to forget and it's not working."

That was what made this whole thing worse. If Jack was just another guy, someone who didn't matter, she would have easily taken control and there wouldn't be an issue.

But he did matter and it was an issue. He was a coach now, a coach she wanted to kiss again; a coach who could threaten everything she'd built for this team.

If Barry was right.

Claire sighed. "Maybe we should have sprung for the girls' movie. There's something you're not telling me."

Laurie started to protest but Claire held up a hand, cutting her off. "I'm not blind. I happen to have a daughter quickly approaching the teenage-madness years, and I know when someone's holding back."

Laurie's mouth clicked closed. Put like that, she wasn't about to argue. Not like she had any idea what Claire was talking about.

Attraction to Jack was one thing. Feelings, if there were any feelings and she was sure there weren't, was another matter entirely.

"I don't know why you're worried, but if you ever want to talk, I'm here for you." Claire stopped and took both of Laurie's hands in her own. "I mean it. We're on this team because of you, and we're staying because of you."

Claire glanced away. "Suzie and I wouldn't have survived the divorce if it hadn't been for you. Don't forget that, no matter what happens, you're our coach."

"Thank you." Laurie could only nod and pray that little glimmer of hope would be enough.

Her stomach twisted and as she watched Jack finally glanced their way. His eyes meeting hers and he smiled, big and proud.

Her heart quickened and she knew it wouldn't be enough.

CHAPTER 28

"*Give him a chance.*" Hugh's advice tumbled through Laurie's head as she stared at the empty field, waiting impatiently for the day's games to begin, waiting for her girls to take the field.

Jack was with Lacey and Elizabeth, watching both girls warm-up, having them go through their pitches. She watched as he spoke to Lacey, whose eyes were big and eager to please—the first time Laurie had ever seen Lacey want to please anybody.

"*Give him a chance.*"

Hugh was right. She needed to take a step back, to give Jack the lead, a chance to grow comfortable as the *Angels'* coach. She was just terrified of him becoming *too* comfortable, of what Barry warned of coming true.

From across the field, Laurie watched as Kent warmed up the *Rascals'* girls, as he kept a hard eye on his pitchers, looking to see who was throwing the best.

Kent always threw his best girls against the *Angels*. Almost like he was trying to prove something to Laurie—that he was worth her saying yes to the dinner he always asked her to.

She shook her head. Beating her team was definitely not the way to a dinner date, and neither was holding her hand a tad longer than necessary. No matter; he was harmless.

Not like Jack. Jack was far, far from being harmless.

"Psst," Claire whispered through the fence. "Stop worrying. I thought we were supposed to have fun on this team?"

Laurie cracked a smile. It was hard, but she did smile. Claire was right too. Everyone was right, except her. She was the one who couldn't seem to get it together and just let go.

Let the past stay in the past.

"Stop that. I mean it," Claire chided. "Have fun or you can't have this little treat I brought you." She lifted a coffee cup and Laurie could practically smell the vanilla drifting on the early morning breeze.

"You're a lifesaver."

"I know." Claire grinned. "But you can only have it if you promise."

What was she supposed to say? When temptation was right there, her still sleepy, overworked, and nervous brain would agree to just about anything. It was blackmail, and Claire knew it.

So when Jack walked over, all smiles and telling Laurie how Lacey and Elizabeth looked, she took a deep breath and did her best to play fair—to be on the same team as Jack. After all, she'd promised.

"I think Elizabeth should start today," Laurie said, "and I think you should call her pitches."

Jack tossed his glove on the bench and turned. Even her tired, nervous brain could see she'd surprised him.

"You sure about that?"

No. "Yes. You've been working with her. I think it'll be good for both of you."

She hid her nerves and fears as Jack searched her face. She would give him this chance and she would do her best to make room for him. Somehow, she'd show Barry he was wrong about Jack. And the last thing she wanted was to push him away the way she'd pushed Hugh away.

Jack nodded, slowly, as if unsure how to respond. "We never did have a chance to go over anything..."

They both glanced at the batting line-up, the one Laurie had put together while he was warming the girls up. Trust wasn't something that came easily to her, but she had try to trust him, otherwise the team would fall apart before they'd even started.

"No, we didn't." Partly because of Nancy showing up that day in the hammock, but mostly because Laurie had been too afraid to call and meet with him.

She unclipped the board and handed it to him. "You know the way I coach, but I don't know the way *you* coach."

It was the hardest thing she'd done since the day she quit softball. Even harder than the letter she'd written to her father telling him she'd quit. Okay, maybe that was still harder.

Still, Laurie held out the board to him and her hand didn't shake, not in the least. She would step back; she would let him coach.

"Jack, I want you to coach my girls. Tell me what you'd like me to do."

He hesitated. "Are you sure?"

Their coaching styles were different. She'd already seen enough to know that, but maybe she could learn something new from him too. He did have more experience, professional experience, while she'd only played in college ball.

Not that there was much else when it came to woman's pro softball, but still. His experience counted for a heck of a lot.

"Yes, I'm sure."

He reached for the clipboard, but instead he took her hand and held it for several seconds. Warmth spiked through her, shot right through the middle of her fears.

"Just because I'm a coach now doesn't change anything."

"What do you mean?" She licked her lips and Jack's eyes narrowed, watching her with something she was sure wasn't appropriate for their co-coach relationship.

"You can still threaten to hit me with your bat."

She smiled. It was small and tentative, but it was still a smile. "I'll remember you said that."

'Give him a chance.' Okay, Hugh. She'd give Jack this chance and

hope it wouldn't hurt her girls. As for herself and Jack, though, that was a whole other story—one that didn't matter until her team settled in with their new coach.

Laurie stepped back and let Jack take the lead.

In truth, the first game went great. A little shaky at first as both Jack and her girls were a little nervous, a little new working together. But the girls listened to him, and even though she'd given Jack the go-ahead to take the lead, he didn't.

He'd turn to her, a lift of his eyebrow, and ask what she thought about a particular batter or what had gone wrong with a play or if he should have told Suzie to steal on that bunt.

Laurie couldn't help it. She relaxed. She sat next to Jack, their buckets side-by-side, knees brushing each other's every once in a while. And every time that happened, she felt a blush from her face all the way to her stomach.

Her stomach didn't listen when she reminded it, yet again, that they weren't going to deal with the attraction between her and Jack. The team came first, and only then would she deal with the very hot, very steamy kisses.

Every once in a while he'd glance at her and smile, the kind of smile that sent her stomach fluttering and her heart pounding. This, of course, wasn't helping her convince her stomach of anything.

Oh, and there were whispers from the parents, whispering that seemed to pick up every time Jack leaned into her ear and asked a question.

But the way his breath tickled and caressed her skin, the parents had every right to whisper, because all she could think about was his lips being even closer, lightly touching her skin like they had in the hammock and…

The loud, unmistakable *crack* of a bat knocking the stitching off the softball jerked Laurie from her hammock fantasies. Elizabeth had pitched a curve that went straight down home plate instead of curving. The big, heavy-hitting batter got every piece of that ball.

It blasted into center field. A straight and true hit. Shit.

"Damn." Jack jumped up from his bucket and Laurie was right behind him.

Suzie snatched the ball on the second bounce and threw it towards home plate. A runner rounded third. Laurie bit her bottom lip. A slower runner. Thankfully it wasn't one of the other team's faster girls, otherwise the coach would have sent her home.

It's what Laurie would have done.

With only one out in the inning and the fifth batter coming to the plate, a girl Laurie knew had no problem hitting home runs and getting runs in, the situation was looking pretty dangerous for Elizabeth.

"Lacey's warmed," Laurie said. "She's ready if you want to pull Elizabeth."

Jack frowned, clearly trying to keep his cool. "I want her to work through this."

"You sure?"

He didn't answer.

"This is your call, Jack."

He hesitated, torn between being parent and coach, and she waited for him to decide. Finally, Jack gave a firm shake of his head. "She made a mistake. She can battle her way out. But have Lacey throw some more. It might push Elizabeth to work harder."

"I'll take care of it." She called Lacey to warm-up. This was always the fine line she had to walk, between coaching and pushing her girls. Today it was Jack's call.

Elizabeth needed to work, needed to battle her way out of this. Maybe that'd help her confidence too, maybe it'd help see her she was more than what her mother thought.

And Laurie needed to stand back and trust Jack. Of course, that was much easier said than done, especially when Jack touched her shoulder leaned in and whispered, "It'll be all right. Trust me."

His breath tickled her ear. She shivered, and for a brief moment, their eyes met, held. Those blue eyes of his seemed to darken. Even with the game moving around them, with Elizabeth fighting on the mound, Laurie still felt the spark between them as if it couldn't wait for even one inning, one extra pitch.

Desire? What she felt swirling through her stomach and burning her skin was definitely not desire. Oh, no. She'd gone way beyond desire.

And Jack knew it, too.

He broke the contact, ripping his gaze back to Elizabeth and the game. He cheered Elizabeth on, told her to hang in there and stand up straight.

Laurie grabbed onto the fence for balance and took several gulping breaths. What... what was that?

"Coach?" Lacey tugged on Laurie's shirt. "You all right?"

Laurie's face, all nice and flushed thanks to that smoldering look she'd shared with Jack, just got hotter. Shit. What had she gotten herself into?

"I'm fine. Come on, let me get my glove and I'll warm you up."

And hopefully it'd help Laurie cool down now that she had some nice, safe distance from Jack.

Laurie patted Lacey on the shoulder and went onto the field. It wasn't until she stepped onto the dirt, the coarse grains crunching under her cleats that the hairs on her neck raised and she felt a familiar set of eyes on her.

Not comforting, not in the least. She didn't need to look to know who it was, but she did anyway.

Kent watched her from the third base coach spot. Even from here she could feel his gaze and his anger. He must have seen the look she and Jack shared, and the very open, very obvious attraction between them.

Great, just great.

First she had an annoying, uncontrollable attraction to Jack and now she had to deal with Kent. One of the few coaches who still couldn't take a hint.

Jack, at least, didn't seem to notice. That was good. Right now, she wanted all his energy on her girls.

She could take care of herself, and if Kent couldn't take no for an answer, well, it'd been a while since she'd used her bat.

"Come on, Laurie," Lacey called. "I need to be ready at any minute."

Laurie shook her head and trotted after the once always angry and unhappy young girl. At least Jack had already done one good thing for the team and that was making Lacey happy.

The other question, the one she didn't want to think about, was whether or not he could make her happy. And if she wanted him to.

CHAPTER 29

*J*ack was pretty certain that if anyone ever commented on how easy it was to coach their own kids, he was going to call bullshit and give them a piece of his mind.

Easy? Hell, this was probably one of the hardest things he'd done.

Laurie headed off to the side with Lacey. At the mound, Elizabeth wiped the sweat from her chin using her shirt. Her attention flicked to Lacey, then back to her dad.

He saw her question, saw the hesitation.

Time to give her the pep-talk and see if she could get through this or not.

Jack called time to the umpire and jogged out to the mound. Elizabeth didn't meet his eyes. Not like he could blame her. One more line drive to the outfield like that last one and they'd lose the game.

This was the last inning with the winning run now on first. It wasn't an easy call to make, to leave Elizabeth in or call for Lacey, and he'd half hoped Laurie would give him a hint—make a decision so he wouldn't have too. But that was why he was here, wasn't it?

Dirt and sweat smudged Elizabeth's cheeks from when she'd slid into second base earlier. "I'm sorry, Dad. That last curve, it didn't..."

Didn't curve. Not one bit.

He nodded. "You've pitched a great game. I'm proud of you."

"Really?" She glanced up.

"Really. And I know you showed those other girls what you're made of."

"But you're still going to take me out?"

Jack glanced at Lacey as she threw another pitch. Laurie easily caught it, then tossed the ball back. She turned and met his gaze. She was waiting, waiting to see what he'd do.

He nodded at her, then focused his attention back to Elizabeth. "You tell me. You got one more out in you?"

Her eyes widened. "Do you mean it? You're going to let me stay?"

"I'm asking you. If you tell me you can do this, I'll let you do it."

What else could he say? He hadn't seen her look this confident, this hopeful in how long? Way too long.

"I can!"

"All right then." He gripped her shoulder and squeezed. "Now listen up. This next girl likes to crowd the plate. You think you can throw a couple inside pitches? Maybe a little chin music?"

She smiled and Jack knew, whether they won or lost, it no longer mattered. Not any more.

Although, when Elizabeth threw those next pitches exactly like he'd asked (even if they weren't as fast) and the batter grounded out to second base, he changed his mind about the win.

A win felt damn good right now. He clapped and cheered right along with Laurie, and when the girls came in for their high-fives, Elizabeth was first.

"I did it, Dad!"

"Like I had any doubts." He winked at Laurie. After all, she'd been the one who pushed him to make the decision, and he was glad he had.

It wouldn't always turn out this way, but that was just another part of the game. Elizabeth—his daughter—had gone and done the rest herself.

The *Angels* huddled around each other and gave the other team a quick, good-game cheer, then lined up to high-five each other for a game well played. This was the sort of thing he hadn't done since little league, before he'd gotten serious with baseball.

It felt good to do it again, to do it here on this team.

He and Laurie hung in the back of the line, and when he motioned for her to go first, she shook her head. "This one was all you, Coach. You go first."

"I had help."

She smirked. "Not that much help except for calling pitches when you ran to the bathroom."

"First base coach, warming up Lacey, calming Suzie down when she popped one up to the catcher. I'm really grateful for that. I'm not too good with crying."

"You'll get better if you want to last on this team." But she smiled and held out her hand. "You're right, though. It was a team effort. Nicely done, Jack. I'm impressed."

He didn't take her hand. Instead, he leaned in closer. "Impressed enough that I passed the test? Am I one of your coaches?"

She lowered her hand, but didn't step back. "Yeah, I guess you are."

He didn't know if she was afraid to admit the truth or just afraid to say the truth aloud. But he was a coach—he was one of *her* coaches— and he wasn't planning on going anywhere.

That was just something she'd have to get used too.

"Impressed, huh? I'm glad to hear it. After all, that's what I was going for." He would have kissed her, would have shown her exactly what he was going for, except Elizabeth tugged on his shirt.

"Come on, Dad. You have to go shake hands. That's what the coaches do and you're a coach now."

Laurie laughed. "Whether I like it or not, I guess I can't exactly get rid of you now, can I? The girls would probably mutiny."

"That's right," Elizabeth chimed in. Then she frowned. "What's a mutiny?"

Jack spun her towards the line. "Never mind. Laurie's just ticked that I had such a good first day."

Elizabeth didn't get that either, but she shrugged and joined her teammates. Laurie, however, did understand and right before they reached the other coaches she leaned in.

"You did have a great first day. Thank you. You really did a great job with my girls."

He knew what she was thanking him for, that it was more than just winning the game. She was thanking him for the trust she'd placed in his care, a trust he knew wasn't easily given.

"You're welcome," he said.

Now, he was hoping she'd trust him with more. That she'd trust him with herself. That game, however, would be the World Series, not just softball, and it was one he planned on seeing to the final game.

The other team's head coach, Kent, cleared his throat. "Sorry to cut into this conversation." He stepped forward and shook Jack's hand. "Great game out there, Coach."

A firm grip, strong and challenging. Kent didn't hide the way his gaze flicked to Laurie, who stood beside Jack as she shook the other coach's hand.

Jack's good mood vanished.

Laurie stiffened beside him, as if she could feel Kent's eyes on her. It was slight, so slight that Kent didn't notice. Jack did. He noticed everything about Laurie, noticed the way her shoulders arched back, preparing to face Kent. Or punch him.

He'd been so focused on the game he hadn't thought much of the way Laurie had kept her distance from this team's coaches. She was always warm and friendly with other coaches, chatting with them both before the game and during.

Not this time. Jack had noticed, but he hadn't really *noticed*—not what it meant. He did now and he sure as hell didn't like it.

"Nice to meet you, Kent. Charles has mentioned you a few times."

None of them good. Jack smiled, knowing Kent would hear and know, Jack's unsaid message. But Laurie didn't need Jack to defend her. If the anger radiating off her was any indication, he knew damn well she could take care of herself.

Kent still hadn't let go of Jack's hand, as if that was showing his dominance. *Whatever.*

Jack was really hoping Laurie would lay Kent flat on his ass and end this ridiculous pissing contest. He'd been in his fair share of those; hard not to after playing ball with Barry, and compared to Barry, Kent was an amateur.

But if Jack had to bet on anyone winning this particular contest, it'd be Laurie. And if Kent was too stupid to figure that out, that was his issue, not Jack's.

"Not bad at all for your first time," Kent said, pulling Jack's attention away from Laurie. "The team really came together for you in the end."

Jack smiled right back, all white and shining teeth. The kind of smile that said, 'back off asshole.' "Might be my first time coaching, but I've been in my fair share of games."

"Of course."

Kent held Jack's grip for another moment, the barest tightening of his fingers. "How could any of us forget the star baseball player? But I've got to hand it to you, you managed to get this one here to play nice."

"I always play nice." Laurie turned from the other coach—Jack had already forgotten the short, mousey one's name—and gave Kent the same friendly handshake.

But there was nothing friendly about this handshake, at least, not from Kent and not from where Jack stood. Kent placed his other hand over hers, trapping her.

"I was planning on getting a bite to eat," Kent said. "It'd be great if you could join me."

Laurie's back straightened. She was definitely going to punch him. Jack knew because that was the same look she gave him right before she reached for her trusty bat.

"I have plans."

"Oh?" Kent's smile slipped.

"That's right. With Jack. It's a team tradition for the coaches to eat out after a game. There's a lot to talk about."

Jack's eyebrows lifted. He was pretty darn sure she and Hugh only ate out after the Sunday games, but, hey, this worked fine for him. He tucked his hands in his jean pockets, rocked back and smiled.

Who knew having a tough, softball goddess for a coach could be so entertaining? And to think about all those dinner dates he got out of the deal. More opportunities to end up in that hammock together...

Jack blinked, finally noticing the trickling of parents leaving the stands had slowed. Instead of collecting their kids and heading to their cars, they lingered by the fence watching and whispering (if that loud gossip could be called whispering).

"You know, one of these days you'll have to say yes and have dinner with me." Kent stroked Laurie's knuckle with his thumb.

Unfortunately, Kent didn't see the danger he was in, didn't realize he was the lowly number nine batter who never got to hit and was now facing the league's meanest, batter-hitting pitcher. Jack almost didn't stop her.

Almost.

It was Elizabeth waving at them that got him moving—not something he wanted his daughter to see, Laurie pounding the snot out of this guy. He slipped between them, yanking Laurie free just a bare second before she snapped off Kent's thumb.

"I gotta tell you, Kent, if I can't get a lady to say yes after the second or third time, I'm man enough to realize I've lost the game."

Kent swayed back, barely out of Laurie's furious reach, while Jack kept a firm grip on her.

"Stay out of this, Jack," Kent snapped. "She doesn't need you defending her."

"And let my coach beat the living snot out of you? In front of my team? And let's not forget all those nosy, vulture-gossiping parents."

Kent paled and Laurie finally stilled. Good. They finally realized they were standing in the middle of the field and gathering quite the audience.

"Right." Kent adjusted his uniform shirt and waved at his team, who'd stopped cleaning out the dugout to stare. "Anyway, I just wanted to say good job and all that. I thought we'd had it in the bag, but I wasn't expecting Elizabeth to toughen up. Didn't know she had it in her."

"You'd be surprised what she's capable of," Jack growled.

Now it was his turn to want to punch that condescending smile off Kent's face, but then Laurie was there, pressing her hand on Jack's shoulder.

It was a light touch, but enough to hold him back. He wasn't ready to think on why just yet.

"Elizabeth," Laurie whispered to him, just to him.

She turned to Kent and that other coach, who'd nearly backed into the dugout to get distance from them. "Well, gentleman," she said softly. "Now we've got all the parents and nearly two-dozen twelve-year old girls staring at us. Who wants to be the one to throw the first punch?"

Jack managed to push down his temper, just enough to flash her his most charming, Jack Evans smile ever. The kind of smile the photographers always loved and guys like Kent hated.

"Actually, I was kinda hoping it'd be you."

"Funny."

She smirked, taking the bite out of her voice, and he knew they'd be all right. They'd gotten through the games today and even Kent's little stunt hadn't changed the fact that they'd made a good team.

"We'll see you next weekend, Kent." Jack gave him the barest of nods before turning back to his team. His girls.

"You know," Laurie said as she caught up to him, "I'm the one who's supposed to be pissed off. It wasn't your hand he was stroking."

"That's the point. It was *your* hand."

And he really didn't like anyone but him touching—and definitely stroking—her hand. Or any part of her. Ever.

"Jack." She touched his shoulder, the same place she had earlier. "It's fine. Kent's just... jealous, I guess."

"How many times as he asked you to dinner?"

"Every game, but he usually isn't like this."

She rubbed her hand and tried to shrug it off, but he could tell it had shaken her. She didn't have to say that it'd felt like a violation, even if only a small one. He could see just by looking at her. He nearly stalked after Kent just to throw that punch.

"Just let it go, Jack. It's fine."

"It's not fine."

The team had gathered in right field, pulling off their cleats and socks, waiting for their team meeting. A handful of parents waited nearby, half to pick up their kids, the other half to hear what had happened with Kent.

"Look, let's just forget it okay?" Laurie asked. "Besides, you're the one who made it worse."

"And how did I do that?"

This time, Laurie blushed. Her cheeks turned into the delicate red color he enjoyed so much. Much better than the discomfort he'd seen moments ago.

"So," he murmured, "since we're having dinner tonight, mind telling me where I'm taking you?"

"I didn't, I mean I only said that so—"

"I don't care why you said it, only that you did and you're eating dinner with me tonight."

And tomorrow.

CHAPTER 30

*L*aurie should have said 'no' to dinner. The very second Jack pulled up with the top down on his Ferrari, she should have canceled, claimed she had a headache and needed rest.

Laurie glared as their waiter dropped the largest meat-and-vegetable-topped pizza on the menu (adeptly named *Joe's Special*) and couldn't decide who she hated more: Jack for roping her into this, Claire for telling him about her secret love of pizza, or herself for her inability to say no to pizza.

If only Jack hadn't suggested they go to *Joe's Pizzeria;* the second he did she knew she'd been outed.

He and Elizabeth leaned over the pizza and took a big, long whiff of the steam curling off the world's best pizza. Okay, maybe she wasn't being very fair. It was only half Jack's fault that she couldn't stop thinking about him; couldn't stop thinking about how well the day's games had gone.

Or how much she wanted to lean across the table and kiss him. *That* was why she should have said no. Because she wanted to kiss him; because she knew before he dropped her off at her car tonight, she would.

"Aren't you glad you came now?" he asked.

"I hate you." And then she served herself the two biggest slices, got one for Elizabeth, and then made Jack get his own. The jerk.

"Why do you hate my dad?" Elizabeth tilted her head, trying to stuff in as much pizza as possible into her mouth. "I thought you liked him."

"I do." That was the damn problem. "I hate him because he already knows how to bribe me."

And they'd only known each other for a handful of weeks.

A handful of weeks and she was already wondering how it would feel to have his hands running up her sides, to feel his skin sliding over hers.

Laurie shook her head. *Focus.* Daydreaming was not helping.

Jack smiled, that same lazy smile that said he knew exactly what she was thinking. She looked away.

She should have said 'no' because what she needed, more than anything, was space. Space away from Jack, space where his knees weren't brushing against hers. That when she turned it wasn't him she always saw, wasn't him that her gaze immediately searched for.

It also didn't help that she couldn't stop thinking about kissing him. All freakin' day. Well, at least after she'd realized he wasn't about to cause her team to spontaneously combust and explode when she handed the coaching reins to him.

Ugh. Laurie took a long swig of her beer.

Joe's had the usual crowd. As a favorite after-game hang-out for the teams, all the big tables were packed and it was hard to hear. Laurie didn't mind, mostly because she didn't have to listen, didn't need all her attention to focus on the girls.

Instead, tonight she could just kick back, enjoy her cold beer, and watch as the kids kicked up the wood shavings strewn across the floor. Elizabeth waved when Claire and Suzie pushed aside the swinging tavern doors and Laurie knew she'd been more than outed.

She'd been set up.

Before she could even take a breath, Elizabeth snagged another slice of pizza and ran off to sit next to Suzie. This, of course, left her and Jack. Alone, with their knees still brushing.

And then there was that smile of his.

"Did you plan this?"

"Me?" He asked, all innocent-like but he didn't fool her. Laurie had been coaching girls for years. She knew all the tricks.

She scowled at him. How did she get herself in this mess?

Not that it was a bad mess to be in, but it was one where she didn't have firm grounding, didn't know what the other team (in this case, Jack) was planning.

Jack slid across the booth, until his thigh was pressing against hers.

Shit. Laurie nearly fumbled her beer and spilled it in both their laps.

"Easy there, last I checked I hadn't bitten you."

Laurie blushed. Thinking about Jack and biting her...not good. "Look, I guess it's time we have this conversation, you know. About us."

"Okay. What should we talk about?"

Everything. "Jack. You're now a coach and—"

"First I was a parent and I took that concern off the table. Now you're making up another one." He leaned in. A strand of hair dangled just above his eyebrows, tantalizing, as if she should just reach up and brush it back.

"See," he murmured. "I'm pretty sure you're attracted to me and I'm sure as hell attracted to you. What's the problem?"

What was the problem? She had a hard time thinking with him leaning so close.

After all, hadn't she been wrong about him? Hadn't he proven that he could be a good coach and not just some parent who wanted to push his kid until softball became a job and not a game?

When she first met him, ex-pro baseball player and all, that was who she'd been expecting, not this caring father who gave up everything for his daughter.

"I..." She fiddled with her napkin, but Jack only touched her chin, drawing her to him.

"Tell me."

She was afraid to trust him. She'd barely trusted him with her team and now he wanted her to trust him with... well with *her*.

"What if this doesn't work out?" she blurted instead. "What if we give it a try and it doesn't work out? It's not just us involved. There's the team. There's Elizabeth."

Jack's face closed up, not much, but enough that Laurie realized one thing Jack hadn't mentioned.

"You haven't told her, have you? You haven't told Elizabeth. I care about her. She's... she's fragile and I don't want to be the one to break her."

"Thank you for that, but there's been nothing to tell. And I won't. Not until I know for sure there is something."

But there was something.

Man, there'd been sparks between them the first time they met— even if she had hated his guts.

"She loves you," Jack said. "She can't stop talking about you."

Laurie kept herself busy by eating another bite of pizza. It didn't taste as good as it usually did, but she figured that was her swirling stomach's fault and not the pizza's.

"She loves her mother," Laurie pointed out.

"Her mother doesn't give a shit about her."

"Fair enough, but that doesn't mean Elizabeth sees it that way."

They both knew she didn't. They both knew how much Nancy's attention meant to Elizabeth.

Laurie watched Elizabeth and Suzie played the old arcade machines and from what Laurie could see, Suzie had quite the gun hands at the zombie-shooter game.

Elizabeth's smile, her laugh, it was completely new. Neither had been there when Laurie first met her. Elizabeth was happy, and whether or not Laurie was afraid to admit it, she couldn't deny the truth. She was part of the reason Elizabeth was happy.

And Jack was part of the reason Laurie was happy, why she had looked forward to this weekend—even though her nerves were on overload worrying about their coaching chemistry.

Hugh had been right about giving Jack a chance on the field. Now maybe she needed to give him a chance with her heart.

Laurie set her pizza down. She hadn't felt like this since the last time she'd stepped onto the mound, the last time she'd pitched at her league's championship game. There was excitement mingled with the very obvious feeling of needing to throw-up.

Excitement and fear.

She looked up and met his eyes. "Okay, Jack. You promise me you'll talk to Elizabeth and promise me that no matter what, this doesn't affect the team."

"And? I can hear an 'and' in there."

"I need to know the truth, about you and Barry."

Calm, easy-going Jack disappeared the minute Barry's name slipped out. This was something Laurie needed to ask him, needed to understand. She didn't give Jack a chance to close up. She told him about her conversation with Barry and his warning.

"Whatever he said... do you believe him?"

She shook her head, but Jack's hand clamped down on hers.

"I need an answer."

A real answer, not a head shake. Again, she had no idea what had happened between these two men, but she'd be honest.

"I don't know. Not because I don't believe in you.. .but because I was scared he might be right. That you might take my team away from me."

His hands slipped free from hers. He didn't look at her. Instead, he focused on Elizabeth and Suzie, a frown darkening his face.

"And now?" he asked.

This was the real question, the real test whether or not this thing between them was real, and whether or not it'd go a step further.

"After today? No, I don't think you will."

A weight lifted from her chest. She couldn't tell how upset he was, if she'd ruined any chances of them being more than just coaches. But if that's what happened, well, that was the way it was meant to be.

"I think these girls mean a lot to you, and I don't think you're holding onto to your baseball past, trying to re-live it through them," she said.

Jack reached for his beer and took several long gulps, which made Laurie blink. She'd never seen him act like this before. Was he nervous? Had she said something (other than the obvious trust issue)?

"Barry's not totally wrong." Jack set the bottle down. "We played together, had fun together, swore we'd always play together no matter what. That's when my career took off. His was doing just fine, but..." Jack shrugged.

"It wasn't like yours," Laurie added. After all, Jack had gotten the 'Rookie of the Year' award. She could see how it had skyrocketed his career.

"Barry resented me for a long time; still does, if he warned you about me. I don't blame him either."

There was more to it than that, Laurie knew, but she didn't want to push.

From across the restaurant, Elizabeth yelped while Claire carefully handed out the next batch of quarters. Claire glanced at Laurie, sending a small smile and a nod.

Claire must have known she and Jack needed this talk. She'd have to find some way to thank her later.

"What did you mean," Laurie asked, "about Barry not being wrong? I've seen you with Elizabeth, heck I saw you coaching today."

Jack's smile tightened. "Part of me *is* still holding onto baseball, still longs for it. I wasn't a good person back then, and I did some pretty screwed-up things."

Laurie didn't ask. She had a feeling he'd tell her, but she didn't want to know. Truth was, she didn't need to know.

She placed her hand on his and their fingers curled together. "Do you think it'll get in the way? That it'll affect your coaching?"

"I work every day to make sure it doesn't." His gaze met hers. "I wouldn't hurt your team, Laurie. I know how much it means to you."

And like that, with this simple promise, she knew she could trust him—trust him with her team and more. If she was brave enough to let him.

That was the question, wasn't it?

How brave was she?

"Okay, then. That's what I needed to know. We'll give this a try—and I really hope I don't regret this."

As quickly as Jack had changed at her mention of Barry, he changed again. This time, though, the change sent shivers of pleasure rushing through her.

He leaned in. She felt his hand slide around her waist. She didn't even know when he'd moved it there, but she yearned to be closer, to be pressed against him.

She didn't move. They were, after all, in a restaurant.

And yet, he was only holding her and it felt... felt like so much more.

"Why would you regret this?" he asked.

With him so close, with him holding her like this, holding her in a way she couldn't remember the last time she'd been held, Laurie had no idea why she'd regret anything.

Except if he didn't kiss her right this moment, they were going to have some serious problems.

Screw it. Who said he had to kiss her?

Laurie closed the distance, pressed her lips against his and the rest of the world dropped away. The noise, the other teams, the wonderful pizza now growing cold.

None of it matter except Jack.

It was just a kiss.

A simple, light kiss.

Nothing like some of the ones they'd shared previously. And yet he felt wonderful. Just as she imagined every inch of him felt wonderful and perfect. And he probably was, the same perfect as the day he'd walked away from pro baseball.

All hard, lean muscle.

All from one light, delicate brush of their lips while Jack's arm circled her waist.

"Dad?"

Laurie and Jack bolted apart. Both their faces flushed as Elizabeth stared at them, eyes wide. She held her empty pizza plate in her hands.

How could she have forgotten? Was she so out of control that she could possibly forget his daughter?

Jack took a deep breath, but was careful not to look at Laurie. "Do you need another pizza?"

Elizabeth bit her bottom lip, then slowly set the plate down. "No. I'm not hungry."

And just like that, the hunted, unsure child Laurie had first seen was back.

"Jack," she whispered. "I'm sorry."

He shook his head and she could see the regret in his eyes. "I think we'll go home now. Can Claire give you a ride back to your car?"

"Sure." She'd take a cab if she had to. "I'll see you tomorrow."

Tomorrow. At the game. Laurie stifled a groan and smiled at Elizabeth, hoping to set the girl at ease but Elizabeth wouldn't look at her, wouldn't even glance in her direction.

Jack, though, did. There was definitely regret there as he handed her some cash for the food. Laurie held up her hand to stop him.

"No. It's okay. I got it."

He didn't argue for once, not when Elizabeth was already out the door. She could tell he wanted to say something, but they both knew there was nothing he could say. Not until he talked with Elizabeth.

"I'll see you tomorrow."

The second the swinging doors swung closed, Laurie buried her head in her hand. "Brilliant move, Laurie. Just brilliant."

Just because Jack was a coach didn't change the fact that he was still a parent. It didn't matter that for a few seconds she'd forgotten that; but the truth of the matter was, she had.

"Didn't go well?" Claire asked, sliding into the spot Jack had just left. "I'm sorry. I was hoping to keep them focused on the games."

"No, it was my fault. I should have known better."

Claire reached across and grabbed a slice of pizza. "Known better? You should have been kissing that man a lot sooner than tonight."

Laurie buried her head further. "I was."

"Oh." Even with her ears half covered she could hear the surprise in Claire's voice. "It's about time you found someone who excited you more than softball."

Laurie peeked through her hands. "I'm not excited about softball."

She wasn't. Hadn't been for years. Coaching was just something she did, something to pass on her knowledge.

Claire snorted.

Okay, maybe Claire had a point—even if it was only a small one.

Claire took a bite of the pizza. "Of course, maybe catching the two of you kissing wasn't the best way for Elizabeth to find out."

Laurie hid her head again and groaned. Boy, didn't she know that?

"I'm guessing you need a ride."

"That'd be great."

And then she'd figure out what the heck she was going to do tomorrow. Hopefully Jack would be a gentleman and give her a heads'-up if they were acting like nothing had happened—or if Elizabeth wanted to find a new team.

The thought sent a sharp, painful stab of fear through her. Elizabeth couldn't quit.

Laurie pressed a hand to her stomach. All this time, she'd wanted Jack gone—off her team and out of her life. Now if he left, she didn't know what she was going to do.

He couldn't leave. But he would. If that's what Elizabeth wanted, if leaving was best for Elizabeth, he'd do it.

So where did that leave Laurie? And did she even have a choice?

For the first time in years, Laurie realized just how lonely she was. A loneliness she hadn't known was there, not until Jack stepped into her life and filled it with something more.

CHAPTER 31

"*E*lizabeth!" Jack ran across the gravel parking lot, just a few steps behind Elizabeth as she darted to his car. "Wait up."

"Why?" She shot back over her shoulder. She yanked on the car's handle, but it was locked.

Jack slowed as he reached her. "So we can talk about this. Look, I…I handled that badly in there. I'm sorry."

She didn't turn around, not even when he was close enough to see her shoulders shaking. Crying.

Jack's stomach twisted. What had he been thinking? Kissing Laurie right in front of Elizabeth?

"Elizabeth. I'm sorry."

"Why? Why should you be sorry? You like Laurie."

He wanted to look at her, to get some idea what she was thinking —other than feeling hurt and betrayed. It was pretty damn clear he'd bungled this.

"I do like Laurie. I like her a lot, but that doesn't mean I can go around kissing just anybody. Not after it's been just us for so long."

'Us' because Nancy had refused to be part of their family. Laurie was right. He should have talked with Elizabeth long before he'd pursued any kind of relationship.

"Hey." He touched her shoulder, and when Elizabeth didn't pull away, he hugged her. "You don't need to cry. Your dad was an ass and I'm sorry."

She shook her head. "Mom's always got guys with her. I know she's... well she's... you know. You're not... you're not going to cheat on Laurie are you?"

That damn newspaper. Jack swore. "I'd never do that. Never."

"Because you like her."

"I do." He liked her a hell of a lot, a liking that had crept up on him faster than he'd expected. "Things with me were messed-up back then. I'm not that guy anymore, Elizabeth."

"I know." She rubbed her eyes and after a moment, turned around in his arms.

He hated that hurt look in her face, the red cheeks and red eyes. Hated that this time he was the cause, him and not Nancy.

"I hurt you," he said. "I'm sorry."

She bit her lip as if trying to keep anymore tears from falling. "I just, I just wanted mom... I just wanted us to be a family again."

Jack pulled her closer and rested his chin on her head. "I know, sweetheart. Your mother will always be your mother and no one is going to replace her. Ever."

"You mean it?"

"As long as you want."

Until Elizabeth finally realized Nancy wouldn't come around, until she realized there were other people out there who actually cared for her.

"I can try better too," he said. "I can be nicer. I can call her and invite her to the games."

"Really?"

"Yeah, really."

He pulled back and wiped at a tear before it fell off Elizabeth's nose. "We'll do our best to get your mother around more, but it's her choice to come or not. Fair?"

She nodded.

"Okay. And if you don't like me dating Laurie, then I won't. You come first. And," his stomach twisted. It wasn't fair to Laurie, but she had to understand—had to—that he was a father first, regardless of what he might be feeling for her.

"And," Jack said, "*if* you don't want to play on the *Angels* anymore, I understand. We can find you another team."

"No! You can't, Dad. I don't want another team."

"What about Laurie?" He couldn't get the words out *'Laurie and me.'* "You like her."

"It doesn't matter." He'd walked away from baseball, a sport he'd once loved for his daughter. He'd do it again. "You come first."

Elizabeth shook her head. "That's not fair. You like Laurie... and I like her, too."

He had no idea how much he needed to hear those words. "You're okay then? You're okay if I date her? Even if we're your coaches?"

"Yeah, I'm okay with it." She shuffled her shoe in the dirt, before smiling, still tentative and unsure, but at least it was a smile. "Plus, Lacey's going to be so jealous when I tell her tomorrow."

"Do you mind if I tell Lacey, first? Actually, do you mind if I tell Coach Laurie first?"

Elizabeth giggled. "That's probably a good idea. She's probably worried you already dumped her."

She would be, he knew, but she'd understand too. "That'll just make tomorrow an even bigger surprise."

Jack swung Elizabeth off her feet, his back only mildly protesting (after all, Elizabeth wasn't as small as she used to be) and plopped her into car without opening the door. She giggled. It was something they did all the time when she was smaller, but she'd never get too big for this. Not for this.

"What do you think Laurie's going to say when I tell her?"

"Yes, of course." Elizabeth sat all prim and proper in her seat as she buckled up. "And if she doesn't then I'm going to have to bench her or something."

"Good."

He kissed Elizabeth on the forehead and for the first time in a long time, Jack felt light on his feet. He hadn't completely screwed-up the dad thing, and Elizabeth wasn't mad at him.

Maybe Laurie had been right about him, maybe he wasn't a too bad of a father.

And somehow, he'd even told Laurie a small bit of his past and the person he was ashamed of being. He'd told her and she hadn't judged him. Even now, with him putting Elizabeth first, she understood.

Now he just had to continue convincing Laurie they could make this work. Oh, she'd use tonight as an example of why she couldn't date him, but he wasn't going to give her a chance to protest, not when he was damn sure he needed her in his life.

He would make this work. Because somehow, in these few weeks he'd known her, she'd become important to him.

CHAPTER 32

$\mathcal{L}$aurie paced up and down the dugout, rearranging the bats for the third time, unclipping and reclipping the line-up board. Nerves. Damn them. This was silly. She was acting silly. She had nothing to be nervous about.

Jack had called her, told her he'd talked to Elizabeth and everything was fine.

But it wasn't fine.

She knew better than to just kiss Jack, in public no less, and with his daughter right there. His daughter, who needed such a delicate touch and she'd nearly ruined everything.

All because of Jack. All because she couldn't see past him. Couldn't see past her own feelings.

She managed not to kick the ball bucket on her fourth pass, but only because last time she'd hurt her toe (and it was still smarting).

"You look a little nervous there, Coach." Laurie spun around, recognizing Hugh's voice instantly. He leaned in the dugout entrance, one hand braced on the fence.

"Hugh!" She gave him a hug, which he happily returned. "I was wondering when you'd show your ugly face."

"I had to give you and your new coach a chance to adjust. Don't need me leaning over your shoulder or anything." He pulled back. "You gonna tell me what's got you in such a tizzy?"

She snorted. "Your new coach, who else?"

"Oh? I heard the games yesterday went well."

"They, uh did."

"I see." Hugh rubbed his chin and gave her that all-knowing grin.

Why did he have to come by today? Why couldn't he have waited another week or two (*or maybe a month or two*) so she could figure things out between her and Jack?

"Does this mean it's going well?" Hugh asked. "Between you and Jack?"

"How should I know?" She shoved him out of her dugout. "He hasn't gotten here yet. And it's none of your damn business."

Her girls were already warming up in the outfield, throwing balls back and forth. Even Lacey was smiling.

"Stunning," Hugh murmured, catching where Laurie was looking. "I don't think I've ever seen that girl smile."

"Jack's been working with her. He said she's got a natural curve ball." Laurie had seen it, but with Lacey's temper, every attempt Laurie had made ended in absolute failure. She'd kept her distance, offering just a few nuggets of advice.

Sometimes Lacey would take them, handed out as carefully as they were; other times she didn't. Jack, though, couldn't say anything wrong. He was already Lacey's hero, as well as hero to more than a few girls (and mothers) on the team.

"You were right about him, you know. He's good with the girls."

Hugh nodded. "I thought he would be. He seemed to have that same drive you had. Different, but still the same. You sure you're all right?"

Laurie jerked her attention from the parking lot. "Fine. Why?"

"I've never seen you this distracted."

"Well, there's been a lot of changes going on."

"Like your new coach?"

"Yeah, like Jack."

And whether or not she and Jack were dating.

Laurie twisted the end of her ponytail around her finger. They shouldn't be dating. Last night was a clear enough indicator of that; she just needed to be man—or woman—enough to tell Jack.

"Ah, here's your long-lost coach now." Hugh pointed and Laurie forced herself to turn, nice and slow, like she only half-cared that Jack had finally managed to show up.

Then she saw him and she swallowed. He had his leather jacket on over his uniform shirt and he strode across the parking lot with the kind of purpose she instantly recognized. The kind that said he had something important to do and nothing was going to stand in his way.

Her stomach plummeted, but she forced herself to keep her head high, to keep all these swirling emotions locked away until she could be alone.

Hugh stepped forward and waved at Jack, but Jack merely nodded and then walked right past him, sweeping off his sunglasses with a single, perfect movement.

Laurie blinked. What the...?

She backed up a few steps before she realized she'd moved. Jack didn't stop, didn't break his stride until he stood in front of her.

With her back against the fence—when had she gotten there? All she could do was lift her chin and say good morning.

With his eyes shuttered like that, she couldn't get a read on him. Except for his intensity, which she could practically feel radiating off him in waves.

"Jack?"

"I told you that Elizabeth and I talked last night, but I didn't tell you what we talked about."

What?

"I thought in person was better."

"Oh."

And this, then, was the part where he broke up with her, which was silly since they hadn't actually been dating so she shouldn't be upset because it was just attraction and...

Laurie found herself nodding. "Of course, I understand."

Elizabeth poked her head around Jack. Laurie had no idea where she'd come from. But strangely enough, Elizabeth didn't seem upset, not in the least, not with that giant smirk on her face.

"You're right, Dad. I don't think she gets it."

Laurie's head spun. She glanced back and forth between the two. *What was going on? Didn't Elizabeth not want them to be together?*

"No," he agreed. "I don't think so either."

"So?" Elizabeth asked. "Aren't you going to kiss her already?"

Laurie blinked. "Excuse me? I thought, I mean..."

"A kiss," Jack said, "is a fantastic idea."

Then, before she could twist away, stammer any kind of protest, or just have a second to get her head on straight, Jack grabbed yanked Laurie towards him.

She flattened against his hard chest and that solid wall of muscle—still perfect from his baseball days—didn't move. His mouth, though, did, thoroughly claiming her mouth, and her complete attention.

She barely heard the cheering girls or the clapping or the who-the-heck-cared—all that mattered was Jack and his amazing kiss. Her arms wrapped around his neck even as his circled around her waist.

He held her as if he'd never let go.

Jack easily picked her up and spun her towards her girls.

Laurie pulled away, laughing. "Is that your answer, then? You're not leaving?"

Part of her had thought, had feared, he'd leave. That she'd be alone again.

"My answer, Elizabeth's, and I hope yours as well. I promise, we're not going anywhere."

What could she say to that? She pressed her forehead against his as he set her on the ground. "You think we can make this work?"

"Would I have kissed you otherwise?"

Laurie lifted her eyebrows. "Yes."

Jack laughed. "Got me there, but yes, I think we can. I'm willing to try anyway."

That was all she could ask for. She'd try, too. She trusted him with her team and now she'd trusted him with a lot more—she'd trust him with herself.

"Come on you two." Elizabeth tugged on Laurie's shirt. "We have a game after all. Sheesh. You'd think you never kissed a boy before or something?"

Elizabeth, however, wasn't the only one smiling. They had drawn quite the crowd, especially for an eight o'clock game. All the parents, the two field umpires, heck, even Charles seemed to be hanging around, watching.

That's when Hugh gave her the double-thumbs up. That sneak had known this would happen from the beginning!

But how could she blame him for trying to make her happy, even after all these years? She sent him a silent thank-you.

Laurie released Jack and tossed a ball to Elizabeth. "For the record, your dad is definitely *not* a boy. Now, go warm up. And be sure to tell your *dad* you were late to warm-ups again."

"Sure thing." Elizabeth grinned and then took off to join her teammates.

Jack leaned in. "Late?"

"You were both late."

"Glad to see you noticed." He held her gaze again.

As if she wouldn't have noticed.

She slapped his hand away even as it crept back around her waist. "I've got work to do and you, don't you pull that 'making me wait' on me again. That wasn't fair."

Jack raised his hands in surrender. "Whatever you say, Coach."

That's right, they were coaches and they were coaching Laurie's *Angels*. This time, when she stepped onto the field to shake the umpire's hands, getting ready for the coin toss to see who batted first, Laurie wasn't worried about what would happen next, if she and Jack would work out - both as coaches and as something more.

For now they had a game to play and a lot of fun to have.

CHAPTER 33

"You sure you don't want to join me?" Jack swayed back and forth in the hammock, relaxed, and enjoying the cool, summer evening. He causally sipped his beer, watching as Laurie came onto the porch, score-book in hand.

As if there was anything causal about that comment. Or the way his eyes darkened.

Laurie placed her hands on her hips. "You're not getting me near that thing."

"Suit yourself."

The weeks had flown by and they were already halfway through the summer season. She couldn't remember a season going by so quickly, but then again she hadn't ever dated her co-coach either. That probably had something to do with how eagerly she looked forward to games and practices.

She even found herself scheduling extra practices, just so she could have an excuse to see Jack—then immediately discarded the idea. After all, if she wanted to see Jack, she could just pick up the phone and call.

He took another sip, his mouth tilting in that teasing way she couldn't help but notice, couldn't help but want to lean in and kiss him.

Something she'd been wanting to do all day.

She shook her head. "No kissing right now."

"You sure?" Again, there was that little tilt.

"Nice try. We have work to do."

She pulled up one of the lawn chairs (as if something that had as many cushions as her couch could be called a lawn chair) and flipped open the team's score book.

"You weren't kidding about work." He smiled at her, nice and lazy-like, then closed his eyes and rocked back and forth in the hammock. "What happened to having fun on this team? Coaches need to have fun too, you know."

She grabbed his beer and when he protested, tossed him the score book. "The sooner we can focus, the sooner we can get done."

And have fun.

"Good," he said, "because I'd much rather be focused on you."

Jack waited long enough for her to put the beer down and when she leaned over to show him the near double-play the girls had almost pulled off in the second inning, he grabbed her hand and pulled him onto his lap.

Into the hammock.

"Jack!"

That was all she could get out, because then there were his lips and *oh, my he felt so good.* Her hands slid down his chest as if they had a mind of her own. Her hips surely did.

All it took was feeling his long body underneath hers and all good sense flew out the window.

What the hell, hadn't she been wanting to do this all day? All yesterday too?

He didn't stop his kissing until she was curled against him, tossing the score book onto the deck.

"That's much better," he murmured.

"For us, yeah, but not the team."

"The team can wait." He kissed her again and she moaned. "What do you always say about having fun? This, I think is way more fun."

She had to agree with him. Completely.

Jack fiddled with the end of her shirt, then slowly slid his hands up her back. She shivered.

"Jack," she whispered.

Every inch of her ached, needed to be touched, needed more of him. This was usually the point she reminded him about Elizabeth and that they should slow down.

They'd agreed on moving slow. Elizabeth might be okay with them dating, but Laurie spending the night was another issue.

But she was damn tired of slowing down, damn tired of being the responsible one. And as much as she'd enjoyed these past few weeks, of figuring out how to be a couple and coach at the same time, it was also complete agony.

Why?

Because waiting sucked.

Jack's hand stilled and he tensed under her. She pulled back, thinking this time she'd been the one who'd gone too far, but then her eyes met his and knew that was the last thing on his mind.

No, right now he wanted the same thing she did.

His hips lifted and lightly touched against her, the hard length of him—she swallowed. Yes, she was ready for this.

"Jack." Part moan, part plea.

The sliding glass door opened, and then slid closed. Laurie closed her eyes and allowed herself an internal groan. She thought Elizabeth was in bed, or, if not asleep, at least in her room watching movies or something.

She moved off Jack, glimpsed the four inch stiletto heels tapping on the deck, and froze. Nancy.

Didn't the woman knock? And why the hell had Jack given her a key?

"Oh, I seem to be interrupting."

"Damn it, Nancy." Jack shifted Laurie off him, but he wasn't trying to hide her or the very distinct bulge in his pants.

Nancy's gaze flicked down. "My, I see the rumors are indeed true. You're dating, how cute. Elizabeth told me, you know, but I guess I just didn't believe it. But then, you are a much different man than the one I married, aren't you?"

"Better believe it," Jack snapped. "A better man."

Nancy crossed her arms over her busty, nearly spilling- out dress. Laurie hadn't a clue how she managed to get that skinny, tight thing on to begin with.

"Maybe I should have invited Barry over."

Laurie bit her tongue to keep from saying anything she'd regret. Not that she'd regret anything she said, just that Jack might. This woman, this slutty, harpy of a woman was Elizabeth's mother. Not that she deserved a great kid like Elizabeth.

"Nancy," Laurie gave her best smile. "Good to see you."

"I'm sure you're just thrilled to see me." Nancy flicked her blazing red fingernails at Jack. "Where's Elizabeth? You always complain to me about displaying intimacy in front of her and here you are."

"She's in her room. And I don't have problems with you kissing your male friends around Elizabeth," Jack said. "It's when you can't keep your damn clothes on."

Nancy lifted her eyebrows. "Who I sleep with isn't our daughter's business."

"It is when you flaunt it front of her."

Jack got out of the hammock, somehow managing the feat and thankfully not overturning Laurie in the process. She really hoped this was the last time she'd be caught in a damn hammock by Nancy.

"Now," Jack said, "is there something you need other than wanting to meet the woman I'm dating. Again."

"Hmph. You called me, remember?"

"And you never returned my calls."

Laurie scrambled out of the hammock. This was definitely the time when she said goodnight. She couldn't always run from Nancy, but things between her and Jack were still so new, so unsure. Right now, he needed to get his own life straight before she butted her nose in.

But if Nancy glared at her one more time in that know-it-all kind of way, all bets were off. Laurie was going to toss her and that pretty little dress into the damn pool.

"I think I should go and let you two work this out," Laurie said.

"No." Jack shook his head. "You don't have to leave just because she showed up."

"I thought that's what you've been wanting me to do?" Nancy purred. "Spend some time with Elizabeth?"

"You didn't come here to spend time with Elizabeth and we both know it."

Laurie had enough. "Elizabeth. Boy, isn't that nice of you both to think of her? I'm sure she just wants to come downstairs and overhear you arguing. Again."

It hadn't taken Laurie long to figure out just how this relationship turned sour. Nancy really didn't hide who she was, and what her priorities were. She wanted the fame and fortune, but she hadn't wanted the daughter.

Jack, however, had.

It only made her opinions of him rise even more, but he sometimes had a hard time seeing through the red haze Nancy seemed to carry around like perfume.

Even now, she still got to Jack.

"Elizabeth is still up," Laurie said. "I'll see how she's doing and say goodnight. If you're not finished by then, we'll catch up later."

Laurie gave Nancy a barely tolerable smile and made sure to shut the sliding doors all the way. While she was upstairs, she'd make sure Elizabeth's bedroom window was shut, too.

So much for her plan of a productive evening working on team strategy and picking Jack's amazingly knowledgeable brain about tactics. Or, so much for Jack's plan of a romantic evening—one that Laurie could tell had included her staying over.

"Not going to happen tonight," Laurie muttered as she knocked on Elizabeth's door. The least she could do was keep Elizabeth occupied until the flames died down.

Even if it meant she was going to spend the night alone. Again.

'Going slow' in a relationship, especially one that involved Jack, really sucked.

CHAPTER 34

The second Laurie closed the sliding door, Jack spun towards Nancy. "What the hell are you doing here?"

"Good to see some things never change, like your temper."

"The only person I ever had a temper with was you, which we both know you deserved." Even now. "I'm not going to ask again. What are you doing here?"

She waved her hand, dismissing him as if he were a child. "I'd hoped to ruin your nice little romantic evening. Elizabeth said you and *Coach* Laurie always have dinner after your games. Looks like I still have a little bit of luck on my side."

Jack forced himself to swallow his anger. It didn't help that he'd just shared a look with Laurie, the look he'd been waiting for. The trusting look, the one that said she'd stay the night—stay the whole night.

He ran a hand through his hair. What the hell had he been thinking marrying this woman? Being young wasn't an excuse for being completely stupid.

"Is this how it's going to be?" he asked. "Are you going to come over every week and try your best to ruin my happiness? Elizabeth's?"

Nancy frowned at the paper-plates on the table, the leftover pizza box and half-finished beer. "Why not? After all, you ruined my happiness. It seems only fair."

She knelt down and picked up the score-book. Her dress barely covered her ass.

Jack snatched the book from her. "Fair? You had the perfect life. The only thing you had to do was take care of Elizabeth. It's not my fault you couldn't do the job."

"You were the one who got to travel. Who went to all those fancy restaurants, who had all those women all over you." Nancy stabbed his chest with her finger.

Damn nails must be made of cement. She probably filed them too, making them as sharp as possible. He wouldn't put it past her.

"You had fun." Nancy stabbed again. "You had the life, and I had to stay home with a whining baby who never stopped crying. And then you walked away from it and left me in the cold."

Jack pushed her hand away. "How many millions did I leave you with? I hardly count that being left in the cold."

"You might as well have. I lost everything when you gave up baseball."

"You're forgetting who sold those pictures to every tabloid on the stands."

"That was only to get your attention."

"Yeah, well it worked."

"You're so cruel. You were supposed to forgive me." She sniffled and pulled out an embroidered silk handkerchief from her cleavage.

Gee, came prepared did she?

When she realized the act wasn't working, Nancy threw down her handkerchief. "Oh, screw you, Jack. Both you and your new little friend."

"No problem. Now, why don't you tell me what the hell you're doing here so we can both get on with our lives?"

"I already told you," Nancy snapped. "I want my old life back, but thanks to you that can never happen. So. You want to be happy with your new girlfriend, you want Elizabeth to replace her mother?"

"Yes."

Nancy tugged down her dress, revealing even more cleavage, not that it surprised Jack. She had more cleavage than some of the boob-jobs he'd seen in his baseball days.

"Well, that's not going to happen. You ruined my chance of happiness and now I'll repay the favor in kind."

He didn't trust her smile. He didn't trust that Nancy would only strike at him, that she wouldn't leave Elizabeth out of it.

That wasn't Nancy's style, never had been. She played for keeps and the second she stepped up to plate, she was batting for blood. Elizabeth definitely wasn't safe.

"If you hurt Elizabeth..."

"What about your little girlfriend? Aren't you worried about seeing her hurt?"

"Laurie can take care of herself, and trust me, if you want to tangle with her and she flattens you, that's your problem. I'll cheer her on the whole way."

Nancy's smile only sweetened. "I wouldn't think of hurting either of them, dearest. Not that I'll need to do anything."

She swayed her hips forward, bumping him out of her way. "You'll do it all on your own. You'll screw up. You'll fail at what you wanted to be most. A father. And then when Elizabeth realizes her father cares more about the woman sleeping in his bed than her, who do you think she'll come too?"

"I have no intention of failing."

Or of letting Elizabeth feel that way.

He wouldn't stop being a good father. No, with Elizabeth smiling and confident, he'd fight Nancy every step of the way.

Nancy slid open the glass doors. "You failed at baseball and your marriage. If you'd been a stronger person you'd never have gotten caught up in the drugs, in the alcohol. What makes you say you won't fail at this? That you won't just give up when it gets too hard?"

She didn't give him a chance to respond, snapping the door closed as she left as quietly as she'd come. Not bothering, of course, to see Elizabeth.

"I won't fail. And I'll do everything it takes to show you."

He grabbed the empty pizza boxes and went into the house, locking the door behind him. When he turned he saw Laurie lingering on the stairs, one hand on the banister as if she wasn't sure whether she should be there or not.

His anger at Nancy, at himself for letting her get to him—once again—wouldn't leave him.

"I'm sorry about that."

"It's not your fault. She's not making this easy for you."

"No. And she won't."

Laurie nodded as if she expected nothing less. He had to admire her for that, for standing up to the mean, vindictive woman he'd been married to.

"I'm not making this any easier," she said. "And I'm sorry."

"It's fine." He tossed the boxes into the trashcan. "She would have acted this way regardless of who it was."

"I see. You mean, any woman who you brought home?"

Jack glanced at her, watched as her eyes shuddered, closed off from him. "Damn it, Laurie. I didn't mean it that way."

"Damn? First time you've ever swore at me, Jack." She crossed her arms in that same way Nancy had.

"That is not what I meant." He strode the short distance between them. "You're the first woman I've been with since the divorce; and yes, I've had plenty of chances to bring women home. Lots of women."

"That's really not making me feel better."

What the hell was it with this strong woman and her not listening to him?

"It *should* make you feel better," he said, "because you're the only one I can't stop thinking about."

He circled his arms around her and pulled her towards him. She fell easily to him, not resisting. For a brief moment, the smell of Laurie surrounded him. Her smiles, her laughter, the joy she'd so easily and so quickly brought into their lives.

And with one swoop Nancy was threatening to take that all away. He wouldn't let her.

"You're the only one I don't want to stop thinking about," Jack whispered.

Laurie's face softened. "Jack, I'm—"

"Don't apologize. She gets to everyone, and she sure as hell gets to me. Don't ever apologize for her." He leaned his forehead against hers. "And don't let her ruin such an amazing night."

"Amazing?" Laurie smiled. "I thought I was going to pick your brain about strategy."

"And I thought I was going to pick your clothes off."

He kissed her, the same way he'd kissed her in the hammock but this time he gave more of himself, showed her just how much he needed her.

"Don't let her ruin this," Jack breathed against her lips. "Stay."

He felt her shake underneath him. He had no idea if it was a good shake or a bad one. He couldn't bear the thought that it wasn't a good one.

They could figure out the rest tomorrow, and he'd figure out how to be the amazing dad he needed to be for Elizabeth. And for Laurie.

"Stay the night," he breathed again.

Laurie lifted her head. Her eyes met his. She didn't look away, didn't hide from his need, or in this moment, the weakness he knew he wasn't hiding.

With Nancy, he'd always had to hide. From everything, from joy to happiness to fear. Everything except anger. And right now he needed joy.

Laurie lifted up, standing on her toes. She kissed him lightly, so light her lips barely brushed his. "Yes, I'll stay."

CHAPTER 35

*L*aurie stretched her bare arms above her head. Sunlight drifted in through the open window, seeming to light Jack's simple, yet elegant bedroom in a perfect, after-morning glow.

Perfect. Just like last night had been. Even with the Nancy interruption.

Laurie rolled onto her stomach and came face to face with a very glorious, very handsomely naked Jack Evans. She smiled.

"Sleep well?" he asked as he ran his hand down her back. Even now, even after last night, his touch still sent shivers through her.

"I don't think I ever slept so well in my life."

"I'm glad." He kissed her, long and lingering and more than her brain started to wake up.

She pulled away. "I didn't say it had anything to do with last night. This bed is fantastic."

Truly it was the most cushiony, comfortable bed she'd ever slept on. And silk sheets? Oh, yes, she definitely wanted a pair of her own.

"So you're saying you'll come over just to sleep in my bed? It has nothing to do with me?"

"That's right."

He slid on top of her and Laurie's eyes widened when she felt his hard length press against her. He gently kissed her forehead and then her cheek. "I guess I'll have to convince you otherwise."

"I guess."

Laurie was really glad they had a late game today. No eight o'clock game start. No, this time their eight o'clock morning began right here.

And somehow, even after their hurried breakfast and Elizabeth complaining about having a Pop-Tart for breakfast (though she complained with a complete smile on her face), they even made it to the field on time.

Actually, they were a tad late and that was because Jack didn't seem to understand all the softball gear wouldn't fit in his Ferrari. So, after some hassling that took Elizabeth making her dad shut up other-wise she and both their coaches would be late, they finally managed to squeeze everything into his tiny sports car and drive off.

Jack pulled into the unusually packed parking lot. Most Sunday games were slower, more relaxed compared to the Saturday crowd. Laurie got out and slid the seat forward for Elizabeth.

That's when she noticed the sleek black car parked at the front, the car with quite the crowd hanging around it. Like Jack's car, it was the kind you couldn't forget—and Laurie definitely couldn't forget this one.

Not that she had any idea what kind of car it actually was, just that it cost a ton of money. More money than even Jack had sitting around.

Barry White. Shit. Nancy hadn't been kidding when she'd told Jack she wanted to ruin his life.

So, the woman failed at ruining their amazing night, so now she was trying to ruin their games? Elizabeth's mother or not, that woman deserved to be thrown into the batting cage without a helmet and the machine cranked up to maximum speed.

She nodded towards the car, hoping Elizabeth wouldn't notice. "We have guests today."

He followed her nod and his eyes narrowed. "Shit."

"Yeah." Shit was right. "You tell me how you want to handle this."

Elizabeth got out. "Handle what?"

It was easy to forget Elizabeth was there sometimes, she was always so quiet—but Laurie had no doubt about her sharp mind. It took her a whole two seconds to notice the car and to realize what it meant.

"Really?" Elizabeth asked, almost not daring to hope. "Do you think Mom's here?"

"I don't know." Jack slammed his door closed. "She might be. Hey, hold it, Missy. Don't you have to warm-up?"

Elizabeth paused mid-step. Laurie could see every inch of her wanted to run towards the crowd, towards Barry. Laurie grabbed Elizabeth's bat bag from the backseat, swinging it on top of her own.

The extra weight helped her focus, helped her rein in her temper. "Come on. I think our team's waiting for us."

Elizabeth paused, torn between searching for her mother and her team.

"Besides," Laurie said, "I think I already see Lacey warming up. Must be her turn to start, right Jack?"

"No. It's my turn."

Laurie gave Elizabeth a long look. "I thought you wanted to find your mom?"

Elizabeth grumbled. "I'm going, I'm going."

There, Laurie thought to herself, that wasn't too bad. She turned, hoping to share her pleasure with Jack but his scowl knocked her smile right off.

No, he wasn't pleased about this. Not at all.

"Hey," she whispered.

He didn't move, didn't tear his gaze off the crowd. "Will you see the team warmed up?"

"Sure. Do you want to start Elizabeth? It *is* her turn."

Jack's mouth pinched. "No. Start Lacey."

And like that, she felt the man she'd spent the night with pulling away from her. As if the Jack she'd known all these weeks was disappearing, turning into someone else—someone angry and frustrated.

Before he could move away, most likely to hunt for Nancy and Barry, Laurie gently touched his shoulder. This time he stopped.

"She'll have to pitch in front of her mom at some point," Laurie said.

"I'm hoping her mom won't stick around long enough."

"You're not in this alone, you know."

He squeezed her hand. "I know."

Laurie leaned in to kiss him, tender and gentle to show him that she did care, and that no matter what happened with Nancy, she was there for him. And for Elizabeth, too.

That's when the camera's snapped.

Laurie jerked back, but Jack was already there, already pushing her behind him. There were a half dozen cameraman and reporters, but from the noise and the way their words jumbled together it sounded like there were three dozen.

Who were these people? And why were they at her field?

"Jack!" The nearest guy shoved a microphone into Jack's face. "Is it true you and Barry White have made up after all these years? Have you resumed your friendship with the famous baseball player?"

Jack's grip on Laurie's arm didn't loosen. He held her to him, but she didn't know if he was shielding her or if it was the other way around.

"I have no comment." Voice, low and dangerous, Laurie didn't recognize it from the man she'd spent the evening with—and the morning.

"Jack? What's going on?"

As if her speaking was all the permission they needed, the cameras descended on her.

"Who are you?"

"What's your relationship with the former Major League All-Star baseball player, Jack Evans?"

She could barely see with all the flashing lights and the microphones shoved at her. "It's none of your damn business. That's what it is."

And reporters or not, she was going to shove them aside and use them for batting practice if they didn't get out of her face.

Now.

"What she means is 'no comment.'" Still holding onto Laurie's arm, Jack shoved his way past the reporters and photographers.

"God-damned Nancy," Jack growled, low so the cameras didn't pick it up.

"Is this her doing?"

His gaze flicked to her. "It's not the first time she's set me up. They probably got quite a few photos of us."

Laurie tugged her hand free. She didn't need to be dragged around like a child. "Gee, I didn't realize kissing in public was news-worthy material."

Jack stopped. Laurie stopped beside him.

"It is," he said, slowly, eyes shuttered. "It is if you're kissing *me*."

She knew what he meant. The photos in the newspaper, the article about his fall into drugs and women.

"Jack. You know that's not what I meant."

He shook himself. "I know. I just, I just wasn't expecting this. Not again. I need to find Barry and Nancy. You'll take care of the girls?"

What about you? she wanted to ask.

She didn't.

Laurie let him go even though she had a feeling this was a bad idea. The way he practically stormed towards the crowd—the place Barry probably was. He was ready for a fight.

Laurie had no doubt he'd get one.

She shifted the bags on her shoulder. No matter what happened, she'd see her girls through today—and through every game Nancy decided to grace her presence with. And Elizabeth. And Jack.

They would get through this. Together.

Her life, this team, everything was finally falling into place and she wasn't about to let Nancy ruin this. Not when Laurie's happiness, and her team's, were on the line. No freakin' way would Laurie let her.

CHAPTER 36

It wasn't hard to find Barry. All Jack had to do was follow the crowd.

What was hard was getting through the legion of dads and baseball fans, the mothers who dug in their purses for pens and scraps of paper. One even proudly produced a rumpled up grocery receipt for Barry to sign.

Jack pushed his way through, cursing his luck that Barry wasn't out of town at an away game this weekend.

Eventually he made it through and found Barry lounging in the stands—the *Angels'* stands—talking with good ol' Charles. Oh, not to mention the second, larger group of reporters who were managing to hold their tongue while Barry had his conversation.

That was one good thing about Barry, his temper. Also that he was so much bigger than everyone else. Even the reporters backed off when he told them to.

To a certain distance, anyway.

As he got closer, Jack heard Barry's deep, rumbling voice while Charles nodded and scribbled in his notebook.

"I've seen the kid play," Barry said. "Good speed, good attitude, but I'm not sure she'll pan out. Kind of like her dad that way."

A reporter butted his nose in. "Is that true Mr. White? But I'd heard that you and Jack Evans had patched up your falling out?"

Barry flashed his sparkling white teeth. "I only call it like I see it."

Jack ground his teeth and nearly ran over a small boy who darted in front of him.

"Is that so?" Charles asked. "Interesting. What makes you assume this?"

"Same spark, same talent." Barry shrugged. "You play ball long enough you recognize talent for what it is and you recognize those who have the balls to stick it through to the end."

Charles made another scratch in his notebook. "I never thought of Jack's career that way."

"Trust me," Barry said. "I have and so has he. I can guarantee you he's regretted it every day of his life."

"Actually," Jack said, unable to keep his mouth shut any longer, "the only thing I regret is my marriage—since I got Elizabeth out of the deal, I can hardly say that, now can I?"

Charles jumped to attention and the reporters, sensing blood, whipped their cameras and microphones at Jack.

"Jack! Do you have any comments about repairing your friendship with Barry White?"

"It's the first I've heard of it. Unless you count the reporters who mentioned it when I got out of my car." He kept his smile on, as easy as it always was, putting forward a good face for the cameras.

It didn't feel like it'd been four years ago. It felt like yesterday.

Barry merely glanced over his shoulder. "Morning, Jack. Heard you had a good night."

"I'm guessing you did too, seeing as you're here nice and early."

Barry always hated morning games. Always.

Barry's eyes narrowed, but then he shrugged. "What can I say, I'm a changed man? Or maybe I just had a fantastic reason to get up early, like watching your kid play."

Jack stepped forward. He felt the crowd gathering close, trying to listen in or get a better view. He didn't give a shit, not when Barry was trying to harm his daughter.

"Funny," Jack said, "this will be the first time you've watched her play, and already you're giving my friend Charles here the inside scoop?"

"I don't need to see her play," Barry said. "I've seen you play. That's good enough for me."

Charles fumbled with his notebook. "Ah, gentleman, I do appreciate your insight but I assure you I've made quite a few of my own observations and—"

"Good," Jack said. "Especially since Elizabeth is only twelve and has quite a few years before she needs to worry about college. She's here to have fun. You remember what that's like, right, Barry?"

He knew the cameras were recording every word and they better be sure to quote him right. That's right, he thought, spoiling all your plans Charles.

Let the world know what these college scouts were stooping to.

Barry's eyes narrowed, but before he could reply, a familiar manicured hand touched Barry's shoulder, pulling him back from the cliff he was about to run steaming off of.

"Good morning, Jack." Nancy slipped between Charles and Barry before giving Jack her most radiant smile, a smile she never wore honestly this early in the morning. She turned that smile, very purposefully, towards the cameras.

They loved it, of course.

"Surprised to see me?" she asked Jack.

"Not at all." Not after her threat last night. "Elizabeth is looking for you."

"Oh, isn't that nice? Maybe I'll just have to go over and give her a kiss. If, of course, that's all right with you, Coach?" Nancy batted her eyes and Jack just wanted to throw-up.

He'd thought it'd be easier than this. He hoped it would be.

"I'll walk you over. I have to get to the team anyway." Jack swept his arm out in front of him. "Besides, Mr. White has a few eager fans waiting for him to grace them with his presence. And maybe a comment or two for our friendly reporters."

The ploy worked well enough. Barry loved attention and Nancy loved making Jack feel miserable. So Barry did his celebrity thing—the thing Jack had always hated—while he walked with Nancy across the suddenly long distance to left field where Laurie was warming the girls up.

"So, she stayed the night?" Nancy slipped her arm into Jack's.

"It's none of your business."

"You do have a look about you, you know, the 'after you get laid' look. There's a glow about you."

She leaned closer and he felt her breath on his neck. He clenched his fists—and it was the only thing that kept him from flinging her away.

"And there's that walk of course. That confident, 'I-just-made-a-woman-come-madly' walk." She nodded towards his legs. "And with that little spring I'm betting you got lucky this morning too."

"I told you," he growled.

"I know, I know. It's none of my business." Nancy tucked a stray curl behind her ear. "How did Elizabeth take it?"

"Fine."

And that was all he was going to say about it.

"Be that way," Nancy said. "I'll just have to ask her. You do know I'll be coming by more, right? So maybe you should be more careful exactly where you plan on sleeping with your girlfriend."

"Nancy."

"No, I promise I won't go into your bedroom, but honestly, other areas should be off-limits just in case Elizabeth were to walk in. Like the kitchen counter; or that little, fluffy rug by the fireplace. I know how much you liked that spot."

Jack dug his shoes into the soft ground. "I thought you wanted to say hello to Elizabeth. If I'd known you wanted to rehash the places where we had sex during our very short marriage, then I'll take you back to Barry. You can do it in front of the cameras. They'd like that."

Nancy pouted. "That's not very nice of you."

"Well, you're not a nice person, yourself."

Laurie, he noticed, hadn't wasted any time getting the girls moving. They may have been a few minutes later than normal, but the girls were already through with stretching and Laurie had started their running drills.

Elizabeth was at the head of the pack. He could tell she was putting even more energy into it, could see the way she'd glance at him and Nancy, and then quickly look the other way.

Nancy noticed his gaze and hummed thoughtfully. "She does have your speed."

It was more than that. She had the kind of heart and love of the game he'd lost not long after he'd realized just how good he was. And the kind of Major League opportunities waiting for him.

"She's got more than my speed. And I don't appreciate Barry badmouthing about her. Tell him to stop, Nancy. I mean it."

She blinked up at him, confused at first, then thoughtful. "I'll talk with him."

"She's got a lot of talent," he said. "You may not like Laurie and that's fine, but Elizabeth does and thanks to Laurie, she's already getting her confidence back."

"Isn't that sweet? Defending your girlfriend against the wicked witch."

"Hardly." Jack smirked. "I'm just asking you not to screw it up. Elizabeth's working hard and I don't want either of us—you or me— taking that smile away from her."

Nancy's eyes narrowed, and he thought he saw a flicker then. Not kindness exactly, and definitely not understanding. The only thing Nancy was capable of 'understanding' was money and what was in it for her.

"I promise. I'll play nice, but only if you play nice to that lovely scout, Charles."

Jack was ready to get this over with, but her words stopped him cold. "What about Charles?"

"Didn't you hear him talking to Barry?"

He had, but not only hadn't he liked what he'd heard, he'd also dismissed it. Elizabeth was only twelve; college ball was a long, long way off.

Nancy shrugged as if it was no big deal herself, but Jack felt her hooks digging into him.

"Charles has his eye on Elizabeth. Weren't you the one who always told me there was a future for Elizabeth and women's softball?"

"Elizabeth, isn't a woman. She's twelve."

"Like Barry said, it's best to start training them up early. I'll bet by the end of the game Barry will have already convinced Charles to hold a spot for Elizabeth, even if her senior year is a long way off."

Nancy gave him cunning smile and released Jack's arm, calling out to Elizabeth, who immediately broke away from the group. She ran towards Nancy, arms wide and the biggest smile he'd seen in a long while.

It was a smile Elizabeth reserved only for her mother, even if her mother never deserved it.

Nancy turned towards Jack and smiled. "Honestly, Jack. I thought you wanted what was best for our daughter?"

CHAPTER 37

*L*aurie rubbed her right shoulder, kneading the muscles that always tightened after a particularly bad softball day. So much for the fun weekend she'd hoped for.

She leaned back against the metal bench, watching from the dugout as parents led their children to the parking lot. A few lingered by the stands, chatting and gossiping like Dan Richards, but most had simply vanished.

Thank God the reporters had gone. Once they'd realized Jack wasn't going to give them a story, they'd lingered around Barry for a while before seeming to grow bored of him as well.

Of course, there had been the one or two interested in her—thinking that she was actually some news-worthy story just waiting to be cracked open. She'd given them her thoughts on this, quite clearly, and they'd left her alone.

No parents offered Laurie their typical handshakes or waited around to talk about what their kid did right or that bad-luck catch by the other team's third baseman.

Not that she could blame them. After all, it hadn't been a fun day. Not for the coaches and certainly not for the girls. Not with Jack as tense as he'd been or the way he'd raised his voice, sharper than usual. More commanding.

She winced as she worked the muscle, a muscle that refused to let her forget her pitching days, or the past. Not that she was surprised; not with Barry White in the stands today.

If Jack's presence had been the trigger bringing in the college scouts, it was Barry's presence that, swiftly and suddenly, changed the mood of all the teams here.

Competition.

That was the theme of the games today. She'd seen it in her own girls and in the others. The *Angels* always had fun. The girls played on her team because it was fun.

Today hadn't been fun.

She squeezed the muscle and winced as she pinched it. The muscle reminded her that the past, the one she worked so hard to forget, was happening again, right now, right in front of her.

At the other end of the dugout, Jack lifted Elizabeth's bat into her bag, and paused. Barry, who was speaking with Charles by the still-open food stand, waved Nancy over.

Elizabeth, Laurie noticed, was with her.

Jack straightened.

He'd hardly spoken to Laurie since Nancy and Barry had shown up this morning. Their conversations had been short and focused strictly on the game. She tried not to feel hurt, tried to convince herself that he was having an even worse day than the rest of them.

But that still didn't make the feeling go away, that she'd been brushed aside, that what had happened last night and this morning didn't matter.

Jack was a dad, first and foremost, and he was worried about Elizabeth.

She watched as Charles shook Elizabeth's hand, watched as Elizabeth blushed and looked away, as if embarrassed.

Laurie leaned closer to the fence. She didn't have to be close to know what Charles was saying. She'd heard it all before, had heard it a hundred times.

Congratulating Elizabeth on a game well-played, on her base running and scoring the game's winning run. The subtle seeds, the subtle hooks turning softball from a fun, enjoyable sport into something more.

Into a job.

Jack had a reason to be worried.

"You can go, you know." Laurie didn't glance at Jack. "I can finish cleaning up here."

"She's fine."

"Fine?" she asked.

With her shoulder reminding her of once standing where Elizabeth was, of once listening to those same sweet, promising words, she couldn't stay quiet.

Those same words that didn't tell the other half of the story, the darker, less-forgiving half of the story. She had to intervene.

"Jack, she needs you."

"I told you, she's fine." He slammed Elizabeth's bat into her bag. "Charles is a nice guy, and as much as I don't like it, her mother's with her."

A mother they both knew didn't have a mothering bone in her body. A mother who couldn't look out for her daughter's best interest; as if Nancy would even know what that was.

Laurie couldn't let him get away with this self-loathing attitude. He needed to be there.

She rested a hand on his shoulder, but Jack twisted away.

"Charles is great at saying all the right things, making girls feel like they're on the top of the world, the best player he's seen in a decade. It would be good to have someone grounding her, that's all."

"I told you." Jack swung Elizabeth's bag over his shoulder and glared at Laurie.

He hadn't come any closer, but it suddenly felt like he was right beside her, staring her down, and not at the other end of the dugout.

"Elizabeth is fine."

Laurie blinked, not understanding where this sudden anger had come from. "All I'm saying—"

"Is that I don't know my kid. That I'm not a good father."

"I'm not saying that at all. I think you're a great father. And I also think you're scared to death of losing her."

"I'm not losing her." He shifted the bag up higher. "And I have nothing to be scared of."

"Fine. Then why have you been an ass all day?"

"I haven't been an ass. I've been focused."

"You've been a jerk to me and the girls, but you sure smiled sweetly to the cameras when they were on you."

"Smiling to cameras is a habit, but trying to win a few games makes me a jerk?"

"It does when you snap at people like that."

Laurie crossed the distance between them, feeling her old anger sparking, her own softball memories sizzling, now that they were so close to the surface.

"And if this is how you treat women after you've slept with them, no wonder why your wife is so bitter."

That last part sort of jumped out, sneaking free from that place she'd buried her feelings. She watched as Jack jerked back, watched as his face paled.

"Is that what you really think of me?"

"What am I supposed to think when you treat me like I'm invisible?" Laurie yanked her own feelings aside. She hadn't meant to say that, even if it was true, even if that's what she felt. "No, I didn't mean that."

"Yes, you did."

She shook her head. "I *am* hurt and I know... I know what I'm feeling doesn't matter right now and it can't. You're worried about Elizabeth. I get that, Jack. I always have."

What she didn't like was feeling so far down, as if she wasn't even second or third on his list of things to worry about.

She sucked in a breath. Right now, this wasn't about her; *it couldn't be about her.*

It was about Elizabeth—and Charles sweet-talking her, right at this very moment.

Jack didn't reach for her, didn't try to bridge the distance now separating them. Laurie forced herself to breathe, to not think about her feelings, about the pain worrying its way in her chest.

Jack glanced at Elizabeth and at Charles who was giving her a solid slap on the back as if they were long-lost pals.

"You need to go to her," Laurie said.

"She's okay. Charles is harmless."

But Jack didn't tear his gaze away, didn't even bother to glance at Laurie when he turned, not when he left the dugout and headed towards his daughter.

He didn't even say goodbye.

She clenched her fists, and then after a moment, yanked her bag from the floor.

"If you think Charles is harmless, than why were you so worried when you saw them together?" she muttered at his departing back.

Because he'd known. Deep down, Jack knew and understood why Laurie was so worried. He knew because that had been him at one point, except it had been Major League scouts and not college ones.

Jack knew, even if he didn't want to admit it.

Bitterness swept through her. Laurie blinked back a sudden swell of very annoying tears. She hated crying, hated it most of all when it was about softball.

In truth, she'd never stopped crying over softball. The difference was she'd been better at hiding it—well, except for Hugh. She'd played with him, coached with him for far too long. He'd seen her at her best, and her worst, since she was also twelve years old. But didn't it figure that the one person who'd stir up those memories the most, those feelings, was the one person she'd let into her life? She'd stopped crying over softball a long, long time ago.

She watched as Jack strode past Nancy, as he shook Charles's hand with a practiced ease. For a moment, Laurie didn't recognize him, didn't recognize the charming, alluring man who easily stepped into the conversation and took control.

He even took the control away from Barry.

If Nancy was bothered by Jack's appearance, she didn't show it.

Instead, she swept her red curls over her shoulder, chuckled, and snaked her arm with Barry's.

But at least Elizabeth's dad had stepped up for her, was protecting her best interests and not her future 'softball career' interests.

"I guess this means I need to find another ride home."

Footsteps padded on the hard ground, stopping behind her. "That's something I can help with. That is, if you want me, to."

Laurie wiped at the few traitorous tears before turning, and somehow managed to swallow a groan as Kent leaned into her dugout looking as proud and full of himself as a peacock with a new display of feathers.

This time, Jack wasn't here to step in.

Not like she needed him. Not like she'd ever needed a man to step in and protect her. She did just fine on her own and alone.

Just fine.

CHAPTER 38

"Thanks for the offer, but I'm fine."

Kent's smile dropped a notch, but he didn't back away. Instead, he stepped into her dugout, blocking the exit. "I just overheard you mentioning needing a ride. I wanted to help. Besides, I noticed your team had a rough day. You had a rough day."

"It happens."

And right now she needed a convenient excuse to get out of here without killing the man. Whether she liked it or not, she still had to see him (and play against his team) on most weekends. Killing, or maiming him, wouldn't be good sportsmanship.

"Then let me take you home. Maybe we can grab something to eat and you can tell me about it."

"Kent. I thought I was pretty clear last time."

"Of course, you're with Jack."

Kent purposefully shifted his attention to Jack—who Laurie refused to look at. If she did, if she saw Jack ignoring her, there was no way she could keep the hurt hidden.

Kent would see; and she didn't want anyone, especially Kent, to know just how hurt she felt.

"Jack's busy right now," she said. "Being a dad and all. It's a full-time job."

Not like she'd know. She was only the coach after all.

"I thought being with someone you cared about was, too. Or maybe I was mistaken. Maybe you were mistaken about Jack."

Laurie swallowed her tears. She turned, unable to help herself, but before she saw Jack she spotted Claire and Suzie heading to their car.

Claire.

And like that, Laurie had her freedom.

"I wasn't wrong about Jack—and if he hadn't gone to his daughter right now, I would have been. Excuse me. My ride's leaving."

She didn't give Kent a chance to object, in fact, she practically ran him over, her bag smacking him on the shoulder as she passed.

Laurie sprinted towards Claire, her heart thumping madly, praying that Claire wasn't in a hurry, that she might show some compassion and get Laurie out of this terribly embarrassing situation.

One that she completely deserved.

She'd known better than to get involved with a parent, than to get involved with Jack. She'd known and hadn't been able to stop herself, not even when the attraction started turning into something more.

This was her own fault.

Claire paused as she opened the car door and saw Laurie. "Laurie? What's wrong?"

Laurie bent over, resting her hands on her knees as she caught her breath, letting her bag slip to the ground. "I need a favor."

Suzie poked her head out the open window. "Coach Laurie, are you okay?"

No, not at all. "Yeah, I just umm...I just need a ride. To my car."

"But I thought..." Claire glanced towards Jack.

"He's busy right now."

"Who?" Suzie asked. "Jack?"

"Hush, Suzie," Claire said. "Laurie, are you sure? I mean, I thought..."

Thought that she and Jack were a couple? Well, so had she.

No! Laurie shook her head. She wasn't being fair to him. After all, hadn't she told him to go to Elizabeth? That's where he needed to be right now.

"It's just, well I don't have anyone else I can call."

Or ask.

She didn't have anything or anyone else in her life besides softball. Not even the other teachers she worked with. She'd had too much practice keeping to herself, standing on her own feet.

"Of course I can give you a ride. Suzie, can you move to the back? We always have room for you. Whenever you need it."

Right now, what Laurie needed was a friend. Someone who didn't care about her being a coach or about softball. Someone who might feel just as hurt and angry and betrayed as she did with those cameras showing up.

Actually, what she really needed was Jack to just look at her, to worry, even for a second, about her.

"I don't want to ruin your night. If you can just give me a ride to my truck..." Laurie looked away. Her truck, that was still at Jack's. "I guess this is what I get for getting involved."

Claire swept around the car and pulled Laurie into a tight hug. "Don't ever think that. *Ever.* And I'm not just going to let you drive off and be miserable. We'll grab some of *Joe's* pizza—take-out—and have ourselves a nice girls night. After the festivities today, we definitely need to watch some cheesy movies or something."

For a second, Laurie couldn't breathe. She didn't remember the last time she'd had a relaxing evening, didn't think about softball.

It was frightening and wonderful all at the same time. And she wouldn't be alone.

"I think that's a great idea." And just what she needed to get her mind off of Jack.

Jack, who hadn't come to her rescue with Kent. Who'd forgotten that he'd been her ride home because she'd spent the night with him.

But when she opened the passenger door, just before she slipped inside, she couldn't help herself. She looked at him.

Jack, who was looking right back at her.

For a second, their eyes met. Laurie's heart lurched. It felt like she was frozen, like she couldn't move a single muscle.

She couldn't see his face at this distance, couldn't see if he was hurt or at least sorry that he'd forgotten about her.

Claire touched Laurie's shoulder, the half of her that was in the car. "He'll be fine. Talk tomorrow and work it out."

Claire was right. Laurie nodded, got in and closed the door. She couldn't seem to move her hand from the door handle, so she left it there.

"You're right, about being a parent. It's not easy." Claire started the car.

Laurie didn't say anything. There was nothing to say. Not when they both knew she was right.

Tomorrow was another day and so long as Jack could keep Elizabeth, and maybe the rest of her team, from Charles's clutches and his college promises, then it would work out all right.

Even if, in the end, she was the one left standing on the field alone. After all, that was her choice in this and she was fine with that.

Or, she would be once she got her heart to stop hammering and once she convinced her eyes they didn't need to water, to cry.

AFTER TWO FUN, girly movies with the perfect mix of cheesy romance, Claire dropped Laurie off at her truck.

The lights in Jack's house were on, even though it was just past midnight. She didn't let herself think about the lights, or that Jack might still be up.

"You going to be okay?" Claire asked when she rolled down the window.

"I will, thanks to you."

"Do you want me to wait?"

Laurie shook her head. "Suzie's home alone. You should be with her."

Claire nodded, wished Laurie goodnight, and told her to call tomorrow if she needed anything.

Laurie wouldn't call. They both knew that.

She needed to work this out for herself, even if it didn't end well. She'd need to face Jack and what had happened today.

As well as facing what her churning, rolling stomach was trying to tell her.

"Damn it." Laurie wiped at her eyes. Hadn't she worked all this out earlier?

She was not hurt or upset. She was fine.

Laurie slid her key into the truck's door and unlocked it. In fact, Jack might not even be home. She didn't remember him turning off the lights when they left this morning so it was entirely possible he was still out with Nancy and Barry.

Which was for the best.

The front door opened.

Possible, but completely unlikely. Not if Elizabeth had come home with him.

The door closed, nice and quiet because it was so late. The night itself was so quiet that she heard Jack's unmistakable footsteps, the confident stride that seemed to be part of his make-up, part of who he was.

Laurie rested her forehead against the truck's door. She had just managed to find her good mood thanks to Claire and Suzie. They'd taken her into their home for the evening, and for once, she'd felt like she was part of a family rather than standing on the outside, always watching.

She didn't want to talk to Jack, didn't want to feel her insides melt when she saw him, when she was forced to accept—yet again—that being part of his family was impossible.

Jack stopped. "I waited up. I was worried about you."

"I went out with Claire." She didn't turn around.

"I saw."

They said nothing for several moments, just the distant honk of car horns, because in a place like southern California, there was always someone up at every hour and always more than a few people driving on the roads.

"I'm sorry," he said. "I'm sorry about earlier, about leaving you alone like that, about the whole stupid thing with the cameras and Nancy."

Laurie swallowed the tears she felt creeping up her throat. She really needed to get control over her emotions and this sudden need to cry all the time.

He said he was sorry, but she wanted to know exactly which part of 'earlier' he was sorry about. Sorry he'd forgotten her? Or sorry he'd allowed his frustration and fear to take control of his coaching, allow it to affect the team?

But she didn't ask because that would be admitting to herself, and to him, she was hurt.

Hurt more than she'd realized.

Hurt because regardless of whether or not she wanted it to be true, she loved him.

Laurie closed her eyes. "It's fine, Jack. I know. You had to go to her."

He moved closer. She felt him behind her, but he didn't reach for her, didn't touch her.

"That still doesn't forgive me; forgetting you like that."

No, it didn't but then being a father who was worried about his daughter forgave a lot.

Laurie steeled her will and turned. Jack stood behind her, just as she'd thought. His hair was slightly rumpled as if he'd fallen asleep on the couch and had slept terribly.

She managed a wobbly smile. "How did it go? With, Charles, I mean."

"It doesn't matter."

"I guess not."

She was done with this conversation, done before the tears she hated came. She half-turned, opening the door with her free hand. "I guess I'll see you at practice?"

Jack moved, so quickly that Laurie in her emotional, tired mind, couldn't follow. He closed her door.

"Don't."

"Don't what? Jack. It's late and I just...," she just wanted to go home and forget about him. But she couldn't because she would see him at practice, and then at next week's tournament.

Because he was a coach on her *Angels*.

"I just want to go home," she said.

"Stay."

The word rumbled through her, deep and low and promising. She couldn't do this, not right now.

"Jack, please."

"I was an ass to you and I'm sorry. Please don't go."

Laurie's hands shook. She shoved them into her shorts pockets. There was so little space separating them, even that tiny movement seemed to bring them closer.

"I don't think I should."

"Why?"

Because I love you, because if I do you'll only hurt me more. But Laurie didn't say it, didn't say any of it.

How could she when he leaned in like that, when he lifted her chin, forcing her to meet his eyes. His very intense, very open gaze. This was the man who'd worked his way into her heart; this wasn't the man she'd seen smoothly chatting with Charles.

She'd finally seen what he meant about baseball, about how there was a part of him that would always remember, that he would always be part of that world.

"Besides," he whispered. "If I don't bring you inside Elizabeth will never forgive me."

Laurie blinked, the mention of Elizabeth breaking the mesmerizing hold he had over her. "Elizabeth?"

"She was furious when she realized you were gone." His fingers tightened, then immediately loosened. "She was furious when I said you went home with Suzie and Claire."

"Oh."

At least one member of this family cared about her.

"Come inside. Sleep in tomorrow, let me make you breakfast in the morning." His head dipped and he brushed her lips with his. "Let me make it up to you."

She couldn't.

Laurie stepped back and Jack's hand fell away. "I'm sorry, Jack. I don't... I don't think I should."

Even if it was already too late.

Too late because she'd already fallen in love with him and the person he loved most in the world wasn't her. Couldn't be her.

Not when he had Elizabeth.

CHAPTER 39

By the time Jack dragged himself out of bed the next day, morning was well on its way. A good thing it was summer and school was out, otherwise Elizabeth would have been late.

He showered, dressed, and then headed down from a much needed cup of coffee. Or two.

He didn't remember the last time he'd slept so terribly, a complete contrast from when Laurie spent the night. And while they hadn't actually gotten much sleep, when they had slept, he'd slept like a rock.

This? This was just him barely functioning.

He hadn't been able to stop thinking of Laurie, about how much he'd hurt her, of the look in her eyes as she got in her truck.

Elizabeth was at the dining room table, her usual bowl of cereal in front of her. She didn't look up at him when he came in, her spoon held suspended.

"Morning, honey." Jack poured himself that giant cup of coffee, breathed in the most wonderful smell in the world, turned back toward his daughter, and froze.

Elizabeth still sat there, spoon frozen in the air as she looked down as if she was reading...

"Son of a bitch."

Jack slammed the cup onto the counter with a splash and yanked the newspaper away from her.

Just like he'd thought.

Barry White made the front page of their local newspaper—and who else was beside him but Jack, looking as pissed-off as ever.

That wasn't the worst.

The worst was the picture below the one of Barry. A picture of him and Laurie, her leaning in just as she was giving him that kiss, the kiss the cameras had interrupted.

Nancy. This had been her plan from the beginning.

The headline was even worse: FORMER MAJOR LEAGE BASE-BALL PLAYER PICKS UP SOFTBALL—AND THE SOFTBALL COACH.

"Dad?" Elizabeth finally looked up, tears in her eyes. "You, you promised it wouldn't be like this again."

He had.

He'd promised and with a single phone call, one perfectly place rumor, Nancy had broken that promise for him.

Jack scrunched up the newspaper and threw it. "I did promise. And the only one who broke this promise was your mother."

Elizabeth's bottom lip trembled. "Mom didn't—"

"Your mother called it in Elizabeth. Just like she did the last time."

He didn't know why he said it, why after four years of silence, he finally told her the truth. Maybe because now it wasn't him taking the heat for Nancy's schemes. Laurie was, too. And so would the team.

"You're lying."

"No, Elizabeth. I'm not." His shoulders fell, his temper falling with them. "I'm sorry."

Elizabeth fled to her room and Jack let her go. She needed time alone, time to cry, time to hate him.

He had something else to do.

Jack grabbed his keys, didn't bother combing his hair, and drove to Nancy's.

She was up, clearly expecting him. In fact, she opened the door before he rang the doorbell.

"Jack! Good morning."

She also, had on the thinnest, most revealing nightgown and robe ever created. She held out her arms, as if expecting a hug.

Jack glanced behind him. "Are you expecting a guy to jump out with a camera so you could get scandalous shots of us to hurt Laurie?"

Nancy's arms dropped. "Of course not."

"You know, for the first time in your life, stop being a bitch."

That brought her up short. Good.

"Jack, you have no right—"

"The hell I do Nancy." He made himself stay right where he was. He couldn't trust his temper if he came closer. Not after what she'd just done.

She flicked those harpy nails at him. "Are you really so upset about that article? I thought the picture of you and Laurie was simply captivating."

"Elizabeth saw the paper, Nancy."

She shrugged. "She reads the paper? Good for her. It's good to have some worldly views."

Jack ground his teeth. *Focus. Calm.*

"She also saw the one you put in about me four years ago. Remember that one? The one revealing all my dirty secrets to the world?"

Nancy's smile dropped. "She didn't. She was only like, what, eight?"

"Trust me. She saw it. And you've got no idea the damage you caused her, damage I'm still trying to fix."

She chuckled a little, as if trying to cover for her sudden surprise. "Well, you got what you deserved, Jack. I mean, cheating on me like that."

Right. Like she hadn't joined in on a few of those sessions.

He took a deep breath, sought for some amount of calm, found only a tiny shred. It was the kiss Laurie had given him, the gentle one on his cheek.

The promise to see him through this.

"The problem, Nancy, is that I never told Elizabeth you were the one who gave them the pictures."

"You? What?" She touched her chest. "You never told her?"

"I didn't. Not until this morning."

"Jack. You... you didn't say anything?"

Nancy's robe slipped down her shoulder, but she pulled it up, didn't even try to use her body against him.

He realized, with some surprise, that this was probably the first time he'd seen the real her.

A shame really; she could have been someone he wanted to get to know. Maybe marry even.

But she'd had her chance. And she'd had her chance with Elizabeth.

"I'm done, Nancy. I'm done with all of this and your games. I didn't say anything before because you were her mother and she loved you, worshiped the ground you walked on."

Jack stepped back, thrusting his hands in his pockets. "Now. Well, now I think she's old enough to see the real you."

There was one other person he needed to talk to, needed to explain things too. If Laurie gave him a chance. If she wanted to listen.

CHAPTER 40

*L*aurie wasn't surprised when she opened the door and found Jack waiting there, hands tucked in his pockets, hair disheveled. Even his shirt was untucked.

She'd never seen Jack like this before.

But then, she'd never seen what he looked like after being in the front page of the papers. She'd also never seen herself either.

She'd also never felt this, what was it? This level of betrayal before?

This wasn't about her dad pushing her for all those years, forgetting her happiness. This wasn't even Hugh walking out on her team and not even having the balls to tell her himself.

This was Jack.

This was someone she'd fallen in love with.

And someone who'd hurt her.

She closed her eyes, forcing the tears down.

"Laurie."

The way he said her name, it was almost like a punch to the gut. He stepped closer but she raised her hand.

Her fingers trembled. "Did you tell them those things?"

"No. Of course, not Laurie."

She nodded. She hadn't thought so. It was more up Nancy's alley, the claim that Laurie was using Jack's famous connections, his celebrity status and his money to attract the big scouts and attention for her team.

"Laurie, please."

Again he tried to step forward, to wrap his arms around her and hold her close. She stepped back, out of reach.

Oh, she wanted him. She so badly needed him.

The thought made her cry.

"Don't, Jack. Just don't."

He froze. "Laurie. It was Nancy."

"I know. I know it was her. I just, I just didn't expect it to hurt this much."

This wasn't Jack's fault. He didn't bring this down on her life, but he was still the root cause. None of this would have happened if he hadn't come into her life. Even the scouts like Charles would have eventually gotten bored and drifted away.

They might have come because a few of Laurie's legacy players had done great things, but they wouldn't have stayed.

But they did.

Because of Jack. Because of the promise he brought to the team.

Taking them, all of them, to the next level. The one place she just couldn't, *couldn't*, go.

"I know," she said again. "I know it's not your fault. You didn't ask for this, but it followed you here. It followed you onto my team."

She wiped at her eyes, swallowed and until she could talk without her voice breaking.

He wanted to come to her. She could see that, in every inch of his being, he wanted to come to her.

She wanted him, too.

But she couldn't. Not now, and maybe never again. Not until this hurt went away.

"I need some time, Jack. Time before I can make any kind of decision."

Decision. The choice of whether or not to have him in her life. In her personal life.

In her bed. In her heart.

Jack's eyes narrowed, his face darkening, but then he looked away. Whatever was there, whatever was on his face, he wanted hidden from her.

"I understand."

Laurie tried not to think about her heart, and how she felt it breaking as he turned and slowly walked away. But she needed time, even if time would never alter the fact that she loved him.

CHAPTER 41

She'd known it wouldn't be easy seeing Jack so soon after the newspaper incident, but she knew they'd get through it.

Laurie hadn't gone to Wednesday's practice, asking Jack to handle it for her. He had and hadn't asked why.

But now it was a game weekend and if last weekend had been a mess, this one was turning into one giant disaster. Since the first pitch of their first game this morning, Laurie knew they were in for a long day.

Jack had barely looked at her and she'd had spoken even less. They needed time apart—she needed time apart.

Too bad they had to coach the same team, too bad they had to talk —and to get along—regardless of whether or not she'd had enough 'time.'

Laurie winced as Elizabeth threw another ball in the dirt. Mandy scrambled for the wild pitch but by the time she'd gotten it the runner had already made it to second base.

This was why she needed to get over her feelings, to work through this with Jack instead of being silent. Their team needed them focused, needed them working together and not this silent treatment.

Jack sat on the overturned bucket and gave Mandy the next

pitching sign. She could tell he was holding his tongue, trying to keep his temper locked in place.

She'd hurt him, too, and he deserved to be angry with her.

Laurie grabbed her bucket and moved from the other end of the dugout to sit next to Jack.

He didn't glance up at her. "What? You ready to speak with me again?"

"Right, like this is all my fault?" she snapped back. "And no, I'm not ready to talk about what those papers said about me or about our relationship."

This was not meeting half-way, she thought to herself.

"Okay. I thought we should at least try being civil," Laurie said. "Especially considering the entire team, along with the *Rascals* and their nosy parents, know we're having a fight."

"We're not fighting."

Still, he didn't look at her.

"Okay. So not talking or not looking at each other counts as what?"

His mouth pinched into a tight line. "What do you want me to say?"

Other than that he was sorry? Sorry his ex-wife got loose again and tried to ruin not only Laurie's life but her team's as well? Maybe he could say he loved her and she wasn't the only one hurting?

"You know, what? Forget it. I thought we could do this, have a relationship and still be coaches but I guess I was wrong." She'd kept her voice down, hoping the three girls on the bench wouldn't over-hear, but Lacey was practically on the edge of her seat.

So much for privacy.

Laurie growled to herself and started to rise, but Jack's hand clamped onto her leg, pinning her there.

"Look. I'm sorry. And everything that happened last week, with Nancy and Barry, the reporters."

Finally, he turned towards her. For a brief moment, he let her see the man hidden behind the cool, anger.

A man who been just as hurt as her.

"Maybe we moved too fast," he said, "maybe I moved too fast with you, but I want to make this work. Both with the team and with you."

She wanted to forget about last week, to forget about everything that had happened. She couldn't. "We need to talk about this."

He nodded. "That's all I'm asking."

He was asking for so much more, but he wouldn't know how much unless she told him.

Laurie's hand slipped over his. He turned his palm and they sat there, holding each other's hands, their attention turning back to the game, back to Elizabeth who noticed them and gave them a small, shaky smile.

"She really does care about you," Jack said. "She knows we've been fighting."

"The whole team knows."

"She also the read paper."

"Damn it."

His fingers tightened around hers. "I don't want to fight anymore."

She let out a breath she hadn't realized she'd been holding. "Then I guess we should stop, huh?"

After all, weren't they here to have fun?

Jack smiled. It wasn't the same big, joyful smile he'd given her when he'd kissed her in front of everyone, but it was a smile.

They'd get through this. Somehow, they would.

At least, she thought, until she glanced up and saw the one person she'd never seen in the stands. The one person she'd never expected to see, because she'd told him in no uncertain terms, that he wasn't allowed anywhere near her games.

Her dad.

CHAPTER 42

*H*er dad stood there, waiting by the stands. His usual Mount Forest College hat planted firmly on his head. He still wore it, even though she'd left the team almost twelve years ago.

But then he was never without a hat, and even now, it was still a softball one.

He watched her, small brown eyes studying her the way they always did, but there was no accusation in his stance, no complaint on his lips for something she didn't do right.

Something she didn't do perfect.

Breathing suddenly became a lot harder.

"Laurie?"

Jack. He stood up, blocking her dad for a moment, taking her hand in his.

"Laurie, what's wrong? Tell me."

She moved her lips, but the words didn't come. What was he doing? Why had he come?

The worst, the worst part of all was that him just standing there, looking all reasonable and like some regular, ordinary parent made her freeze.

Twelve years! Hadn't that been long enough for her to move on?

Jack followed her gaze, sliding an arm around her shoulder. "That's your dad, isn't it?"

She nodded. "Yes, yes that's him."

"Charles noticed him. He's heading over."

Laurie closed her eyes. Felt a tremor work its way from her legs to her hands. Jack's hold on her increased. He was the one holding her up. Even after she'd dismissed him, refusing to hear his explanation about the reporters, he was here for her. Right now.

Right when she needed him most.

"Jack," she whispered even as a tear escaped.

"It's okay; your dad's shaking his head. Charles is leaving."

Jack paused and finally asked the one thing Laurie didn't want to hear because she knew it's what she had to do. "Do you want to talk with him?"

No.

She hadn't wanted to talk with her dad about softball since that day she'd thrown down her glove and quit.

But he'd come to her game. He'd come to see her team.

She had to talk to him.

Her dad didn't smile when she ducked out of the field and headed towards him.

He didn't smile much anymore, at least around her.

Softball had been the one thing they'd shared. The one thing that had been just 'him and Laurie.'

Once softball was gone, there hadn't been much else to fill its place. Sure there was the general talk: how was work, how her mom was doing. Usual stuff, but nothing personal.

He never asked about the *Angels* and she never talked about them.

Her dad waited until she was close enough, then nodded off the vacant benches, away from the stands, away from her team. She was grateful for the gesture. This was hard enough for her as it was.

But when he turned, when she saw the slight downturn of his mouth, his tense posture and hands tucked in his jean pockets, she realized this wasn't easy for him, either.

He wasn't angry.

He was nervous.

Somehow knowing that made this meeting just a tiny bit easier. Even if her hands couldn't stop shaking.

"Dad."

There. She'd said it. Said the first word. "What are you doing here?"

"I had to come. I mean, I saw the paper last week, and..."

Of course he'd seen the paper. Everyone had seen the paper.

"It was your mother's idea," he continued, "she wanted to make sure you were okay."

"I'm... I'm fine." Laurie pulled off her hat and rubbed her forehead, needing something to distract her hands, the shaking she felt. "I mean, I'll get through it. The things they said about me, they're not true."

"I know they aren't."

"I mean, Jack and I are together. That was true. The rest of it..." her voice trailed off, left it unsaid. The part about Laurie using Jack's fame and his money to attract the scouts.

Her dad laughed. Not a funny laugh, but a dry one. A mocking one. Mocking himself. "Trust me, Laurie, I knew they weren't true. I learned the hard way, remember?"

As if either of them could forget.

They stood like that for several minutes, neither speaking. Probably because they were both afraid to.

Even though Jack was still in the dugout, she felt him watching her. She felt his strength, almost as if he was standing there right beside her, holding her hand.

She could either learn to forgive the past, or she could continue to let it rule her, to control her life.

It wouldn't be easy.

It wouldn't happen today.

But she could make a start.

"Thanks, Dad. Thanks for checking on me." She half-turned, ready to go back to her team, but then she saw Elizabeth giving Jack a hug and remembered a time when she'd given her dad that same hug.

Given it to him because she was happy. Because she'd just struck out a batter.

And he'd been proud of her.

"You can stay if you like," she said. "Stay and watch the game."

Her dad didn't move and most of his face was shadowed because of his hat. His shoulders didn't loosen any, but he nodded. "Thanks. I just might do that."

Maybe it was a start. For both of them.

That's what she was thinking when Laurie headed back to the dugout and realized Jack was now the one standing, tense, glaring at the stands.

Nancy.

Apparently today was the day for unscheduled, and unwelcome visitors.

This time, Nancy was alone. She wasn't even wearing her trademark designer heels. Instead she looked more normal, more down-to-earth.

More like the rest of the moms, though still better-dressed than them.

Jack had been concerned about having Elizabeth pitch while Nancy was around. That was why the week before—as soon as he saw Nancy—he'd suggested Lacey to start, even though it was Elizabeth's turn. Pitching required the kind of concentration, the kind of bravery to stand front and center, with everyone's eyes on you.

When the pitcher screwed up, it hurt the team. When the pitcher wasn't focused, it hurt everyone.

And today, Elizabeth was pitching.

How had they missed seeing her? Of course, the lack of cameras, reporters, and fashion-magazine clothes probably had something to do with it.

Laurie was at Jack's side before she realized she'd even taken a step. "Ignore her. Elizabeth needs us right now."

He didn't seem to hear her, his attention completely focused on Nancy.

"Jack."

He blinked. "What?"

"*Elizabeth*. Do you want to call time? Do you want to talk her?" If they were going to do it, do anything for that matter, now was the time.

"No. Let her pull through this."

His gaze strayed back to Nancy.

"I can't keep hiding her from Nancy."

Laurie knew he was right, but she also knew that Elizabeth didn't have the right mind frame for this. Of course, she didn't have the right frame of mind either, herself—she was still shaking from speaking with her dad.

This was Jack's call, and if he thought Elizabeth could pull through this, then she'd let him.

She didn't like it though, especially when Elizabeth glanced at the stands to see what had her dad's attention. The second her posture stiffened and red flamed her face, Laurie knew she'd spotted her mother.

Elizabeth straightened, even held her head up a little higher. It didn't help. The next pitch was a curve that didn't curve and the batter hit a line drive right at Suzie in center field.

Suzie raced forward, catching the ball and immediately threw it to third base. It didn't matter. The runner on second had been waiting for the catch and was already safe.

Laurie slapped the fence with her hand. Damn it. This was the last thing Elizabeth needed right now.

Meanwhile, Laura Taylor, also known as "Ball-Killer," stepped up to the plate, and Elizabeth, her attention now split between her mother and yet another failed pitch, threw another please-hit-me ball right over the middle of the damn plate.

The sharp crack of ball hitting bat was all Laurie needed to know it was a long, hard hit to the outfield.

The runner on third scored, and Ball-Killer Taylor just hit a freakin' triple.

CHAPTER 43

"**S**on of a bitch!" Jack kicked the ball bucket and walked onto the field, yelling 'time' to the umpire.

The umpire gave him a nod and Jack did his damnedest to ignore the other team's cheers as Taylor slid safe into third base, killing the ball Elizabeth had so stupidly thrown right down the middle of the plate.

Their catcher, Mandy, stayed behind home plate, which was fine by him. He and Elizabeth needed to talk.

Elizabeth with her face red and eyes downcast, fidgeted on the mound. "I'm sorry."

"Sorry doesn't change the fact that you just threw two fat pitches down the plate."

And probably cost us the game, but he managed to keep that part in.

"What's going on? Why isn't your head in the game?"

It was a stupid question, especially when he knew the only person to blame was himself. Their whole team's head wasn't in the game.

Jack clenched his fists. He didn't have time to think about Laurie or their relationship, if they even had one anymore. After last week, he doubted it.

Even though he'd been there for her when she saw her dad, it didn't change anything. They'd both probably made a mistake deciding to try to be coaches and… well, whatever they had been.

Just like he hadn't changed anything when he'd confronted Nancy about the newspapers, told her that Elizabeth finally knew the truth. Sure, Nancy had looked upset, but that sure lasted a long didn't it?

She was back to her usual tricks, trying to upset Elizabeth.

And right now, he needed to get Elizabeth's head in the game, to focus.

"No. I just, I just made a mistake." She looked once at the stands, then back at her feet. "Mom's here."

'Mom' was the last person Jack wanted to talk about. "You're not focused. You're distracted."

Just like him. Especially like him.

Damn it, why did women always get under his skin? Always cloud his thoughts, his judgment?

"I'm fine."

"Fine." He growled the word out. "I have Lacey warmed up and ready. Can you finish this inning or do I need to pull you?"

Elizabeth wiped at her cheeks. "No, I can do it. I want to show Mom how good I've gotten and… and she came, Dad. She came."

Jack ground his teeth.

The umpire touched his wrist. Time was up. If Elizabeth wanted to get out of this, fine. She'd see what it took to be a star player—and it wasn't easy.

None of it was ever easy.

"I won't pull you. You leaned forward on those last two pitches. Stand tall. Drive with your hips and don't cost us the game."

Elizabeth's bit her bottom lip and nodded. "Okay."

Jack stormed back off the field. Laurie stood in the dugout, hands on her hips, nostrils flaring.

He didn't have time to deal with her; he couldn't think whenever she was around.

Not to mention that with Nancy here, he needed a clear head. He was barely keeping Elizabeth and all her hopes and dreams out of Charles' clutches. All thanks to Nancy butting into their lives.

"What?" Jack snapped.

Laurie's eyes narrowed. She took a deep breath and then stepped aside, letting him back in. It was only after Jack got his seat and flashed Mandy the sign for a fastball, high and inside, he finally noticed Laurie hadn't sat back down.

"What?"

"What did you say to her?"

"Nothing."

He didn't want to talk Laurie, didn't want to talk to anyone.

He wanted Elizabeth to get out of this inning so he could deal with Nancy and get her the hell away from his team.

Even if Elizabeth wanted her mother there.

And once he dealt with them, then he'd talk to Laurie and figure just what the hell was going on between them.

No, he hadn't been with many women since Nancy left, hadn't had any serious relationships, but no woman had ever gotten under his skin like this, gotten him so tangled up it felt like he was lost and alone. Just like he'd felt when he realized Nancy wasn't the woman she thought he was.

"Lacey!" Laurie called from beside him. "Get ready."

It took a moment, but the second her words registered, Jack was on his feet and rounded on Laurie. "What are you doing?"

"What am *I* doing? I'm doing what *you* should have done in the first place instead of making her stay out there."

Jack's eyes narrowed. "She's working through this. How do you expect her to get better if you pull her at the first sign of trouble?"

Laurie stepped closer and grabbed a fistful of his shirt, pulling his closer so their noses nearly touched.

"And how do you expect her to get better when she's out there doing everything she can to not cry in front of everyone? In front of her mother?"

What?

Jack pulled back, turning towards Elizabeth. Even from here he could see her puffy, red face. She wiped again at her eyes and did her best to smile when she saw him.

From the stands he heard Nancy's lazy clapping. "Come on, honey, show mommy how good you are."

It took all his energy, every inch of his control not to run into the stands and pull Nancy down by the hair. She was doing this, hurting Elizabeth, just to hurt him.

Laurie released his shirt. "You need to get her out of there."

"I can't."

He needed her to fight through this, to show Nancy she was a good ball player, that she wasn't a failure.

That he wasn't a failure as a father.

"Jack."

The way Laurie said his name it felt like a slap, a nice hard sting right across his face.

"She can't do this, not right now, not with her mother watching."

She was right. Damn it, how he hated Laurie in that moment, but she was right.

Elizabeth was still young, still had growing to do, and it wasn't easy for any pitcher to get through tough innings like this. But with her mother in the stands, a mother who paid attention to everything except her daughter?

No, Elizabeth wasn't ready.

But he needed her to be.

"She's staying. Let her fight through this."

Laurie jerked back as if he'd slapped her. "Jack. She can't."

"She's staying out there."

Laurie swung her attention to the field, to the home-plate umpire; Jack grabbed her arm before she stormed onto the field, calling for a pitcher change.

Elizabeth threw the next pitch. This time, she managed to stand up tall, but her fastball had lost its earlier kick.

Still, Elizabeth kept the ball inside like Jack had asked, and the batter couldn't get her arms fully extended. Instead of a hard hit, it was an easy out to third base.

Yes! One more out to go, and then he could deal with Nancy. Deal with her and show her that he and Elizabeth weren't failures.

They could do this; they would do this.

"One more, Elizabeth," he whispered. "You can do it."

"You need to pull her," Laurie whispered. "I mean it Jack."

Laurie's voice caught. He glanced at her, eyebrows raised, but Laurie had already turned her head, blocking his view.

"You need to pull her," she said again.

"Let her finish it." But even as he said it, he knew it was selfish, knew it was wrong.

Elizabeth wasn't focused. She'd been torn between worrying about her father and his growing relationship with Laurie. Then Nancy had shown up and he yelled at her.

"Fine." Laurie turned back, eyes glistening with unshed tears. "If you won't, I will."

She didn't have a chance.

It was with the very next pitch he wished he'd listened to Laurie, had listened to his own pinching gut.

This time, the hit didn't just bring in the runner on third. This time, it was a freaking home run.

Elizabeth burst into tears and ran off the field. Jack stepped forward, but Laurie pressed her hand against his chest.

"Move," he growled.

"No."

His eyes narrowed. "Damn it, Laurie. I need to go after her."

She pushed back. "You will do no such thing. You will stay here and get your team out of this mess."

"My daughter—"

"You have more than just your daughter to worry about Jack," Laurie hissed. "This is your team now, remember? You're a coach."

The hell with that. My daughter just ran off the field in tears and I'm not about to—

Laurie's grip tightened. "You're her coach *and* her father. And you're also half the reason she took off crying. Do you really think she wants to talk to you right now?"

"I..."

The tension pushing him to run after Elizabeth faded. It didn't go away completely, not when every instinct told him to run after his little girl, to hold her and tell her everything was going to be all right.

But it wasn't, because he was the one who'd pushed her.

Half the reason. Jack glanced at the stands, where Nancy was already making her way down. He couldn't let her near Elizabeth, not now.

Hell, he couldn't get anywhere near Nancy either. None of this would have happened if she hadn't shown up.

"I'll take care of Elizabeth," Laurie said. "You take care of my team."

Jack took a deep breath. Laurie was right. He was the last person Elizabeth wanted to see right now.

"You said Lacey's ready?"

At Laurie's nod, Jack stepped onto the field and took back control, at least as much as he could. It was one thing to be a father, but being a coach had more responsibilities, ones he hadn't counted on.

Like not being able to run after Elizabeth when she needed him.

CHAPTER 44

*L*aurie left the dugout just as Jack called for Lacey to take the mound. Elizabeth was running to the same bathroom Laurie would have run to—to run and cry where her father couldn't see.

Laurie gasped, trying to breath. Tears choked her.

It was happening all over again.

She tried not to think about how this was the same bathroom where Jack had stolen a kiss from her. Or she'd stolen from him. Just weeks ago, back to a time when her life had been a whole lot simpler. When she hadn't been in love with him, which made what happened out there, him yelling at Elizabeth on the mound, just that much harder to deal with.

And with her dad there, watching.

The tears kept coming. Laurie didn't fight them.

She was done fighting them. Right now, her tears didn't matter.

The only person who mattered was Elizabeth. She needed Laurie, needed the one person who understood what it felt like to be on the mound, to feel like you were disappointing your coach, your team, your father.

Every step closer to the bathroom, the more Laurie's fury rose, dissolving her tears. By the time she reached the bathroom, Laurie wanted to kill Jack. The hell if she loved him and could barely imagine herself living without him, if he'd been standing beside her she would have killed him.

She had promised herself years ago she'd never allow one of her girls to cry, not like this. Not running off the field.

Not because of a parent, not because of a coach.

Never, ever again would she let one of her girls feel like this. And she'd blown it. It had happened right in front of her, regardless of how she felt about Jack, and she hadn't done anything to stop it.

Laurie pushed open the swinging door, some of the blue paint peeling off at her touch. The same blue paint as when she'd ran into here years ago.

"Elizabeth?"

Elizabeth didn't reply, she just sobbed. Sobs that pulled at Laurie's heart.

Laurie sprinted to the last stall and when the door easily opened, found Elizabeth on the floor, head pressed against her knees.

Laurie forgot where she was.

All she could remember was how many times she'd rocked back and forth in that same position, that some spot, hiding her face and her tears from the world.

She'd only cried after the game, always when no one was looking, when no one would see Laurie, the star player, hiding in the bathroom and crying.

At least, if she could help it.

Sometimes she couldn't, and like Elizabeth today on the mound, there were times when nothing in the world would make those tears stop.

"Oh, honey." Laurie knelt beside Elizabeth and scooped her into her arms. "It's okay, I promise. It's okay."

"No... no it's not." Elizabeth sobbed. "My mother was there and she saw... she saw me throw those horrible pitches. And we've lost... we lost the game because of me."

And just like that, the truth poured out of Elizabeth. How scared she was to disappoint her dad after all the work they'd done together, and most of all, how she didn't want to be a failure.

"My mom isn't proud of me. She hates me."

Laurie bit her lip. She'd beat Nancy to a pulp later, right after she got finished with Jack. But right now anger was the last thing Elizabeth needed.

"That's not true."

Elizabeth, more than anything else, needed her mother—and her mother was the one person who would only hurt her further.

"You're doing great," Laurie said. "Really. Everyone has a bad day."

"But my mother was there!"

"So what? You had a bad day. No one is perfect. I'm not perfect. I had bad days all the time and I would end up in here, just like you, crying. Even now. Did you know my dad was in the stands? And look at me," Laurie pointed to her face, "he's still making me cry."

And this time, he hadn't done anything.

This time it had been the memories. Memories triggered because of Jack's anger.

Elizabeth glanced up. Her eyes were all puffy and red and she was breathing through her mouth. Laurie rolled up a bunch of toilet paper and handed it to her.

Elizabeth didn't argue, and she blew her nose several times. "You cried in here too?"

"More times than I like to remember."

"But why? I thought you were the best player."

Laurie closed her eyes and rested her chin on Elizabeth's head. "I was, but... but I didn't have a dad like yours. My dad loved me, worked so hard to make me the best softball player ever."

Laurie's voice caught. She had to say this, had to share this with Elizabeth. "My dad tried hard. A little too hard, and he pushed me. Just like how your dad wants to push you, help you get better. He cares so much for you, and he wants to see you happy. More than anything else, he wants you to smile."

Elizabeth sniffled again. "Are you sure? He was mad today."

"But that's not your fault," Laurie pointed out. "He's mad at me and at your mom."

Elizabeth wiped her nose. "Why? I thought you liked each other."

"We do, but sometimes it isn't easy and things with your mom..." Laurie fumbled for the right words.

Elizabeth still loved her mother, regardless of how she was treated.

"My mom doesn't make things easy," Elizabeth answered for her. "I saw the papers. Dad told me. He told me she did it."

"Yeah, he told me the same thing too. But you know what? Your dad is definitely proud of you and he wants to see you do your best."

She tightened her hold on Elizabeth. "And he wants to show your mother how good you are, too. He wants to show her just as much as you do."

Probably more considering he lost his temper.

"And you're lucky your dad cares about you so much," Laurie continued. "Otherwise he wouldn't be here, working with you every day, coaching your team. He's proud of you."

Jack was proud of Elizabeth, Laurie had no doubts about that, but she wouldn't say the same about Elizabeth's mother.

Laurie stretched her legs out and pulled Elizabeth in closer. She didn't remember the bathrooms being this cramped, but then she'd been Elizabeth's size at the time and, unlike Elizabeth, Laurie hadn't had an adult on the floor with her, trying to make her feel better.

"Really? Do you really think he's proud of me?"

"I promise. Your dad is proud of you. And so what if you had a bad day? Everyone makes mistakes and seeing your mother surprised you."

Elizabeth looked away, but Laurie wasn't going to let her off that easily. She touched Elizabeth's chin until she looked at her.

Elizabeth's bottom lip trembled. "She thinks I'm a failure."

"Does your dad think that?"

Again, another lip tremble.

Laurie shook her head. "You know very well your dad doesn't think that. He loves you. He walked away from baseball because of you, and I know for a fact he never regretted it."

She'd known the moment she had walked into Jack's office and seen all his old baseball trophies and photos. And when he gazed at them, she hadn't seen regret. He'd made that decision with eyes open and he'd done it for his daughter.

Now if only she could get him to back-off and let Elizabeth be a kid for a little while longer, but even that was somehow tied to Nancy.

They stayed on the bathroom floor until Elizabeth's sniffling quieted. They stumbled to their feet and Laurie waited while Elizabeth washed her face.

"Do you feel better?" she asked.

Elizabeth gazed back in the warped mirror and for a second it looked like she was going to cry again. Then, she took a deep breath and nodded. It was a tentative nod, but she held herself up.

"I'll be okay."

That was the best anyone could hope for, at least for now. She wanted to see Elizabeth smiling again, smiling and happy.

They walked out of the bathroom and Laurie nearly ran into Elizabeth's back. Jack was standing by the entrance to the girl's bathroom, face drawn tight as he paced back and forth in front of the girl's bathroom. Nancy, who'd started going after Elizabeth, was back at the bleachers, hands rubbing together, not once looking away from them. From Elizabeth.

Jack froze when he saw them and Laurie knew she hadn't lied in there. Jack did care. Jack loved his daughter.

The problem was he didn't love *her*.

Laurie swallowed the hurt, swallowed those feelings until only a strange numbness was left behind. A numbness because she knew now, staring at him, face drawn and tight with worry, what she had to do.

It was the only thing she could do.

"Elizabeth," he whispered, "I'm sorry."

Elizabeth glanced at Laurie before slowly walking over, letting him hug her close. Laurie heard Elizabeth's own 'I'm sorry' back to him.

The game was over, which wasn't surprising. Her girls probably hadn't gotten any hits, not with Jack distracted and Laurie and Elizabeth gone.

Not her girls, she thought to herself, not any longer.

Jack lowered Elizabeth to the ground and held out his hand to Laurie. "Thank you."

"It was nothing."

She didn't take his hand.

Claire, Laurie noticed, had taken charge, ordering the girls to clean up the dugout and their gear, giving Laurie and Jack the time to help Elizabeth. Claire was a great friend, definitely more than Laurie deserved.

Jack squeezed Elizabeth's shoulder. "I should have listened to you out there and I didn't. I'm sorry."

The ache in his voice, in his words, made Laurie pause, look at him closer.

Her dad's voice had never ached like that. Never.

Not even today. But she knew her dad regretted what had happened between them. That's what she'd seen in his eyes, that's why he'd come here today.

It only just made her decision now more clear. She'd failed in her promise.

She might not have been her dad, the one yelling at Elizabeth on the mound, but she'd been just as bad.

She'd stood by and let it happen.

"I wasn't okay," Elizabeth told Jack. "I shouldn't have told you I was okay, but then I saw Mom and I just wanted to make her proud of me. She came to see me and I messed up."

"No, you didn't mess up. I did," Jack said. "And don't let anyone tell you differently, you hear?"

Laurie wiped at her eyes, pushing away the tears before anyone noticed, especially Jack. "No, I'm the one who messed up."

Both Jack and Elizabeth looked at her, and it was almost like Jack was surprised to see her there.

Surprised, huh? That really said exactly where she fit in his life.

"Laurie, you didn't do anything," Jack protested.

She raised her hand, stalling him. "You're right. I didn't. I didn't stop you and I should have."

She hadn't been able to. She'd frozen, and she didn't know if it was because of seeing her dad or if was because of her feelings for Jack.

The reason didn't matter. All that mattered was she'd stood by and done nothing.

"I promised myself I'd stand up for my team, that I'd never let a girl go through...go through what happened to me."

This time, there was no hiding the tears. Not when they had a life of their own.

She didn't fight them.

Jack came forward, reaching for her. She moved before he could touch her, hold her.

It would have only made it worse.

"I can't." She shook her head. "I'm falling apart. Everything, everything about this game is tearing me to pieces and I couldn't stop you out there. I let you yell. I let you... I let you become the same man my father was."

Her stomach rolled at the memory, at the feelings Elizabeth had awakened in her.

"Laurie," Jack whispered. "That's not true. That was my fault. I let my temper get control of me."

Elizabeth moved beside Laurie, taking her hand the same way Laurie had done earlier. "Laurie? What's wrong? Why are you crying?"

Laurie brushed at the tears and forced herself to meet Jack's eyes. "Because I can't do this anymore."

CHAPTER 45

"I'm quitting."

Laurie's words slugged him in the chest. Smacked into him so hard he stumbled back.

"Quitting?" Jack could barely force the words out. "You can't quit."

She couldn't. The team needed her.

He needed her.

Laurie shook her head, tears streaming down her cheeks. This was her team; the *Angels* were her team.

"Laurie." His voice cracked. "I'm sorry about what happened out there. I didn't think, didn't realize with your dad there, and then I saw Nancy..."

And he'd lost his temper. He'd become the man her father had been, just like she'd said.

Damn it, he knew what that would do to her; he knew how much it meant that her girls—all of them, including her—have fun on this team.

He wanted to hold Laurie, to show her just how much he needed her. She held out her hand—a hand that for the first time since he'd known her, was shaking.

He was causing her to shake.

Jack froze.

"This is my fault," she said quietly. "I should have stopped you, Jack, and I didn't. I couldn't. If I can't do that, then the best thing for me to do is walk away."

Elizabeth squeezed his hand and her voice broke as she started crying again. "Laurie, you can't leave. We need you."

"I'm sorry, Elizabeth. This time... this time I'm done with softball. For good."

She swept past them, the edge of her uniform lightly brushing against his arm. He couldn't go after her.

This whole time he'd been so worried, so concerned about Elizabeth, he hadn't given a thought to Laurie, to the one person who believed in him, who thought he was a good father and a good coach.

"Dad," Elizabeth tugged at his arm. "You have to go after her."

He couldn't move.

"She's hurting and you need to talk to her."

All this, all of it, was his fault. He'd done exactly what Barry had warned Laurie about. He'd taken over her team, stolen it, even though that had never been his intent.

"Dad!" Elizabeth smacked him in the arm. "I thought you loved her!"

Elizabeth's words knocked him back. He stumbled.

Loved her? Did he?

He didn't know, hadn't thought love was even possible when his life revolved so completely, and so focused, on Elizabeth.

A slight clearing of a throat made Jack stand, made Elizabeth stiffen beside him.

Nancy smiled at them, hair still in its perfect, sprayed-on position. "Jack, I just wanted to see how Eliza—"

Jack rounded on Nancy. "See how she was doing? Continue to taunt her? Is this really some sick, twisted game to you?"

He was done playing. He'd told her that and still she'd come.

Her very presence had pushed him over the edge, had caused him to hurt Laurie.

Nancy's mouth opened and closed. "I didn't mean to, I, really did just want to see Elizabeth play."

It was that slight hesitation that made him pause, made him believe, even for a moment, she might mean it.

"So is it true?" Nancy asked. "Do you love her?"

"If I do, don't you think she should be the first one to know? Not you?"

His voice, hoarse and low like he hadn't used it in years, scratched his throat. He needed to go after Laurie.

He needed to tell her.

Because it was true. He did love her.

Elizabeth braced her hands on her hips, took two steps forward until she stood protectively in front of him. She glared at her mother. "Of course, he loves her. And he's going after her and bringing her back."

Jack blinked and Nancy did the same. This couldn't be Elizabeth. This couldn't be his daughter.

Nancy's eyebrows arched high. "So, you do have Jack's courage, don't you? I never saw it before."

Elizabeth straightened, both her hands and back shaking. She'd stood up for him. She'd stood up to her mother, the one person whose attention she always wanted and never got.

For him.

Nancy wiped at her eyes.

Jack was surprised to see there were tears. Real ones.

"She's right, Jack. You need to go after her. You need to tell her you love her." Nancy smiled, but it wobbled slightly. "That you love her in a way you and I could never love each other."

When Jack didn't move, Nancy shooed him with her hands. "Go, Jack. Don't ruin the best chance you have at being happy."

He had to go after Laurie. She was leaving her team behind. Leaving him behind.

He wouldn't let her. He'd do whatever it took to bring her back.

Elizabeth spun towards him. "You have to go after her!"

"Elizabeth—"

"Don't worry about the team. I'll get Hugh and Claire." She slapped him on his arm. "You go bring back my coach."

He knelt in front of Elizabeth, holding her shoulders. "Are you sure?"

"Of course, I'm sure. You love her, don't you?"

"I do."

From the minute he'd laid eyes on her.

"More than Mom?"

He glanced at Nancy, then Elizabeth. "Yes. More than I ever loved your mom."

"I know, Dad. I've known since forever. Now will you please go after her?"

Jack didn't wait for Elizabeth to tell him again. He'd always known he'd had a smart, good-looking daughter. He'd just had no idea how much until today. And how lucky he was to have her.

CHAPTER 46

$\mathcal{L}$aurie leaned against her truck, hand on the door handle, but didn't have the strength to open it. Her legs shook, barely keeping her upright.

She'd just wait here, wait here until it was safe enough to drive, until she got her feelings under control.

She wiped at her eyes and the tears that just didn't stop.

This time, the past and her father had nothing to do with it. They weren't the ones to blame.

She was.

She'd been the one who'd frozen out there, who hadn't stopped Jack, who hadn't kept him in line like a coach should.

She'd failed.

Just like she'd failed back then, being too frightened to stand up to her father.

"This is the best thing," she told herself. "Just walk away while you can, before you cause any more harm."

She couldn't stop shaking, couldn't stop hurting. She'd failed her team. Her girls.

"Don't tell me you believe that." Jack. His rumbling, familiar, soft voice rolled through her.

Hurt her.

Laurie squeezed her eyes shut, willing him to go away. Needing him to go away. She couldn't move on if he was there. Couldn't stop crying.

"But you do, don't you?" he asked. "You believe that."

She didn't turn around, just leaned further into the truck, her head pressed against the driver's-side window. "I already told you. Please, just go away, Jack."

She heard his distinct stride as he came closer, felt his heat as he came up behind her.

"I can't go away. At least, not until you've given me the chance to tell you how I feel about this."

What was there to say? He'd wanted to be a coach, he'd wanted her team. Well, he got it. All of it.

"Laurie." A hand brushed her ponytail to the side. His fingers brushed her neck. She shivered, even as more tears squeezed out.

Even now, she was paralyzed. Couldn't move.

"I can't go away, not until I tell you the truth. Please."

She forced herself to turn, forced herself to meet his eyes— promising it would be the last time. She only had to be strong for this one moment more, and then she'd never have to see him again.

Would never have to be hurt by him again.

Jack gazed at her, so close their breaths mingled, intertwined together. His hand reached up, gently touching her cheek.

"You can't quit. The girls need you. I need you."

She shook her head, but his hand immediately stilled her.

"You're irreplaceable, Laurie Stevens. Get it through your thick head. The girls will not be the same if you leave, and I sure as hell won't be."

"That's not true, it's—"

"It is true," he snapped. "It's true because they love you. I love you."

"You... you... what?"

He jerked back and ran a hand through his hair, frustration in every movement.

"I love you, Laurie. I love you and I'm not going to let you walk away from me. I'm not going to let you walk away from this team —*your* team. Do you hear me?"

The truck was the only thing holding her up. If she'd been standing on her own power, she'd have sank right down onto the dirty, parking lot asphalt.

"I love you," he said again. "And I'm not letting you quit. Not me, not this team."

He reached for her. She didn't back away.

Jack pulled her to him, so close their noses brushed each other. He sighed, breathing her in as if she was the only thing he needed.

"And I need you out there," he said. "I need you to tell me when I'm being an ass, when I'm going too far. I can't do it without you."

Laurie reached her arms around his neck, holding him close to her. "The girls need me?"

He snorted. "Who else can spot a shark like Charles? Of course, they need you. Even the idiot parents like Dan Richards need you around."

He paused, his hand pressing against her neck. "I need you, too."

Laurie closed her eyes. She heard the cheers from the nearby fields, the softballs smacking into gloves, the nearby stands erupting in applause.

Applause. For her. For Jack.

They straightened, but she didn't pull away from him. Sure enough, her parents, her girls were clapping and cheering, with Elizabeth right up front, Hugh by her side.

And her dad.

He'd taken off his hat and watched her, a small smile on his face. But that's not what made her eyes water. It was the look he gave her.

He was proud of her.

She'd walked away from softball, threw out all her chances of college and the Olympics.

And he was still smiling at her.

He was still proud of her.

It might be too late for Laurie's memories and her own softball years, but it wasn't too late for these girls—this team that depended on her. A team who needed her to keep them on the straight path, a path of having fun in softball for as long as they could.

Jack was right. They needed her.

"Will you stay?" he asked. "Will you stay with us?"

She met his gaze, a gaze that held the same longing as hers, for both the game, and for love. He was her *Angels'* coach, but he was more than that.

He was everything that had been missing in her life.

Maybe, just maybe she had another shot at the championship game, at the game that really mattered. And just maybe, another chance at hitting a home run.

The only thing left to do was step up to the plate.

OPEN YOUR HEART. MAKE A WISH.

Any Normal person thinks magic a myth. Anyone worth knowing, knows differently. Magic wanted and it took. Free pizza delivery, free Wi-Fi, freewill.

All of it, fair game.

Blessa of the Blessings Bridge made sure all her landing platforms, from the golden arches to the inter-dimensional voids, remained clear of seaweed and seagull shit. An important job, really. Essential, even.

Too bad she hated it.

"The Blessings Bridge" will transport you to living, breathing world where magic resides alongside freeways, fishing piers, and funnel cakes. A world you never knew about, but always knew existed... right outside your backdoor.

By joining my list you'll receive wonderful benefits such as being notified of upcoming book releases as well as the free story, *The Blessings Bridge.*

To enjoy your free copy of *The Blessings Bridge* and keep up with the latest news and releases, go to chrissywissler.com/free-book/ and chrissywissler.com.

SEARCHING FOR SANCTUARY

Find your home. Find your heart.

Searching for Sanctuary: An Enchantment Avenue Novel, on sale now
from your favorite retailer. Turn the page for a sample chapter from
this book.

Not all animals handle magic well. Even ones bred and hand-picked
for the job.

The massive lion laying there. Hot breath blowing the tattered
pink too-too. Aisha standing outside the cage, dust swirling all
around. Completely helpless.

Another one. Lost.

Set in the dazzling world of Enchantment Avenue. A story of those
discarded when their use fades, and the one woman willing to take
them in, imperfections and all. Hope and redemption, love and magic.
All possible.

CHAPTER 1

$\mathcal{A}$isha leaned against the cage's rusted chain-link fence. The hot surface heated her dark skin, but she ignored it.

The tiger Lanhi lay sprawled and uncaring on her wooden hovel of a house's flat roof. Massive paw hanging off. Not even swinging in the nonexistent breeze. Not the way she used to, like she was batting at some stray hopping-kangaroo mouse that'd wandered in from the southern pen enclosures.

It'd only happened once, not long after Lanhi had arrived, when she'd barely had the will to even eat her food. Aisha hadn't respelled the mouse enclosure lock against hair-thin whisker-picking abilities (the hopping-kangaroo mouse's master having not informed Aisha of their peculiar talents—the same talents that'd gotten them banned from hearth and home and a much nicer, much more expensive Familiar Sanctuary).

But the little adventure of hopping-kangaroo mice had given Lanhi (and the mice) some of their own spark back. Both sides had survived (thank goodness), and while the doors were now safely locked and secure, the spark had held.

Especially for Lanhi.

Until today.

Until whatever had made her change, made her revert back to the tiger with barely the will to live.

And yet, even now Lanhi lay on her roof with her paw hanging down as if the memory of the mice was still with her. Still hanging on. Perhaps even a small spark remained for her to be on guard for the next silly hopping-kangaroo mouse foolish enough to come into her domain of faded and tearing circus posters, elephant stands, and flung-about clown noses on the dust-dirt floor of her enclosure.

Even though her paw just hung there. Unmoving. Uncaring.

"Come on, sweetheart. Please." Aisha felt the magic within her gut stir. Slowly, as if reaching out to the tiger…testing and unsure.

Aisha held her breath.

She hoped Marcelle had reported wrong. Hoped her magic would prove otherwise, that their dancing Lanhi was fine.

Lanhi ruffed and grumped. A hot puff of air spewed from her massive mouth of teeth and tongue, blowing at the tattered, pale-pink tutu hanging from a skirt hook.

The sparkly sequins, no longer sparkly.

The ruffles wrinkled and limp.

The tutu had been a recent addition. As had the clown noses. Insisted by Lanhi's master, the witch Ghazille.

Fat lot of good that had done Lanhi.

The unrelenting Simi Valley sun beat down on Aisha, the outside cage, the lines and lines of other Familiar cages in her Waystation, barely a narrow, dirt footpath between them. Even the tiniest movement caused a small twister of dust to billow upwards. The dust didn't even spare poor Lanhi, her no longer shimmering, no longer carefully groomed orange-, white-, and black-striped coat and instead, now dull and faded. The Waystation's famous dust coated every surface, made Aisha's skin look a pale tan instead of the dark, sun-kissed skin of her grandfather's people, the Hadzabe tribe.

A tribe she couldn't *actually* remember.

Aisha snapped her eyes closed. Squeezed them shut.

She needed to focus on Lanhi. Focus on someone she *could* help. Who *wanted* help.

Sweat trickled down Aisha's forehead. Dripped off her nose. She didn't move. Not even when the salty sweat slid into the corner of her eye.

Any movement, sudden or even slow, could send the tiger Familiar into another set of fits.

It was one of the main reasons Lanhi had been banned from her previous sanctuary. An uncontrollable Familiar was a handful; an unpredictable one, a danger to everyone. The kind of Familiar those high-end Sanctuaries didn't want to help.

But Aisha did.

Her magic continued to circle. To rise up from her chest, reaching her throat. Still tentative. Unsure. Trying desperately to reach out, to find some connection between Aisha and Lanhi, something that would help her understand—would help the tiger keep wanting to live.

She almost wished Lanhi would have those fits again. Anything to bring the tiger back to her usual spirits. Anything at all to show that she wasn't withering away.

Just like so many of the other retired, abused, and often forgotten Familiars.

Lanhi ruffed again. Blew another a sigh of hot air. Made the tutu's ruffles dance just the slightest, but nothing like the way those ruffles had danced before Lanhi had been sent to the finest Familiar sanctuary in the Northern Hemisphere, Paradise Grove Familiar sanctuary —before, of course, coming to Aisha's barely-holding-together Waystation.

There wasn't even the tiniest bit of excitement behind those hooded orange-gold eyes.

The magic in Aisha's stomach settled into a cold, hard stone.

Not even a stirring remained.

"Damn," Aisha whispered. "Not another one."

Aisha swept off her felt-brimmed cowboy hat. Slapped it against her khaki pants. Dust billowed up and into her nose, tickled it. Right alongside the tang of animals and sweat, rotting meat, and just plain hot-dry Waystation.

She sneezed. Then sneezed again.

Felt a familiar ache for home, a longing to go back to another time. Funny how a sneeze could remind her of the hot summers at her parents' thriving sanctuary in the Serengeti Magical Proper. Back when her life was going just fine and climbing upwards, upwards to where no sky, no magic was the limit.

She slapped the hat back on her head.

She'd never change that clock, though.

Never.

This was exactly where she needed to be.

Who she needed to be.

Aisha gave one last look at Lanhi. She'd have to call the witch, Ghazille. Not that the woman would care. Not that any of them did, not after their Familiars wound up in the Waystation, the last stop on their abandoned, unhappy, and too often short lives.

At least for these Familiars.

Not all Familiars led the perfect lives the Enchantment Avenue Council (hell, even that great and powerful High Council) liked to preach from their safe havens of magic and strength. They pretended ignorance when it came to abuse and misuse of Familiars, turning a blind eye especially when it came to the highest among them.

But Aisha knew better, and so did the Enchantment Avenue Council.

Her Waystation was living proof, and they knew it, too. Did their best to keep it all under wraps. An open, unacknowledged secret.

Even if they needed her.

Needed someone to take in the Familiars who couldn't handle the strain of performing like a monkey for unrelenting magical masters. The kinds of masters who didn't even deserve a pet, let alone the special, magical bond shared with a Familiar.

An old argument, though.

She sighed, knowing there was nothing she could do. Not about the Council and not for Lanhi. And all the Familiars like her.

But she wouldn't let them go out alone.

Whatever it took, she'd be there for them.

To continue reading *Searching for Sanctuary*, visit ChrissyWissler.com or your favorite bookseller.

ABOUT THE AUTHOR

Chrissy Wissler's writing has garnered praise both from readers and professional writers. Readers love her characters and the emotional grip she engenders.

About her novel *Home Run, New York Times* bestselling author Kristine Kathryn Rusch said: "Wonderful book, chockfull of unexpected surprises. If you like sports novels, you'll like this—even if you don't like romance. If you like romance, you'll like this—even if you don't like sports novels."

Chrissy's short fiction has appeared in the anthologies: *Fiction River: Risk-Takers, Fiction River Presents: Legacies, Fiction River Presents: Readers' Choice, Deep Magic,* and *When Dreams Come True.* She writes fantasy and science fiction, as well as a softball, contemporary series for both romance and young adult.

Before turning to fiction, Chrissy also wrote nonfiction for publications such as *Montana Outdoors, Women in the Outdoors,* and *Jakes Magazine.* In 2009, *Inside Kung Fu* magazine awarded her with their 'Writer of the Year' award.

Follow her online at ChrissyWissler.com. To enjoy another story by Chrissy Wissler and to keep up with the latest news, releases and more, go to: chrissywissler.com/free-book/

For more information:
www.chrissywissler.com
chrissy@chrissywissler.com

Hidden in Time: Novel

Hidden in Lore: Collection #1

Hidden in Myth: Collection #2

Hidden in Legend: Collection #3

Little League Series

Swing Away: A Little League Novel

Prom Dates & Softball Bats

Throw Like a Girl, Catch a Date

Fly Away

No Crying in Softball

More to Life than Softball

A Pitcher's Unexpected Date

A Catcher's Christmas Wish

Stolen Bases, Stolen Kisses

Softball Baby

Off-Balance

Batter-Up Pucker-Up: Collection

Everlasting: Collection

All or Nothing: Collection

9 781949 056020